SERGEANT VERITY
PRESENTS HIS COMPLIMENTS

Also by Francis Selwyn

**SERGEANT VERITY
AND THE BLOOD ROYAL**

**SERGEANT VERITY
AND THE SWELL MOB**

**SERGEANT VERITY
AND THE IMPERIAL DIAMOND**

SERGEANT VERITY PRESENTS HIS COMPLIMENTS

FRANCIS SELWYN

day books

A Division of STEIN AND DAY/Publishers/New York

For Gordon Grimley,
who named Verity

FIRST DAY BOOKS EDITION 1981
First published in hardcover in the United States of America, 1977
by STEIN AND DAY/*Publishers*.
Copyright © 1977 by Francis Selwyn
All rights reserved
Printed in the United States of America
Stein and Day/*Publishers*/
Scarborough House
Briarcliff Manor, N.Y. 10510

Library of Congress Cataloging in Publication Data
Selwyn, Francis.
Sergeant Verity presents his compliments.

I. Title.
PZ4.S4693Sg3 [PR6069.E382] 823'.9'14 76-41724
ISBN 0-8128-7064-6

Contents

1

Joseph Morant-Barham, heir to the heir of Earl Barham, honourable only in title, laid two cards on the smooth green nap of the miniature gaming-table. At nineteen years old, his flushed face showed a smooth and almost dimpled petulance to match his pigeon chest and shock of dark, perfumed hair. Cornet of Horse in the 12th Lancers, young Morant-Barham's reputation at faro, baccarat or loo had driven such games from the mess-room to more private apartments where his brother officers were not obliged to invite him. It was not said that Cornet the Hon. Morant-Barham cheated at cards. He might do, but such things were not said in the mess of the Lancers.

It was common knowledge that before the regiment embarked for the Cape there had been a row of some sort at the Beargarden Club in St James's. Complaints were said to have been laid before the club committee over Morant-Barham's conduct at cards. It was even suggested that the committee had drafted a request for his withdrawal from membership. But a future Earl Barham was a considerable adornment to the club and its finances. Joey Morant-Barham might be 'an uncommon bad fellow for a hand at loo', but he seemed to care little how much he spent on the club otherwise. Being only a year out of Harrow, and a likeable young man into the bargain, he was merely informed that his fellow members had decided not to 'recognize' him in the card-room for the next twelve months. In every other room of the club, he would be their friend and crony. In the card-room, the older men would ignore his very presence. However, it was not supposed that a future Earl Barham would show such deplorable form as to go where he knew that he must be unwelcome.

For the moment, the Beargarden Club was ten thousand miles away. Not one of the other subalterns at the table was from the 12th Lancers. In their own dull and lack-lustre mess-rooms they were whispered of as 'fast' young men, but once the story of their evening with Earl Barham's grandson was out, they would shine with the glory of undisputed rake-hells.

When Morant-Barham laid down his cards, a hundred sovereigns were at stake. His hand of a five and a three was closer to beating the bank than any player had come in the past half hour. The cards lay on the antique baize, its walnut surround polished to the gloss of liquid honey. The young man looked up, moistening his lips and glancing at the other four men. Opposite him sat the banker, Lieutenant John Ransome of the 73rd Foot, brushing his silky black moustaches against the brick-red of his face, a complexion acquired by several years of Indian service. Like the others, Ransome was bare-headed, his scarlet tunic with its gold braiding open and crumpled. With a deep, enigmatic smile, he laid his two cards on the baize. The seven and two of diamonds, a natural and un-beatable nine.

There was a general intake of breath at the narrowness of Morant-Barham's defeat, as well as at the size of the stake he had lost. The young man's mouth twisted ner-vously. His companions sat in silence and heard far below them the deep reassuring double beat of HMS *Birkenhead*'s powerful engines, the three steel fists of the pistons spar-ring forward and down in succession. The fins of the ship's paddle-wheels beat the surface of the South Atlantic in a light, rapid putter, just below the level of the cabin-ports, where the hissing paddle-wake bubbled and broke. Beyond this luminous froth, the surrounding ocean swell had long since grown black in the late twilight. Four or five miles astern, the coast of southern Africa was now indistinguishable from the dark water, except where the fire of an isolated kraal flamed briefly and then vanished. Morant-Barham's boyish face dimpled in a grimace of self-disparagement.

'Gilt, I think,' said Ransome smoothly, 'tick being no go. When a fellow may be fighting the Kaffirs tomorrow, he oughtn't to start issuing paper for what he owes tonight.'

Morant-Barham drew five little pillars of gold coin towards him, checked their number and slid them hard across the table.

'Curse it!' he said, mocking his own misfortune again and slewing the coins with vindictive force. The gold columns slithered and fell. Bright, tiny sovereigns spun and rang in the rich oil-light, bouncing and rolling in every direction, over the gilded wooden chairs, under the small ornamental tables with their alabaster lamps and silk-tasselled shades in rose pink, into the recesses of the fine Regency sofa with its cerise velvet, all of which accompanied Cornet the Hon. Morant-Barham, even on a troopship.

'Come now, Joey!' said Frank Chamberlain on his right. 'What's the good of being beastly ill-natured? A man must learn to take his licking and not squeal. You ain't down to your shirt-tail yet by a long chalk. And your old governor don't keep you short. By George, he don't!' Chamberlain indicated the comforts of the cabin with a general wave of his hand. Morant-Barham said nothing. For the chance to call him Joey, to chaff him about his people, and then to boast of the familiarity in their own mess-rooms, men like Chamberlain were prepared to lose unquestioningly at baccarat. Morant-Barham saw no cause for complaint, especially since his guests were now about to part with their money more freely and more willingly than they themselves had ever imagined.

'Ain't it time to be getting down to the pasties on the old green baize again?' said Charley Keston of the 84th Foot. 'Cut and shuffle, Jack Ransome!'

'Have the goodness to wait,' said Morant-Barham coldly, 'while the servant is called to fetch the yellow-boys off the floor.'

'Hold hard, Joey,' said Chamberlain good-humouredly. 'A fellow don't play in front of his batman. Colonel Seton won't have faro or baccy on shipboard, and the servant isn't born that wouldn't peach on his master if it paid him.'

'My servant don't peach, Frank,' said Morant-Barham. 'And I've a mouth that's dry as a whore's bush for a hock and seltzer water.'

He clapped his hands over his head with the impatience of a schoolboy summoning one of his minions. His four guests sat in their unbuttoned tunics, the smoke from their Flor Rothschild cheroots drifting, greenish-grey, into the rich tawny oil-light overhead. The door opened.

'Fetch in some seltzer water and German wine,' said Morant-Barham languidly.

'Very good, sir.' The voice was a soft but pert cockney treble. Chamberlain looked at John Ransome.

'By thunder!' he said. 'Joey's got a bum-boy!'

'No I ain't,' said Morant-Barham smoothly. 'It's a doxy. She won't pass for a Grosvenor Square lady but she's a sight better than having one of the soldiers' or sailors' women. She only dresses like a valet so she shan't be spotted easy. And if Colonel Seton should come on me for it now, I shan't have to look far to know who peached.'

The others exchanged glances, marvelling and congratulating themselves at the same time on the richness of the story they would have to tell, how they had gamed for a hundred sovereigns a hand with young Lord Barham and his woman in a sumptuously furnished cabin on the *Birkenhead*, outward bound from Simon's Bay. When the girl returned with the hock and seltzer water, each of them turned in his chair to admire her.

'Over here, Miss Janet, if you please,' said her young master gently.

Her dark hair was shaped close to her head, its length pushed up into a pretty top-knot with the aid of a tortoiseshell comb. Soft features and a faint freckling were illuminated by the apparent timidity of her brown eyes. Morant-Barham's guests moistened their lips thoughtfully at the shapes revealed by the white cotton shirt and dark brown tights, which resembled the costume of a footman. The girl was a little stocky, but the slight heaviness of her thighs, the proud swell of her hips, and the soft roundness of her breasts were all displayed with a cunning which belied the modesty in her eyes. Charley Keston screwed his eye-glass into place and swallowed hard. Frank Chamberlain was clutching the edge of the table, unaware that his whitening knuckles betrayed his enthusiasm. The *Birkenhead* had embarked the depot companies of ten regiments at Cork on 7 January 1852. It was now 25 February and few of the subalterns on board had even spoken to a woman in two months. When choosing his guests, Morant-Barham selected those for whom the deprivation had been most severe.

The young brunette served the men with hock and seltzer water. Then she stood before him, waiting to be dismissed.

'There are some Victorias and half-sovs on the floor,' he said, as though it were almost too tiresome to mention. 'Pick 'em up and fetch 'em here.'

Flushing a little and keeping her eyes lowered to avoid the eager gazes of the men, she dropped to her knees and began to search. A coin had lodged between the thighs of Ransome's breeches and there was much amusement as he insisted that she must hook it out with her own timid fingers. Frank Chamberlain ostentatiously picked up a coin and dropped it into his own lap. When the girl stooped for it, he seized her wrist with one hand, holding her while the fingers of his other circled the tips of her soft breasts.

'Have a care, Frank,' said Morant-Barham softly, and the fierce little subaltern released her. He was prepared to be familiar with the young Barham but not to fight him.

Presently she was searching under the little sofa, kneeling with her forehead almost on the floor. Charley Keston was confronted by the spread and rounded seat of her dark brown tights. As though the girl were entirely innocent of the effect, the plump cheeks of Janet's bottom wiggled and squirmed at him as she stretched after an elusive coin.

'Ain't Miss Janet got a backside on her, old fellow!' said Chamberlain wonderingly to Keston.

'She ain't a twelve-year-old virgin, Frank,' said Morant-Barham, 'which all your mess-room says is what you prefer.

The cove who kept her before me got careless and she dropped a cub on him. She won't see twenty again.'

'And you still a schoolboy last year!' said Ransome derisively.

'It ain't age, Jack Ransome, it's being the master of a doxy that counts. Not that this frisky little filly ain't taught me a French trick or two!'

Before allowing the girl to leave, he instructed her to freshen the glasses, which obliged her to lean far over the table to reach Chamberlain's. Again Chamberlain seized her wrist, looking her hard in the eyes, moulding and fingering her breasts through the tight cotton.

'And that's where it stops, Frank,' said Morant-Barham quietly. Chamberlain became reproachful.

'Dammit, Joey! She ain't going to be Lady Barham, is she? She ain't exactly wearing her bubbies like a young countess! A fellow can share a doxy with his chums. Where's the harm?'

'No harm, Frank,' said Morant-Barham. 'Only when a fellow invites four chums to his cabin, and when he loses the bank and a hundred sovs and more in two hours, he ain't in a sharing mood. I know it's square, of course, only a fellow can't help being a bit down, all the same.'

'That's gammon!' said Chamberlain determinedly.

'No it ain't, Frank, it ain't gammon at all. If a fellow was to win back his sovs, and perhaps a bit over, there's no knowing what he mightn't do for the chums he won from. He might turn into such a jolly dog that he'd call his doxy back and let them give her what-for. There's no knowing but he mightn't.'

They stared at him. The future Earl Barham pimping for his street girl! This was going to be an evening to remember, a story they would tell in mess billiard-rooms and club smoking-rooms when they were tired old majors and colonels on half-pay. How they went on the randy with Joey Morant-Barham, or Earl Barham as he would then be, and how they ploughed a doxy with him.

It was Lieutenant John Ransome, the oldest of the men, who set the tone and smothered any remaining scruples in his companions.

'You damned young rascal!' he said, almost laughing. 'You've pulled this thieving dodge before!'

Morant-Barham shrugged.

'I ain't a thief, Jack Ransome. But I ain't exactly green as a new leaf either. I know you older subalterns think any young griff ought to be, but he ain't always. And I don't ask you to share my doxy. There's a hundred soldiers' women below decks that might give you a serving of greens for the asking. Crabs and all.'

During the pause which followed this, Ransome looked carefully at the others. Then he looked back to Morant-Barham.

'Well, then, old chums,' said Morant-Barham lightly, 'shall we say a bank of two hundred sovs to make the wheel go round easy?'

James Seton, Lieutenant-Colonel of the 74th Highlanders, walked slowly along the narrow, iron-ribbed passageway which led aft from the troop-decks behind the bilge-tank. The majority of the five-hundred men under his command were already asleep in the hammocks slung from the massive deck-beams overhead. Others slept huddled in blankets on the bare boarding of the deck itself. Behind Seton, at a regulation distance, walked the orderly officer, and behind the orderly officer came the orderly sergeant. Strict discipline was almost impossible on a troopship and, in some respects, undesirable. Yet in the hold, secure behind bars, lay Private Suitor, a hulking Irishman whose court-martial sentence of fifty lashes for drunkenness had been confirmed by Sir Harry Smith, Commander-in-Chief at the Cape. Tomorrow, at morning parade, the man must be roped to the triangle and flogged. Suitor was an old offender, his brawny back marked by the thin white scars of several previous ordeals.

It was Seton who had relented so far as to allow Suitor to be visited by Fusilier Atherton, a lantern-jawed towering soldier with a Nottingham brogue, who had acquired a reputation among officers and men as leader of an evangelizing movement among the soldiers themselves, forswearing strong drink, oaths, and every form of immorality. Colonel Seton had overheard Atherton in the cell, endeavouring to comfort the condemned man, urging him to put aside the fear of the drummer's lash and to seek instead a release from the eternal pains of hell which must search the souls of the damned. And all the time, Suitor had whispered, 'Save me, Mr Atherton! Save me!' There was no fear in his voice only an urgent confidentiality, as though he were asking Atherton to show him the secret of a conjuring trick. Seton knew the game. The man guessed that Atherton might speak to Major Moxon, who was sweet on the 'evangelists', and Moxon might 'beg him off' the flogging. But Sir Harry Smith had signed the order, and there was nothing that begging could do.

The memory of all this was wakened in Seton's mind by the sound of Atherton's voice in a recess by one of the mess-deck openings, and by the sight of an unkempt young woman close by him. The girl bowed her head, eyes downcast, fingers twisting awkwardly together.

'Ah don't know,' she said softly, 'Ah don't know that Ah could make mesel' worthy by enduring such things. There must be other roads to repent, sure?'

'If thou art my woman thou shall endure!' whispered the tall Fusilier fiercely. His lantern-jaw seemed to hang slack of its own weight and his pock-marked face shone with the heat between decks.

'Not here!' she looked about her in the gloom. 'Not this minute!'

'Thou fool!' he said, with a kind of stern affection. 'This very night thy soul may be required of thee!'

'Ay,' she said thoughtfully, and moved closer to his side.

Seton chose not to notice. Once a commanding officer tried to regulate the affairs of soldiers and their women there was no end to it. He thought, however, that a word in Major Moxon's ear might not come amiss.

Further aft, a row of glass panels offered a view of the deep well of the *Birkenhead*'s engine-room. The massive and polished hammer-heads of the three pistons drove forward and back through their elipse with the power of trapped animals seeking escape. There was a pervasive smell of coal dust and hot oil. Through the open door of the stoke-hold, the black silhouettes of the stokers appeared against a tapestry of flame, like figures already consigned to Fusilier Atherton's hell.

Among the polished brass and steel, the engineer officer of the watch surveyed his little kingdom, while the paddles beat their throbbing rhythm alongside the hull. The telegraph was set at 'Full Ahead' for the night as the ship cut the ocean swell towards Algoa Bay, where the first of the depot companies were to be disembarked. Chalked on a little board, for the engineer officer's information, were the locations of the senior officers on the vessel. Captain Salmond, RN, commander of the *Birkenhead*, was already in his cabin, having retired at the first opportunity.

Seton turned about and dismissed the orderly officer and sergeant, returning their salutes punctiliously. It was past one in the morning, but the knowledge that his men might have to face the ubiquitous fire of Kaffir marksmen the next day had prompted this final tour of inspection. Seton's satisfaction with the quiet orderliness of his men was not equalled by general admiration for their officers. His own 74th Highlanders were well led, and some of the other infantry companies were adequately commanded, but he felt the natural antipathy of a foot soldier and a Scot towards the dandy officers of cavalry. The smooth, affluent young wastrels of the dragoons and lancers displayed a peacock arrogance which he found loathsome. As he walked slowly along the carpeted corridor, the cabins of the 12th Lancers on either side still showed cracks of light at their doors and emitted a muffled hum of voices and the occasional boisterous guffaws. A door opened, illuminating the unbuttoned figure of Lieutenant Chamberlain. With tunic open and breeches askew, the young man belched and moved unsteadily towards the infantry berths. The door closed before Seton reached it but he caught the warm stench of sour wine and stale cigar. He made no attempt to call Chamberlain back. Officers were to be reprimanded when sober. Chamberlain blundered into the cabin which he shared with Lieutenant Keston. Seton heard the voices and subdued laughter of the two young men. Thoughtfully, he entered his own stateroom in the stern of the ship. As he lay down, the engines of the *Birkenhead* beat their strong, soothing double rhythm. Five hundred men and their hundred and thirty women and children slept their deep final sleep.

Joseph Morant-Barham was alone in his cabin with Lieutenant John Ransome after the other three subalterns had left. The two men sat either side of the green baize table, lolling in their chairs. Between them was a litter of empty glasses and piled cigar bowls, scraps of paper on which the reckonings had been made, and several scrawled IOUs with Charley Keston's signature.

'Two hundred and eighty,' said Ransome, taking the cheroot from his mouth. 'Two hundred and eighty your departed guests left us, not counting the damned paper you let young Keston issue for the last half hour. Paper's a blue look-out, Joey. You and I shan't be rich while you let fellows pay you with that gash.'

Ransome fanned out Charley Keston's promissory notes, as though they were a hand of cards, and shook his head ruefully.

'Dammit, Jack!' said Morant-Barham pettishly, 'we mayn't be anything, the way you call it, if you pull that dodge with your tunic-sleeve too often. They must be blind not to see!'

Ransome's sun-reddened face broadened in a tolerant smile for the boy who was hardly more than half his age. He spoke softly.

'You'd be blind not to see, Joey, sitting where you are, but then we're two of the closest pals a man ever saw, ain't we?'

The young man slapped his hand down like an angry child.

'They could have seen, Jack! It don't excuse the risk!'

Ransome grinned and slowly shook his head again.

'Joey, Joey! The art of it is that even when a fellow sees, he looks away rather than have a beastly row. A gentleman don't care to quarrel over cards, not even when he knows there's huggery-muggery. And the beauty of it is, they each lost a piece to you, and then you were so obliging as to lose it all to me. It takes suspicion off you, and if you don't complain over losing it to me, then why should they?'

'Fairground faking ain't worth the risk,' said the boy sullenly.

Ransome's face coloured up, as if at some implied insult.

'Risk?' he said sardonically. 'With Chamberlain blind drunk? With Keston's breeches busting each time your Janet showed her fat backside? When three gentlemen in turn have ploughed another gentleman's doxy, they don't generally start a rumpus over what may have happened at his card table!'

Morant-Barham's face dimpled in derision and he tossed his black curls contemptuously.

'Ploughed her! They took her in the other room for the look of it, to boast what whoremasters they were tonight!'

'Joey,' said Ransome, grinning gently, 'I wasn't so green as to miss having from her own mouth every word of what went on in there. Two of them rode her so hard she couldn't lie still after it. Keston was the rummy cove. Put her on her back and held her legs like a wheelbarrow. Then has your Miss Janet over a bolster with her bum in the air. Last of all, has her kneeling at his chair, her face going down on him and her parts displayed in a mirror behind her. I don't risk Keston busting up and not paying his ticks.'

Ransome tossed the IOUs on the table, and Morant-Barham brightened.

'Take his paper in your share, Jack, if you can squeeze him.'

'No, Joey. Share and share, gold and paper.'

'I told you I must have gold,' said the boy, almost whining. 'Dammit, Jack, you know there's a broker to be paid.'

'You all the halfpence and me all the kicks, eh?' said Ransome. 'A broker won't brave the Kaffirs to follow you. There's a hundred and forty each in gold, and half Keston's paper.'

'Jack,' said Morant-Barham coaxingly, 'I signed a bill for £200 two months ago, from a damned little money-changer in Fetter Lane. I never had £200 nor anything like, but the bill was at three months and the cash must be sent.'

'You'll be on the other side of the world, Joey. Sleep easy.'

Morant-Barham clasped his hands and closed his eyes.

'It must be paid, Jack. Really it must. . . .'

'Because?'

'Because, dammit, it ain't my name on the bill!'

Ransome sighed with undisguised satisfaction and the boy looked up sharply, tasting for the first time the sick fear of having begged a respite from the hands of a professional blackguard.

'Jack, it must be bought back. I only did it for a safe spec. If that bill goes to the fellow whose name's on it, there's all hell to answer! God, Jack, you can see that, can't you? You can see how a fellow might be so driven that he'd do it for a sure spec?'

Ransome sat very quietly, as though hardly able to credit his good fortune in having stumbled on the young man's criminal foolishness.

'Borrowed £200 and put another man's name to the debt?'

Morant-Barham nodded.

'Take the paper,' he urged. 'Squeeze Keston for it. Take the £80 gilt, and whatever else you please.'

Ransome sucked his teeth and whistled softly. The possibilities for plucking the imprudent young heir to the Barham estates were so enormous, given this piece of information, that he needed time to assess the opportunity more fully.

'Jack,' said the young man suddenly, 'take the £80 and the paper. There's £200. And take my bill at three months for £120 more!'

Ransome laughed softly and shook his head.

'And when the bill ain't met, Joey? What then?'

There was a pause, Ransome continuing to whistle softly.

'Jack,' said the boy again, 'take the girl! She's worth more than all the rest. You can't ask for one better broken to the saddle! Dammit, didn't you see her work for me? She's taught to do the same for any man that runs her and, between whiles, keep him at a stand a hundred ways. Only think, what you might do in India with her!'

Ransome got up and opened the door leading to the sleeping quarters. By the dim illumination of a single lamp he could see Janet lying on the bed. She was still naked but for her stockings, perhaps expecting further demands upon her soft pale body. Ransome approached, calling her to him, telling her to turn, stretch, or bend herself in the most convenient manner for his examination. With unconcealed amusement he questioned her gently, compiling an inventory of the acts practised on her. The girl replied in timid murmurs as Ransome's hands ran like a whisper over the smooth, milky contours of breasts, hips and bottom. Then, with the patting and probing done, he left the girl and returned to his host, standing before Morant-Barham, leaning with one hand on the gaming table, his smile betraying nothing of his decision.

'Well?' asked the boy impatiently.

Ransome steadied himself on the table as the hull of the ship vibrated uncomfortably, the helmsman turning hard to starboard and causing one of the paddle-wheels to spin clear of the water with the incline of the ship. The *Birkenhead* righted herself and then seemed to rise on a sudden and unexpected swell. Ransome braced his feet apart and clutched the table with both hands, his dark eyes narrowing as though with suspicion. The ship swung violently, there was a distant clatter of china and one of the glass shades in Morant-Barham's cabin toppled and smashed to tiny sparkling slivers on the carpet.

'The deuce of it!' said Ransome, relaxing his grip a little.

But the long rising swell came again, stronger and steeper, the *Birkenhead* heeling as though in the trough of a great storm. Just as it seemed that the worst might be over, the hull rolled precipitously, the rattle of falling furniture smothered by a great crash which echoed through the ship as though every gun-port had been stove in simultaneously by a heavy sea. Morant-Barham was thrown from his chair by the impact, while Ransome lost his footing and fell backwards among the scattered furniture. Two of the oil-lamps had smashed, leaving only one whose guttering flame cast a fitful shadow-play over the wreckage and confusion.

Morant-Barham, conscious of a swelling bruise above his left eye, struggled to his feet and found that the floor of the cabin sloped upward a little towards the stern. Yet when he began to walk it seemed as if the angled deck was shifting under his feet with the weight of every step. And then the schoolboy subaltern lost his fear of Ransome in a still greater apprehension. The mighty engines of the *Birkenhead* were ominously still and somewhere inside the hull there was an echoing inrush of water.

'What in God's name was that?' he asked, shivering.

Ransome picked himself up from the littered fragments of glass and the overturned furniture.

'Get your bitch dressed!' he said, brushing down his tunic vigorously. 'Get on deck!'

But Morant-Barham was peering into the wrecked cabin, kneeling and fumbling in the gloom.

'The sovs, Jack, the sovs! All on the floor somewhere!'

'Damn the money! Get up, unless you want this brig for a coffin!'

The hull of the ship was coming alive again with voices and footsteps in the passageway. Ransome pushed Morant-Barham through the shuffling files of men, along narrow passages and up iron ladders in the warren of the *Birkenhead*. They moved almost in silence, the majority of them having been shaken from their deepest sleep by the blow. A party of foot soldiers, moving at the double, crossed the path of the escapers. Steam hissed from the safety-valves as the hull moved again under their feet, wallowing in the ocean surges like a dead whale. Deep in the ship's entrails they heard the funereal clang! clang! clang! of the first iron hand-pump which the soldiers had manned.

'Now,' said Ransome, pushing forward, 'sharp's the word and quick's the motion!'

As the ominous tolling of the pumps echoed through the emptying hull, Captain Salmond, commander of the *Birkenhead*, and Colonel Seton, as senior military officer on board, reached the quarter-deck. On the main deck, below them, where the tall thin funnel breathed its smoke and sparks into the night air, the depot companies were pushing and mingling as they strove to assemble by regiments. The officer of the watch presented the charts to Salmond.

'Point Danger five miles to port, sir,' he said, gesturing through the darkness towards the African coast. Salmond looked at the chart briefly and then waved it away. There was nothing marked in the ship's path but any East India captain knew that a hundred reefs off the coast of Cape Colony had never been charted. Danger Rock, several miles off the Point, was the unmarked grave of a dozen vessels but thousands had passed it in safety. It was a remote chance, not even a chance in a thousand, but HMS *Birkenhead* had hit the saw-toothed ridge of the reef at 2 am, bows-on, and full speed ahead.

On the main deck, below Salmond and his officers, the troops swarmed like bees from an overturned hive, surging from the hatches and companionways. The junior officers, the first on the scene, endeavoured to restore order.

'Depot Company, 73rd Foot, fall in! . . . 12th Lancers! Fall in, lads! Fall in!'

'She'll tear herself open on the rock if she stays fast in this tide,' said the officer of the watch, not quite out of Salmond's hearing. The men on the quarter-deck could feel the ocean swell and the strong night-wind pulling the stern of the ship round and then swinging it back again. At each movement there was the shrill bird-shriek of metal twisting against rock.

Salmond called sharply,

'Mr Hetherington! Two turns slow astern, if you please!'

'Two turns slow astern, sir!' Hetherington's voice echoed down the speaking-tube. The engine-room telegraph rang its familiar and reassuring code. Among the steam released by the safety mechanism during the ship's immobility, the engineer officer wiped his forehead with his sleeve and closed the valve. The mighty pistons of the paddle-axle recoiled once and then twice. The finned wheels threshed the water in two precise strokes.

The *Birkenhead* seemed to glide clear of the obstruction and there was a subdued cheer from some of the troops on the deck. But no sooner had the paddles stopped than the sea carried the hull forward again. The grinding of metal on rock and the rending of timbers rang hideously loud in the stillness of the night air. In the forward troop-deck, the last of the riflemen to push their way towards the companion-ladders heard the sound at their backs and turned to see with horror the entire bulkhead buckle and burst under the thundering weight of sea. Far below the ship's waterline, there was no escape for them. Men and their equipment were caught in the swirl of dark water, clutching at chairs or tables as the foul bilge water reached them first. It was no sudden death. Ten or fifteen minutes might pass before the last obstinate pocket of air was driven out and the few survivors were forced against the upper deck-beams, holding their breath against the cold flood overwhelming them until their lungs burst.

On the main deck, Colonel Seton had established order among the survivors of the depot companies, his company commanders taking up the cry, 'Fall in, in drill stations!' Seton himself was with his 74th Highlanders when Frank Chamberlain slipped across to take his farewell of young Joey Morant-Barham.

'Well, old fellow, I don't suppose we shall all of us come out of this with our feet dry. But if you do, and I don't, and if there should be a court of inquiry, do tell them that the drivelling old idiot commanding the ship sank us by going astern off a rock, when the only thing that might save us was slow ahead. I ain't a wet-bob but I know that much!'

They shook hands firmly, and Chamberlain marched away to his regiment.

On the bridge, Captain Salmond heard the inrush of

water at the bows swelling to a mighty flood. Belatedly, he came to the same conclusion as Frank Chamberlain.

'Let go the bower cable, Mr Hetherington! Keep her on the rock, if you can. Once she slips off now, there's no holding her.'

But the tone of the messages brought by runners from the lower decks was hardly encouraging. The forward holds were under water and there was nothing for it but to draw the soldiers and their hand-pumps back, abandoning part of the ship to the sea. It was ten minutes since the *Birkenhead* had struck the reef and already the stern was beginning to lift clear of the water as the bows settled. The paddle-wheels hung idle and the trail of smoke from the thin black funnel was replaced by the whistle of escaping steam.

'Mr Archibald,' said Salmond softly to his gunner, 'fire the pivot-guns. They may be seen by some of the settlements or by another ship.'

As the gunner doubled away, Salmond's officers looked down and saw the troopers of the 12th Lancers herding their chargers from the horse-boxes on the main deck, driving them towards the port gangway-opening. One after another the terrified animals were half-pushed and half-thrown by the men over the side of the ship and into the dark surges.

'Poor brutes!' said Hetherington.

'Those poor brutes can swim, Mr Hetherington,' said Salmond tersely. 'They don't like it, but they may reach land long before you or I.'

The gunner reappeared, breathless.

'The entire foredeck is awash, sir! No way through to the magazine and in any case the shells for the pivot guns must be under water already.'

A great weariness appeared to settle on Captain Salmond.

'Very well,' he said. 'Mr Hetherington, order the firing of the distress rockets.'

The officers on the quarter-deck busied themselves in letting off the flares. The dark blue flash of the rockets lit the surrounding water in a garish pyrotechnic display.

A score of the sputtering missiles rose in their long arc and then glided down, settling on the sea like so many malevolent birds, continuing to burn with a slow blue fire which cast its sickly light over the wreck of the *Birkenhead*.

The last of the horses, hysterical with fear, had been pushed into the purplish gloom with a floundering splash. Regimental companies waited in drill order, their commanders before them and a group of women and children huddled close to each formation.

'Mr Hetherington!' called Salmond, 'an account of the ship's boats, if you please.'

Hetherington consulted the list which had been brought him.

'Both main pinnaces wrecked by falling spars, sir, at the moment of striking the rock. Port and starboard paddle-box boats ready for lowering. Ship's cutter prepared, and two small gigs, sir.'

'And the complement now?'

'Four hundred men mustered, sir, all others lost below decks. Fifty crew, including Royal Marines on guard. All women and children safe, sir, one hundred and thirty of them all told.'

Salmond straightened up from the rail on which he had been leaning.

'My compliments to Colonel Seton. The boats must be lowered at once. Will he have the goodness to see the women and children safely into them? The men must stand fast or their numbers will swamp the boats.'

As he spoke, the hull shifted again under their feet and there was a distant sound of crumbling wood and metal. Steam from the boilers was now escaping in a deafening hiss but Salmond was so absorbed in his task that he hardly seemed to notice such distractions. His officers looked down on the scene below where their men scurried to lower the two boats carried on the paddle-boxes. Ropes had been hoisted over one of the yard-arms to form makeshift davits for the port boat. Teams of pig-tailed sailors hauled on the lines until the boat swung up and over the ship's rail, suspended with the swell of the sea below it. As the little craft hung just under the level of the yard-arm there was an abrupt crack and the makeshift tackle snapped. The stern of the boat fell with a splintering of board on to the rail of the *Birkenhead*. Like actors in a grim farce, the sailors left the wrecked lifeboat and raced across to the starboard paddle-box to assist in lowering the other boat. The soldiers of the depot companies stood impassively at attention, their faces lit by the faint blue light of the rocket-floats.

Salmond watched them swing the starboard boat up from its paddle-box and clear of the ship's rail. But he could see that the ropes were too thick and the blocks too small. This might not have mattered so much if the crane-pins and sheave-pins of the lowering gear had been scraped free of rust regularly and coated with tallow and black lead to preserve and lubricate the mechanism. But there was no time for such luxuries in the routine of a ship like the *Birkenhead*. The starboard lowering-gear creaked and then jammed hopelessly, leaving the lifeboat suspended at a steep angle half-way down the ship's side. There seemed no question of being able to free it in the time that was left.

On the other side, however, the cutter had been lowered. Even there, when the boat was ten feet above the waves, the forward tackle gave, parting with a loud snap, so that the bows crashed to the water, spilling into the breakers the four men who had been paying out the tackle within the boat itself. By the time that the angle of the boat had been righted, there was no sign of the heads which had bobbed briefly among the waves.

The gangway was open, the rope ladder thrown down the wet and pitching plates of the hull. Colonel Seton strode across to the rail with two of his officers and, to the surprise of the onlookers, the three of them drew their swords.

'Let the women and children through,' he said firmly. 'The women and children first.'

Salmond heard him and thought to himself that the cutter would not hold a quarter of the women and children. One or two smaller boats might be got away in the time left. Perhaps they would hold the remainder of the men's families but it would be a damn close-run thing. For the men themselves there was nothing but to remain as they were on the sloping deck of the doomed ship, in regimental order as precise and well-disciplined as if it had been a review at Woolwich or in Windsor Park.

The cutter was already full and pulling away from the ship's side under the command of a youthful midshipman. A huddle of women and crying children who had been left behind attracted Cornet Morant-Barham's attention. He watched them miserably. Presently a small pinnace was lowered and Colonel Seton, glancing down once to see that it was secured, called softly,

'Down you go then! Smartly as you can!'

When the women and their children had already over-loaded the frail craft, he held his sword across the gangway opening.

'No more in this one,' he said gently.

Morant-Barham saw to his horror that one of the distraught women who had been turned back was Janet, and that she was coming towards him, weeping incoherently with fright. He moved to her, not knowing what to do. At that moment, the last of the fugitives to be permitted through, tousled, grimy and aged beyond her years, turned and saw the weeping girl. She ducked back under Seton's sword.

'Ah'm staying wi' Atherton,' she said firmly, and limped away to find the Fusiliers so that she might take up her vigil as close to him as possible.

Morant-Barham caught Janet by the arm, thrusting her forward. As he did so, he drew from his pocket a little wash-leather bag, heavy with the weight of sovereigns, and pressed it into her hand.

'Now's your chance, old girl,' he said encouragingly. 'It ain't much of a chance, even if you get safe to England. But such as it is, you shall take it.'

He thrust her past Seton and turned away again before she was helped down the rope ladder by the sailors.

From the quarter-deck, Captain Salmond could see by the light of the flares that two of the little boats had pulled far enough away from the ship to be out of any danger, while a third was just casting off. There was a deep rumbling, far down in the hull of the *Birkenhead*, and the frame of the vessel shuddered more violently. Not a man of the ten depot companies moved. One of Salmond's midshipmen noticed a dozen women still waiting with several small children clinging to their skirts and howling. He called to an officer beside this forlorn little group.

'The last of the boats is trimmed!'

A captain of the Highlanders escorted them to their final hope of rescue from the sinking troop-ship. At this critical moment, for the first and last time, one of the ranks of a depot company broke. Three soldiers, maddenened by the fear of death and drowning, knew that their fate would be sealed in a minute more. They broke from their comrades and rushed the gangway opening where the rope ladder hung above the last of the boats. Morant-Barham turned to his groom at his side and took his pistol, which the man was holding for him. He aimed it carefully at the back of the nearest fugitive and fired. The soldier stopped suddenly as though he had run into an invisible wall, and fell. The sword of a lieutenant of Highlanders flashed dully in the gloom and a second man crumpled to his knees, his hand scrabbling feebly behind him at the long wound. The third man reached the rail and seeing the pinnace cast off, threw himself over the ship's side in an hysterical resolve to reach it. He fell into the water, his head bobbed briefly and then, with arms uplifted in a last appeal, he sank beneath the dark waves.

There were no more boats to lower and the sudden inactivity produced an uneasy calm on the ship. The grinding of the bows on the reef, under the pressure of the long rolling swell, was heard clearly by those in the little boats. Then the men on the main-deck were thrown in a convulsive rolling movement as the *Birkenhead*'s prow seemed to leap into the air and fall back. A long splintering of heavy timbers mingled with the demonic shriek of torn metal as the ripped bows of the ship broke clean away and subsided into the churning water to boil and foam by the reef.

In the blue light of the distress flares the women and children in the boats could still see the regiments paraded on the deck. For all the crashing of the waves against the broken hull, it was possible for these survivors to catch some of the shouted commands as the men were marched aft to the greater safety of the ship's stern. Presently there was another sound, softer and more general. It grew in volume as more and more of the men on the decks took it up. It was not a prayer nor a hymn, but both prayer and hymn, and something more to the doomed regiments. The first words were lost but the women in the boats soon made out the rest and wept at the hopeless bravery of the men who defied their fate.

> . . . *Send her victorious,*
> *Happy and glorious,*
> *Long to reign over us. . . .*

At that moment there was the crackling of a giant hand crumpling tinsel. The funnel of the *Birkenhead* snapped in two under its own inclining weight, the top half breaking from the restraining cables and crashing to the deck in a shower of sparks from burning soot. The angle of the ship was steeper now, the stern clear of the water, the rudder hanging in mid-air, the paddles aloft like huge and idle mill-wheels. With the toppling of the funnel, nothing remained of the superstructure but the mainmast and main-topmast at the stern with sails reefed. Captain Salmond turned to the paraded regiments and cupped his hands.

'All men who can swim, leap overboard and make towards the boats!'

The men waited, expecting Colonel Seton's order. But Seton was in stern conference with his officers. A moment later he turned to the ranks of waiting soldiers.

'Every man must understand,' he said firmly, 'that the boats containing the women and children are already full.

It is our duty to stay steady here and give those others their chance of life. If the boats are swamped or capsized, then no man, woman, nor child will survive in the sea. By accepting our fate as Englishmen, by doing that duty which our Queen and country expect of us, we may at least save those whose lives must be dearer to us than our own. Let every man remember that the eyes of posterity are upon him and his conduct now. All regiments will stand fast!'

The red lines of the foot soldiers in their white blanco'd webbing, the blue and gold tunic'd files of cavalry, stood stiff and motionless. Not a rank was broken again. Subalterns and senior officers walked slowly before their companies, speaking encouragement during the last agony of the *Birkenhead*. Fifty men of the Royal Marines, part of Captain Salmond's complement, stood guard at their posts on the sloping deck. There was no knowing exactly how long the stern and midships section of the wreck might survive in the rising sea and the fresher wind which now whipped and snapped at loose rope-ends and chilled the men's faces. It might be half an hour, it would certainly not be an hour. The men concentrated their thoughts on the hope which remained for the women and children. They put sternly from their minds their own fates and those of the few men who survived trapped far below in the hull, gasping in the hot and fetid pockets of air while the foul bilge-water lapped round their shoulders and the remainder of their lives was measured in long aching breaths.

The only stroke of mercy shown by the elements came in shortening the suffering of the men. Scarcely ten minutes after Colonel Seton's last order, the shattered hull of the *Birkenhead* was lifted by a powerful swell. A mighty crack reverberated like the parting of a great beam. Those in the lifeboats watched in silent terror as the ship slid into her final plunge, the men of the depot companies slithering forward and being drawn down in the strong suction of the water that closed over the dark hull. For a minute or two the maintopmast at the stern remained above water, a score of men clinging to the cold and slippery timber. One by one, they surrendered to the aching numbness in their hands and fell headlong into the sea.

A general wail of despair and fear rose from the women and children in the boats as the *Birkenhead* went down. Then there was a complete and terrible silence with nothing visible on the broad surface of the sea but the heads of a few men who clung to the flotsam of beams, broken spars and decking which the first impact had torn from the ship. All their comrades had been dragged down in the whirl of the lethal undertow. The deep blue lights of the rocket floats began to flicker and then, each in turn, the flames dwindled and vanished. In the last moments of the faint blue light, the survivors heard the screams of men in a pain that was more swift and rending than the agony of drowning. It was a sound which caused some of the women to stop their ears, while others saw the sinister black peak of fins cutting the water, against the guttering blue light of the floats. Fast and sure, the sharks closed upon the debris of the wreck, weaving among the flotsam to snatch their human prey.

There was no help that those in the heavily-laden boats could offer as they drifted away from the horror of Danger Rock, carried by the swift tide. The last boat to be launched, the little gig, drifted further and faster than the others until it was separated from them by almost a mile of ocean. There was just light enough from moon and stars for its occupants to make out the faces of their neighbours, some weeping and moaning, others sitting in deep, silent shock. Not twenty minutes after the *Birkenhead* had foundered, one of the women in the gig cried, 'Look! Look! Look here!' There was a confused struggle. At first her companions, searching the starlit sea for sign of rescue, had not realized that she was pointing to something in the boat. Then two or three of the others joined her, wrestling to tear the cloak which was wrapped tightly round one of the survivors.

'Dear God!' said an old woman, 'it's one of the men! In a woman's cloak!'

''e's a hofficer too!' said a young woman softly.

'Saved 'isself in women's clothes, on'y kep' 'is tunic and breeches underneath!'

There was a long, wailing, ululating cry, a communal howl of loathing, more chilling in its way than anything else in the terrible hour since the *Birkenhead* had struck Danger Rock.

'Leave me!' shrieked the man. 'Listen to me! Hear me, for God's sake!'

'You brute!' said the old woman. 'Our men died rather than do what you did!'

'Look at 'im! Took a woman's place in the boat, and left her to die in the water!'

'No!' cried the man. 'Never! I was detailed aboard the boat as guard by Colonel Seton! I swear it's the truth!'

'And sat there, hid in a woman's cloak, and never said a word!'

The derision grew around him. Not one of them wanted to believe the wretch.

''e must a-done for the poor soul to get 'er cloak!'

'He killed her to save 'isself!'

'The bastard shan't be saved! Not if I swing for 'im!'

The brawny sailor's woman, who spoke last, moved from the oars where she had been pulling and crouched forward at him.

'It's my woman's cloak!' he shouted. 'Hear me! For God's sake!'

But they seized him, a dozen of them, each as strong as the pampered young man who had cheated or murdered his way into the boat. As they bent his back over the side and his head almost touched water, his fear broke in a screaming and convulsive hysteria. He exhausted this and lay whimpering and trembling.

'Get the brute's feet up and have his head under!'

'Take a care with that,' said the sailor's woman, 'or the boat may be overset. Best roll him into the water easy. Now!'

There was a final arching and struggling, and then a cry of defeat.

'May he drown slow and hard,' said the old woman, while the others thought silently that even the sound of his cries would bring the black fins shearing the water towards him with deadly speed.

'Save him,' said a young woman, as though to herself.

'Too late, dearie. What's left of him ain't worth saving.'

They huddled in the boat, hardly caring where the tide swept them. The faint light shone on cheeks moist with tears. Several children cried with fright. As cold streaks of day caught the wave-crests, there was no sign of flotsam nor of the three other boats, which had gone their own way. Worst of all, the faint outline of Point Danger and the African coast, which had appeared like a watercolour wash on the horizon the evening before, had now vanished completely. An early mist limited visibility to a few hundred yards but even when the damp piercing cold of the first hours of daylight gave way to a clear noon with the sea reflecting the fierce heat of the sun like a burning-mirror, there was still no horizon-trace of land, no sign of any other vessel.

Among these survivors, the burly sailor-woman alone seemed undismayed. From the point of sunrise she knew the east, though as the day went by with no indication of the passage of time her sense of direction appeared less certain. Most of the children were crying in real distress and no longer from mere fright. The women, hardly hearing this any more, bowed their heads or sat staring vacantly ahead of them, lost in the depths of their own thoughts. But several of them still took the oars with the sailor-woman, whose bare muscular arms and broad sun-darkened face bore witness to her determination. Even in their self-absorbed reveries the others heard from time to time her urgent but resolute encouragement.

'Row hearty, my dear souls! Row hearty!'

A group of three of the *Birkenhead*'s boats, which had contrived to remain in convoy, was picked up by a coastal schooner, the *Lioness*. The search vessel HMS *Rhadamanthus* was despatched to the scene of the wreck soon after.

There was little enough to be done there and the *Rhadamanthus* was soon detailed to confine her operations to a search of the long unexplored coastline where men who might have swum ashore from the wreck would now be wandering exhausted. Sixty-eight men of the five hundred troops on the *Birkenhead* were recovered.

Two days after the *Rhadamanthus* abandoned her operation, the Portuguese trader *San Francisco de Goa* was eighteen miles south-west of Simon's Bay, homeward bound to Lisbon from the trading settlements of Portuguese India. Soon after first light the officer of the watch heard the look-out call, and bringing his spy-glass into focus saw the little gig with the name *Birkenhead* painted on its stern. The oarswomen were resting on their oars and the other occupants packed into the boat slumped upon one another.

Captain Ignacio Ramon, called from his berth, brought the shabby little steamer close alongside and stood on deck while his first officer went down the wooden rungs of the rope ladder. The sea was calm and the manoeuvre was simple. Before he set foot on the stern of the gig, the first officer knew that he was boarding a vessel of the dead. The bodies of the oarswomen, faces already shrunk and taut, were hard as statues in their hunched postures. Their passengers were sprawled, half fallen from their seats, eyes open and jaws dropped, in this floating charnel-house. The first officer shuddered and turned his back, seeking the ladder again. Captain Ramon had no need to await the officer's report. The tragedy of the *Birkenhead*'s gig was plain to see from the deck. Even in the cool openness of the early morning, the sweet, overblown odour of decay reached him. It crossed his mind that with a score of bodies there was little more the *San Francisco de Goa* could do than consign them to a mass grave in the ocean.

The first officer had just caught the wooden rungs of the ladder when he heard something which almost made him let go in his fright. From the boatload of corpses behind him there came a whimper and a sudden faint cry.

He turned about, not knowing which of the bodies might still have life in it. It was a child's cry, of that he was sure. Hanging by one hand, and with his foot on the gunwhale of the gig, he looked carefully at each of the eight children in the boat. At least six of them were dead beyond all question. And then he saw a slight flickering facial movement which betrayed life in one of the other two. It was a girl of about seven years old who was the sole survivor.

It was not entirely a feeling of pity which prompted the first officer as he picked his way through the dead, hardened limbs and lifted the child up. With this duty done, he thought, no more would be expected of him. Someone else could assume the disagreeable responsibility for the funeral of the victims in the growing heat of the ocean sun.

During the remainder of the day, the crew of the *San Francisco de Goa* cared for the child with great tenderness. There was no doubt that she would not have woken from this last sleep unless the gig had been spotted at that time. But warmth and care gradually overcame the effects of cold and exhaustion. Though she looked dully about her, drink and food restored her parched tongue and some of her physical strength. She seemed a sturdy youngster, the daughter or casual foundling associated with any group of soldiers' or sailors' women. Her robust young body had endured much in the past few days but had survived it. By great good fortune she had either not seen or not recognized the deaths of so many of her companions. Her spirits revived considerably and by the time that she reached Lisbon there was little sign of the ordeal she had suffered.

The British Consul thanked Captain Ramon for his Christian burial of the bodies of the victims and for his care of the one survivor. Ramon had observed a certain knowingness in the girl during the period of her recovery and he now suggested that perhaps it would be a charitable act if he were to adopt her, unofficially. The Consul was grateful but regretted that such informalities were not possible. It was necessary that the girl should be returned to England. She must go to her family, or if there were none, to the workhouse to learn a useful trade. It was a pity, but it must be so. Captain Ramon nodded and took his leave of the Consul. The last small tragedy attendant on the disaster of the *Birkenhead* seemed now to be complete.

2

Sergeant William Clarence Verity of the Private-Clothes detail, Whitehall police-office, was in his element again. It was a year since he had returned from secondment to the Intelligence Department in Calcutta during the final stages of the Mutiny and the disappearance of the great Kaisar-i-Hind diamond. Now, at the end of May 1860, he bore no worse marks of his ordeal than a faint brickish tan which still overlaid the pink roundness of his moon face. With his black hair plastered flat for neatness and his moustaches carefully waxed at the tips, he strode on his night-beat through the bright streets and murky court-yards of the West End. His shoulders were a little hunched, his hands clasped behind his back, and his movements suggested an overweight performing bear. The night-beat was an unpopular duty among the men of the Private-Clothes detail, but Verity relished the dark coolness after the nights of near-suffocation in Bengal and the torment of the prickly heat on his soft plump flesh.

At two o'clock in the morning, the Haymarket was so thronged with men, women, and children that Verity had to shoulder his way vigorously through the pressing crowd to make any progress at all. In his Private-Clothes outfit of worn stove-pipe hat, threadbare frock-coat and matching black trousers he was as conspicuous as a race-course swell at an evangelical meat-tea. He passed slowly by the coffee-stall with its tall steaming urns, where the crowd was densest. Regent Street 'aristocracy' from clubs and night-houses, resplendent in silk hats, embroidered waist-coats and chains, eyed the girls of the town who paraded slowly up and down their allotted stretch of pavement, one hand coquettishly twirling a parasol, the other hold-ing up the train of their skirts from the foul moisture which condensed on the paving in the cooler air of night.

A pair of sparring 'snobs' in loud check coats gave way to allow Verity past, grinning at him. Raffish sporting gents watched him, put their heads together confidentially, and then shouted with laughter. Inspector Henry Croaker of Whitehall police-office could have done the magsmen and the doxies of the town no greater service than to allot their beat to this fat fool. Verity's shabby 'private-clothes' were so well known that, far from disguising him, they marked him out at a hundred yards to the greenest stickman in the game. It was true that one or two lags had fallen victim to the portly sergeant. Ned Roper and a doxy or two were sweating out their time in Australian convict settlements. But the opinion up and down the Haymarket was that Ned and his bullies had been soft as new cheese.

With his mind fixed determinedly on the business in hand, Verity plodded onwards. In the side-streets there was no illumination except for an occasional gas jet flaming and flaring. But the main artery of pleasure, which ran from Pall Mall, up the Haymarket and the curve of Regent Street to Regent Circus and Langham Place, was brilliant with white gas-light. From before midnight until the first lightening of the dawn sky it was the territory of painted cheeks and brandy-sparkling eyes, the stench of bad tobacco which never cleared even in the open air, the sound of raucous horse-laughs and shrieked obscenities. Verity crossed to the splendid Nash quadrant of Regent Street. The colonnade had lately been pulled down so that there should be no shelter for street girls in front of the shops. They gathered there, all the same, offering themselves for sale under the harsh glare of gas-light and the windy roaring of its flame. Verity did not so much as glance at them, but they knew him.

'Don't yer feel frisky, old mole?' shrieked a girl of fourteen or fifteen, her pink cotton gown matched by a porkpie hat and tall feather.

'Cut it, Beth!' said a demure-looking girl in a Jane Clarke bonnet and black silk dress. 'That's Mr Verity, that is. That's the brave detective officer, that is!'

There were hoots of derision from a dozen girls along the pillared shop-fronts.

'Oh,' said the youngster, ''im as went to 'indoostan in the Mutiny, and was took prisoner by the natives, and had his apparatus removed in a dungeon!'

Screams of merriment rolled and reverberated the length of the pavement. Verity strode on, not deigning to notice such insults. 'A man that's seen what I've seen happen to such young persons don't need to answer 'em,' he said to himself firmly. Even from where he now stood he could look at houses and remember the scenes within them. Nell Jacoby, once tall and queenly, lying in her own filth on the floor of a barred attic, her body covered with the marks of ill-treatment by her keeper. Miss Amanda, whose greed led her to marry a rich tyrant and connive at his murder. They respited her from the gallows, Verity thought, but only to put her literally into the hands of hardened criminals on a convict hulk, where she might be raped and abused so many hundreds of times that the form and features of womanhood would hardly be recognizable in a year or two more.

Oh yes, thought Verity, he could put the wind up any Regent Street whore, but there were more important things to be done just now. Mr Croaker had been very insistent about it. Verity was to go and listen to two men talking. He might wait all night for them to meet and talk. He might wait in vain. But if the conversation took place, Mr Croaker was most anxious to have the substance of it reported to him. One of the men would be Charley Wag. The other might be any one of a dozen of his victims. The subject of the conversation would be blackmail or extortion. Blackmail seemed to be all the go in London that summer of 1860, though the success of the blackmailers was questionable. Many of those whom they approached, faced with public ignomiy, had apparently chosen another solution to their difficulties. The series of suicides among men who were wealthy, well-born and of doubtful habits had reached the proportions of an epidemic. 'Only,' as Sergeant Samson remarked to Verity, 'I never before 'eard that self-destruction was catching like the cholera.' But young Lord Clifton, the Earl of Reade, Lords Latham, Marlow and Chevenix, the Hon. Augustus Hall, and Sir Fraser Willoughby, had all seemed to contradict Sergeant Samson with the aid of penknives, shotguns and the noose.

Inspector Croaker had painstakingly put together scraps of information from men of his own detail and from informants who were sometimes members of the 'criminal classes' and sometimes not. Mr Croaker had no doubt of the identity of the architect of the blackmail conspiracy. He was Charley Wag, *alias* Carlo Aldino, who had risen from a hawker of obscene snuff-boxes at country fairs to be the proprietor of a Regent Street flash-house. However, it was necessary to confirm suspicion by a little evidence. Referring to the conversation which must be overheard, Mr Croaker with his dark little eyes and the autumnal yellow of his sickly complexion had said, 'It will require a certain resource on the part of the investigating officer, sergeant. Should you find that the surveillance is beyond you, report back to the duty inspector. He will know whom to send.'

Verity's pink cheeks swelled with wind, partly the result of indignation and partly of a hastily consumed 'veal and hammer'. Beyond him! A sergeant who had run to earth the finest cracksman of his age and foiled the success of the famous train robbery! A sergeant who had gone to India, rescued poor lost girls from the harems of the mutineers, saved himself and his companions from the fortress prison of the Nana Sahib, and retrieved the great Kaisar-i-Hind jewel! Beyond him to track down a common whoremonger like Charley Wag and listen to a few words of conversation! Who the devil did Mr Croaker think he was speaking to? And Verity blew his moustaches upwards in a burst of exasperation. The street girls, recovered now from their helpless laughter, watched him go. In that outfit, they knew he would never get anywhere near Charley Wag.

Verity knew it too, and his plans were laid accordingly. Soon he had passed the blaze of light which shone dazzlingly on to the pavement at half-past two from such night-houses as the Blue Posts, the Burmese, and Barron's Oyster Rooms. The interiors were wide open in most cases, showing the spacious rooms with their costly fittings. Brilliant gas illuminations from chandeliers and wall-fittings were reflected by numerous ornate mirrors, giving the atmosphere of a fairy palace to each room.

He turned into a narrower thoroughfare, where a dimmer light from the little houses showed round the edges of drawn green blinds. Chalked on the blinds themselves were such phrases as 'Lodgings for single men', 'Model lodging house', or, more precisely, 'Beds may be had within'. Between Rose Burton's and Jack Percival's night-houses was an establishment better lit than any of the others in the street: Ramiro's Oriental and Turkish Baths. It was no secret that Ramiro was Charley Wag and that the baths with their facilities for scented vapour, steam-cleansing, and 'shampooing', as it was delicately termed, were a profitable extension of the flash-house. Here, too, Charley Wag conducted his business during the hours of darkness. Strangers who had dealings with him no doubt felt at a disadvantage, naked and vulnerable among the warm, scented mists of steam. But there were few strangers. Charley Wag's visitors were generally his subordinates and, like a Roman emperor in the luxury of his bath, he lay at ease and gave his instructions. The words were spoken softly but carefully. Next day, a dishonest brothel-bully who had pocketed the takings was met with and crippled for life by the blow of an iron stave across one of his legs. An awkward girl was seized, bundled into a carriage, and taken somewhere very private. For several days afterwards she could not bear to be seen, let alone touched, but her awkwardness was cured. One of Charley Wag's debtors, an unsuccessful gamester, was beaten just sufficiently to encourage prompter payment. If he was a police officer or a man of influence, however, it was suggested to him that his debt and much more would be forgiven in exchange for certain favours towards Charley. There were half a dozen 'traps', as he called them, who owed their livelihoods to Charley Wag.

From Sergeant Samson's information, Verity had a plan of the Oriental and Turkish Baths in his mind. Behind the velvet and plush of the front reception room was a long marble corridor. To either side of it, the baths led off. At the far end was a door, beyond which lay the more magnificent baths where Charley held court. There was a steam-bath and, according to Samson's information, a finishing bath large enough for the Wag and his companions to swim in. His companions were, for the most part, female but they were not the doxies of the flash-house. Charley had never acquired a taste for English girls and he disliked using street-women. Instead, he was plentifully supplied with young girls from his native land – and Charley liked them very young – who acted as naked houris in his strange seraglio.

Verity entered the reception room from the street, his hat in his hand.

'Steam-bath, cold dip and towel, if you please, miss,' he said to the rouged and whitewashed creature at the table. She took his shilling, from which he saw to his dismay there was no change, handed him a linen towel, and motioned him towards an archway concealed by heavy curtains in rich ruby velvet. As he approached this, the curtains were drawn back by a woman on the far side, an elderly Italian duenna, thick-set and with hair dyed black, who said something to herself in her own language. Then she looked down the mottled white and pink marble corridor and shouted, 'Simona! Stefania!' There was no response. The woman shrugged and sat down again on a little stool.

The corridor was carpeted in a Turkey pattern, the doors on either side being of plain oak. At the far end, facing down the passageway, was a door whose solidity left no doubt that, as Samson insisted, it was the way to Charley Wag's private domain. Verity walked slowly and casually. The baths to either side of him were empty but it was necessary that he should be as close to Charley's presence as possible. It must be the last room opening off the passageway which adjoined the Wag's apartments. Wisps of steam hung in the pink and white marble rooms, the warm air heavy with the aroma of flowery perfume, the sourness of dead cigars and the stale scent of overheated bodies. From each room came the whisper of steam and the faint ripple of water on stone.

At three in the morning the baths seemed deserted. Verity reached Charley Wag's door and then turned into the last of the little rooms adjoining it. He pushed the plain oak and found, first of all, a porch where his clothes might be left. The street-girls were quite right, he would never have got near Charley Wag in his familiar 'private-clothes', but what better disguise than to be entirely naked in a place where nudity was the universal fashion? Verity puffed a little with satisfaction as he undressed, hung up his clothes, bolted the door behind him, and stepped into the marble cubicle with the towel in one hand. But he was not alone.

The girl who lay on her stomach on the couch was the fairer-skinned of the two, though her large dark eyes, her shock of black hair and the soft pallor of her naked body were unmistakably Italian. From the whispers of the two girls, Verity deduced that this was Stefania and that her companion, standing over her, was Simona. Simona, petite but well-rounded, her olive skin and tawny fair hair giving her the look of a Neapolitan street urchin, was the leader in the present game. Down the curve of Stefania's naked back were several blue artificial flowers, with several more tucked between her thighs so that the heads showed. Simona was obliged to take each one in her mouth and remove it, her lips brushing the sensitive flesh. Verity took the scene in at a glance and his eyes grew round. Simona bent her head over the back of Stefania's thighs while the other girl's fingers played over Simona's round bottom and legs.

''erel' said Verity sharply. His strongest feeling was one of annoyance that a carefully devised plan to eavesdrop on the Wag had been frustrated by the presence of the two girls. They were no doubt two of Charley's private collection. Simona gave him a sly glance and then bent to her task again, opening herself more fully to Stefania's advances. Verity took a step forward.

'Hook it!' he said. 'Sharp!'

They looked at him and sniggered. With the towel wrapped round his loins, he opened the door and stood in the corridor, waving indignantly at the duenna. The old woman waddled towards him and entered the cubicle. There was a stream of vituperation and then a series of loud wet slaps accompanied by cries of indignation. The performance was repeated. Followed by the woman, the two girls, rubbing vigorously at the hand-prints, hurried snivelling from the room. The woman pursued them down the passageway, muttering to herself. Fortunately, Verity thought, in her anxiety over the girls she guarded, she had not bothered to suggest that he might choose one of the dozen empty baths.

The persistent trickle of water and steam made it impossible to hear anything through the wall which separated the bath from Charley Wag's rooms. Verity looked round quickly at the sunken marble trough and the couch where Stefania had stretched out to be 'shampooed' by Simona. The pipes ran along the wall behind the couch and there were two little wheels which must operate stop-cocks of some kind. Verity took the wheels in a large ham-coloured fist and turned them gently. The whisper of steam and the chuckle of water dwindled and died. There was almost perfect silence, except for the faint grumble of voices beyond the wall. Verity's heart beat faster with expectancy. It was all to be as Sergeant Samson had promised. High in the wall was the little grating, but not so high as to be out of reach with the aid of the couch and its serviceable marble top. Once the precise words of the speakers could be heard, the blackmail conspiracy might be unmasked. As he pulled himself up, Verity had a series of mental images in which the Wag confessed all under his stern questioning, and Inspector Croaker grasped his hand in a manly, congratulatory gesture. 'Think of me as your friend, for the future,' said the mythical Croaker. And finally there was the moment when Charley and his accomplices were sentenced and the judge called before him the worthy and methodical officer who had brought the villains to book.

In the reality of the Oriental and Turkish Baths, Verity

pressed his ear to the grating, listening hard. Charley Wag's voice was easily identifiable by the intonation. But it was the other voice, bluff and throaty, which spoke first. It reminded Verity of an overweight, frog-eyed colonel who had commanded his regiment in the Russian War.

'I've been on the square with you, Mr Aldino, damned if I ain't! You've been paid for those papers and I shall be obliged to you for giving 'em me!'

'One moment,' said Charley Wag with a voice like velvet, 'it is not my concern. I act as your agent only because you wish. What is in those papers is very bad business, but it is my sister who has them. I go between.'

'I ain't going to be put off, Aldino,' said the other man. 'Either I get those papers or a reckoning shall be had.'

'You have the papers, milor,' said the Wag softly.

'All the papers!'

'*Some* papers,' said Charley. 'The rest another time, eh? My sister is a greedy woman. She say, the more you dissect such things the better they cut up. You understand that, eh?'

The other man cleared his throat with a churning cough.

'See here, Aldino! You try screwing a fellow up too far, and you'll come up with nothing but a handful of shine-rag and the skin taken off your back. Don't think I couldn't hire a crew of ruffians to settle with you cheaper than I could pay all this.'

Charley Wag began to laugh, as though at a child's pleasantry.

'Signor! Why you do that? You got enough tin to buy all those things and the pretty pictures too! Why you want such nastiness? You don't forget what is in the letter, eh? You don't forget what happen to you if the truth is told?'

The other man roared like a wounded animal in his rage.

'You damned brute! You blackguard!'

And Charley Wag laughed and laughed, moving about a little as though he might be holding off a puny assault with one hand.

'You must buy from my sister, milor! My sister a very greedy woman!'

Verity, on tip-toe, tried to see if the grating gave any view of Charley Wag's steam-bath, but the iron slats were angled carefully upwards. It was the Wag who did the spying on the unwary and indiscreet couples who used the bath which Verity had hired. At that moment, both Charley and his visitor moved. There was the sound of a scuffle and their voices became indistinct. Verity decided that they must have gone into the finishing bath, from which the sound would not carry clearly to the grating. He could eavesdrop only by going out into the corridor and standing at the Wag's door. With the towel still wrapped round his loins, he walked softly into the passageway. It was only as he looked more closely at the door dividing the row of baths from the private apartments that he noticed that it was entirely smooth. There was no handle and no keyhole on the public side, no means by which it could be opened except by those inside. No search detail was going to burst in on Charley Wag unannounced. And despite the thickness of the door, the voices were louder here. The Wag was exultant and his victim, the fight terrified out of him, was pleading.

'I tell you,' said the Wag, 'you try to hit me twice. I hit you once for sure. And now I hit you again for sure, but this time with my bellissima. Where you want Charley should mark you, milor? You want it where it not show? You say where and Charley give it you, otherwise on the face.'

There was a quick movement, a scampering, and a scream of fear from the other man. Verity had been entirely unprepared for this development. He wondered whether duty required him to turn a deaf ear while some well-heeled weakling screamed and retched under Charley's blows and knife-wounds. Or should he break off the surveillance, reveal his identity, and prevent the fearful injury about to be inflicted upon the unknown lordling? Before he could give the matter any further thought, there was a bare footfall behind him. He turned and saw Simona and Stefania at his heels. Simona screwed her face into a mask of frenzy and screamed, 'Carlo! Carlo!' The old duenna had emerged from the velvet entry curtains once more, followed by a pair of muscle-bound draymen. There was no doubt that they recognized Verity for what he was.

It was all timing now, he thought. He too shouted, 'Carlo! 'Carlo!' to the entire dismay of the others. He shouted as though his life depended on it, which in a sense it might do. To his relief, the trick worked. Charley Wag, hearing the uproar, cautiously opened the door a little on his side. Verity, the only one close to it, flung his weight forward at the most vulnerable point, his bare shoulder and upper arm numbed and bruised by the impact. But the door gave, as Charley Wag failed to hold it, and Verity was through the space in an instant. He threw himself back upon the panelling and the door slammed shut. Whatever the odds against him, the muscle-bound bruisers and their companions were now securely locked outside.

The room into which he had forced his way was the finishing bath, an oval pool some fifteen feet long set into the pink and white veining of the marble floor. Charley Wag, with the square and solid good looks which suggested a middle-aged Roman emperor, was wrapped in a towel so large that it might have served him as a toga. He stood six feet tall, his jaw set, his lips parted in a smile of derision, and his nostrils distended in expectation of a brawl. Crouched against the wall, wiping his mouth on the back of a blood-smeared hand, was a hatless, broken-down man in a shabby green coat. Verity was distracted by the incongruous appearance of the victim, thinking that Charley must have fallen on exceptionally hard times if he was obliged to fasten on such genteel paupers as this. He turned his attention, reluctantly, to the Wag.

The blade was eight inches long, thin and elegant, the dulled steel of its edges showing that it had been whetted to a razor's fineness. The handle was nothing but scarlet cord woven round a steel core. Verity felt a tingling vulnerability as he saw the knife-point angled precisely at his belly-button. At least there were none of the Wag's bullies in the room, but their arrival through some inner door of the apartments could only be a matter of a few minutes.

Circling carefully round Charley Wag, Verity consoled himself by thinking that he had fought bigger odds than this. Indeed, the sight of the stiletto gave him a moral advantage. He had been brought up to believe that an Englishman's weapons were his fists and that only women and cowards resorted to knives and such things. Beneath all the bravado, Charley would prove to be the craven degenerate of his type.

But that hardly solved the immediate problem. The Wag was hunched about ten feet in front of Verity, the blade tilted forward and upward, daring him to come on. Verity decided to accept the invitation. It was no good playing a waiting game. In a few minutes at the most the Wag's ruffians would reach whatever secret way led from the flash-house to the private baths. He must settle Charley by then and hold the door against them.

Charley Wag studied the portly, half-naked man, the belly folds and the faint quiver of surplus flesh. The face was the colour of port-wine from heat and exertion, the dark eyes narrowed and the black waxed moustaches bristling up with the scent of battle.

'Avanti!' said the Wag softly, thinking that a slit from the pubic bone up the soft belly to the solar plexus would open the affair admirably. The man was going to die, of course, but Charley had to know who he was and why he came. A careful cut below the belt would take the fight out of the plump red-faced intruder and, if deep enough, would put him in such misery that he would tell his questioners whatever they wished to know in order to earn his quietus. Charley judged the distance and then stopped in amazement. The fat man had drawn the wet towel from his loins and was standing entirely naked.

Verity drew the towel through his fingers and flicked it with a snap at the Wag's knife-hand. It missed by several inches but the Wag stared in astonishment. What was this man that he played such games with an opponent who faced him with a steel blade? The towel flicked again, catching the Wag on the side of the face. It stung him sufficiently to make him step back with an oath. The oval bath set into the floor was just behind him and he moved warily. At the third snap, the towel wound itself round Charley's right arm, enabling him to snatch it but causing him to drop his knife in the process. He began to reach for the fallen blade but Verity's huge clenched knuckles slammed into his face between nostrils and jaw, drawing blood from the nose and the torn lips. The Wag lurched sideways to avoid the bath at his back and in doing this he gave Verity an opening. From long experience of Cornish wrestling in his childhood, as well as criminal encounters later on, Verity knew that to get an opponent's head 'in Chancery' under his own arm, forearm tightening on the windpipe, was the readiest answer to any weapon. With a movement like an abortive standing-jump he got the Wag's neck in the crook of his arm and bent him with short, abrupt impacts, supported by the weight of his entire body. Charley bowed and cursed, gargling in his throat as the lever of Verity's forearm tightened.

'You just act very quiet and reasonable, my man,' said Verity breathlessly, 'if you know what's good for you!' And he brought a little more pressure to bear. Charley Wag gave a desperate gurgle and a rasping scream. His body seemed to slacken and crumple. Verity tried to hold him, half sensing what was coming, but Charley was on his knees and then, in a mere second, a red-hot pain streaked across Verity's right shoulder. All strength and leverage in the arm had gone, and the Wag was dancing free, fencing with the knife which he had retrieved from the floor.

Even the towel had gone, and it was now Verity who was held at bay. With every lunge of the blade, every withdrawal or evasion on his own part, the minutes were passing until the rear door would be broken in and the bullies of the Wag's flash-house must overpower their master's assailant. Twice Verity tried to close on the toga'd and muscular Wag. The first time Charley attempted the belly-cut but Verity swerved away with such improbable speed that he felt only the brush of the slicing blade, like the sting of a nettle. The second time he made the mistake of turning away too slowly, exposing his flank for an instant and allowing the dancing blade to flash diagonally across his rib-cage, laying open the flesh as though it had been soft butter and bringing a flow of blood over his hip. And then he began to despair. There was no way that he could fight the Wag without being cut to pieces, but unless he fought and won in the next few minutes he would be cut to pieces anyway, more leisurely but just as certainly. He was not fool enough to suppose that Charley would allow a spy to escape him.

With despair rising in his throat, Verity dodged the knife and managed to close on Charley in a last attack. The two heavily-built men gasped and sobbed for breath as they clutched at one another and the marble wall resounded to the slap of wet, blubbered flesh falling against it. Verity was almost driven back by the weaving blade. There was so much blood smeared on his body now that he could hardly tell how many times he had been cut under all the slipperiness. He held tight to the Wag's toga and smashed a blow to the jaw, with such effect that the man went spinning backwards, the toga unwinding as he tottered away and fetched up with a naked thump against the opposite wall.

But the knife was still there and the brawny body, now stripped of all covering, looked like the frame of a gladiator with its tensed muscles and olive colouring. Charley saw that the fat, pale sergeant was almost done for, his wind gone and his breath drawn in deep snorts. It was time to finish the matter. The Wag caressed the handle of the stiletto and took a step forward.

Just at that moment, behind Charley Wag, there was a scamper, a whimper and a splash. The shabbily-dressed man who had sat against the wall, covering his face with the back of his hand, had drawn a small package from the breast pocket of the battered green coat. As though coming to a sudden decision in the matter, he pulled himself to the edge of the oval finishing bath, ripped open the package and allowed a score of loose papers to flutter into the water. The ink upon them began to spread in pale blue drifts.

Verity bit back the exclamation that was on his tongue, catching the uncertainty in Charley's eyes. The Wag could not see what was happening behind him and had to know the origin of the sounds.

'Mario?' he called questioningly, but there was no reply. 'Mario? Alfredo?' Still receiving no answer and fearing an attack from behind him, he kept his knife blade angled to hold Verity and for an instant his face turned slightly towards the sounds and his eyes flicked to and fro. In that second Verity was upon him again, fighting with the desperation of a man who has been given an unexpected last chance. A savage blow to the Wag's wrist sent the knife clattering from the open hand even before the curse of pain was uttered. With unexpected agility, Verity shot out his foot and the knife spun, slithered across the marble and dropped into the oval bath with a plop. Now, he thought, it was all Cornish style.

'Mario!' Charley Wag drew back, confusion clouding his dark eyes. 'Alfredo! Simona!' He was no longer asking but calling the assistance of anyone within hearing. Whatever the Wag's bullies might do to him later, Verity knew that he could win now. He slammed into his tall, burly antagonist. A massive blow with the right fist directly above the Wag's heart stopped him and bowed him forward. A short upward jab took him on the jaw and lifted him as though he had risen in the saddle. But his footing had gone, his feet skated on the wet floor, his heels rose and he went down with a crack which Verity found deeply satisfying. At last, Charley Wag lay face down at the edge of the oval bath, quite senseless, his right arm trailing in the water.

'He ain't too bad,' said Verity for his own information. 'Why, he ain't bleeding half what I am. You over there! What was them papers you threw in the water?'

The florid-faced man, despite his shabby appearance, assumed a well-bred indignation.

'I don't know who the devil you may be, sir,' he said breathlessly, his composure returning, 'but it's none of your affair.'

'I'm a police officer,' said Verity, closing on the man, 'and there ain't a caper you could name that ain't my affair!'

He looked at the pulpy drifts of paper in the pool. The leaves had been thin and had disintegrated quickly, the writing washed away almost as soon as the water swirled over the ink. A thin gruel of pulp and water was all that remained of the evidence in the great blackmail investigation. With that evidence intact, the case against Charley Wag and his accomplices would have been irrefutable. With the evidence in its present, ruined state, the Wag could not even be brought into court and the chances of a Private-Clothes man getting near him again were nil. For this, the men of the detail had worked since the previous year. Two of them had been beaten unconscious in a rear court of Beak Street by several of Charley's swells, whose delight in muzzling a peeler had led them also to garrot a young sergeant so severely that he never walked a beat again. The shabby military man, who now cowered before Verity, had brought it all to nothing. There was no mistaking the intention in Verity's eyes.

'Keep off me!' said the red-faced man. 'Keep off, damn you!'

Verity had him by the collar, shaking him frenziedly.

'Help me! Help me!' gabbled the man. 'Police! Police!'

'I'm the police,' said Verity quietly, and he hit the shabby military man with his big, bunched fist, so that the red face jerked back like a puppet's head on a wire. The breath was driven from the body as the man hit the wall, and then slid to the floor with a front tooth protruding at an absurd angle from his gaping mouth.

'And what I want you to remember,' said Verity, as though continuing an amicable conversation, 'is that you ain't got half what you deserve. You destroyed evidence what three good men nearly died to get, all to save your foul rotten carcase. Decayed you may be, but you got the manner of a gentleman, the look of having been a soldier, and you ain't no business to be a coward. And if you left some poor little wife to sit at home and weep for your debaucheries, and if there was some lady mother whose grey hairs you brought in sorrow to the grave, you done worse than turn your back to the enemy. All things considered, my man, I let you down light.'

At the door which led to the more public baths, there was a sudden hammering, though the lock could only be opened from Verity's side. It sounded from the hum of voices as though there must be a crowd of considerable size in the corridor beyond. A loud and familiar bellow drowned the rest.

'Open this door at once, in the name of 'er Majesty! Open it up!'

For good measure a heavy boot crashed unavailingly against the stout panelling. Verity picked up the towel, wet and blood-smeared, and wrapped it round his middle. The blood on his bare flesh had thinned to a pale red with the water and perspiration as he walked majestically to the door. He opened it and stood before a score of men and women who had forced their way this far into the sanctum of Charley Wag. The whiskered face of Sergeant Albert Samson, red mutton-chopped, peered forward from the crowd.

'Dear Gawd, Mr Verity. You had it a bit 'eavy, aincher?'

'Have the kindness to come in and keep them out, Mr Samson,' said Verity faintly, nodding at the crowd of onlookers. 'And I ain't particular to 'ave to listen to your profanities neither, on top of other trials.'

Samson, whose beat covered the area of the Oriental and Turkish Baths, shouldered his way past the door and looked about him.

''ere, Mr Verity! You ain't 'alf set the cocks a-going! I never saw so much blood since that slap-bang throat-slitting down in Lambeth! Cor, you must a-fought like a brick!' Samson's blue eyes widened and his sandy features expanded in a broad grin at the thought of it. 'And 'oo might these two coves be?'

'That's a gentleman as was in a spot of bother,' said Verity indicating the red-faced man who was picking himself up unsteadily and fingering his mouth.

'Ransome,' muttered the man. 'Captain John Ransome, late Her Majesty's 73rd Foot.' In identifying himself he found it hard to conceal the self-justifying tone of the professional beggar.

''e'll want to be on his way, I expect,' said Samson pointedly. 'And this?' He joggled the Wag's ribs with the toe of his boot.

'That's 'im 'imself,' said Verity proudly. 'That's Charley

Wag, *alias* Ramiro, *alias* Carlo Aldino. That's who that is.'

Samson squatted down beside the motionless figure and turned him over on his back. The Wag's head flopped backwards as Samson struggled with the inert muscular body. And then Samson listened very carefully and got to his feet.

'That's who he *was*,' he said, correcting his colleague gently. 'That's who he was, before he went to his last long home.'

Verity's eyes bulged with indignation.

'Whatcher mean? I 'ardly touched him! There's not the blood on him! I've seen a Michaelmas goose bleed more 'n that!'

'Coves don't bleed a lot when they've snuffed it,' said Samson patiently. 'Being dead, the flow stops. I'm surprised you was never given to understand that, Mr Verity.' He tested the Wag's pulse and heart again, then shook his head.

'But I never did half to him what he did to me!' Verity seemed distraught with the unfairness of it all.

'It ain't what you did, my son,' said Samson, 'it's what the marble coping of that pool did when he fell. You ought to come and see this side of his 'ead! Skull and all broke open like split fruit! Might a-been no stronger than a pumpkin the way it's bust. You get that sometimes with these heavy-looking coves,' Samson concluded conversationally.

Verity stood, fat and dejected, in the bloodstained towel.

'I never thought he'd go that heavy,' he said gloomily.

Samson stood up again.

'Chance medley,' he said with a flourish, 'that's all it was. A slice o' chance medley with no blame attaching to you whatsoever. I'd say you ain't got a thing to answer for. Except to Mr Croaker, in the line of duty.'

'It was Mr Croaker's idea!'

Samson looked about him at the blotches of watery blood on marble walls and floor, the body of Charley Wag, its eyes rolled back to show little more than the whites, the soggy pulp of evidence floating in the bath, where the recently departed Ransome had thrown it.

'Not this,' said Samson quietly, 'not this wasn't Mr

Croaker's idea. And I can't say it was mine. When you was covering yourself with glory in Injer, me and Ziegler and Meiklejohn was walking our feet off to catch Charley at his game. Months of it. And then you was asked in to listen to a simple conversation relating to blackmail. Half an hour later the evidence is destroyed, the only witness is sent packing, and Mr Croaker's pet and only suspect is gone to a 'appier place! There ain't one bloody thing that leads anywhere any more!'

Verity felt dizzy, whether as a reaction from the exertion of the fight, or loss of blood, or the sight and smell of blood all about him, he could not tell. He leant heavily against the wall.

'It ain't fair,' he said feebly.

'No,' said Samson unsympathetically, 'there's a lot ain't fair in this world. I daresay me and Meiklejohn and Ziegler is going to feel it ain't fair either.'

'Mr Samson, you got it wrong, all of you. It ain't blackmail. It can't be. Charley Wag isn't – wasn't – so stoopid that he'd try to blackmail a broken down old captain like Jack Ransome with no money to his name.'

'No?' said Samson unimpressed.

'No, Mr Samson. Captain Jack ain't held a commission in five years and was last known of going the round of fairs and race meetings doing the old three-thimbles-and-a-pea trick.'

'You let them as have worked on the case be judges of that,' said Samson wisely. 'You done enough.'

'I never killed a man before, not fighting face to face, Mr Samson. And I wouldn't a-done now, but it was him or me.'

Samson walked over to the door to admit his two accompanying constables.

'Being your acquaintance, Mr Verity,' he said, 'I'm glad, in course, that it was you came out of it. But I can't say that Meiklejohn and Ziegler wouldn't rather have had Charley Wag and a road to follow home.'

Smells of horse dung and warm straw rose faintly from the stable beneath the kitchen of the little mews dwelling. Julius Stringfellow's possessions, the old silhouettes in mahogany frames, the ornamental plates celebrating the coronation of William IV, and the forage cap worn at the siege of Bhurtpore thirty-eight years ago, were now penned in by the newly-acquired treasures of his daughter and son-in-law. There was an imitation French clock under a glass dome, a steel engraving done from a photograph which showed the young round-faced Queen seated with her Consort standing beside her, there was even a brand-new Windsor chair with its tall pointed back in the shape of a Gothic arch.

Below the kitchen, in the mews stable, Lightning, the elderly cab-horse, snorted in his sleep. Stringfellow moved lopsidedly across the kitchen on the wooden leg which had served him ever since the loss of his own at that same siege of Bhurtpore, in the war against the usurper Doorjun Saul. The old cabman paused and regarded the plump detective sergeant, once his lodger and now the husband of his beloved child, Bella. Verity sat dressed in his baggy trousers on a small stool. His shirt was off and the extent of his wounds displayed.

'You had it bad, chum,' said Stringfellow thoughtfully.

'I've had it worse before now, however,' said Verity, tight-lipped.

Stringfellow hobbled to a cupboard, unlocked it and took out a china bottle. There was a faint aroma of brandy as he pulled the stopper with his teeth.

'Course,' he said, 'I ain't saying you'd want to be a cab-man. What I say is, if you *did* want to be a cabman, there ain't no reason you shouldn't apprentice yourself along of me and, consequential, be your own master after my time.'

He tipped some of the brandy on to lint.

'Paddington Green ain't a bad area for it,' he continued, pausing for reflection, and then he applied the raw spirit to Verity's wounds. Verity's eyes widened, his mouth worked and puffed, and at last he emitted a windy groan.

From the open doorway of the little kitchen there was a stifled whimper. Stringfellow's dark, bushy eyebrows gathered in a frown as he peered through the darkness. He moved a pace forward and pointed at the leather thong which secured his wooden leg.

'Miss Bella!' he said, 'see this? Now I ain't going to tell you again that this ain't proper work for a woman. But if you ain't out of here in two seconds, I don't care if you'm married and have a cradle going upstairs. Off comes this 'ere strap and leathers your hide for you smart enough to keep you dancing for a week after!'

'Run along, Mrs Verity,' said Verity faintly and there was a scampering on the stairway.

'I know the spirit do catch the rawness,' said Stringfellow, retrieving the lint. 'Howsoever, I wish the regimental surgeons had had it to spare after Bhurtpore. I'd a-got two legs now.'

He examined Verity's arm, blood seeping from the deep wound where Charley Wag had cut himself free from the head-lock.

'That ain't a-going to heal of its own accord,' he announced. 'It'll weep like that until it festers.'

Humming a little tune, he rummaged in a drawer and produced a needle and thick twine. He twisted the needle in a candle-flame.

'What can mend a 'orse can mend a man,' he said philosophically.

Verity looked away and Stringfellow went to work.

'You no idea the satisfaction of a cab,' he said, as Verity bit back a gasp of pain, 'jogging on, seeing places.'

'Don't prose so!' said Verity breathlessly. 'I was a sojer against the Rhoosians at Inkerman, and in a manner o' speaking I'm a sojer now against Charley Wag and his kind.'

Stringfellow broke the twine in his teeth.

'Likewise,' he said, 'I have had cause to remark that you was never obligated to fight the Rhoosians in Paddington Green, nor expect your wife to caper about like one of Miss Nightingale's ladies.'

'Mrs Verity ain't soft,' said Verity at length.

Stringfellow stood back a little to admire his surgical skill more fully.

'Soft?' he said thoughtfully, 'she went soft the first night you set foot in this 'ouse! Whimpering to see the brave sojer that'd beat the Rhoosians at Inkerman! And then pining after the brave policeman that beat Ned Roper and all the swell mob, one-handed. Mind you, if Mrs Stringfellow 'adn't gone off with the cholera that summer of the Hyde Park exhibition, there'd a-bin a firmer hand on 'er! See her married to a 'usband that comes home four o' clock of a morning, cut to tatters, and sits in the kitchen a-bleedin' 'isself silly! A cabman's daughter, too!'

'If it's all the same,' said Verity weakly, 'I ain't particular to discuss cabs tonight.'

'What don't get discussed is liable to be forgot,' said Stringfellow sternly. 'Mind you, though, an old 'orse do get you by the throat a bit these warm summer nights, don't 'e?'

3

'Sergeant William Clarence Verity, you have been paraded on a charge of having made an unwarranted and brutal assault upon a member of the public, Captain John Ransome, late 73rd Foot. Of that charge I find you guilty. It is my duty to reprimand you severely and to inform you that you will lose twelve months' seniority in the rank of sergeant for this offence. The nature of the offence, the finding and the punishment will be entered in the divisional record. It is also my duty to warn you that you have now been reprimanded three times in all, once for insubordination and twice for assaults upon members of the public, and that a fourth such breach of discipline must result in your automatic dismissal from the force.'

Inspector Henry Croaker looked up from the papers on his desk as he spoke the final words. There was an expectant gleam in his eyes at the promise of one mere reprimand standing between him and the dismissal of the portly, self-righteous sergeant. Hero of Inkerman or not, another reprimand would be the end of him. Croaker's dark whiskers were finely trimmed and his thin yellowish face, the colour of a fallen leaf, seemed a perfect match for the dry withered tone of his voice. At Verity's back, Sergeant Ziegler, the escort, breathed heavily on the nape of his neck, as though he might be chewing something slowly.

'Defaulter stand fast!' said Croaker in his brittle voice. 'Escort dismissed!'

Ziegler stamped about and marched from the room with the slow, swinging gait he had perfected for such occasions as this. It was the usual form. Once the official proceedings were over, the unofficial 'roasting' of the culprit followed. Verity stared ahead of him. When the house in Whitehall Place, Scotland Yard, had been a gentleman's residence, thirty years before, Croaker's office had served as upstairs drawing-room. Through the panes of the window Verity, stiff at attention, watched the coal wagons and collier brigs of Whitehall wharf. Beyond them the waves of the murky river sparkled in the morning sun. Penny steamers trailing a banner of black smoke from their tall stacks bore their top-hatted passengers across from Surrey to the Middlesex shore.

Croaker kept him at attention, pushed back his chair a little and for several seconds indulged in the sheer pleasure of surveying his victim.

'Sergeant Verity,' he said at length, rolling the words on his tongue as though savouring them, 'you imagine, I suppose, that you have come easily out of this affair?'

'No, sir,' said Verity firmly, presuming that an answer was called for. 'Never thought that, with respect, sir. Still 'ave considerable twinges in the arm and side, sir.'

'Do you?' said Croaker, as though the news brought him deep satisfaction. 'Do you?' He sat silent for a moment and then asked, 'And what of your colleagues, sergeant? What of the men who devoted months of hard, unremitting work to the discovery of a vile criminal conspiracy, only to see their efforts destroyed by you in the course of a simple and routine piece of surveillance?'

'Don't see that, sir. With respect, sir.'

'Don't see it, sir?' said Croaker derisively. 'Don't see it? In the first half hour of your part in the investigation, you destroy the evidence, murder the chief suspect, and assault the only available witness! Don't see it!'

''ave the honour to suggest, sir, as it wasn't me that destroyed the evidence. It was Captain Ransome as threw them papers in the water.'

'And you, a trained detective officer who had been present throughout, did not even see fit to suggest to him that he ought not to do so!'

'Wasn't like that, sir. I was engaged with the person Aldino.'

'And killed him!'

'Didn't mean to, sir. 'ad to lay 'im cold, sir, or he'd a-coopered me and Captain Ransome.'

'So you say. And who would Captain Ransome have coopered?'

'Don't follow, sir. With respect, sir.'

'Why was it necessary to break his teeth for him?'

'Just it, sir. When I saw what he'd a-done with the evidence, destroyed it and all, I wasn't quite meself for a minute. Loss of blood and faintness it must a-bin, sir.'

'You were overheard by a witness making some foolish remarks about Captain Ransome's treatment of his wife and mother before you hit him. Was that the result of faintness or loss of blood?'

'Must a-bin, sir, or I wouldn't 'ave done it, would I?'

Verity was relieved to see that this shot brought Croaker down from his flights of official irony.

'I will just say this, Sergeant Verity. For some reason of his own, Captain Ransome has declined to bring criminal proceedings for assault against you. Had he done so, there can be no doubt that you would not only have been dismissed the force, you would now be serving twelve months in Horsemonger Lane Gaol, attended by hard labour on the treadmill and the crank. Do I make myself clear, sergeant?'

'Yes sir. Very clear, sir. One thing to say, sir.'

'Well?'

'There's a funny smell about it, sir. I don't think you got a blackmail case, sir. Least, not ordinary blackmail, sir. Captain Ransome is known on race-courses and fairgrounds and such places. He ain't got two groats for a farthing. Charley Wag wouldn't a-wasted time squeezing him.'

'Indeed?'

'Yes, sir. O' course, there's blackmail going on. But that ain't the heart of it, somehow. However, if I'm given permission, I'll find out what is, sir.'

'Four of your colleagues have been arranging that matter for several months, sergeant. They were within arm's length of the heart of it, as you call it, when you intervened. It is not intended that you should be given any further opportunity to display your peculiar skills in this case.'

Verity swallowed.

'Sir?'

'Yes, sergeant?'

''ave the honour to request, sir, what duties I shall be allotted to, if it ain't the blackmail dodge.'

'Have no fear, sergeant. You will very shortly find out that duties have been found to match your talents in every respect.'

Inspector Croaker rarely smiled and would never have permitted himself to do so in the presence of a subordinate. But there came into his eyes, as he regarded the fat perspiring sergeant, a dark glitter which suggested a deeply-felt and almost animal satisfaction.

The room in which the dozen men of the Private-Clothes detail paraded reminded Verity of Hebron Chapel School in his childhood, the masters and ushers standing at the front, the pupils lined up before them. Inspector Swift, as duty officer, was about to combine the roles of educator and disciplinarian. While the men waited, Samson, who was next in line to Verity, said from the corner of his mouth,

'You never came to the wake for Charley Wag, then?'

'No!' said Verity, shocked, ''ow should I?'

'Some of us went,' whispered Samson. 'Wasn't half a do before they packed him off to Kensal Green! Porter and gin, and that gassy foreign wine what do fizz up your nose. And them fancy pies and cakes. Oh, my eye! Ain't they prime, though?'

'Mr Samson! 'ow could you a-done it?'

'Those two doxies,' whispered Samson happily, 'Simona and Stefania, what no one had a use for. I went into their room with them. Stripped off in a twinkling. The dark-haired one gets on her back, and that young baggage Simona gets over her with her tight little bum waggling in the air, and then. . . .'

'Parade: 'Shun!'

There was a scraping of boots and Samson stood rigidly to attention, staring piously ahead of him in his obedience to the demands of duty.

Inspector Swift detailed the men for their various beats, one by one, until all had been accounted for except Verity. He dismissed the others to their tasks.

'Sir?' said Verity hopefully.

'Downstairs, sergeant,' said Swift, half sympathetically. 'The ground-floor back, I'm afraid.'

Verity swallowed with visible apprehension.

'Ground-floor back, sir?'

'The hiring-room,' said Inspector Swift sadly. He was a large freckled Irishman who was reputed to love Mr Croaker like a dose of rat-bane. 'Orders of your own Inspector,' he added gently.

Verity turned away slowly, bewildered at the sentence passed upon him. After the death of Charley Wag, he had been prepared to face dismissal from the force or even criminal proceedings, but the ground-floor back was a crueller fate than either. It was the hiring-room, as Swift called it, where detective officers without suitable employment in the division were paraded for hire by members of the public. In practice, their employers came from a very limited class of the wealthy and the noble who had chosen to explore some family mystery, or wished to exercise surveillance over an errant wife or scapegrace son. It was a place generally reserved for officers who had not given quite sufficient pretext for dismissal but whose age or habits made them of little value to the detail. As Mr Croaker well knew, a man who was relegated to the hiring-room had only one path ahead of him, the path of rejection by his peers and superior officers alike.

Verity walked towards the ground-floor back, and for the only time in his police career he felt that he was close to tears. Other officers of the Private-Clothes detail were busily setting out on their beats and assignments. With their departure the building grew silent. Verity opened the scrubbed oak door of the room, which was sparsely furnished with a few wooden benches and painted in a lime-coloured wash which since the eighteenth century had been supposed to render police offices and prison cells proof against typhus and gaol fever. Four other men sat, widely-spaced, on the benches. One, a ruffianly-looking fellow, kept his head lowered and picked his teeth. Another sucked with furious energy on a short clay pipe. There was an emaciated dark-haired sergeant whose breath betrayed the sweet acidity of gin as Verity passed him, and a well-dressed man, neat and clean, who had been sent to the hiring-room merely because of his grey hair and advancing years.

Verity found a space on one of the benches, as far removed from the others as possible, and sat down glumly. From time to time, the duty inspector would enter and call the men to attention. They stood in an irregular line, aware that from some spy-hole they were probably being surveyed by an intending customer. 'Like whores on a fucking pavement,' the cadaverous sergeant remarked in his slurred voice, after each intrusion. The entire morning passed and not one of the customers was inspired to make his choice from the men in the hiring-room. After a time, Verity found a natural empathy with the cleanly, neatly-dressed old man who sought only a tolerant if unresponsive audience for his conversation. He talked of gardens and flowers, of roses he had grown and of roses he proposed to grow. Verity nodded and made acquiescent sounds, which seemed to be all that was required. The ruffianly detective sneered at the old man's gentility and the cadaverous drunkard complained of the noise.

As morning turned to afternoon, the old man unwrapped a spotless 'kingsman' or neckerchief, and cut his bread and cheese. Verity refused the proffered slice. The emaciated sergeant moaned for a pull of crank or sky-blue or mexico, while the two rougher men suggested he might stash his gab.

It was mid-afternoon when they were called to attention again. Shortly afterwards, Inspector Swift returned.

'Mr Cuff,' he said gently. The elderly man got up, turned to Verity with a half-bow, and followed the Inspector out with great jauntiness. Verity and the others waited in a morose and depressed silence. At four o'clock or thereabouts another call to attention came. The four men stood in varying poses of rigidity, the thin drunkard half leaning on Verity's shoulder. There was a pause before Swift reappeared.

'Sergeant!' he said in an abrupt whisper, and Verity saw that he was looking at him. Swift beckoned and Verity followed him out of the room. In the passageway the Inspector turned to him.

'It's not much, sergeant, but you may work at it. It goes hard to see a good man sitting in that room. Whether you care for the job signifies little so long as it gives you your quittance.'

'Not like it, sir?'

'No,' said Swift. 'Your employer is Mr Richard Jervis.'

'Mr Jervis, sir?'

'Younger brother of Lord Henry Jervis, deceased.'

'Oh,' said Verity, '"im!'

'Quite,' said Swift. 'There are three brothers, Lord Henry deceased, Lord William, who now holds the title and estate, and Mr Richard, the youngest. A month ago, Lord Henry was killed in a shooting accident. The party was beating for game on the Jervis lands at Bole Warren in Sussex. Lord Henry was following a raised stone path with a ditch below it, when he stumbled and fell. The rifle he was carrying hit the stone, jarred and went off. The bullet passed through his skull on the right-hand side, killing him at once. There was never a doubt that the bullet was fired by his own rifle, and there was no one within thirty yards of him when it happened. There must have been a dozen witnesses. The coroner's jury returned accidental death and the police investigation confirms it. There were rumours – just gossip, you understand – which said that Lord Henry might not have stumbled, that he shot himself deliberately.'

'Destroyed 'isself, sir?'

'Quite, sergeant. There is, of course, no evidence that he did and not the least reason for him to do so. It was never suggested at the inquest.'

'Then why am I sent for, sir? With respect, sir.'

'Mr Richard Jervis is a crippled gentleman,' said Swift softly, 'and as such he mayn't undertake much investigating on his own behalf. The suggestion of Lord Henry's suicide has greatly distressed him. He does not believe that his brother destroyed himself, nor does he believe there was an accident.'

'Don't follow, sir. With respect, sir.'

'Mr Richard Jervis,' said Swift patiently, 'claims that Lord Henry was murdered.'

'Don't see 'ow, sir. Not if he was killed with his own gun and there wasn't no one near him at the time.'

Swift spread out his hands.

'There is no way that the police or the coroner's jury could see, sergeant. But young Mr Jervis is insistent that he will have a new and private investigation into Lord Henry's death. It is his money, sergeant, and his privilege.'

'And the present Lord William, sir?'

'The present Lord William is a captain in the Royal Navy, sergeant. He is at present at sea in HMS *Hero*. He is also the companion in pleasure of some of the highest and – between ourselves, sergeant – some of the lowest in the land. His interest in the family, the estate, his brother dead and his brother living is not intense. It is Mr Richard Jervis who will be your employer.'

''ave the honour to request, sir, do I 'ave to be 'ired for this? There ain't nothing to be investigated, sir!'

'Sergeant Verity,' said Swift gently, 'be a good fellow and do as Mr Jervis asks you. It is not your fault if his belief about Lord Henry proves wrong. Walk smartly and talk sensibly. When you return here, it will not be to the hiring-room. But if you choose to be troublesome now, be sure that Mr Croaker will give you very little grace in the hiring-room before submitting to the commissioner of police that there is no further employment in the force for which you are suited.'

Verity swallowed again.

'Yessir. Very good, sir.'

He followed Swift into an office furnished with black leather chairs and a satinwood bureau. A young man in his late twenties sat at a fine walnut table. He was, thought Verity, groomed neat as a fashion plate, his fair hair trimly worn and the dundreary whiskers carefully barbered. It was clear at a glance that the young man was prey to some long-established sickness. The wan, pinched face gave the blue eyes with their large pupils a disproportionate size and brightness. The pallor, visible as clearly in the thin elegant hands as in the face itself, was enhanced by a black silk coat, black stock and cravat, and the mourning gloves in black kid which lay folded on the polished walnut. Verity faltered at the prospect of being immersed in the young man's grief and sickness.

'Mr Jervis, sir,' said Swift in his soft Irish voice, 'this is Sergeant Verity, of whom I spoke.'

Richard Jervis looked up slowly and surveyed Verity with a long and careful stare. He nodded, as though in reluctant approval, and addressed all his remarks to Swift.

'He is experienced in the detection of murder? In distinguishing between murder, misadventure and self-destruction? He is, shall we say, *au fait* with the evidence and the methods?'

'As are all our officers, sir,' said Swift with the merest hint of reproach.

Richard Jervis nodded, as though he had heard all that was necessary. Swift intervened again.

'I trust, sir, you will find no cause for complaint with Sergeant Verity. However, sir, you must know that an officer can only detect what there is to be detected. He cannot make murder where there was none.'

'And he should not convict a poor soul of self-destruction, whose life was robbed from him,' said Jervis sharply. 'But I must be guided by you, Mr Swift, must I not? I am to do as you bid, as all of you bid in the matter. And so I shall. But I will have justice, sir, for all that. I will have justice done!'

'It is to be hoped you will, sir,' said Swift blandly.

Verity looked furtively at Richard Jervis, the brightness of the eyes reflected and intensified the bitterness of the voice.

'As to the matter of a fee,' said the young man more composedly, 'have the goodness to direct to my steward at Upper Berkeley Street, Portman Square. Whatever is customary shall be paid.'

Swift bowed his head a little and Jervis laid his pale hands, side by side, on the table.

'Please to call for my man and leave us,' he said quietly.

Swift motioned Verity from the room, went to call Jervis' servant and then returned to the plump sergeant.

'Remember,' said Swift in a whisper, 'he can't bear to be watched when he's moved.'

Verity turned a little and saw a man of indeterminate middle-age entering the room where Jervis sat. He took in the bull-like shoulders the shabby bottle-green coat, the dark hair and moustaches now dusted with grey against the burnt face, the dark spaniel eyes. He turned to Swift again.

'Captain Ransome, sir,' he said softly, "im as was in with Charley Wag that night! Wot the 'ell's he doing as valet to Mr Jervis?'

'Alack and alas, sergeant,' said Swift, in his gentle, ironic manner, 'that is something which you are not paid to investigate. If a gentleman chooses to employ Honest Jack Ransome as his valet, what of it? Charley Wag knew of some peccadillo and he bled poor Captain Jack even of his miserable half-pay allowance.'

'The person Ransome threw the evidence in the water and destroyed it!' said Verity indignantly.

'Ah,' said Swift, 'and so might you have done in his place, sergeant. What was evidence to us was disgrace and shame to him, stories of Captain Jack and another man's wife, or Honest Ransome and a stable lad or two.'

'Captain Ransome and the thimble-and-pea caper at every fair and race meeting!' said Verity sceptically.

'And so it was once,' said Swift genially, 'when times were hard for an old soldier. But now, like many a rough and tough old warrior, Honest Jack finds shelter in a gentleman's employment.'

Half-turning his head, Verity glimpsed the slight pale figure of Richard Jervis, manoeuvring himself forward with a pair of sticks while Ransome's heavy arms supported him with unexpected gentleness. The gentleman and his valet turned a corner.

''ave the honour to request, sir,' said Verity to Swift, 'if I'm to ride to Portman Square on the box of the gentleman's coach now.'

'No, sergeant,' said Swift. 'Whatever your movements, you may make them on foot or by twopenny bus. Learn thrift, sergeant. There's no end to what a man may do, if he'll only be thrifty.'

'That's very true, sir.'

'First collect your belongings, clothes, accoutrements. Then proceed to Mr Jervis' town house. Upper Berkeley Street, Portman Square. When a man is hired, he lives in. You'll find the servants' quarters comfortable enough. Many a uniformed officer on the beat and living in a station-house might envy you.'

'Then I ain't to live 'ome, sir?'

'Sergeant,' said Swift gently, 'an officer, when hired, serves his master. Like all servants, he may have a half day off from time to time, or even a Sunday. But he mustn't expect to be paid for working in one house when he lives in another, any more than if he was a butler or valet.'

'Then I ain't to live with Mrs Verity!' said Verity aghast.

'A man doesn't join the force for who he can live with!' said Swift reproachfully. 'But now you know why such good care is taken to avoid the hiring-room. You mayn't be your own master in the division, but you're never less your own master than when on hire.'

'I might a-took the Queen's shilling again and done no worse,' Verity said with a growing sense of grievance.

'So you might,' said Swift, 'and then again you might have took it and been shot like a blackcock in some foreign war. You be thankful for a snug billet, my lad, and that you aren't sleeping tonight under the bridges or the Adelphi arches, like twenty thousand other poor wretches. When a gentleman hires you and pays your board, you've got a lot to think yourself lucky for!'

4

'Course,' said Stringfellow reasonably, 'you can't 'elp feeling for the poor young gentleman. You can't 'elp being sorry that his brother met a bloody end and that self-destruction and all its attendant 'orrors was hinted at.'

Playbills outside the Britannia at Hoxton or the Coburg, advertising the latest melodrama, were Stringfellow's favourite reading and their style was apt to influence his own in speaking of the great issues of life and death.

'It's me I feel sorry for,' said Verity bitterly, 'put to an investigation what the coroner's jury and the constabulary have already finished. 'ow the mischief can it be anything but an accident? The bullet came from the poor young fellow's own gun, which was in his own hand and which hadn't been tampered with. And there was no one in thirty yards of him. He must a-shot 'isself, accident or not.'

''e was never victim to the fell demon of self-destruction!' said Stringfellow incredulously. Verity shook his head.

'Not unless there was more to it than appears. Why, he'd got the title and the estates. True, he 'adn't yet got a wife but there was every prospect. He was a well man, 'ealthy and 'olesome I don't see self-destruction in it.'

They stood in the Upper Berkeley Street mews which led to the rear of the Jervis town house. Two kitchen-boys were struggling with a polished wooden box whose lid bore the initials 'W.C.V.' It had accompanied the twelve-year-old Verity from the miner's cottage at Redruth to the grandeur of Lady Linacre's house in the Royal Crescent at Bath, where he was first page and then footman. His father had painted the initials on the lid, with their scrolling and flourishes. His mother had papered the inside with a rose-patterned paper so finely textured that it felt like damask. The varnish was a little cracked and the gloss somewhat dimmed but the sight of the box brought back so many poignant images to his memory that it seemed entirely fitting that it should contain all his worldly possessions. The two boys struggled through the doorway with it and began the ascent of the narrow wooden stairs at the back of the great house, leading to the servants' attics. In one of these little garrets, Verity was to live during the period of his hire by Richard Jervis.

Stringfellow and his son-in-law stood forlornly in the yard, Stringfellow's vehicle, a lumbering square coach in bilious yellow with green wheels and axletree, waiting just behind them. On the door was a faded coat of arms which resembled a dissected bat. Lightning, the old cab-horse, stood with drooping head, his scanty mane and tail twitching as he winced and rattled the harness. An apple-cheeked old woman in cap and apron appeared at the kitchen steps and gestured at the two men.

'Coach!' she shouted.

Stringfellow moved towards her with the rolling gait which his wooden leg gave him.

'I ain't for 'ire just this minute ma'am,' he said apologetically.

'Do have done, then!' said the old woman laughing. 'Course you ain't for hire. Do'ee just put some straw under the animal's feet and take a drop of the right sort.'

Stringfellow's face brightened and he beckoned Verity.

'I'm Mrs Butcher,' said the old woman, 'housekeeper here since the time of old Lord Samuel Jervis, him that was father to Lord Henry and Lord William and Mr Richard.'

They followed her into a pleasant little parlour with a brick floor and a doorway which gave on to the kitchen, showing its stoves and hot closets, its scrubbed pine tables and rows of copper pans. Mrs Butcher opened a corner cupboard and produced a dark bottle and three glasses. She went to a small oak sideboard and returned with an earthenware jug of water and some sugar lumps in a blue and white china bowl. Stringfellow placed seats for the three of them and they sat down round the table.

'A drop of the right sort don't come amiss after a journey,' said Mrs Butcher, winking at Stringfellow.

'I shouldn't say no,' Stringfellow conceded, 'but Mr Verity ain't got much use for it.'

'Just a little drop,' said Mrs Butcher firmly as she prepared the potion, 'a little drop o' gin with cold water and a lump of sugar to take away the sharpness of it.'

They raised their glasses.

'Your 'ealth, Mrs Butcher,' said Stringfellow, taking a long pull at the gin and water, then emitting a contented sigh.

Mrs Butcher turned to Verity.

'And you'm the detective officer that's to bring Lord Henry's murderer to light?'

Verity was thunderstruck that what he had taken to be a confidential assignment was known to the servants of the house.

''oo says there was murder done?' he asked suspiciously.

Mrs Butcher pulled a face.

'Someone must a-said it, Mr Verity, or you wouldn't be sitting 'ere now, would you?'

'You seen what was in the papers, Mrs Butcher. The bullet that killed Lord Henry had the marks of his own gun on it. It was fired from his own gun, which was in his hand, and no one in thirty yards of him when it happened.'

He supped at his gin and wiped his moustache on the back of his hand. Mrs Butcher pulled another little face, as though she did not greatly care either way.

'It ain't everything that gets into the papers,' she said.

'Meaning?' asked Verity.

'Meaning,' said Mrs Butcher, 'that I ain't going to repeat gossip and be got in trouble for it. You find what you can find, and if it looks to point towards a certain party, you come and tell me. Then I can say if it matches what I know.'

They drank in silence for a minute or two.

'Mrs Butcher,' said Stringfellow presently, ''oo might it be as is master of this house?'

'Of old,' said Mrs Butcher, 'it was Lord Samuel Jervis', the house here and the country place at Bole Warren, down

Lewes way. Lord Samuel died and it went to the eldest son, Lord Henry, who was very taken with being a clergyman at Oxford, but never did. Very bookish 'e was. With his head and his money, 'e might a-bin a bishop if he'd gone through with it. Instead, he goes for a sojer in the Rhoosian war and then comes home to this 'ouse and the country estate. Never married, though who can say he mightn't in a while more? When he died, everything passed to the present Lord William. Being a naval gentleman, he's as often at Portsmouth or Plymouth as he is here. And though I ain't particular to talk about it, even when Lord William is in London he ain't in the house much. There's dances in the season and shooting parties at Bole Warren, but for the greater part of it, poor young Mr Richard might be master here if he chose.'

'So all the inheritance don't mean much to Lord William?' said Verity hopefully.

'The rate he's racketing along,' said Mrs Butcher, 'it'll mean something when he has to raise every penny on it to keep him out of a debtor's prison.'

She spoke with a finality indicating that she had already said as much as she proposed to on the subject of the Jervis family. Verity and Stringfellow took their leave of her and retired to the cobbled yard again. Lightning raised his head slightly and regarded them with equine disinterest. Stringfellow braced his good leg on the coachwork and hauled himself up on to the box where an old greatcoat was spread for comfort.

'Seems to me,' he said philosophically, 'that the entire house thinks there was murder done.'

'Servants' gossip,' said Verity indignantly, 'that's all it is. Why, Mr Stringfellow, I thought you'd a-known better than to truck with that sort o' thing when you know the evidence is all the other way. It's evidence that puts gossip in its place!'

Stringfellow looked down at the smug pink moon of his son-in-law's face with its neatly waxed moustaches.

'I ain't averse to a bit o' gossip,' he said firmly. 'It helps to make the day go round smooth. And if you think it ain't evidence, Mr Verity, then you got a bit to learn about evidence!'

The room in which Richard Jervis received Verity on the following morning resembled a counting-house rather than any domestic apartment. It was the place where the master of the house might have called his steward or his butler to account. Jervis, appearing slim to the point of frailty in his mourning suit, sat in a black leather chair. His slightly crouched posture suggested distortion as well as paralysis of his body from the waist down. In their first meeting alone he seemed to Verity to exhibit an invalid's tetchiness in his resentment of sympathy and a manic determination to show himself master of events. The blue eyes searched Verity's face carefully.

'Mr Verity, I am a careful man. I pay attention to detail and though I have more than enough money for my needs, I spend it scrupulously.'

'To be sure, sir.'

'I say this because there are those who will tell you that I am about to waste your time and my money on a foolish investigation. What I want from you is no less than a full inquiry into my brother's death.'

'With respect, sir, I can examine the evidence at the scene of the tragedy. Only being some weeks since it 'appened, there won't be so much to be found as there was when it was first examined. I can examine the rifle, sir, though it's been done by men whose business is rifles. And I can talk to the gentlemen who saw the tragedy, sir, one of whom is yourself. But I don't suppose there's any questions that haven't been asked already. 'owever, I gotta say, sir, that when all's said and done, I can't make a murder out of an accident, nor I mustn't neither.'

Richard Jervis' pale blue eyes narrowed, the sharpness of his pale face accentuated by the trim triangle of his fair beard.

'Pray God you bring my brother's murderer to justice, sergeant, or there shall go back such a report to your inspectors as shall live with you and them the rest of your days!'

'Evidence is evidence, sir, and accidents is accidents,' said Verity softly, rocking a little on his heels.

'What do you know of accidents, Mr Verity?'

'Don't follow, sir. With respect, sir.'

'Do you not? Then I must lead you. You will no doubt have heard that I sit here, a man with half a body, because of what they call a hunting accident.'

'I 'ave understood so, sir, and very sorry I am it should be so.'

Jervis slapped his hand on the table.

'No, sergeant, you have not understood. I see the hunters in my mind as clearly as I see you now. I see them close upon me, the devil masks of hate. Even in my dead limbs I feel the blows. Can you imagine, Mr Verity, what it is to feel blow after blow and to know that each one is doing such damage to your body that can never be mended?'

Verity was aghast, his face creased with incredulity.

'I 'ope to God, sir, you don't mean you was maimed deliberate?'

'What else should I mean, sergeant? Don't I make it plain?'

'But the villains that did it, sir? Who might they be, and why never brought to account for what they'd done?'

'Their faces were changed to devil-masks, Mr Verity. I could not name them. It is many years ago and it may be that some of them are now dead. But those who killed my brother are not dead.'

'You don't suspect the same persons, sir?'

Richard Jervis sniffed and said in his most level tone,

'There is a curse upon our house, it seems.'

He became silent, sitting in deep thought, as though no longer aware of Verity's presence.

'Sir,' said Verity gently, 'I must have evidence. The villains that 'armed you, them that you say made away with Lord Henry Jervis, I can't touch 'em without evidence.'

'Justice,' said Jervis flatly, 'vengeance. What of that?'

'It goes on evidence, sir. It must do.'

'And where there is no evidence, the evil man must go free?'

'Yessir. But there always *is* evidence, sir.'

Richard Jervis slapped his hand upon the table again.

'Then, by God, sergeant, you shall have evidence enough. There shall be nothing in this house or this family hidden from your eyes. You will go first to Bole Warren and examine the scene of Lord Henry's death. I will instruct the gunmaker who testified at the inquest to make his evidence and the gun available to you. My late brother's physician, Dr Jamieson of Burlington Street, shall answer your questions upon the medical evidence. He was with the shooting party at Bole Warren when my brother met his death. My brother's private apartment in this house has not been opened since the inquest. You will be given access to it, and you will search the contents.'

'Search 'is private things, sir?' asked Verity in some alarm.

Richard Jervis' mouth twisted slightly.

'I am not interested in repeating the mistakes of the previous investigation, Mr Verity. Your inquiry is to be complete. You will act on my instructions and my authority. If it is at any time suggested to you that there is something you had best leave alone, that is the very thing you will examine most diligently. Do you understand your instructions?'

'Yessir. Being as the weather might turn to rain, sir, I shall make it my business to see the place where it 'appened first off, sir.'

'Good,' said Jervis. 'See it done tomorrow.'

Verity's tone indicated a change of topic.

''ave the honour to request, sir, 'ow I may stand with regard to Captain Ransome. It ain't my business, of course, who may be your valet, sir, but he does have a certain reputation.'

Jervis nodded.

'I take people as I find them, sergeant. Jack Ransome was a brave soldier who met with ill fortune. I do not employ him in any confidential manner but merely as my servant.'

'See, sir,' said Verity, relieved.

'However,' said Jervis, 'Jack Ransome owes you some explanation, which he now makes through me. His dealings with the person Aldino, which you came upon, were not the result of Aldino attempting to blackmail him.'

'No, sir,' said Verity, 'didn't see 'ow they could be, Captain Ransome not being of enough substance to satisfy Aldino.'

'No,' said Jervis. 'Jack Ransome had gone on the part of a brother officer to obtain compromising material held by Aldino or his associates.'

'Ah,' said Verity with soft satisfaction, 'that was it then! And 'oo might this brother officer be?'

'Captain Ransome will not tell me, Mr Verity, and you may be very sure he will not divulge the confidence to you. However, he acknowledged his debt to you for saving him great injury and now forgives the blow you struck him. He was pressed, I understand, by one of your inspectors to lay an information but quite refused.'

''andsome of him, sir.'

'Indeed,' said Jervis, 'it was Captain Ransome who advised me in the matter of selecting you from among the officers whose services were tendered.'

'*Very* 'andsome, sir.'

Verity sought some way of steering Richard Jervis back to the story of the hunting 'accident' in which he had been so savagely crippled, but the young man was calm again by this time and it hardly seemed propitious to excite him further. At least the role of Ransome was clear. He was exactly the type whom one of Aldino's victims might have employed as go-between in order to avoid entering the Wag's premises.

Richard Jervis unlocked a drawer in the table, took out a metal coin-coffer, unlocked that as well and counted off three sovereigns.

'You are to take these, Mr Verity, so that you shall be supplied for your journey. The sum will be discounted against your final payment. Perhaps you will have the goodness to sign a form of receipt.'

With this mundane transaction, Verity took his leave.

A stormy east wind strained at the yellow-green of the trees in their young foliage where the broad gravelled carriageway passed between weathered limestone pillars, marking the boundary of Bole Warren. Spruce trees arched

overhead in a natural vaulting which obscured the low sky
and the rain clouds, the colour of a drawing in Indian ink,
lowering on the Sussex weald. Having dismissed the dog-cart
which had brought him from the station, Verity followed
the directions Mrs Butcher had given him. The terrace and
gables of the house, the two little towers with their conical
roofs, grafted on in a moment of chateau-inspired building,
were hidden from the gates by the intervening woodland.
Copses and spinneys, the carefully landscaped view of a
retired East India merchant seventy years before, had run
riot. The dark bridle-paths and alleys, where only the
faintest dappling of sun penetrated, had become the
paradise of the hunter and keeper with dog or gun.

In accordance with Mrs Butcher's instructions, Verity
turned left where the gravel carriageway forked, veering
away from the house towards the scene of Lord Henry's
death. The driveway dwindled to a path with dark
leafmould underfoot. Those trees which rose on either side
to interweave their thin branches above him seemed to
Verity as dark and leafless as they might have been in
winter. All about him he heard the measured dripping of
the rain as it ran through the tangle of twigs and fronds,
soaking deep into this gloomy arboreal cavern.

He stopped abruptly, seeing ahead of him a recently-built
structure in the centre of the bridle-path. It was the
mausoleum of the Jervis family, the greater part of which
rose above the ground, though it was approached by steps
leading downwards to the iron latticework of the gates. In
general appearance, it resembled a huge and ornate hearse,
copied in stone and set down in the dank parkland. Iron
posts and chain surrounded it, a pair of stone lions sat
timelessly at the beginning of the steps, and the tomb-house
was topped by an octagonal Gothic column. Its precise
setting, in the centre of the path, strengthened the
impression for Verity of being in the darkened nave of a
dilapidated church. He approached cautiously.

The mausoleum had been built a dozen years before,
under the will of Lord Samuel Jervis, father of the three
brothers. A more ancient house would, of course, have had

its own parish church upon the estates, but the Jervis wealth was new wealth. Where there was no church on the land, a fashionable tomb-house would serve the purpose. Lord Samuel's inscription was already darkened by the dampness of the place, the characters partially obscured by mosses and lichen. Below this, the new lettering was cut lighter and sharper.

> *Within this mausoleum are deposited*
> *the mortal remains of*
> LORD HENRY FREDERICK JERVIS
> Master of Arts of New College, Oxford
> Captain, Duke's Own Infantry, before Sebastopol
> Justice of the Peace
> Born 12 March 1827
> Died 4 May 1860
> *'Thou standest in the rising sun,*
> *And in the setting thou art fair.'*

Verity removed his tall, worn hat and stood in respectful silence for a moment. To his mind, at least, the late Lord Henry seemed to have been an unexceptionable, even admirable, young man. There was, of course, no accounting for the fancies some murderers took to people but the admirable Lord Henry, with his mild manner, sense of civic duty and hesitant inclination towards Holy Orders, seemed an unlikely choice for homicide. The moment of respect passed and Verity put his hat back on.

'Leastways,' he said softly, 'if we should require Lord Henry in the course o' investigations, we shall know where to find 'im.'

The pathway narrowed still further and Verity soon found himself knee-deep in wet bracken, which soaked the lower legs of his baggy black trousers. None the less, this was the way the shooting party had come, beating the undergrowth to rouse their prey. He looked about him in the silence and the dankness of the place, the only sound coming from the now intermittent splash of rain dripping from leaf to leaf. Across a veritable sea of bracken, through which he was wading, there was no more than a thin screen of saplings.

The wood opened out at last and he could see the so-called sunken fence on which Lord Henry had been walking at the time of the accident. It was really a stone wall built against a rise in the ground to hold the earth back so that it resembled a rough terrace. This was the point at which the wooded area ended and a more cultivated slope of lawn – or grass, at least – led up to the house. The raised ground with its crude stone facing stretched across the entire view ahead of him. Not hard to see, Verity thought, how an accident might happen if a man was walking along the edge and stumbled. Not hard to see, either, how a man like Lord Henry, shooting only because it was expected of him and secretly giving his mind to other things, might lose his footing from time to time.

It was just as he was lifting his left foot upwards and forwards through the tall fronds of bracken again that there was a sound within an inch of him, a reverberating, metallic crack, as though a pile of iron sheeting had fallen almost on his head. Verity jumped with the fright of it, starting forward, and in so doing saved himself the worst of the injury. For all that, he found his leg absurdly immobilized, half raised from the ground. Something deep in the bracken and yellow-brown as the bracken itself had seized upon him. There was a deep slow consciousness of pain in the left leg, but he had not been hurt badly. It was the ample black cloth of his trouser leg which had fed the fearsome maw. Gingerly he put his left hand down and felt the cold, encrusted teeth. He drew his fingers back quickly.

'Ugh!' he said with a shudder of revulsion, 'Mantraps!'

He tried not to think of what might have happened if the mechanism had not rusted, if he had not moved faster instinctively at the first faint sound, if the thick cloth of his suiting had not gagged the obscene and cruel teeth. Again he put his hand down. The loose fold of the trouser leg was held fast in the iron mesh of the teeth. There was nothing for it but to tear himself free. He stooped down to see if he could wrench the worsted cloth apart on the blunt iron. Even as he did so, there was an explosion from somewhere behind him and a 'twing-g-g . . . twing-g-g' just above his lowered head. A sudden shower of torn leaves fluttered down upon him as he crouched, helpless, in the bracken. There was another abrupt report and this time the shot came whipping among the fronds where he crouched, scything off the fern-like heads. It crossed Verity's mind that whether or not someone had killed Lord Henry Jervis, they were certainly intent on killing him. He planned quickly and instinctively. First rip the cloth loose at any price. Second lie still. Let them come at him. Then jump. If they stayed back, wait for the dark and then crawl through the bracken towards the boundary of the estate. His first wrestling with the trouser-leg was interrupted by a voice, closer now.

'You just stand up, my fine lad, where I can see you nice and clear. You won't poach me out of my cottage, not you nor the rest of your bastard tribe.'

The tone was triumphant rather than angry. It did not sound to Verity like the voice of a murderer.

'If you ain't a-going to stand,' the voice said, 'then it'll be my pleasure to raise 'ee with a pound o' soft shot up the arse.'

Verity clambered to his feet, scarlet with indignation. The man who approached him with gun levelled was slight of build and wiry. His dark eyes seemed restless and cunning, his mouth and chin bristling with coarse, hard stubble. His mouth hung open with the appearance of a ghastly smile, quite unconnected with good humour, so that his few discoloured teeth gave him the look of a panting dog. He was dressed in a high-crowned hat, limp neckerchief, a shabby old greatcoat, breeches and gaiters. The hands which held the gun were rough and coarse, the fingernails long, crooked and yellow. Seeing Verity caught by the trap, he rested the gun against a tree.

'You'm new to this caper, my fine friend,' he said thrusting his grinning face towards the helpless sergeant.

'You'll answer for this, my man!' said Verity furiously.

The gamekeeper laughed uproariously.

'I'll answer for it! Oh, I will, will I?'

He busied himself with a clasp-knife, cutting a long thick switch from a spruce tree.

'You get this contraption off me, sharp!' roared Verity. 'You'll answer in the dock for setting cruel and unlawful devices!'

The gamekeeper whittled away at the stout switch.

'We don't a-set nothing,' he said, 'only there was so many set under the old law that we ain't never found the half of them. And when a poacher do step into one, and his friends hear of it, you've no idea how they avoid this place for months after.'

'Don't you 'ave the impudence to call me a poacher!' said Verity struggling.

'And what might you be then?'

'I'm a police officer,' Verity snarled, 'Scotland Yard division.'

'Oh!' shouted the wiry little man, 'that's good, that is! Police officer!' And he laughed till he had to wipe his eyes on the back of his hand. 'Now,' he said more seriously, 'I got one way with poachers. No law, no fuss. While you're in that trap, I'm going to thrash you with a big stick. When I'm done you shall go free. You'll probably have to crawl from here, on account of hurting too bad to walk, and you'll keep your bed a week or two. Then you'll be able to hobble about, and the end of next month I daresay you'll be as good as new. Only,' the voice grew sharper, 'you'll be in no hurry to come back poaching on my lands. I got a snug little lodge and a full larder. I ain't a-going to lose my place through villains like you. And as for the traps, there's notices set, "Attention. Mantraps". Supposing you can read 'em.'

He raised the stick.

'There's no notice at the main gate,' said Verity quickly.

The gamekeeper lowered the stick.

'You never came in through the main gate?'

'I'm here on the orders of Mr Richard Jervis.'

'Never mind that. If you came through the main gates, a poacher would hardly do that. Hold on a minute.'

The man walked away and emitted a low mellow whistle. He entered the trees and there was an exchange of voices. Ten minutes passed before he returned.

'Your name ain't Verity, is it?' he asked suspiciously.

'Course it bloody well is!' said Verity angrily.

'You never said so.'

'Fat chance I had of saying, or you of listening!'

'Rumer,' said the man, 'that's me. Jem Rumer. Gamekeeper to Lord Henry and his father before him, and now to Lord William.'

He took a tiny key from his pocket and knelt at Verity's feet. There was a click as the toothed iron relaxed its grip.

'They never said,' Rumer remarked, as casually as though he and Verity were now old acquaintances, 'never said about you coming today. What they know up at the 'ouse and what they tell me about it is two quite different things.'

'You'll answer to Mr Richard Jervis for this,' Verity muttered, freeing his trouser-leg from the iron fangs. Rumer shook his head.

'No I shan't, Mr Verity. Mr Richard don't own a stick of furniture nor a leaf on one of these trees. This is Lord William's land and I'm his lordship's man. It was old Lord Samuel Jervis', then young Lord Henry's, and now Lord William's. The part you was on, I got very strict orders about. That's the scene of the tragedy, that is,' Rumer continued with relish. 'Lord William won't have a soul near it. Not even you. Mr Richard ain't got no rights there, Mr Verity. And nor have you.'

'Should you happen to know why I'm here?' Verity asked, in a calmer, professional tone.

'Course I do,' said Rumer, surveying the damaged trouser-leg. 'There ain't a person in Bole Warren don't know. Mr Richard, being a poor crippled gentleman with nothing to do but fret, gets to thinking. Thinking ain't much good to a person, Mr Verity, when it's fretful thinking. He gets to believing that poor Lord Henry was 'orribly murdered.'

'Which he wasn't?'

'Mr Verity, I ain't saying a word against poor Mr Richard. But when a man is shut in a chair all day, when he can't have the comforts of an ordinary man, it takes his mind, somehow, and gives it a funny turn. Things you or I wouldn't notice gets turned into a funny way.'

'And how might you, Mr Rumer, come to know just what happened?'

'A-cos I was standing not fifteen feet from where we are now, Mr Verity. There was me and the boy and four men hired as beaters that morning. Way behind us, there was the half-sovs, which we call half-sovs because that's all they tip. Up in front there was Lord William, Lord Henry, Mr Richard, and the sovs.'

'How many sovs, Mr Rumer?'

The keeper's mouth opened in the same mirthless smile, displaying his scattered yellow teeth as he thought the matter over.

'There was four. There was Dr Jamieson, Lord Henry's physician. There was the Reverend Mr Cartwright from Bole Warren and the Reverend Mr Harrison from Lewes that was Lord Henry's friend. And there was Captain Loosemore that was a naval gentleman and friend of Lord William.'

'And where was Captain Ransome?'

Rumer laughed.

'He ain't a sov, Mr Verity, nor even a half-sov. He was stood in the trees, as he might be one of the beaters.'

'And might you have been able to see the gentlemen near Lord Henry, Mr Rumer?'

'What I saw,' said Rumer, 'was Lord Henry on the edge of the sunken wall there, walking along it, and a great space all about him. The others was walking through the trees.'

'Not Mr Richard,' said Verity reprovingly, ''e wasn't walking anywhere.'

'No,' said Rumer, ''e was in a wheelchair. Used to ride a shooting pony until his legs got worse. But he'd shoot from a chair all right.'

'And you saw Lord Henry fall?'

'Saw 'im fall, Mr Verity, and heard the rifle go off.'

'Saw the puff of smoke?'

'No, Mr Verity. Never did. Ain't that odd?'

'It ain't odd, Mr Rumer. Lord Henry was using that Prooshian powder, which don't make smoke. It shows you an honest witness, though. If you'd said you'd seen smoke, I should have been obliged to disbelieve every other word you said.'

Rumer grinned again, eager and gratified.

'And you say,' Verity resumed, ''e couldn't a-bin murdered?'

'Mr Verity,' said Rumer earnestly, 'with these eyes I could see poor Lord Henry walking along that sunken wall and I could see clear round him on every side for thirty feet or more. He was there alone. He fell and the gun went off. I saw and heard. When they picked the poor gentleman up, they saw the bullet had come from his own rifle. He was the only gentleman that carried a rifle that day, Mr Verity, and it was clutched in his poor dead hand in a death grip which showed he'd never let it go.'

'And why should he carry a rifle, Mr Rumer, 'im alone?'

Rumer smiled wistfully.

'Lord Henry wasn't much of a shooting man. He never scored high. But his position obliged him to entertain other gentlemen and to join the sport. However, he carried a rifle to kill sure and clean, thinking that a burst o' shot might injure an animal and not finish the job. 'e'd never even sight a rabbit or a hare unless he could take it from the front, for fear poor puss might not be killed clean. And he was always glad to have the shooting parties over.'

'Course,' said Verity, 'you wouldn't 'appen to think of any reason why any man should want to kill Lord Henry?'

'Not a man that was here that day nor any other.'

'Not a poacher that had been sentenced in his court?'

'Lord Henry never sat on the bench here, nor elsewhere I shouldn't think. There might be a man or two who hated Lord William, now. But not Lord Henry.'

They walked back along the path Verity had followed, towards the lodge.

'In course, you'll take a pot of ale?' said Rumer hopefully, remembering the illegality of mantraps.

'Why,' said Verity, 'I do think I will.'

At the scrubbed table of the tiny lodge kitchen the two men sat, each with a pewter pot before him, as though they had never had a quarrel between them. Verity raised the tankard of dark ale and tilted back his head. His throat moved in a long resonant rhythm. He lowered the pot.

'You must be a 'appy man, Mr Rumer, in your position 'ere?'

'I am, Mr Verity. Very content.'

'A good master, I daresay? That makes a difference.'

'I ain't got a master, Mr Verity, Lord William being a naval gentleman. Five months out of six he's with the *Hero* or in town.'

'*Hero*?'

'It's what they call a frigate. Ninety-one gunner. He must be her captain, I should say.'

'Funny,' said Verity, 'at the town 'ouse, they reckon he don't live there neither.'

'You'd find him at the White Bear with a suite of rooms, then,' said Rumer knowingly, 'or in one o' them 'aymarket houses. Dubourg's or the like.'

'Ladies' man, is he?'

Rumer winked.

'He ain't Lord Henry. He's got a roar to him and he likes a girl that's easy. But he won't bring 'em here. Nor Portman Square, I daresay.'

Verity sighed.

'No use for his town house, nor his estate.'

'But the money he can raise on 'em, Mr Verity. Think o' that!'

Verity thought.

'To spend on whores, Mr Rumer?'

'And the rest,' said Rumer. 'Lord William ain't a yokel to be took by a young madam. Highly connected, he is, in course o' playing for high stakes and pleasuring the finest ladies.' Rumer leant across the table, as though they might be overheard by some concealed witness. 'He was instrumental in introducing 'is 'ighness to a hand at baccarat.'

' 'is 'ighness?' said Verity with a grimace of doubt.

Rumer sat back and nodded confidentially. He opened his mouth carefully and, making no sound, he slowly shaped the words, 'Prince of Wales!'

'Well I never,' said Verity. For the first time he was taken aback by one of Rumer's knowledgeable revelations.

'You'll 'ave another jug?' said the gamekeeper hospitably.

'Don't know as I should, Mr Rumer, when duty presses. What I should like most is an understanding between us that I might come back here, if need be, without a soul knowing about it. Not even Mr Richard Jervis himself.'

Rumer sucked his teeth, shook his head and whistled softly.

'It ain't my place to let you, Mr Verity. Nor Mr Richard's.'

'But I gotta do the job proper,' Verity protested. 'I can't just go where Mr Richard Jervis thinks fit. 'e ain't a detective policeman. 'e wouldn't know murder from plum pudding nor a Seven Dials magsman from Prince Albert, poor crippled gentleman.'

Rumer continued to whistle significantly. Wrestling over a decision which caused him visible distress, Verity drew from his pocket the remaining two sovereigns of the three for which he had signed a receipt to Richard Jervis. The keeper's yellow-nailed fingers closed over the coins.

'Don't alter what belongs to Lord William, however,' he said quietly. 'What I don't see don't hurt. But what I do see, I must act upon. I got a place to keep, Mr Verity.'

Verity's face flushed a deeper, port wine shade.

'And that's where I thought we had our understanding, Mr Rumer. You was to be my friend in the business and, consequential on you being such, I wasn't to say a word to a soul about them cruel and felonious traps that has been left about the estate, quite contrary to 'is lordship's instructions, I'll be bound.'

Through the tiny Gothic window of the keeper's lodge, he saw the dog-cart waiting. Rumer nodded, acknowledging that justice, albeit harsh, had now been done.

In blazing June sunshine, Verity walked eastward along the Strand from Northumberland Street. Coats in summer linen were unknown in the Private-Clothes detail, so that he still wore the black trousers which were shiny with age, the threadbare frock-coat and tall stovepipe hat. His red face and faint air of decrepitude suggested a long-employed counting-house clerk whose advance in age had not been accompanied by any rise in his professional status.

The square-paned windows of the select little shops caught the sun at a dozen different angles. Someone had called it the finest street in Europe. It was certainly one of the most expensive. A smart olive-green brougham with the crest of a noble family on its door in small, discreet gold figuring, rolled to a gentle halt, and a shopman in a baize apron ran out to its occupant. In the broad thoroughfare, between the rows of pleasantly proportioned buildings, a slow procession of drags, carts, rattling little omnibuses, four-wheel cabs and hansoms, saddle-horses, broughams and chaises, rattled and jangled from Trafalgar Square to Ludgate. Here and there a splendid chariot with the coachman perched on a brilliant hammercloth and with liveried servants behind moved sedately through the throng of vehicles in aloof self-confidence.

Beyond the glitter of the river in the summer afternoon, the dark tenements of Southwark sprawled in close and narrow streets. Their occupants were rarely to be seen in the Strand however, for a wise authority had imposed a penny toll on Waterloo Bridge, which obliged most of those who lived on the Surrey shore to walk round by Westminster Bridge in order to save twopence a day. None the less, Verity noticed a pair of girls, fourteen or fifteen years old, dressed in black and seeming the daughters of the poor, who walked with great self-assurance, gazing in at shop windows. His natural suspicion was aroused. Then a man in a black silk hat and cloak approached them. He spoke to the elder girl, while her sister began to draw away. As Verity passed he heard the bigger girl scolding the younger impatiently. She took the youngster's arm and pulled.

'You are a *fool*. Oh, you fool! Come, he wants us.'

There was nothing the law of the land required him to do and Verity, moving on uneasily, reflected that his first allegiance now was to the employer who had hired him. Before the windows of Somerville and Pope, gunsmiths, he halted and surveyed the goods offered behind the small square panes. The specimens of the gunmaker's art were such that a man hardly needed to be a follower of the sport in order to admire their beauty. The stocks of the rifles shone with an immaculate auburn gloss, the fine grain polished to a liquid perfection. Brass and filigree blazed like gold in the summer sun, steel barrels sleek as satin and the entire ensemble displayed on velvet of the richest green. Verity pushed open the door.

Somerville looked as though he had returned hastily from a battue on a country estate and had not had time to change into his town clothes. Shooting jacket and gaiters exuded an air of fresh moorland among the smoke of the town and the faint stench of the city river. Around him, the tall glass cases and the solid leather chairs gave the little shop the impression of a gun-room in a country house.

'I was expected,' said Verity firmly, 'with Mr Richard Jervis' compliments.'

'So you were,' said Somerville with a faint Devonian burr which almost matched Verity's intonation. 'To see the rifle.' He seized Verity's hand and shook it with anxious sincerity, then turned about, unlocked a tall display-case and took down a gun from one of the upper shelves. Verity noticed that a label had been tied to it.

'You come,' said Somerville, as though his visitor did not know it, 'about poor Lord Henry. Well, sir, this is the gun that did the bloody deed. Beautiful as sin and twice as treacherous.'

'Might there have been something amiss with the weapon, then, Mr Somerville, sir?' Verity asked with an appearance of innocence.

'Amiss?' Somerville could hardly believe his ears. 'Amiss?

With our finest piece? Why, sir, we made it for Lord Henry five years since, we fitted him for it as though it was his wedding suit. Stock snug to the shoulder, barrel true to the eye.' He raised the gun in demonstration and lowered it again. 'See, Mr. . . .'

'Verity,' said Verity.

'See, Mr Verity. Do see, now. Touch there. That stock is smooth as a girl's skin, ain't it. And the barrels! Damascus laminated steel! Nothing better. None of your old horseshoe nails melted down and beaten round a bar. Them barrels, Mr Verity, I saw made. Best silver steel beaten flat and worked into a beautiful twist. Do touch it, sir, do! None of your Brummagen there. Why, sir, there they still do melt down their old horseshoe nails and make an iron bore. Bust up in no time.'

'It's a fine weapon, Mr Somerville.'

'Rough-bored, smooth-bored, lapped, polished. . . .'

'Rifled, Mr Somerville?'

'French rifling,' said Somerville confidentially. 'None better when this was made. Our weapon, Mr Verity, will hit with unerring precision when held by a steady hand.'

'Your weapon, Mr Somerville?'

'All our weapons, sir! A child might take the top off an apple at a hundred paces, if only he held it steady.'

'That's very nice, Mr Somerville. And what might that bit of ornament be on the piece, that metal bit?'

'Now that,' said Somerville, 'is a game-maker with a little scoring wheel. When a shooter hits his mark, he can move it without altering his hold on the gun. As he does so, the numbers go round on two little wheels. He can mark up to ninety-nine.'

'And what might it say when Lord Henry was killed?'

'Six, Mr Verity,' said Somerville sadly. 'Only six. His lordship wasn't much for the chase.'

'And you, Mr Somerville, having seen the gun, and the bullet what was took from his head, you can imagine how he must a-fell, hit the gun on the ground to jar it, and shot 'isself through the head?'

'Mr Verity,' said Somerville sadly, 'the bullet that killed

him had been shot from this gun, which he was carrying when he died. There was little marks on the stock of the rifle, where it fell. When the gun was taken from his grasp it was empty and had been fired, though of course it was fired anyway that morning at least half a dozen times before.'

Verity nodded.

'Mr Somerville, might a man shoot himself on purpose with such a weapon. I know his lordship never did, but might it happen.'

Somerville looked at him disapprovingly.

'He might, Mr Verity, if he could hold it far enough along his arm to turn the muzzle on himself and still press the trigger. However, a poor wretch that's determined on self-destruction is likely to find fifty easier ways of doing it.'

'But for a man that wanted to destroy 'isself, while making it look accidental, it might be the very thing.'

'It might,' said Somerville, 'and there again it mightn't. But I ain't going to go so far as supposing that self-destruction ever crossed poor Lord Henry's mind.'

'Nor am I, Mr Somerville, no more am I. But us detective police has the habit of looking at a thing all sides up.'

'Generally,' said Somerville coolly, 'it's what's most likely that's true.'

'Generally it is, Mr Somerville. Generally it do turn out that way.'

If Dr Jamieson had been a fat man, he might have been spectacularly jowl'd. As it was, his slack red face hung in creased meagre folds, his eyes watered easily and his general disposition seemed that of profound melancholy.

'It is not my custom to discuss such matters with hired policemen,' he said glumly. 'I set no precedents. What I had to say was said to the coroner's jury.'

He looked up from the broad partners' desk at which he sat. Behind him on the marble mantelshelf a fine Orléans clock with nymphs in bronze ticked sedately and, despite the June warmth, a fire burned crisply in the grate.

'I was given to understand, sir,' said Verity respectfully, 'as you mightn't object to setting Mr Richard Jervis' mind at rest.'

'I do not object,' said Dr Jamieson tetchily. 'I will set his mind and yours at rest. But I will be no party to calumny and family quarrels.'

'Family quarrels, sir?'

Jamieson ignored the question.

'The matter is quite simple, sergeant. Lord Henry Jervis was walking on the sunken fence dividing the woodland from the grass terrace. That fence is four and a half feet high. In the sight of the keepers he stumbled, the loaded rifle which he was carrying hit the ground and jarred, that jarring fired a bullet at an upward angle, entering the skull behind the right ear, being diverted by the bone mass towards the back of the skull and becoming impacted there. The gun never left his hand. Indeed, when he was picked up it was hard to prise his fingers free. He had clutched it in the final instinctive spasm, clutched it in the so-called death-grip.'

'The wound, sir,' said Verity appreciatively, 'just the entry of a rifle bullet?'

Jamieson opened a drawer and took out a sheet of blue notepaper. He unfolded it and took out a small piece of card with an engraving upon it. Verity recognized it. When a photograph was taken of a body, for the benefit of a coroner's jury, it was customary to present it in the clearer and more easily available form of a steel engraving, taken from the print itself. The card showed a tiny puckered hole, impersonal and dehumanized.

'Was he washed before the examination, sir?'

'Washed?' said Jamieson suspiciously.

'Washed for his grave-clothes, sir, when they laid him out. Only there ain't no blackening round the wound, sir.'

'Schultze powder, sergeant. He was using Schultze powder. Smokeless. Whether or not they washed the wound makes no odds; you can't have blackening with smokeless powder.'

'Quite so, sir,' said Verity, handing back the card. 'One other thing, sir.'

'Yes?'

'Might it happen, in any way you know of, sir, that Lord

Henry could either have took his own life or been cruelly murdered?'

Dr Jamieson gave a faint snort of derision.

'Who tells such tales?'

'No one, sir. Only if they're tales then the truth is the best way to stop 'em being told.'

'Lord Henry killed himself,' said Jamieson, 'of that there is no doubt. His gun was in perfect order, there was no sign of anything to trip him up, even supposing a murderer had fancied the remote possibility of staging such a thing. He fell over his own feet. As to self-destruction, it would be cumbersome in the extreme to do it in such a manner, pointing a rifle at his head and then jarring it on the ground until it went off. No, sergeant. There were half a dozen of us close by him, the keepers were looking at him. They saw no such thing. Lord Henry killed himself by pure accident. Dammit, man, he had every reason in the world for wanting to live. He was young, healthy, rich. Tell me that Richard Jervis wants to do away with himself and I might understand why. Tell me that some injured husband has taken a shotgun to Lord William and I might believe you. But not Lord Henry.'

'Yessir. Much obliged, sir. Been a great assistance, sir.'

Jamieson stood up and came round the desk, laying a hand on Verity's arm, man to man.

'Take some advice,' he said in a rich, affable voice. 'Do what you must do and then, soon as you decently can, go back to your proper duties. There's nothing for you here.'

'Yessir,' said Verity stiffly. 'Most 'elpful, sir.'

He backed awkwardly towards the door, bowed clumsily, and withdrew.

The chatelaine at Mrs Butcher's waist rattled its cluster of keys, her starched skirts rustling on the narrow wooden steps of the servants' stairway as she climbed. Once or twice she put a hand to her lace cap, as though fearing that the exertion of the ascent might have dislodged it from its place, crowning her white hair. Verity followed behind her, puffing a little. The arrangement of the Jervis town house

reminded him of a visit with Bella to the Old Vic to see the
Indian Jugglers. Then, as now, the way had lain up bare
precipitous steps to the gallery, a staircase divided from the
more expensive part of the building which led to boarded
and roughly furnished apartments.

'That's a nasty wretch, Rumer,' said Mrs Butcher, 'a cold
cruel man, to be sure. Dr Jamieson I only saw, never heard
speak above a few words.'

'Friend of Lord Henry's, was he?' gasped Verity. 'Friend
and medical man altogether?'

Mrs Butcher paused on a step, drew breath and thought.
She shook her head and began to climb again.

'More Lord William's friend, though he cared for the
whole family o' course. He was more of Lord William's
liking, if you take the meaning, more of a sporting
gentleman and ladies' man.'

Verity puffed a little more.

'I don't see 'ow I should be a sporting gentleman and
ladies' man, Mrs Butcher, not if I was obliged to spend half
the year at sea and most of the rest caring for a great house
like this and the lands at Bole Warren.'

Mrs Butcher chuckled and climbed faster.

'Bless you, Mr Verity! Lord William don't spend more
than two months a year at sea. 'e's in town all the rest. Only,
o' course, he prefers to live where he's accustomed rather
than in Portman Square.'

'Not live 'ome, Mrs Butcher? Not in a fine 'ouse like this?
Now, why might that be?'

Mrs Butcher turned on a tiny half-landing and faced him.

'There's gentlemen,' she said, 'that likes their game with
other gentlemen, wagering sovereign for sovereign with the
'ighest in the land. There's gentlemen that likes ladies who
ain't quite what they should be. In course, they can't bring
'em in a carriage to Portman Square, nor they can't send
'em through the kitchen way neither. Such gentlemen is very
often found to have apartments in the White Bear and such
places. And that's all about that, Mr Verity.'

'And such goings-on might lead to family quarrels, as Dr
Jamieson said?' Verity asked innocently.

'I don't undertake to know what 'e may a-said,' Mrs Butcher announced firmly. 'However, I do know what my place is worth and when I've said enough, even to oblige a sad young fellow what Mr Stringfellow was prevailed upon to take as son-in-law.'

She turned her amply-skirted back upon him and opened a small door on the half-landing. Stepping through it, Verity found himself on a sumptuous landing, carpeted in blue and gold, ending in a fine rounded Georgian window before which the sculpted head of a girl in corkscrew ringlets reflected on its pedestal the afternoon sun with brilliant marble whiteness.

Mrs Butcher bustled along before him, drawing up her chatelaine and selecting a key. They stopped before a massively carved door.

'Never a soul crossed the threshold since the poor young gentleman went to his tomb,' she said, lowering her voice dramatically. 'And you wouldn't be now unless Lord William was with the fleet and Mr Richard had give such express instructions.'

The key turned in the lock and she opened the polished door.

'I'm to stay here, like a sentry at St James' Palace,' she said, 'till you do come out again.'

Verity bowed slightly, in his lumbering awkward manner, and entered the apartments of the late Lord Henry Jervis. The door closed behind him.

His first impression was of a heavy and dusty silence. Even the view of Portman Square from the windows, the cypress grove and beech trees railed in on the broad lawn, surrounded by the cobbled thoroughfare and the houses on the four sides, seemed mute and remote, as though he had indeed passed from the world of the living to the mansions of the dead. A warm stillness, the faint sickliness of dead flowers not cleared from their vases, gave strength to the impression. The apartment consisted of a large drawing-room in front divided from a smaller back room by folding doors. It was furnished in the style of twenty years earlier, the furniture and decorations of Louis Philippe.

Ormolu tables and boule cabinets were ranged about the rooms, each bearing its small bronze statuette or ornament. Above the gilded tables, the walls were hung with brackets and watercolour drawings. Over the cabinets, glass-shades and picture-frames there hung an oppressive sense of gloomy richness.

Looking about him, Verity could scarcely decide what it was that he was expected to do. If these rooms represented Lord Henry's collection of worldly goods, then he could have owned little which bore his personal mark upon it more specifically than a stick of furniture. Nowhere was there any sign of family or personal correspondence, the accounts of Portman Square or Bole Warren. Walking ponderously about the rooms, Verity examined the little tables. Two of them had drawers which opened and revealed no more than notes of the most cursory kind written to Lord Henry by men who could or could not attend his party and would or would not make up a group for a battue at Bole Warren. In the rear drawing-room, where the furniture was more varied, a Chippendale bureau stood, immaculate and inviting. Verity went through it, drawer by drawer, sifting the trivia of the dead man's life. Little bills and receipts, hastily-scrawled notes with half incomprehensible jokes and exclamations intended only for the eyes of a near friend who understood them, a tiny miniature of a girl's face, and lockets bearing the likenesses of Lord Samuel Jervis and his wife. There was a locket of female hair, which might have belonged to a young beauty of the past century as easily as the present. Verity felt a great sadness overcoming him at this glimpse of the loved and loving details of the Jervis family. And it was all for nothing.

On such occasions, there was no cure for melancholy but in work. 'The square of four is sixteen, and you must lengthen your lever proportionate to your weight, is as true when a man's miserable as when he's happy,' someone had once said to him. It rang true to Verity that work gave a man a sure hold of something outside his own uncertain emotions. When the drawers of the bureau yielded nothing further, he turned his professional suspicion upon the structure of the polished furniture. With half his mind dwelling on other things, he tapped and felt, sliding a hand under a ledge of a drawer-opening or running his fingers along an elegant piece of beading in search of some concealed lever.

Such pieces as the bureau were mere toys. No self-respecting criminal would have entrusted his treasure or his confidences to their so-called 'secret drawers'. Why, thought Verity, anyone with an eye for it soon got to seeing where the places were which no other drawer or cubby-hole occupied. Then it was only a matter of tapping to find the hollow sound. And when that happened, a thief would carve his way with a chisel, never stopping to try the genteel method of searching for a hidden spring. It was at that moment that his own finger-tips struck a hollowness beneath the polished surface. He had the flap of the bureau down and was facing the little drawers and pigeon-holes inside. Between two sets of drawers there was a narrow, inlaid panel, four inches across and about eight inches tall. He tapped it again and heard the hollowness once more.

'Ah!' he said with faint satisfaction, 'so that's it!'

There was no sign of a catch, no place where a catch might be concealed nor a knife blade could enter. Verity patiently opened the drawers on either side of the panel, drew them from their recesses and searched methodically in the wooden frame. At last he found the thin strip of springy metal and thumbed it back. Suddenly the entire section behind the panel came free so that he drew it out like an open box, four inches by eight and about a foot long.

At first he expected it to be empty but there were several items in it. He drew out a book, printed in some foreign language which he assumed to be French. The paper was thick and greyish, the cover no more than marbled paper pasted on cheap board. There was another volume, bound in stained and rubbed grey boards with a dingy white spine whose lettering had faded to invisibility. Two more small and recently-printed volumes accompanied these. Verity opened the first at random.

After dismissing the eunuchs, I again drew the couch close to her, and without further ceremony lifted up her clothes. How lovely white was her round belly and ivory delicate-formed thighs! The mount of love, just above the temple of Venus, covered with beautiful black hair. . . .

Verity put the volume down and, picking up the other, glanced at its title: *Venus Schoolmistress: or, Birchen Sports.* He shook his head thoughtfully.

'Poor young gentleman,' he said aloud. There was something loathsome in the duty of dredging the furtive, trivial lusts of the dead in this manner. However, the four books had occupied the greater part of the concealed compartment in the bureau. They were unremarkable in themselves, the broken-down little shops of Holywell Street, just north of the Strand, thrived on such editions of aged erotica. Yet it saddened Verity to think that the books might in some way sully the reputation of the dead Lord Henry Jervis with his unrealized ambition to take Holy Orders.

Beside the books there were four glass-plate photographs, positive prints of a kind which required a sheet of white paper behind them to see them clearly, and an envelope containing what would no doubt be an old love-letter. Verity picked up the four glass plates with care. They were all chipped or broken in some way. Two of them had had a strip of glass sheared away, converting the oblong to a square, a third had lost a triangle at one corner. The fourth was accidentally chipped but the image appeared complete. Verity drew a sheet of white paper from one of the bureau pigeon-holes and slid it behind the first plate.

His heart sank. It was all to be worse than ever he or Richard Jervis could have expected. There were two figures in the picture, the man naked and flat on his back, his neck and head missing where the end of the plate had been sheared away. The girl who knelt astride his legs was petite, trimly-rounded and olive-skinned, her tawny blonde hair worn down her back with the aid of a comb. Her head was lowered to her partner's loins, eyes closed and lips pouting, while she spread her thighs for the man's fingers with their

two distinctive rings. The man himself was distinguished by
a white forked streak where his left thigh and belly joined. It
might be a scar or a blemish on the plate. Of the girl's
identity there could be no doubt.

'Simona!' said Verity softly, and looked again. In the
background was a blurred oval shape. Blurred it might be,
but he knew it for the finishing bath in Charley Wag's
private apartment at Ramiro's. As for the man in the
picture, Verity had seen the Wag naked and knew that the
pale, undeveloped body was not Charley's. But it must have
been a most important client for Charley to have made both
his private bath and his own girl available.

The second plate confirmed his suspicions. Simona and
Stefania, the latter with paler body and shock of dark hair,
lay naked, nuzzling one another's mouths. They seemed to
be on a low divan, a man standing over them, his head and
shoulders missing again where the end of the plate had been
broken off. But the white fork at the join of left thigh and
belly was there again, confirming it as the scar of an old
injury.

The third plate had suffered no more than an accidental
chip. It seemed to Verity the most mysterious of all. There
was no man in it, merely a girl who was fully dressed in a
theatrical costume which suggested the part of a page to a
knight errant in some mock-tournament. He studied the
snub-nosed, narrow-eyed insolence of her expression, the
sturdy figure of a fifteen-year-old tomboy, fair hair spread
loose across her shoulders.

'Now her I have seen,' he said gently. 'Youngest doxy in
Ned Roper's flash 'ouse a year or two back. Name of Miss
Elaine.'

He studied the picture again. There was little in it that
even the Vice Society could have taken exception to. Elaine
was in three-quarter profile, though her head was turned
towards the camera a little more. She wore a 'doublet'
fashioned from a blouse. The lower part of her 'armour'
consisted of very tight trousers in grey-blue material. From
the style of the costume, Verity had no doubt that the girl
formed part of a display which gulls and yokels paid

willingly to watch. The plate showed her as a broad-hipped, sturdy-thighed youngster, the grey-blue trousers stretched smooth over her figure and nipped in narrowly at the waist. From the rear, Elaine's bottom appeared a near-perfect circle, the tight cloth creasing deeply under the full cheeks. It was unlikely, Verity thought, that many of the spectators were much interested in the finer points of jousting or the ways of ancient chivalry. He laid the third plate aside and took up the final one.

The composition was so crowded that at first it was difficult to distinguish the subject. Presently it appeared as something enacted on a stage or dais with a half circle of spectators on the far side. The faces of these men and women were represented in miniature but quite distinctly. They were a fashionably-dressed group in evening clothes, some laughing at what they saw, others staring in dismay. The four men on the dais were naked, as was the girl, all four of them wearing goat-masks, which the girl did not.

Verity examined her, the slender but well-shaped body, the profile and colouring of Eastern beauty tempered by a childhood in the mean streets of Ratcliffe or Wapping. The dark hair rose in an elegant coiffure from her delicately-shaped neck and ears, her cat-like almond eyes lighting the fine oriental mask of her beauty. She knelt on all fours, the four men standing over her, one on each side, one before and one behind. Her slim young shoulders curved down to the velveteen lustre of coppery skin in the small of her back, the smooth paler ovals of her bottom narrowing to firm thighs and trim calves. Lynx-eyed, she turned her head to the spectators, as though their excitement at what she was showing them somehow intensified her own.

'Jolly!' said Verity aloud. 'Wherever there's mischief. . . .'

He paused and looked at the four men. One of them, at the girl's head, bore the same white fork at the joining of belly and thigh. The hand with the bloodstone ring and the gold was hidden by the girl's head, the fingers lost in the dark hair as they guided her face back. Rings might alter, Verity thought, scars never.

There remained only the sheet of paper in its envelope, addressed to Lord Henry Jervis at Bole Warren. Verity drew out the sheet of paper.

Sir — Not many years ago, a great injury was done by you to a poor woman, in consequence of which she died. It was well for you had there been no witness to your cowardice and your folly, if all had perished as that poor soul. I trust to inform you there is one who saw your every act, from first to last, and who lives to publish to the world what you have done. Such an object as you are, so base a villain, must disgrace the dignity of revenge, but yet there is justice requires a forfeit paid. In token of what I might tell of you, receive this ring and recollect where last you saw it and missed it. It shall cost you dear and, never fear, the reckoning shall reach you when next you hear from your faithful correspondent, Anonyma.

For half an hour Verity searched the secret compartment, the papers, envelopes, bureau, and every likely hiding-place for the ring. There was no sign of it. But then, he reflected, it could be any ring. He might find a dozen belonging to Lord Henry and never know which was mentioned by the mysterious lady of the letter. He looked again at the glass plates of the photographs. He must, of course, ask Mrs Butcher tactfully about the rings the young man wore and where precisely the wound might be that Lord Henry sustained when a battery of mortars at the Redan spewed its lethal hail of iron among his infantry. Yes, he thought, the question must be asked, but the answer could hardly be in doubt. The next interview with Richard Jervis was likely to be a difficult one. Far from undermining the evidence of accidental death and establishing a case of murder against persons as yet entirely unknown and unsuspected, Lord Henry Jervis seemed likely to join that procession of the rich and the titled who had embraced violent death in the past eighteen months rather than face the public humiliation which awaited them. It was no ordinary humiliation, for Charley Wag and his minions were artists in blackmail. The revelations which he held in store were precisely those for which each particular victim would die rather than endure.

It seemed to Verity that he might as well inform Richard Jervis at once and close the investigation into Lord Henry's death as speedily and decently as possible. Then he picked up the otherwise innocent plate of the girl Elaine in her tournament costume. For several minutes he stood in silence.

''ang on a bit,' he said at last. 'This don't fit. There's a screw loose somewhere.'

6

'And so,' said Verity in a tone of great secrecy, 'they was obligated to show me into the private apartments. And there, in a secret drawer, was photographs and a letter, compromising the late Lord 'enry Jervis as a coward and debauched wretch!'

Sergeant Albert Samson, who had been crouched forward in expectation of what was to be revealed, sat back against the buttoned leather of the cab seat.

'Well!' he said thoughtfully.

'I had it from Mrs Butcher afterwards,' Verity continued, 'how the rings was Lord Henry's rings that never left his hand and how the white mark at the top of his leg was just the exact wound 'is Lordship sustained on the explosion of a mortar before Sebastopol.'

Samson thought about this too.

'Well!' he said again, more softly. The cab jolted a little as they crossed Westminster Bridge towards Lambeth, the river crowded with barges drifting lazily, their long sweeps splashing the water astern as the bargees guided them. Men and women, their pink dresses and parasols bright in the afternoon sun, strolled across the pavements or loitered in the shell-like alcoves placed above the piers. On the box of the cab, Stringfellow sat with whip held idly and tall hat askew. Lightning, the ancient horse, clopped slowly towards the Surrey shore.

'It ain't half a mess,' said Verity thoughtfully. 'I been hired by poor Mr Richard who swears Lord Henry never died accidental but was foully murdered. Rumer the keeper, Mr Somerville the gunsmith, and Dr Jamieson all swear there was no way of murder. Now to cap it all I must tell Mr Richard that indeed it mayn't be an accident a-cos his brother had some reason for self-destruction. I shouldn't wonder if he wasn't to go off with apoplexy!'

Samson sucked his teeth. He said,

'You never thought, my son, that they might be using you, did you?'

'Whatcher mean?'

'Suppose your Mr Richard and even Captain Ransome knew Lord Henry had made away with himself. How better to draw attention from it than by raising a cry of murder, so that all the wagging tongues say if it wasn't murder then it must be accident. The thought of him doing away with himself ain't to be entertained even by the scandalous. They never reckoned that you might find evidence.'

Verity nodded.

'I 'ad some such thoughts, Mr Samson. Charley Wag wouldn't have blackmailed a broken-down old captain like Jack Ransome. It wouldn't answer any purpose. But then I 'eard that Captain Jack swore he was only there acting for a gentleman who was being blackmailed but didn't care to be seen visiting Charley. And then I got to thinking who that other man might be, Captain Jack being a member of the Jervis household.'

Samson chuckled.

'And Mr Richard, that acts so touchy and flares up like a new wick, he never had the goodness to name the party he thought had murdered Lord Henry?'

'I ain't been favoured with such statement, Mr Samson.'

It was Verity's first half-day off, which he had hoped to spend with Bella in Paddington Green. Instead, in his perplexity, he had sought the advice of Sergeant Samson, producing a tracing he had made of part of the blackmail note written to Lord Henry Jervis by Anonyma. Samson, from his investigation of the general blackmail conspiracy, had identified the writer as Miss Elaine who appeared in one of the photographs in tournament costume. Samson also swore that in the course of the afternoon the girl might be traced and questioned.

'You have no idea,' said Verity conversationally, 'how obliged I am to you, Mr Samson, for this. You and Mr Stringfellow, of course,' he concluded, glancing up at the box of the cab.

'I been watching Miss Elaine and a dozen little bunters for months,' said Samson cheerily. 'It ain't no hardship to find her. 'owever, if you chose to return an obligation, you might go on telling what them girls was up to in the photographic plates.'

'I don't see 'ow they were done,' said Verity insistently, ''ow all the parties was got to hold still for long enough to make an exposure. Two of 'em, with that Simona and that Stefania you was so sweet on, was at Charley Wag's baths. The other was odder still.'

'Jolly?' said Samson.

'Yes, in a place at night with a crowd looking on and four men in masks. Like sort of devil-worship. But 'ow did they do the picture in such conditions?'

'The way you go on about that little minx in the picture,' said Samson, smacking his lips at the thought of it. 'Them sly dark eyes and her gold skin, and that saucy bum stuck out! Wouldn't I give 'er turn and turn about!'

'That ain't the point, Mr Samson!' said Verity angrily.

'No,' said Samson. 'The point is them photographic plates ain't worth a Pandy's spit. It's Miss Elaine and her letter that might tell a tale.'

'Funny name,' said Verity.

'We don't know it is her name,' Samson confessed. 'Being a foundling, she had to take a name for her profession. Seems she took one out of a poetry book by Mr Tennyson, something of King Arthur, to please the quality. So Miss Elaine she is.'

They turned into the New Cut, Lambeth, and Stringfellow reined in the elderly horse. In the hot summer afternoon the pawnbrokers had turned the contents of their small stifling shops on to the pavement, in order to do business in the open. Tables, chairs and looking-glasses blocked the promenade with precarious pyramids of copper kettles and pans. The cheese-dealer in a blue apron stood before the marble slab of his open window with quarters and slices of cheese on stands at either side. White eggs on deal racks were placarded as 'fresh from the country', and large cuts of bacon, 'fine flavour', made up the rest of the ticketed display. Stringfellow drew up the cab outside the second-hand clothes store, where bereaved families came to sell the clothes of the dead. Corduroy jackets, vests and fustian trousers hung from the rows of brass rods under the awning.

'It ain't the work of the world to catch young Elaine,' said Samson thoughtfully, 'but there's no harm in liming your bird good and proper.'

He and Verity got out of the cab. Samson helped Stringfellow down from the box and changed coats with him, so that it was now Samson who appeared, at first glance, as a shabby coachman and Stringfellow who seemed, in the dark interior of the cab, a man who might have ten or twenty sovereigns in his pocket. Stringfellow remained in the cab, holding a silver-topped stick which Samson had procured for the occasion to give a final touch of affluence to the old man's appearance. Samson swung himself on to the box of the cab, tilted his hat forward a little over his face, and appeared to doze in the warm sun. Verity leaned in through the cab door.

'Mr Stringfellow,' he said softly, 'I want you to have this.' He handed Stringfellow a wooden device consisting of a six-inch stem and a small slatted piece which protruded from the upper half of the stem like a flag on a pole.

'What's this, old chum?' asked the cabman doubtfully.

'It's my constabulary rattle, Mr Stringfellow. If there's any cause for trouble, or if the young person should make off, you're to spring the rattle. Press the top and then swing it round for all it's worth. Makes a racket to wake the dead.'

With this promise, Verity withdrew, lurking among the

chairs in green and puce-coloured leather displayed before a furniture shop at some little distance from the cab. The bright, hot summer afternoon passed in dusty silence. A ginger-beer fountain pulled by a pair of ponies rumbled slowly down the street. It resembled nothing so much as an upright mahogany piano with two brass pump-handles and glass containers for receiving the drink. Beyond the motionless perspective of Springfellow's cab and the beer fountain, a small group of men was gathering on a corner. They were stripped to the waist and bore on their bare flesh marks of burns and scalding so horrifying that any passer-by was likely to throw a shilling into the tin mug and hurry on, so that he might avoid being accosted by the injured men. Verity knew the trick of old, 'the scaldrum dodge' practised by beggars who learnt the art of staining their bodies with acid and gunpowder before setting out on their rounds. Under other circumstances he might have intervened, but there was more important business on hand.

'Kind and benevolent Christians!' the voice of the beggars' leader drifted faintly on the warm afternoon air of the street, 'It is with feelings of deep regret and shame that we unfortunate sailors are compelled to appear before you this day, to ask charity from the hands of strangers.'

Sailors, thought Verity, recognizing one of the beggars as Jack Tiptoe who had made a considerable living as a disabled beggar who could not put his heel to the ground. When discovered walking with both heels comfortably on the pavement he had been despatched to six months on the treadmill at Coldbath Fields Gaol. Jack Tiptoe had never been to sea in his life, nor was he likely to unless it was on a convict hulk.

'We are brought here from want, I may say actual starvation. What will not hunger and the cries of little children compel men to do?'

Several small children, possibly associated with the beggars, had approached the ginger-beer fountain.

'When we left our solitary humble homes this morning, our children were crying for food. I assure you, kind friends, we and our families would have been houseless wanderers all last night but, as you may see, we sold the shirts off our backs to pay for lodgings. We are English sailors, British jack-tars. It is hard that you won't give your own countrymen a penny, when you give so much to foreign hurdy-gurdies and organ-grinders.'

A girl of five or six, walking slowly away from the scene of the begging, holding a little tin cup, passed Stringfellow's cab. She stopped and turned a tearful face at the open door and then entered, holding out the cup. Verity began to move slowly and unobtrusively forward.

'I hope and trust,' chanted the beggars' spokesman, 'some humane Christian will stretch out a hand with a small trifle for us. . . .'

At that moment, Verity saw the prey. She was by no means seductive enough for Charley Wag's private collection, though she had served her time in Ned Roper's bawdy-house. At fifteen years old she appeared a loud, defiant youngster as she tossed the fair hair spread loose across her shoulders. Her face was a study in vulgar, snub-nosed insolence, her dark narrow eyes seeming to have the tint of green bronze. She moved rapidly along the street, a rough, striding tomboy, her grey skirt worn as short as possible to display a length of leg. At the cab she stopped, faced the interior and swore at Stringfellow for a dirty, filthy thing. Verity crept closer and Samson, as 'cabman', still appeared to doze on his box. Her voice was loud enough for Verity to catch every word as she swore at Stringfellow, demanding what he meant by trying to rape the little girl of five or six. Then there were hints at the financial cost to 'such a gentleman as he was' of having to face the police, a court case and public shame.

So that was the caper, Verity thought. Perhaps it was an extension of the scaldrum dodge. Elaine working in partnership with the beggars. No doubt it was more remunerative than the fairground display for which she had worn the page's costume.

She was calling now to the beggars, urging them to come and see what had happened. By God, Verity thought, there must be a score of silk-hatted gentlemen, moved to pity by a little girl's tears, who had fallen victim to the dodge and had turned out every pocket and parted with watch, chain, pocket-book and stock-pin to silence the hue and cry of the begging school.

The beggars had fallen silent and were now beginning to move with slow determination down the pavement towards the cab. Verity braced himself for a scuffle. But just then, the hot quiet afternoon erupted with a din of the most raucous and clattering kind. Seeing the advance of the beggars, Stringfellow had sprung Verity's rattle. It was a sound which any member of the criminal class knew all too well. The beggars heard it, paused, turned and ran, scattering in every direction, separating down different alleys and turnings to lessen the chance of capture. Jack Tiptoe led the retreat, sprinting away down the New Cut like a champion.

The little girl ducked away from Verity and ran off. It was not worth giving chase, he thought, and losing the more important catch. With Samson at his side and Stringfellow now out of the cab, he pinned the girl against the coachwork and locked the iron cuffs on her wrists.

'Why, Miss Elaine,' said Samson cheerily, 'fancy you having come to this sort o' caper!'

'You bastards!' she said, in the tone of a belligerent heifer, 'you put this up on purpose!'

They bundled her into the cab, where she landed sprawling on the leather seat, the grey pleated skirt hauled up far enough to display the sturdy roundness of her young thighs.

'Now,' said Samson conversationally, 'bastards we may or may not be, miss, but we ain't here to arrest you. We want you where you can be got and seen from now on.'

The girl's narrow eyes brightened, as though at the thought of what she might make as a police informer.

'First,' said Samson, 'there's got to be a reckoning for the dodge you been working in the New Cut here. You'll be took to Mrs Rouncewell's. . . .'

'No!' cried Elaine.

'You'll be took to Mrs Rouncewell's, dealt with by her,

and put to honest toil in her hygienic steam-laundry. When she's brought you to the right frame o' mind, Mr Verity will ask you some very important questions. . . .'

'Bugger your questions!' she snarled, struggling between them.

'Arrest might be better, Mr Samson,' said Verity nervously. 'Arrest is proper.'

'You want your questions answered,' said Samson, 'you leave my case to me. She ain't going to say a word unless she's obliged.'

He tapped the roof of the cab.

'Mr Stringfellow, 'ave the goodness to take us round to Mrs Rouncewell's Steam Laundry, off Old Kent Road.'

Lightning stumbled forward with a rattle of harness, under Stringfellow's gruff command, and they jogged sedately towards Blackfriars, the Elephant and Castle, and the strange domain of Mrs Martha Rouncewell.

The Hygienic Steam Laundry was a forbidding building behind a façade of soot-blackened London brick, windows with frosted glass and iron bars, its single vaulted entrance which suggested the gate of a workhouse. Mrs Rouncewell was a widow with a living to earn and she was no believer in allowing her working-girls off the premises. Ten years before, she had been a redoubtable police matron who took a lively interest in her duties of close-searching female suspects. After a brief marriage, which proved too much for her spouse, Horace Rouncewell, she undertook the running of his business with vigour and determination. The laundry was a greater success in his widow's hands than it had ever been in his own, and she remained the friend, often the assistant, of any detective officer who took her fancy. To this class, both Samson and Verity belonged.

Even on such a hot afternoon, a fog of escaping steam half-filled the cobbled courtyard as the gate was locked again behind Stringfellow's cab. Beyond the opaque glass of some of the windows, flesh-pink shapes moved to and fro. It was no secret that in such establishments, in the moist heat, the girls' clothes became sodden rags within ten minutes.

Many of them worked stripped naked to the waist and some chose to work naked altogether.

In her parlour, to which the hiss and clatter of the laundry penetrated clearly, Mrs Rouncewell, dark and brawny with two tufts of hair springing from moles on her chin and cheek-bone, surveyed her visitors.

'We 'oped,' said Samson piously, 'that you might favour us with your assistance in a delicate investigation. This young person, Miss Elaine, is to be asked questions of great consequence to a titled and noble family. Only she won't answer. However, she has also been apprehended begging and extorting. Now, for that she might be confined in gaol. But such wouldn't serve the noble family and wouldn't answer questions. On the other hand, if she was brought to repentance by a lady of a firm hand, such as yourself, and taught to answer when spoke to, then her misdemeanour might be forgot. And o' course, Elaine here would be expected to apprentice herself here to you, for which the parish might reimburse you, and for which you wouldn't pay a 'aypenny wages to her.'

Mrs Rouncewell thought about this.

'Quite the best thing for 'er,' she said at last. 'It beats the Old Bailey by lengths. Miss Workhouse! Sister Charity! In 'ere.'

Two burly young women in grimy smocks appeared.

'Her,' said Mrs Rouncewell, nodding at Elaine, 'for the barrel.'

Without another word said the two smocked women seized the handcuffed girl and in a few deft movements stripped off the skirt and the pants she was wearing underneath. One of them pulled aside a curtain, revealing an alcove into which a barrel lying on its side had been securely wedged. Verity, nervously sensing what was about to happen, looked at Samson. But Samson watched with complete calm. The women lifted Elaine and pushed her face down over the barrel. As it was happening, the sturdy adolescent tossed back her fair hair and twisted her face round defiantly. Then her head and shoulders disappeared over the far side of the barrel and Verity could see nothing beyond the full pale cheeks of Elaine's bottom. Mrs Rouncewell armed herself with a switch cut from an ash plant.

'And now,' she said, 'p'raps you gentlemen'd 'ave the goodness just to take a turn down so far as the Elephant.'

As they left the parlour, she turned to her task, measuring the ash-plant carefully across the plump globes which Elaine reluctantly presented.

'A fine mess,' said Verity furiously as they crossed the yard, 'a fine mess there could be out of all this.'

'A fine mess there could be for *you*, my son, if that little whore Elaine won't answer your questions,' said Samson confidently.

There was a sharp smack followed by a shrill cry.

''owever,' said Samson, 'Mrs Rouncewell ain't one to let you down.'

They walked the length of the New Kent Road to the Elephant and Castle, and then turned back. As they entered the cobbled yard once more, the sounds of the confrontation between Mrs Rouncewell and her new apprentice-girl were still continuing. Samson led the way into the parlour. Elaine twisted and lunged convulsively like a fish in a net. Mrs Rouncewell looked up.

'How the minutes fly,' she said in surprise. 'I usually sends gentlemen to walk a stretch. It helps to give me a grip hold o' time.'

Elaine, red-eyed and weeping copiously, struggled upright. Mrs Rouncewell patted her familiarly on the rear, causing the girl to jerk forward.

'Cry away, Elaine my dear,' said Mrs Rouncewell. 'It exercises the lungs, washes the face, and clears the eyes of dust. And it softens the temper. Why, you'll be as meek and obliging for the next half-hour as ever Mr Samson could ask!'

With that Mrs Rouncewell drew her smocked assistants to her and left the girl with the two sergeants. Elaine wore neither her skirt nor pants, both of which garments Mrs Rouncewell had taken as a precaution against her fifteen-year-old apprentice absconding.

'Well, now, Miss Elaine,' said Samson jovially, 'p'raps you'd just care to answer questions as they're asked.'

Elaine snivelled and said nothing, her hands rubbing busily behind her. Samson walked slowly round her, thoughtfully admiring the bare thighs, the triangle of light hair between them, and the nakedness of the girl's body from her waist down to her stockings. Verity produced a pencil and a notebook.

'Now, miss,' he said self-consciously, 'where might you have been when a picture was took of you in tournament costume, breeches and a doublet?'

'Never 'ad a picture done,' she said sullenly.

'Where might it have been done and you not know?'

'Greenwich Fair,' she said, 'Brighton races, Lewes, Lansdown Fair, Newport. There's a thousand places we went.'

'And where might you have written a letter to Lord Henry Jervis, that is now dead?'

'I never did,' she said, nervously pulling at her lower lip with her teeth. 'I never 'eard of him.'

'Miss Elaine,' said Verity softly, 'the letter is found, your hand is identified, your picture with it for good measure. Now, that barrel is still there and it's no inconvenience to put you backside-upwards over it and call in Mrs Rouncewell. So I just ask you again, where might you have writ that letter, signed Anonyma?'

'It was done when I came to town, two months since,' she said grudgingly. 'I was to have had money and never a penny I got.'

'Why did you write it?'

'I was made to. Charley Wag, 'im that was coopered afterwards. He made me do it.'

'Why Lord Henry Jervis?'

'I knew a bit about him, and Charley thought he'd know me.'

'Miss Elaine,' said Verity, 'Lord Henry Jervis died violently. There's suspicion he was cruelly murdered. Now, let's have the truth of that letter.'

But even as he spoke he realized the mistake. At the

reference to murder she looked up, frightened silly at the thought of the noose and the slow throttling death on the public gallows as the trap let her down with a slither rather than a drop.

'I'll tell you!' she screamed. 'I swear it's all! Charley made me write! He told me every word to put! I could never have wrote a letter without it! I pray I may be blasted if I know a word more than that!'

Samson stood close by her, stroking the back of Elaine's thigh gently.

'You don't care about being blasted or suffering the pains of hell, Elaine. You care more about Mrs Rouncewell being fetched in here. That's what you need.'

'Fetch her!' said the girl with sudden firmness. 'There's no more I can tell, a-cos there isn't more to tell. A tanning ain't going to alter that.'

Verity gave a quick glance at Samson and shook his head slightly.

'Then there ain't more for you to do, miss,' he said gently, 'than serve out your time here. You may escape if you try, but I ain't got to tell you how Mrs Rouncewell welcomes back them that's taken again.'

He opened a door and called the proprietress in.

Ten minutes later, Verity and Samson walked away across the cobbled yard, leaving the new washer-girl to her apprenticeship. Samson, evidently giving expression to feelings which had greatly preoccupied him, said,

'You was unfortunate, Mr Verity, you was most unfortunate to 'ave mentioned any suggestion of Lord 'enry being murdered to Miss Elaine. You saw how it shut her up. You scared her so she wouldn't say another word.'

Verity flushed slightly.

'Mr Samson,' he said firmly, 'I ain't so stoopid as not to know what I'm about. Course I scared 'er. If I'd done otherwise, she'd have said nothing in the first place. You'd make a better detective officer, Mr Samson, if you wasn't so quick to judge by the first appearance of a thing!'

Arms swinging a little, the two sergeants marched side by

side out of the gates of Mrs Rouncewell's Hygienic Steam
Laundry in a silence born of mutual reproach.

*Sergeant William Clarence Verity presents his compli-
ments to Mr Richard Jervis and has the honour to
submit the results of the investigation which he was
hired to undertake.*

*Sergeant Verity has examined Mr Rumer, the keeper,
and others who witnessed the death of Lord Henry Jervis
at Bole Warren, who avouch for His Lordship stumbling
and firing his rifle in what appeared an accidental
manner. There was, at the time, no other person within
thirty yards of Lord Henry.*

*Mr Somerville, gunmaker of the Strand, has sworn to
Sergeant Verity that the bullet which killed Lord Henry
must have been fired by the rifle His Lordship was carrying. This can be told by each rifled barrel making its
unique mark on a bullet as fired.*

*Dr Jamieson of Burlington Street has confirmed to
Sergeant Verity that the medical facts are consistent only
with Lord Henry having shot himself on stumbling.*

*Sergeant Verity is possessed of no evidence from any of
these witnesses to suggest that Lord Henry died other
than an accidental tragic death.*

*In accordance with instructions, Sergeant Verity has
also examined the personal effects of the late Lord
Henry. Consequent on this, he is obliged to mention certain items which may be distressful to His Lordship's
family but which his duty requires him to specify. There
are three photographic plates of a grossly indecent
nature, the figure of a naked man appearing in each,
though the section of the plate depicting the head has
been broken away. The man is identified by marks of
wounds upon the body and rings worn as Lord Henry
Jervis. Two of the young persons in the plates are known
to Sergeant Verity as associates of the late Carlo Aldino,
on whose premises the acts photographed appear to have
taken place.*

Sergeant Verity is also in possession of a letter written

to Lord Henry by a young person in an endeavour to extort money. A young person has been found who admits to writing such words at the dictation of Aldino but does not know the intent or purport of same.

With great regret, Sergeant Verity is obliged to conclude that a blackmail conspiracy was attempted against Lord Henry. Sergeant Verity will not go so far as to suggest that His Lordship was induced by this to take his own life. However, he must advise that no pains be spared to keep this in confidence. Once the evidence of extortion is known, there will be no lack of ill-disposed persons ready to attribute self-destruction to Lord Henry.

Verity read through his report and thought for several minutes. Then he dipped his quill in the little china well and added a final paragraph.

Sergeant Verity can only say how extremely sorry he is that he has not been able to serve Mr Jervis more to Mr Jervis' wishes. He is also conscious of the grief which the late Lord Henry's death must cause and hopes he may offer sincere condolence.

Sergeant Verity begs to remain Mr Jervis' obedient humble servant.

Verity signed and dated the report. With a deep sigh of disappointment for himself and sympathy for the Jervis household, he took a cylindrical wooden ruler in his large fist, holding it like a truncheon, and drew the final neat line at the bottom of the page. Leaning forward over the little table again, his tongue protruding slightly through his teeth with the effort of intellectual concentration, he addressed an envelope to Richard Jervis, Esq., Upper Berkeley Street, Portman Square. Since it was the very house in which he was writing, the report was unlikely to go astray.

The room was unexpectedly bright and cheerful, overcrowded by ornaments and bric-a-brac which exemplified the wealth of the Jervis family. A Turkey carpet in red, blue and yellow adorned the floor. A gilded clock beneath a glass bell ticked the seconds away softly. The gold-framed looking-glass reflected a carefully landscaped and sunny rear garden through the open window. Richard Jervis looked up from his chair, his open hand smashed down on the inlaid table with a power which seemed beyond his emaciated frame.

'You blackguard!' he gasped, throwing down the pages of Verity's report. 'You damned scoundrel!'

'Sir?' said Verity, relaxing from his rigid posture of attention in dismay.

'This!' shouted Jervis, threshing the air with the pages of the report. 'Is this what I have paid you to do?'

'Sir?' The bewilderment grew on Verity's plump face.

'Did I hire you that you might malign my brother's character? Have I paid you to traduce him and insult me in this manner?'

'I never. . . .'

'Indecent photographic plates! Letters from a whore! My brother was a man of more virtue than you could ever imagine, more worthy, more righteous. . . .'

Jervis beat his palm on the table in light, rapid strokes.

'It ain't no pleasure to me, sir. . . .'

'Be silent!'

Captain Ransome, at his usual place behind Richard Jervis' chair, stood with eyes lowered, as though from shame on Verity's behalf. Jervis rapped the table and said nothing. Verity paused a moment as the young man's eyes flashed in excited fury at him and then looked down again. The portly sergeant, with an air of injured dignity, drew out his notecase and took from it a single sheet of paper. He placed it on the table before Richard Jervis, who picked it up, unfolded it and read it.

'That,' said Verity sternly, 'was what come from Lord Henry's bureau. And I think, sir, if Captain Ransome ain't no objection to withdraw, you and me had best have a private word.'

'I think, Captain Ransome, you may find matters to occupy you,' said Jervis shortly. Ransome nodded, half bowed to his master, and withdrew.

'First off,' said Verity as soon as the door had closed,

'there's things not said in that report. Such as who the gentleman may have been that Captain Ransome was representing when he went to see Charley Wag. Could a-bin Lord Henry, sir. Could a-bin you.'

Richard Jervis said nothing for a moment. When he spoke again his voice was unsteady.

'How much have they paid you?'

'Paid, sir? Don't follow, with respect, sir.'

'How much have my brother's enemies, his murderers, paid you? How much did they give you to fabricate this tale of blackmail?'

'There's no murderers, sir, only in your imagination. I ain't got to tell you, sir, how bitterly sorry I am things should come to this. But facts is facts, Mr Jervis, and evidence is evidence, like it or not.'

'Evidence!' said Jervis with a sneer. There was another long silence.

'Sir,' said Verity carefully, 'I also got to say that there's reason to think the blackmail mayn't be over. They must a-got hooks into this family and whoever inherits Charley Wag's place may bleed you for Lord Henry's reputation.'

'You fool!' said Jervis with contempt.

'Sir,' Verity persisted, 'I gotta say this. If I was working on this case official, for Mr Croaker, first thing I'd ask now is about Captain Ransome. He ain't always had a good reputation, sir, though he went as Honest Jack. 'im and Charley Wag quarrelled, and fought. What I gotta ask is, could it a-bin thieves falling out?'

Jervis looked up, the triangle of fair beard seeming sharper, the grey eyes bright with fury.

'How dare you!' he shouted in a voice that half rose to a scream, 'how dare you impugn Jack Ransome! That man has been my legs, my eyes and ears. That man has brought me to life again!'

'Very sorry, sir,' Verity mumbled, and he began to feel that he really had behaved badly towards Ransome and Richard Jervis, that he deserved at least some of the wrath.

It was at this point that Ransome returned. He handed several slips of paper to Richard Jervis and Verity recognized them as the tracings of Elaine's blackmail note which he had made so that Samson might identify the writing. There was also a copy in his own hand of the entire note.

'Found in the fellow's room, sir,' said Ransome. 'His practice attempts for the final draft.'

''ere!' said Verity in a purple fury, 'by what right is my belongings searched?'

'Unfortunate for you, Sergeant Verity,' said Jervis bitterly.

'Sir,' said Verity, hanging on to the truth like a terrier to the neck of a rat, 'I got proof that I never fabricated such a note. The girl Elaine admitted writing it, yesterday.' And he told the full story of the day's events.

Richard Jervis sniffed derisively.

'So,' he said, 'you seize your Elaine, a fifteen-year-old slut. You take her to a private place where she first refuses to have any part in your plan. Then your female accomplice strips her. She thrashes Elaine's backside for half an hour. And then, of course, the girl agrees to say that she wrote the letter. Might that not be it, sergeant?'

Verity was about to invoke Samson as a witness. Then he thought that if things went badly it would be better to save Samson rather than that they should both be destroyed. He said,

'Them photographic plates, sir. There's proof of blackmail in them.'

Lord Henry's double drawing-room was on the floor above them. In slow and painful procession they moved to the stairs, Richard Jervis shuffling with the aid of two sticks and Captain Ransome's powerful arms. At the staircase, as though it were the most natural thing in the world, Ransome picked up his master, like a groom carrying a bride, and bore him rapidly up the three sides of the staircase which rose above the central vestibule. At the double door of the drawing-room, Ransome took a key and opened the lock.

'Show us your evidence,' said Richard Jervis. He was breathless and his wan face was pinched with pain.

Verity led the way into the front drawing-room and through the archway to the rear.

'The plates is in the secret compartment of the ornamental bureau, sir, what stands before the rear window at the centre,' he said triumphantly. Then he stopped. Before the rear window in question there was a small occasional table without a single drawer. Verity swung round to 'see where the bureau had been moved to but there was no sign of it in the rear room. He charged like a wounded bull into the front drawing-room. It was not there either.

'Well?' snapped Richard Jervis.

'It's gone, sir. The bureau's gone. Someone must a-took it!'

'Sergeant Verity,' said Jervis, 'if you are indeed a blackmailer, thank God you are also a stupid one.'

Captain Ransome intervened.

'Sir, might not a murderer have left such evidence here for Mr Verity to find, hoping to suggest suicide by Lord Henry? Then, thinking that Mr Verity would never mention such disagreeable evidence to you, might not the murderer think himself safe to remove it after a few days during which nothing had happened?'

'It ain't likely, by God,' said Jervis furiously, 'not without my key!'

'Not just your key, sir,' said Ransome respectfully. 'There's Mrs Butcher's and Lord William's.'

Richard Jervis thought about this, and Verity looked sidelong at the bluff red face of Jack Ransome, a broken-down half-pay captain who had done him an unexpected friendly service by his suggestion.

'It could a-happened, sir,' said Verity encouragingly. 'That or something like it.'

Richard Jervis looked helplessly about the room. Then his gaze swung at Verity.

'Sergeant,' he said sharply, 'I advise you to forget what might have happened and remember instead what will happen. I have hired you and I will not release you so easily. If, in the shortest possible time, you do not provide the service for which I have paid, Inspector Croaker and your superiors shall hear the whole sorry story of your failure. More than that, I shall preserve the so-called blackmail letter and your own scribblings. They too shall go to Mr Croaker, with my compliments and my observations. Do not think, sergeant, that you will get the better of me by perjured evidence forced from a Lambeth street-girl by beatings and threats!'

'I been put up, sir!' said Verity, his voice quivering with anger.

'If you have sold yourself to my enemies, you shall find you have made a bargain to repent of!'

'Sold!' muttered Verity, jowls trembling, 'I been put up, sir, and the villain that done it ain't half got a reckoning to pay!'

7

'Fifteen four and a flush of five,' said Mrs Rouncewell triumphantly.

'I'm low and Ped's high,' added Samson, turning over the dummy hand.

Mrs Rouncewell's healthy masculine features creased in a deep grin.

'Tip and me's game,' she announced. Then she collected the cards which lay on the table and coaxed them into a pack. The single illumination in her dark parlour was the oil lamp at the table's centre, casting a rich shadowy light on the faces of Samson and Verity who sat at play with her. Mrs Rouncewell splashed a careful measure of spirit from a stone jug into the three glasses, adding hot water from a kettle. Finally she plopped a lump of sugar into each.

'Nasty ungrateful wretch,' she said suddenly, recalling an earlier topic of discussion. 'Nasty charity-school creetur. Ran off the first chance she got, not minding the pains I'd took to apprentice her proper. There ain't no reason a girl can't make a respectable living at the wash-house, once she puts her mind to it. It ain't one of your dirty, unhealthy jobs. Clean 'olesome suds and water. Fresh linen. And I never had to give Miss Elaine her licks more 'n two or three times.'

'No appreciation,' said Samson sympathetically. 'But her mother was a whore and if the girl ever has a daughter she'll likely go the same way.'

'I could a-took a fancy to that little madam,' said Mrs Rouncewell wistfully.

Verity took a pull at the unaccustomed heat of the gin shrub and his eyes watered with the effect.

'You never saw who 'elped her out?' he asked breathlessly.

Mrs Rouncewell shook her head.

'Never *saw*,' she said carefully, 'but I know sure enough. Jack Tiptoe and the scaldrum dodge needed 'er. There was two of 'em as they calls Stunning Joe, the fighter, and American Jack, walking the pavement outside 'ere as if they'd been paid to walk a beat.'

'She ain't with 'em,' said Samson, 'not that we can see.'

'No,' said Mrs Rouncewell, 'she wouldn't be where you could *see*, a-cos she knows the consequence. Straight back 'ere for the bloody 'iding of a lifetime. Nasty little slut.'

'She might 'a-gone back to the fairgrounds,' Verity remarked. 'She might be anywhere from York to Bodmin. Contrariwise, she might have got a taste for what Charley Wag put her up to. Them blackmail dodges is easy money for a girl like 'er that doesn't care a fourpenny-bit in the china dog-kennel for what she puts on paper. It don't 'ave to be true. There's a thousand young gentlemen in London, and old 'uns too, that'd pay her a hundred pound rather than have it whispered that they'd dishonoured themselves, even if they never had.'

They finished their gin.

'I'm to walk back,' said Verity to Samson. 'I left the 'ouse in Portman Square before the chains were put on the doors, and I shall go in after they're taken off in the morning. I must start on my way, Mrs Rouncewell, I really must. But I shan't easy forget all the 'elp you gave me and Mr Samson.'

'I'm sure it was nothing, Mr Verity,' said the muscular old woman, 'I only fret for 'aving lost Elaine. Why, she was fed on the best. None o' your padding-ken gruel and slops but lovely rabbit pie. Sich a rabbit-pie! Sich delicate creatures with sich tender limbs that the very bones melt in your mouth and there's no occasion to pick 'em. And for that the little slut run off! Nasty baggage!'

With varying expressions of sympathy for the ingratitude shown by the fifteen-year-old street-girl towards her mistress, Verity and Samson took their leave. Even in the deadest hours of night, the streets just south of the river seemed bright and noisy with buying and selling. At the kerb of the paving stood a block-tin stove baking potatoes for sale to passers-by, a lavish design in coloured lamps erected over it. The kidney-pie stand was advertised by a candle in an oil-paper lantern with characters crudely drawn. One of the ragged boys gathered under the canvas blind of the cheesemonger's shop, earned a penny a night by running to fetch a light from the wine vaults each time the candle blew out. Under the flaring gaslights, the watermen from the Blackfriars Wharf returned with dim and dirty lanterns in their hands and trudged to the ill-lit doors of 'watering-houses' for pipes and rum shrubs.

'You ain't struck a lot of luck, Mr Verity,' said Samson kindly. 'I shouldn't wonder if you wasn't glad to get back to the division. Specially since you was hired under false pretences.'

'Gammon,' said Verity, striding in time with Samson. 'All gammon.'

Samson chuckled.

'Far from uncovering evidence of blackmail, my old son, you helped to suppress it.'

''ow d'yer mean?'

'Lay you odds,' said Samson, 'your Mr Jervis wasn't worried whether Lord 'enry died accidental or not. But he knew there was evidence of blackmail and he wanted it found. So he hires you for an investigation, knowing a detective officer is the most likely to find it. Then, when it's found, he destroys it and calls you a liar for saying it ever existed.'

Verity shook his head.

'Not if you'd seen Mr Richard Jervis,' he said softly.

'Lay you odds?' Samson suggested hopefully.

'I ain't a gamester, Mr Samson. Never was and never will be.'

There was another silence which continued as the two sergeants crossed London Bridge. In the recesses above the piers of the bridge, in arches, and doorless hovels, the destitute huddled in shapeless masses. The mist hanging over the river surface deepened the red glow of fires on small craft moored off the wharves, rendering more dark and indistinct the murky buildings on either bank. Warehouses, stained by smoke, rose heavy and dull from the mass of roofs and gables, among which the tower of St Saviour's and the spire of St Magnus struck three o'clock on the night air. A forest of masts rose from the shipping below, as though in reflection of the thickly scattered spires of churches above.

'Mr Samson,' said Verity softly, 'if you wanted the body of a dead man, 'ow would you go about the business?'

'I s'pose I'd go to an anatomist like men that walk the public hospitals do.'

'No,' said Verity impatiently, 'what would you do if you wanted the body of one man in particular?'

Samson's face creased in suspicion and alarm.

'Opening tombs?' he said. 'Snatching corpses?'

'No, Mr Samson. Legal.'

'Whose body might you want to examine, then?'

'Lord Henry Jervis,' said Verity with a scowl.

Samson threw back his head with a guffaw that roused the sleepers in the niches of the bridge and set them shifting uneasily.

'Cor,' he said at length, 'you ain't 'alf a caution, my son.'

'Never mind that, Mr Samson, 'ow might it be done?'

'Well,' said Samson jovially, 'seeing that the corpse you wish to question is a peer o' the realm, you might first ask his guv'nor. Not Mr Jervis in this case but Lord William. If 'e ain't averse to his brother being uncoffined, then he might ask the Home Office to please grant an exhumation order. Or you might ask Mr Croaker to ask them. Only thing is,' said Samson smugly, 'Home Offices are apt to be fussy about having their clients dug up all over the place and seeing Kensal Green turned into a 'oliday fair.'

'I never even seen Lord William,' said Verity thoughtfully. 'I got no idea how he'd take to it.'

'Likewise,' said Samson blithely, 'you might cut a caper my way.'

''ow's that, then?'

'Smile sweet on a couple o' resurrection coves and have 'is lordship up and about, ready for inspection, without a by-your-leave.'

'Mr Samson,' said Verity sternly, 'I got trouble enough already. It ain't the way I should've chose to make Lord William's acquaintance, but ask him I will.'

Samson rubbed his hands briskly in the pre-dawn chill. He said,

'It ain't no business o' mine, I daresay, but why might you be so desirous to see Lord Henry?'

Verity scowled again.

'Simple, ain't it? I never seen Lord Henry and I only know what I'm told about his scars and his rings. And I never saw the wound the bullet made, only from a steel copy of a photograph. He ain't been in the ground more than a month, so there can't be much alteration.'

'You never mean to have him out of his shroud?' said Samson in dismay.

'That ain't all I mean to do, Mr Samson,' said Verity primly. 'That ain't even the half of it. So far I took everyone's word for what happened, and look where I am! Now I'm going to see for myself.'

They stood on the verge of Covent Garden Market, the sky red and golden from the newly risen sun, the long rows of carts and donkey-barrows loading. Under the dark Piazza bright little dots of gaslight were burning in the shops, while shoeless girls on the steps of the Theatre tied up flowers in penny and halfpenny bundles. Samson looked at Verity's round face as it glowed with plump self-confidence at the thought of seeing for itself.

'God save us all!' he said with faint exasperation.

Verity turned to him with studied dignity.

'Much obliged, Mr Samson, and I ain't a man that takes kindly to profanities.'

Then, in a gentler tone, he bid Samson a good-day and began his slow lumbering walk, north to the thieves' rookery of the Seven Dials, west down Oxford Street, and thence to Portman Square and Upper Berkeley Street. At five o'clock the boy who slept in the kitchen roused himself to attend to the laying of fires, and the chains were taken off the doors.

Captain Lord William Jervis had for many years maintained an appearance of indeterminate early middle-age. He seemed not the least out of place chaffing a group of young men in Dubourg's or the Beargarden, nor in serious debates among senior officers at the Board of Admiralty on the comparative advantages of iron-clad warships and the lighter wooden vessels. It was this last subject which chiefly preoccupied him as he strode up the steps of Portman Square in company with Captain Lord Edward Clay, the two men in the royal blue frock-coats and white ducks of their naval uniform. Lord William bore the same clear-cut features as his brother Richard Jervis, but the older man's face was set more aggressively, the cheeks flushed and the trim whiskers jet black.

'If a ship were to roll heavy,' he said a little breathlessly, 'then of course she must ship water through the gun ports and can't fight her guns. But they need only ask Yelverton. When his squadron was caught in the Portsmouth gale, every ship rolled like a skittle. The iron-clads rolled over so far that a little water was shipped through the ports and made the guns difficult to fight. But, damme, the wooden hulls rolled so far that the ports must be closed tight to stop them shipping every sea that came.'

The two men strode through the open doorway. But for the death of Lord Henry Jervis so shortly before, this would have been the evening of 'Lord Jervis' summer dance', the single event of the London season by which the family distinguished itself. This year it had been decided to substitute a mere private dinner-party, as a token of family mourning, but it was an event which obliged Lord William, as head of his house, to leave the diversions provided for him by a succession of street-girls at the White Bear.

Unobtrusively, the Jervis house had been transformed into a brighter and more agreeable setting for the guests, as though the summer dance had not, after all, been cancelled. The wrought-iron balcony was glassed in and had become a conservatory stocked with orchids and bright, tropical flowers. Every alcove of the hall and stairway had grown a green arbour among fine pilasters, which were in fact no more than painted wood with daubs of heavy gilding. Incense was still being burnt by the servants to kill the smell of paint. A score of additional footmen, kitchen-girls and maids had been temporarily employed, for even a private dinner-party in the Jervis town house required places for thirty or forty couples. Lord William and Lord Edward Clay climbed the stairs together and then separated to the two dressing-rooms set aside for them.

Lord William, in his habitual manner, threw open the door.

'Anstey!' he shouted, looking round for his valet, 'Anstey, damn you!'

There was no reply. His lordship drew a silver-engraved spirit flask from his pocket, poured a full measure and drained it off. He put the flask on the dressing-table. Just then there was a movement from the small adjoining bedroom which formed part of the dressing suite. Lord William, who had drawn off his blue frock-coat and thrown it on the sofa, opened the communicating door. There was Elaine. Having now finished making the bed, she tossed her hair into place and straightened up. Lord William's mouth twisted in a half-formed sardonic smile.

'Well, little madam!' he said, 'why so quiet and secret in here? Did you mean to spy on a gentleman dressing himself?'

Elaine knew how to type a customer from his first words. In Lord William's case, she looked him full in the face with all her snub-nosed impudence, her narrow dark eyes with their tint of bronze-green scanning his features. And then her mouth opened in a slack grin.

'Take off those damned weeds,' said Lord William

imperiously, and he went to lock the door through which the absent valet might otherwise come. When he returned, Elaine had cast off the long skirts and petticoats of her servant's livery. She stood revealingly in a white blouse and a grey pleated petticoat, obviously part of her professional wardrobe, so short that it reached no lower than the tops of her thighs.

'I'm not la-di-da about it,' she said, as though the words were a challenge. Lord William surveyed the broad hips, the sturdy legs and thighs of the young tomboy. Then he sat on the edge of the bed and pulled her towards him, running his hand up and down her bare legs as she stood there. Under the skirt, she was wearing tight pants in white cotton. Lord William began where the waist of the material touched the base of her spine and let his fingers travel over her body, through the warm cotton, running down between the cheeks of Elaine's bottom, between her thighs, finding the sensitive lap of flesh and working it skilfully with his fingers. The girl squirmed her bare legs restlessly, and presently pulled away from him. But Lord William's protests were cut short as he saw that she was freeing the little skirt so that it dropped to her ankles and she stepped out of it. Elaine slipped a pair of fingers where his own had been, as though out of curiosity, and watched him with amusement. She pulled the front of the pants down and showed a little cleft of fair hair. Lord William's colour deepened and his eyes widened. She turned and pulled the knickers down a little way again. Lord William stared intently at the broad pale cheeks of Elaine's backside, the faded marks of Mrs Rouncewell's attentions just visible.

'Damme!' he said with a tone of awe.

Naked but for her blouse, the girl returned to him, kneeling so that her soft young breasts brushed his knees. She busied herself with him for a moment, then lowered her face. Lord William's features were drawn as though by some inner spasm. He tried to free himself from her but she held on with such determination that he could hardly move her head from his lap. He quivered suddenly.

'Curse it,' he said softly, 'you've spoilt the game.'

Elaine looked up at him and grinned.

'Never,' she said, and went back to her previous occupation.

Lord William was bowled over by the youngster's determination. When his vigour was restored, and he drew her on to the bed, she climbed upon him. Then she paused.

'You got three looking-glasses,' she said. 'It's best to turn 'em so you can see me.'

With this done, she resumed her position, drew her hair into a tail and fastened it with a silk band, and then began to exercise upon her lover. During the episode she kissed Lord William as though she intended to smother him, her agile little tongue moving determinedly in his mouth. Lord William, in turn, was moved to a degree of frenzy he had not known for years. In the urgency of desire his teeth found her throat and shoulders, leaving cherry-red blotches. His hands raked her back, as many a woman's had scored his own, and incredible as it seemed to him, Elaine's cries were entirely of pleasure, as though welcoming even the violence of his lust.

At length it was over and after a brief dallying, the girl dressed herself and left him. Lord William pondered on his good fortune in finding such a chambermaid as Elaine, passionate and adaptable at an age when most girls would have been clumsy and nervous. He had never had a girl in his rooms at the White Bear or Dubourg's who had matched such passion. Thoughtfully he rang for Anstey and turned his mind to the dinner-party.

An hour and a half later, Lord William, his medals and sash gleaming and glowing upon his evening clothes, stood in the fine hall with its marble floor, welcoming the guests. At first he had been unable to concentrate on his duties as host for the memory of Elaine kept on interfering. Now he had repressed this until it was merely a permanent awareness of the girl and her capabilities. As soon as the guests had departed again, he thought, he would stoke the little bitch hot and strong, damned if he wouldn't.

Presently, General Lord Bruce was announced, and Lord William collected his thoughts. The elderly General with his air of silver-haired distinction had been a friend of old Lord Samuel Jervis, and was now no less than Governor to the Prince of Wales during the Prince's undergraduate year at Oxford. Lord William saw the figure of the dapper Grenadier Guardsman on the threshold.

It was just then that a footman approached Lord William, bowed and cleared his throat. Lord William looked at the man in his silk knee-breeches and silver buckles.

'My lord,' said the servant, 'a detective person insists upon seeing you as a matter of the gravest urgency.'

Lord William looked further round and saw a portly figure in shabby coat and baggy trousers, red-faced and black-moustached.

'Sergeant Verity of the Whitehall police office,' said the footman mournfully.

'What the devil have I to do with you?' asked Lord William, not daring to express his anger at the intrusion more loudly for fear of being overheard by General Bruce and the other guests.

'It ain't what you got to do with me, Lord William Jervis,' said Verity quietly, 'it's what I gotta say to you. And said in private is best. Just think o' the young person that was in your dressing-room an hour or two ago.'

Lord William looked about him quickly. It was unthinkable that the discussion should continue in the presence of such guests, equally unthinkable that he should have the fat sergeant carried struggling from the hall.

'This way,' he said sharply.

The two men stood face to face in the little steward's room with its counting-house atmosphere where Verity had first encountered Richard Jervis at Portman Square.

'Sir,' said Verity at once, 'you must be told that the person you was with in your room, and 'oo you spent a considerable time in there with, according to your servant, is a Miss Elaine that 'as already admitted to me trying to blackmail your late brother Lord Henry. It ain't my business what you choose to do with her in your own 'ouse, sir, but it's my duty to tell you the truth. She been party to getting gentlemen into compromising positions and then having photographic plates done of same to extort money from them.'

'Has she?' said Lord William enigmatically, as though he might equally believe or disbelieve the story. 'And what business might it be of yours to set my servant spying on me?'

'He never spied, sir. He found the dressing-room locked and barred. After half an hour, the young person Elaine come out and you was still in there. But you ain't to blame 'im, sir. It was only me seeing the girl in the scullery and saying what a bad lot she was that made the honest fellow tell me in confidence of his fears for you. He's a good, loyal servant, sir, the best you could 'ave.'

'So you say.' Lord William turned, as though about to leave.

'Sir!' said Verity, 'I don't have to say how sorry I am for taking you from your guests but I should wish to ask where Mr Richard Jervis might be and when I might see him.'

'Mr Jervis is ill,' said Lord William airily, 'not you nor anyone else is to see him. Orders have been given to all the servants. The least disturbance might increase his malady.'

'And sorry I am to 'ear it, sir,' said Verity, puzzled. 'But p'raps I might speak fair with you, then, sir, as head of your house. You ain't unaware I suppose of the evil being said about the late Lord Henry?'

'Evil, sergeant?'

'Them that says he made away with himself on account of dealings with young persons, and them that hints at him being foully murdered.'

Lord William drew himself up tall and brushed his dark whiskers with the edge of one hand.

'Who says so?'

'Persons of an evil mind, sir.'

'Dammit, man,' said Lord William with a breathless growl, 'what persons?'

'Ain't at liberty to say, sir.'

'Then to the devil with you and them!'

'I might silence such slander, sir.'

'Then silence it, blast your eyes, and have done with me!'

'In that case, sir, I only got to ask for you to authorise a police medical man to examine Lord Henry's injury and make his impartial report.'

Lord William, his face deepening to a weatherbeaten maroon colour, stared at the fat sergeant, who now shifted uneasily.

'Disinter my brother's body?'

'Only for the eyes of one constabulary medical man, sir. Might stop a lot of tongues wagging, sir.'

Lord William looked at the plump, self-satisfied face with its waxed moustaches.

'You drivelling idiot!' he said, his voice quivering slightly. 'It would start every tongue in the country wagging! Dig him up? This is Mr Richard's doing, no doubt! A pair of madcaps, the two of you!'

As though about to engage in some other business, Lord William strode to the little desk, drew out a sheet of paper, dipped a newly-sharpened quill in the ink-well, and wrote furiously. He sanded the paper, folded it and sealed it in an envelope which he addressed. Then he rang for a footman and handed it to him.

'See this taken at once,' he said sharply, 'Whitehall Place for the immediate attention of the commissioner of police.'

The footman bowed and withdrew. Lord William looked up at Verity.

'By noon tomorrow, Sergeant Verity, you and your possessions will be out of this house. The house is mine, Bole Warren is mine, and every servant upon the estate is mine. I, sir, am the head of this family, not Mr Richard Jervis. What he has, I pay for. Damme, sir, but for me he is a pauper. And now, sir, your Mr Commissioner has my solemn word that if you ever set foot in my house or on my land again, I will prosecute you in every court of the realm. Yes, damme, every court of the kingdom!'

Verity swallowed apprehensively.

'And the duties I was hired for, sir?'

'Your duties are terminated, sir! You are dismissed, damn you! Dismissed!'

With a glare of irresistible rage, Lord William straightened his coat and stormed back to his waiting guests.

The stair creaked a little as Verity eased his large boot on to it. Deeply perturbed by the interview with Lord William, not least by the uncontrolled fury of the man, he had determined on finding Richard Jervis before he was dismissed from Portman Square. Lord William had spoken accurately in saying that strict orders had been given to the servants that Richard Jervis was to be held incommunicado. Even Mrs Butcher had answered with a refusal, followed by long resolute silence, when Verity suggested that she might care to open the door from the back stairs to the second-floor landing of the house with the key on her chatelaine. He had watched his chance for half an hour, but there was no possibility of purloining a key for the purpose and no way of entering the main rooms of the house otherwise. While the dinner-party continued, the attention of the servants was directed towards it. Once it was over, Verity's chance of moving about the house unobserved in the time remaining to him was very slight indeed.

'A man what's seen as much of cracksmen as I have can't help picking up a dodge or two,' he said to himself philosophically, and moved casually towards the back stairs, as though going to his attic room to pack. At the second landing, the door which communicated with the main part of the house was impressively solid. The panelled oak was unpolished and massive. The lock, too, was resplendent with brass furniture.

'It ain't a Chubb nor a Bramah, 'owever,' said Verity softly. Humming a little tune to himself, he drew a tin from his pocket and a slender metal rod, thinner than a pencil. The tin contained a yellowish wax which smelt of cobblers' shops. With great care, Verity smeared a thin coating of this on the little rod and stood so that the gaslight on the bare stairway fell full on the keyhole of the door. He inserted the rod, as though it had been the barrel of a key, revolved it gently and withdrew it. At three points along the rod the wax had been scraped away.

'Why,' he said to himself, 'it's no more than three sliders.'
Pocketing the wax, he produced three slender metal

probes and inserted the first in the lock. After a certain amount of juggling with it, he felt something yield and lift. Holding the probe exactly in this place with the heel of his right palm, he began to juggle the second. When two were in place it was child's play to lift the third and turn the lock. The heavy door opened without a sound.

Verity stepped through on to the richly-carpeted floor of the handsome landing, the sounds of the dinner-party carrying up faintly from below through the airy ovals of the fine staircase. Keeping close to the wall to minimize the risk of being seen from the lower levels, he edged towards the door of Richard Jervis' apartments. The young man might be alone or he might not, but that was a risk to be taken. Indeed, he might not be there at all. Verity reached the door and listened. He thought he could hear the sound of a man breathing deeply, as though in sleep, but he could not be sure. Preparing himself for rapid concealment behind the corner of the wall, he tapped sharply on the panel of the door. There was a movement as though of a sleeper stirring.

'Mr Jervis!' he whispered hoarsely, 'Mr Richard Jervis, sir! Are you there, sir?'

'Who are you? For God's sake tell me, who are you?'

It was Jervis' voice, weak from illness or some opiate given him.

'Sergeant Verity, sir!'

Verity tried the door. It was solid oak again and fastened tight.

'No,' said Jervis feebly, as he heard the movement. 'Locked, bolted. They come and go by the door from the other room.'

'Any chance you might reach them bolts, sir?'

'No chance now. Tied me, by the wrists, to the bed.'

Verity looked round quickly, knowing that the conversation must be interrupted at any moment.

'Sir, I been dismissed by Lord William. I'm to be gone by noon.'

There was the sound of a faint struggle and then a moan, as though of resignation.

'Sir, if your brother, the late Lord Henry, was cruelly

murdered, his body oughta be examined again. I can't make Lord William see the use of it.'

To Verity's dismay, Richard Jervis gave a soft, helpless laugh.

'Sir, if I can't have the evidence; and if your brother was murdered, I shan't ever find who the murderer was.'

Again came the soft laughter of the weary, crippled young man.

'I wish you to find how my brother was murdered. Do not concern yourself with the identity of the assassin. I know that already.'

'You *know* 'im, sir?' said Verity doubtfully. 'And who might he be?'

'Oh, Sergeant Verity, only think. Only think.'

'Are you alone in there, sir?'

'Alone, alone, all all alone, alone on a wide, wide sea.'

Verity rattled the door as far as he could.

'Only think, sergeant. Who hated my brother as he hates me? Who coveted Lord Henry's wealth and lands to pay for his own debaucheries? That was the man whom I saw murder Lord Henry, saw with my own eyes. But I do not yet know how it was done. You must tell me that, sergeant.'

There was a sound of footsteps on the stairs, far below.

'Sir, I can't stop longer! Who was the villain you saw?'

'Why, sergeant, how slow you have been, to be sure!'

'Quickly, sir, or I must go.'

The young man laughed softly, as though he could not comprehend Verity's obtuseness.

'Lord William Jervis!' he whispered sharply.

'Mr Verity,' said Bella softly, 'why was you so long from home?' The vivacious blue eyes in the round little face were wide with puzzlement as she stroked his cheek.

'Blessed if I know,' said Verity thoughtfully, 'for all the good it did!'

They lay side by side in the large ancient bed, bought by Stringfellow at the time of his own marriage. A scattering of embers in the grate diffused a reassuring, shadowy glow across the darkened bedroom, silhouetting the cradle at Bella's side.

'But now you're to live 'ome,' said Bella happily.

'I don't see 'ow there could a-bin murder done,' Verity said for the twentieth time that day. 'But I do know that Mr Richard was locked prisoner in his room, vowing that his brother Lord William was the 'omicide. And they'd done something to Mr Richard, I swear. Drugged him to sleep or restrained him.'

'This Lord William,' said Bella, 'was he a cruel man?'

'A tartar on his ship,' Verity murmured knowledgeably. 'Flogged the whole starboard watch when they only made nine knots speed with a bowline.'

'And he isn't to be took and questioned?'

'Rum thing is,' said Verity, 'so soon as ever I got back to Whitehall Place, who sends for me but Mr Croaker. I'm to forget everything that ever happened. I'm to forget I ever heard poor Mr Richard prisoner in his room and what he said of Lord William. I'm never to have dealings with Mr Richard again nor to go near the Jervis 'ouse. Which Mr Croaker keeps saying is Lord William's house anyhow. That's to be the end of it!'

Bella edged her plump little knee between his knees.

'Here,' she said, 'if a man says another man committed murder, ain't it got to be investigated?'

'Not necessarily,' said Verity. 'Not if someone in a high

place says there ain't primer fishy evidence. Then the likes o' me don't get asked, do they?'

'Someone in a high place says you're not to pay attention to that poor crippled Mr Richard?'

Verity laughed significantly.

'It was never Mr Croaker. Higher up, much higher up. Mr Croaker spoke very straight and calm about it all, which he never does when he's speaking on his own account. Sort o' worried and a bit frightened, I thought. Not a bit hisself. Sour as vinegar and mean as a stoat, that's more his usual way.'

Bella turned her head a little, gazed at the ceiling and shook her blonde curls.

'Ain't it a caution?' she said. 'And what's to become of you now?'

'Blackmail,' said Verity with relish. 'Charley Wag may have closed his accounts but there's a score o' young persons of a bad reputation what have took the business for themselves.'

Bella thought about this. Presently she said,

'Mr Verity, when these unfortunates is arrested, might you have to lay hands upon them? Might you have to touch . . . might you have to touch their persons?'

Verity puffed up his moustaches.

''ere now!' he said tolerantly.

'I 'eard,' said Bella, ''ow constables in the parks was turning a blind eye to unfortunates there in return for making free with their fallen virtue.'

Verity sat up in bed.

'You no business to 'ear such things, Mrs Verity! Why, I can't think who'd say as much! And it ain't your place to 'ear. You'd a sight better give your mind to setting an example o' thrift and respectability to the labouring classes round here. That way, there might be a few less unfortunates. You gotta position to keep up, being the wife of an officer of the law!'

At this point, the child in the cradle was woken by the outburst and began to bawl with powerful lungs. Husband and wife abandoned their discussion and turned to one another. A church clock beyond the rattle of cabs and carts on the Edgware Road struck midnight on the warm summer air. Bella gave a deep sigh of satisfaction.

'Oh, Mr Verity!' she gasped. 'Oh, Mr Verity!'

As a concession to the heat of the day and the shortage of accommodation for officers of the Whitehall Division, the Private-Clothes detail was paraded in the police office yard.

'So they never let you dig up Lord 'enry?' said Samson cheerily.

'No,' said Verity shortly, 'never did.'

'Ah well,' said Samson, 'daresay he wouldn't have turned out much of a cove after all. Speaking o' which, you never missed anything o' the blackmail case while you was boarding at Portman Square. Charley's girls have all took it for themselves now. Leastways, if there is a man behind 'em, we can't flush him out. I'd say it was all down to Charley Wag. With 'im dead, I reckon the blackmail must die too. Girls like Simona and that, they ain't got the style. All of 'em gone back to spreading their legs for a living, I'd say.'

'You ain't off the case, Mr Samson?'

'Oh, ain't I? I'm on to something very special now. Seeing after the nobility and making sure they ain't bothered. Be there ready if there's any go at blackmail, that's how Mr Croaker sees it.'

'Nobility?' said Verity uneasily.

'Yus,' said Samson, 'nobility. Not anyone you'd know.'

Inspector Swift called the parade to attention and detailed the men to their duties. Verity's heart sank as he realized that once again he was being kept back, as he had been on the day that Swift sent him to the hiring-room. But Swift's words to Samson and Verity were more encouraging.

'Right, Samson, got your orders, then? Lord Renfrew to be seen safe through London but not to be approached by you nor spoke to.'

'Yessir.'

'And great care to be taken over the Bond Street business with his lordship.'

'Yessir.'

Swift turned to Verity.

'Now, my lad,' he said, 'I've put up surety for you, in a manner of speaking, and I shan't look to be let down. So walk smart, talk sensible, and keep your face clean. Right?'

'Sir!'

'You may find yourself assisting Sergeant Samson, or you may not. It will depend on events. Your duties are to keep surveillance from now until tomorrow morning upon the Temple of Beauty in Bond Street.'

'Temple, sir?'

'It sells preparations for ladies' faces and persons,' said Swift self-consciously. 'Oils, perfumes, soaps and so on. It says "Beautiful for Ever" over the door. But we hear it sells other commodities too. You are to maintain surveillance and prevent at all costs any untoward proceedings.'

'It ain't to be raided nor closed down, sir?'

'No,' said Swift, 'positively not. No action to be taken against it. The Temple of Beauty is to be protected from interference.'

'Don't understand, sir, with respect, sir.'

'Nor do I,' said Swift. 'Nor does your Mr Croaker, nor Superintendent Gowry, nor the Commissioner. You are indeed privileged, sergeant, for the orders which you do not understand come from on high and are to be obeyed as such. Dismissed!'

As the two sergeants marched away, Verity said,

'I never knew such a thing! Me to stand guard on a 'ouse of ill-fame! It ain't to be warned or closed down but protected. And me to see that nothing undignified 'appens there! Why, I might be one of Ned Roper's bullies.'

'Better than the hiring-room, ain't it?' said Samson.

'What ain't better is not being told why. I'm to do such duties without knowing why. Same as I'm never to see Mr Jervis or have anything to do with the family, and not be told a word of why I mustn't. I keep thinking of that poor young man locked away a prisoner and vowing that one of his brothers murdered the other. And then, all on a sudden, I'm told to forget it. Who by? It ain't Mr Croaker's doing. Higher up, that's what.'

Samson eyed the ankles of a flower-girl appreciatively as the two sergeants turned the corner of Cockspur Street.

'Ain't your worry, my son,' he said philosophically.

Verity stopped.

'Yes it bloody is, Mr Samson! It worries me that there's a smell about all this! There's a smell about Portman Square and what happened at Bole Warren as sure as there is over this Temple of Beauty nonsense. I got wind o' it all right, and I'll see you and Mr Croaker and the rest of 'em in hell before I give up!'

Ramming the tall, dusty hat more firmly on his head, his round face purpling with indignation and exertion, Verity took his leave of Samson and strode angrily away past the tall windows of the United Service Club and the leafy opening of Waterloo Place.

The dust of the summer afternoon, raised by the constant passage of rumbling wooden wheels with their iron rims, brought a smart to the eyes and a dryness to the throat. Standing at ease, conspicuous as a mounted guard outside St James' Palace, Verity occupied the archway of a mews entrance and kept his eyes determinedly on the object of his surveillance on the far side of Bond Street. It was the time of day sacred to the Bond Street loungers, whiling away the afternoon in quizzing the young and titled ladies who promenaded there. The tall, elegant houses were interspersed with bow-fronted shops, the pastel wash of their walls highlighted by the sparkling white paintwork of the square-paned windows. Fine gloves, bonnets à la mode, glittering and glowing jewels, cut-glass, lace, and handsomely-bound leather volumes shone with rich desirability in the window displays.

The largest of these establishments, its double front and fine arched portico suggesting a theatre or assembly room as much as a shop, was the Temple of Beauty. From the display of gilt lettering it might have been the premises of a fashionable chemist or an expensive herbalist, serving the affluent area that lay between Pall Mall and Regent Circus. Under the golden-lettered promise of 'Beautiful for Ever', the windows offered 'Royal Arabian Soap', 'Powders for the Complexion', and 'Jordan Water, 10 guineas a bottle'. Fine ornamental boxes, tortoiseshell or lacquered, boasted 'Favourite of the Harem's Bouquet', 'Souvenir de Mariage', and 'Maiden's Keepsake'.

Under Verity's sternly disapproving gaze, broughams and pilentums drew up before the freshly-painted façade. Liveried servants handed down their well-dressed mistresses who duly made their way into the Temple. The premises suggested the warm perfumed aromas of naked female flesh. It was also noticeable, Verity thought, that for every well-dressed woman who arrived there was also an equally distinguished gentleman. After an hour or two the couple would emerge, as they had arrived, separately. But to a careful observer it was possible to deduce from the time spent which man and which woman had had a particular assignation in one of the salons.

Very clever, thought Verity, a place for the indiscretions of the titled and the wealthy, the jewel of a blackmail dodge that would make Ramiro's Baths seem like a child's game. Small wonder that the authorities wished to prevent unpleasantness, while at the same time insisting that the place must not be interfered with. In one form or another, the men and women who came and went were the authorities themselves.

As an exercise in surveillance, Verity's watch on the Temple of Beauty seemed to him less than satisfactory. He was in full view of the Bond Street strollers, the women in their pink or green crinolines and bonnets, the men in their silk hats and summer suiting of cream or pale brown. There was no doubt what he was, standing at ease in his archway in the tall fraying hat and broad barge-shaped boots. But the men and women who chose to deceive husbands or wives with one another disregarded him. They cared no more for what he saw or thought than if he had been a crossing-sweeper.

As afternoon turned to evening and the dinner-hour approached, the procession of visitors to the Temple of Beauty dwindled. It was in the early dusk that Verity saw a man, on foot and alone, approach the portico and enter. There was no mistaking Lord William Jervis, the tall dark captain with his jaunty stride. Verity drew back into the shadows and waited. But Lord William was not followed by any young woman. Instead, he reappeared after several minutes and strode away down Bond Street towards Piccadilly and Pall Mall as energetically as ever.

Verity puzzled over this. The windows of the Temple of Beauty were now bright with gas in the thickening twilight, so that it looked more than ever like a discreet private theatre. Groups of well-dressed men and women, noisy after-dinner parties, arrived by brougham or cab and went inside. In his mind, Verity began to compose the complaint he would make to Inspector Swift next morning on the waste of a whole day's duty.

He was engaged in this mental composition when a cab drew up on his own side of Bond Street and Sergeant Samson got down from it, looking about him anxiously.

'Over 'ere, Mr Samson,' said Verity softly.

Samson, breathless but businesslike, took his colleague by the arm.

'Right, my son,' he said, 'this is where I want your 'elp, as Mr Swift was saying, you're to get in that place and stop in there. It ain't difficult, no more difficult than getting into a penny gaff nor a chanting crib. They don't charge till you're in. Then you pays your way. Once in there, you're to act like a servant or one of the house bullies. Right?'

'And what should I want to be in there for, Mr Samson?'

'You're to be in there to make sure that Lord Renfrew ain't, and that he don't get in there. That's all.'

'But I don't know 'im!' said Verity plaintively.

'I shall be with 'im,' said Samson. 'You'll know when you see me. And you'll know better than that a-cos Lord Renfrew is with two cronies. One's a fair-haired young gentleman, Lord Renfrew being darkish, and the other is Lord William Jervis.'

'You wouldn't know, Mr Samson, that Lord William been here and gone not half an hour since?' inquired Verity sceptically.

Samson pressed his finger to the side of his nose.

'Arrangements,' he said with a wink, 'arrangements for Lord Renfrew to be shown the spicy side o' town life. Only we know, don't we, Mr Verity, that the dear young fellow ain't never going to set foot over the threshold? 'im a mere boy o' eighteen!'

'I don't see 'ow he's to be stopped, Mr Samson, not if 'e's set his heart on such wickedness.'

Samson laughed uproariously.

'Don't you tell me, Mr Verity, that you can't change a boy's mind for 'im. You with your experience!'

And with this genial encouragement, Samson swung himself back into the cab and was driven briskly away in the general direction of Pall Mall. At least the plan of the operation was clear enough. Lord William had arranged to take the young, and no doubt rich and well-connected, Lord Renfrew to the display offered by the Temple of Beauty. The Renfrew title meant nothing to Verity, probably a form of courtesy bestowed on some elder son who had become a midshipman on Lord William's ship. Why Lord Renfrew's moral welfare had become the primary concern of the Private-Clothes detail was beyond Verity's comprehension. But such were his orders. Crossing the street, he entered the portico of the Temple of Beauty.

Once inside, it seemed that the shop itself was a mere foyer leading to a grander salon within. A man with the biceps of a coal-heaver and the shoulders of a drayman, barred his way.

'And 'oo might you be, fellow?' he inquired, the muscles of his face contorting in a grimace of doubt.

'You "fellow" me and you'll have something to answer for,' said Verity calmly, playing out the role he had chosen for himself. 'I'm the valet of Lord William Jervis, I am. And where he goes, I go. His Lordship just gone to fetch Lord Renfrew and the other gentleman, and if he comes back and I ain't here, he won't half set the cocks a-going.'

At the mention of the names, Verity's challenger stepped back a pace and let him pass, though taking care to follow close behind. As they entered the inner shell of the building,

Verity was surprised how accurately his impression of its being a private theatre matched the truth. There was a carpeted semi-circular space, free of all fittings but capable of seating two hundred people if seats had been provided. Where the proscenium arch might have been, there was a platform curtained off from the makeshift auditorium, and round the auditorium itself rose a series of boxes in two tiers, offering the only accommodation other than the open pit itself. The carpeted semi-circle was filled with the chatter of elegantly-attired men and women, drawn by gossip and curiosity to see the display. What that display might be was not indicated in any way.

'And where may Lord William's place be appointed?' asked Verity sharply.

The bully in his tight-fitting jacket stepped round him and led the way to the right-hand box, level with the stage and nearest to it. The vantage-point, Verity thought, was perfect, while the semi-darkness of the box itself effectively concealed him in its shadows.

The place was the size of a private ballroom, such as lay behind many of the grand façades of Piccadilly and the streets which ran off it. The theatrical structure was no more than wood and plaster painted over, but the effect was significant. The entire auditorium was draped in black with phallic torches upon the pillars, and ornamentation which seemed unremarkable until more closely scrutinized, but which then appeared to be of ingenious obscenity. A hot, musky smell of incense drifted over the velvet and the dark silk.

Somewhere beyond the screened platform a gong beat three times. Slowly the conversation in the boxes and among the close-packed groups in the carpeted pit dwindled and died. Behind the gauze curtaining of the platform there was a sudden flaring of light as the gas was turned up, illuminating a horned figure upon a throne with attendants surrounding him. Verity snorted with indignation. A cheap 'occult' trick to attract the rich young gulls of the West End. He saw that apart from the horned 'beast' on his high throne, there were several men and half a dozen girls, all naked except for the goat-masks worn by the men. These actors gave a sudden cry.

'Lord Lucifer!'

The horned figure on the throne raised its head, the face covered by a mask of inexpressible evil, done in bronze which Verity suspected on closer examination would appear to be cheap tinsel. Two of the naked girls turned, took the halves of the gauze curtain and ran them back to the wings.

'Why!' said Verity softly, 'if it ain't Miss Simona and 'er little baggage!'

He felt a great exultation in the discovery. And whatever else he had failed in, he had now identified the last of the four glass-plate photographs in the late Lord Henry's bureau. The devil-masks, the auditorium, the faces of the men and women in their evening clothes. This was where it had happened. The camera must have been in the wing on the far side, facing diagonally across the stage, directly towards the box in which Verity was sitting. Very neat. Whoever sat in that box was number one for being a participant in some kind of satanic celebration.

'O' course,' said Verity softly to himself, 'just to be *sitting* here watching wouldn't be enough for a real blackmail squeeze, so they had 'im up there, stark naked. To be caught just watching ain't enough, except for a very great man indeed. And for 'im it's more 'n enough.'

'O Mighty Satan, Lord of the Dead, Master of Night, Prince of Darkness. . . .'

Verity snorted again, both with distaste and at the tawdriness of it.

'If they wanted the real fear o' hell,' he muttered, 'they should a-heard some of the old preachers in the great ring on Bodmin Moor!'

'Master, hear us!'

The words were coming from a speaking-trumpet held somewhere off-stage. On the platform itself a black-draped altar with black candles and sticks was set before the throned figure of Lord Lucifer. Also off-stage, several voices began to drone an indecipherable liturgy to the light rapid drumming of feet.

The sounds produced behind the scenes transformed the setting into a great pagan shrine filled with the murmuring of a host of worshippers at the feet of their dark idol. Still intent on the details of the photographic glass-plate which he had seen in Lord Henry's bureau, Verity peered about him in the gloom. Even by the light reflected from the stage he could make out the most obvious inconsistency. In the glass-plate there had been the outline of the box, behind the faces of the spectators. But the two boxes on either side of the stage and level with it were not identical. The one in which Verity sat was a plain opening draped with velvet. The opposite box was the one in the photograph, with an elaborate beading. It was further identified by a crack in the paintwork on one side.

'Only thing is,' said Verity to himself, 'that box is to the right of the stage and they took the picture looking to the left. So 'ow the mischief can a box walk from one side of the theatre to the other?'

Then he snorted with derision again.

'Reversed!' he said contemptuously. 'They couldn't even print it right but got a mirror-image instead. What I don't see, 'owever, is how a man might take a picture in so little light. Why, he'd need to leave a plate exposed for ten minutes at least. They never 'eld still that long!'

There was a clash of cymbals, and as the reverberations died away into a great silence the lights about the dark throne grew dimmer. As though from a great distance, there was a chanting of many voices and the continued drumming of feet in a communal dance. The well-dressed men and women in the pit looked at one another and smiled reassuringly. It was, after all, no more than a lark.

The four men with their goat-masks stood about the black altar on which the 'sacrifice' of one of the girls was to be consummated. Then, as though like a snake uncoiling and rising, the girl who squatted, curled and with head lowered, began to rise from the floor with the grace of a dancer. She was petite and dark, her nude body shining like pale gold in the soft light. The almond elipse of her dark eyes, her neat features and small breasts were unmistakable to Verity.

'Jolly, right enough,' he said softly.

She rose upright between the four masked men, her slender dark body twisting and squirming, her trim legs and slim thighs contorting with energy. Her black, sleek hair was piled on her head with the aid of a comb, leaving clear her delicate ears and nape. The gas-light shone on her moving shoulders as on gold satin, while her slim brown back narrowed downwards and then rounded seductively in the paler and softer fullness of hips and bottom. This, Verity thought, was what the gulls had come for, not for the furtive thrill of black arts.

The four men were closing on her now, dragging her back against the black velvet altar, forcing her back upon it so that although her feet still touched the floor the front of her body was a tight bow with her head lying back on the altar itself. Her arms were spread out, clutching the velvet on either side of her and she made no attempt to shield the triangle of dark hair between her splayed thighs. One of the men took what looked like a large egg and broke it so that thick albumen spread slowly over her belly and ran downwards. The man's fingers aided the diffusion of the substance while another goat-masked figure broke his shell over her breasts and on her mouth.

Impassively the throned figure of Evil looked down upon the obscene preliminaries to the ritual, while Verity watched with incredulous anger the waste of enough food to give dinner to the starving family of a Spitalfields weaver. The girl was bending forward over the altar, her hands clasped between her legs, furtively examining what had been done to her. She watched the men over her shoulder, the dark eyes in the cat-like beauty of her face urging them on. The last man stepped forward and she held still. The shell cracked and Miss Jolly's behind streamed with the same protoplasmic fluid. The men were dragging her on to the altar as Verity, probing the darkness, saw where the camera lens must be concealed, diagonally opposite him in the curtains on the far side of the platform. There was a slight movement among the hangings. That was it, Verity thought, but how was it done in such semi-darkness?

The girl was face down on the altar, a silver cup jammed up high between her parted legs to catch the blood of the sacrifice as it ran down her back and between her thighs. Her agile hands were pressed under her loins and she seemed to be tensing and slackening her body rhythmically with impatience. On his black throne, the figure of Lord Lucifer stretched out an arm imperiously and there was a blinding spasm of white 'stage-fire', which made the audience gasp with surprise.

'So that's it!' said Verity grimly. 'That's the illumination for photographic plates!'

Satan's 'fire' flashed again, as Simona and Stefania brought on a market-basket with a small squealing pig inside it. On her altar, the perverse and erotically maddened girl watched eagerly as the knives and ritual implements were laid upon her and the place for the animal's sacrifice chosen. The stage-fire flashed again, more brilliantly than before.

'Mr Verity!'

Momentarily blinded by the glare, Verity looked about him.

''ere, Mr Samson! Over 'ere!'

Then Samson was at his side.

'Quick as you can, my son! Lord Renfrew and party has given the slip and come through another way. You gotta 'elp now, Mr Verity! If they get in 'ere, I'm done for!'

'They ain't in yet?'

'No, but give 'em two more minutes and they will be. They won't take notice of me, Mr Verity.'

''ow important is it this young Lord Renfrew shouldn't show 'is face in 'ere?'

'You got no idea, Mr Verity!'

'Right,' said Verity. 'One sure way he can't get in is if all the rest of 'em is going out fast!'

To Samson's amazement, Verity clambered on to the ledge of the box and took a crashing jump several feet down on to the stage. He picked himself up at once, strode to the centre and faced the spectators. A complete silence fell upon the actors and audience alike, even the squealing of the pig subsiding to a shrill grizzle. Off-stage, the temple noises died away.

'Right,' said Verity again, his round face growing redder with the effort of shouting loudly enough to make himself heard throughout the auditorium, 'I'm a police officer from Whitehall office and in a moment more it's going to be my painful duty to take your names and addresses, the lot o' you!'

There was a nervous shifting among the well-heeled audience.

'And,' shouted Verity, 'in a moment more the lights is going up and the detective photographer is to take pictures of you all, in case you should have to be identified subsequent.'

He stepped back and ripped aside the hangings where he had seen movement. A small, spectacled man crouched down, cowering behind the wooden box-camera on its tripod.

'Stand where you are, the lot of you!' Verity roared. 'There's two constables among you already and a wagonload more on its way. You'll be took for questioning and close search. Gentlemen to Whitehall and ladies to St James'!'

At this promise, the growing horror among the spectators gave way to panic. Those nearest the door turned and bolted, the less fortunate scrambling at their backs in an endeavour to hasten the stampede. On the stage there was pandemonium. Two of the naked men in goat-masks tried to jump Verity. The first he repelled with a fist like a hambone driven with a smash to the nose. The second he got 'in Chancery', swung him round by the head and shot him over the edge of the platform and into the retreating spectators. There was a shriek of terror from several women as the nude figure fell upon them.

The house bullies watched helplessly from beyond the crowd, unable to force their way through to reach the stage. Samson had joined Verity by this time and began to wreak havoc with immense enthusiasm. The priests and priestesses of Lord Lucifer fought the two detective officers and, in some cases, one another in their enthusiasm to get clear before the police wagon arrived. Samson tripped on a body, crashed into the altar, which proved to be flimsy enough under its velvet, and brought it clattering down. He picked himself from the ruins, almost embracing the nude slippery girl who had been lying on it. In her fury, she flew at him, long nails fencing for his face and eyes. Samson dodged, snatched up a length of double, looped sash-cord from the debris and administered a long-range blow to the slim golden-skinned legs. The demoness yelped, turned about and ran, as Samson delivered a parting stroke to Miss Jolly's rear.

During this encounter, Verity had struggled through the brawl to reach Lord Lucifer's throne, from which the Ruler of Hell was endeavouring to descend, gingerly since the entire edifice appeared far more precarious close to than it had done at a distance. Attacking the foundation, Verity knocked the orange boxes from under the chair which they supported and brought the whole structure toppling over. The Prince of Hell picked himself from the ruins, still wearing his mask.

''ere!' he said peevishly, 'wot's all the aggravation about?'

'You'll find out, my man!' said Verity sternly. He reached out for Lord Lucifer, but the man took to his heels, dodged and ran out through the curtains. Within a few minutes the two sergeants had the stage to themselves.

'This way!' gasped Samson. 'Out here!'

In the general scramble for safety, several windows on the premises had been forced open, wealthy young swells and their ladies scrambling through, dropping to the pavement and running for their lives like small boys who had robbed an orchard. As Verity and Samson reached the street by this route, a considerable number of those who had been packed into the building were still wrestling their way out through the doors. The display of 'Royal Arabian Soap', 'Favourite of the Harem's Bouquet', and 'Jordan Water, 10 guineas a bottle', had been wrecked. Tortoiseshell and laquered fragments were all that remained of the expensive boxes, while the promise of 'Beautiful for Ever' hung at a precipitous angle.

'You done it now, my son,' said Samson apprehensively.

'We was detailed to see nothing indecorous 'appened here. Look at this set-to!'

'Yes,' said Verity, 'and if Lord Renfrew was to be kept out of there, not even be seen in there, 'e must be a very important sort o' cove. There wasn't another way. I ain't so soft I didn't recognize a face or two among all them silk 'ats. And if anyone should come on me for what 'appened, I shall name a few names!'

'Over 'ere,' said Samson, unimpressed. 'Sharply!'

Verity caught a glimpse of Lord William Jervis, his hat gone, being borne along in the rush like a cork bobbing in a stream. There was a fair-haired young man close to him and a dark-haired youth with round face and heavy mouth whose appearance seemed distantly familiar.

'Lord Renfrew!' said Samson. 'Get 'im clear!'

The two burly sergeants made for the crowd, thrusting their way in resolutely and ignoring the angry cries of, 'Stand aside, fellow!' or 'Throw him back!' from the men and the squeals of 'My cloak, sir!' and 'Oh, the brute!' from the women. Samson reached the dark young man, there was a murmured exchange and they began to struggle out through the crowd followed by Lord William, the fair young man, and Verity bringing up the rear.

Once clear of the scrimmage, Verity stood at a slight, respectful distance while the others bent their heads together in earnest discussion. Presently they walked, with the two sergeants behind them, down Bond Street towards the house of Mr Poole, the tailor. Verity noticed that the dark young man's coat had been torn open at the seam of the right arm. While Samson and Verity waited outside, the three men were admitted.

'Still think it was a wasted dooty?' Samson inquired.

Verity puffed up his moustaches a little.

'Oh, no, Mr Samson, not for an observant officer!'

He was peering at the window of the tailor's shop.

''ere!' he said, 'there's a picture of Lord Renfrew in a gold frame!'

'Yes,' said Samson, 'I shouldn't concern yourself over that, however.'

'Only,' said Verity softly, 'it don't say anything about any Lord Renfrew 'ere. It says "God Bless His Royal Highness the Prince of Wales". Cor! 'ere! Wait till Mrs Verity and 'er old father 'ear of this! Blimey! I been within six feet of '*im*! I near as anything spoke to 'im! Why, Mr Samson! Now I see why you was so desperate for 'im not to have 'is picture took or even be seen there, grinning at Miss Jolly's bare what's-it!'

'The less you say about it, my son, the better it may be for us all,' said Samson soberly. 'You stick to duties assigned you, that's my advice.'

'Much obliged, Mr Samson, and I ain't greatly in need o' your advice. I done a bit o' duty tonight, afore you came on the scene, that makes being escort to 'is 'ighness seem very small beer.'

'Oh?' said Samson sceptically.

'Yes,' said Verity. 'I recognized that place as where the fourth glass-plate in poor Lord Henry's bureau was done.'

'You was lucky, my son.'

'It ain't luck when a man keeps at his duties, Mr Samson. But that ain't the 'alf of it. I 'ad time in there to work out that when they came to do the plate, they must a-held it the wrong way round. What they got was a reverse image, like in a mirror. Having only seen the plate o' course, I never noticed anything amiss, thinking it was all the right way round. But seeing the place where it was took makes a difference.'

'Do it? How might that be?'

'Why, Mr Samson!' said Verity with a faint chuffing noise, 'fancy a detective officer like you having to ask! You got a bit to learn about constabulary deduction, ain't yer? When I didn't know it hadn't been reversed, o' course there was nothing wrong with that plate. But if it was reversed, then only think of that funny fork-shaped scar Lord Henry had. Don't yer see? In that one picture alone, he was wearing it on the wrong leg!'

9

The damp walls at the rear of the patched and stained

houses enclosed the square grassy plot of the little burial-ground. Here and there the low mounds of paupers' graves were interspersed with carved stones almost lost in tall grass. Elaine hitched up her skirt as she cut across the ground towards Shoreditch High Street, reached by a narrow cobbled tunnel between the buildings on one side. It was almost midnight and soon there would be an easy trade as the gin palaces and the beer shops began to empty.

Already the foul moisture, which the cooler night drew from the grimy warmth of the stones, glistened upon paving and wall. Even the grass, taller than the girl's knees, was wet, so that she hitched her skirt up almost to her waist to keep it dry. A more distant gas-lamp cast a pale light on Elaine's sturdy young legs and thighs.

Half-way across the plot, she heard a sound behind her and saw the man's shape following. She had no doubt that he was one of those who gloated over the sight of accidentally-revealed female limbs. Even at fifteen years old, Elaine had a proper sense of values. She made money by her body and a man who derived enjoyment from it without paying was as much a thief as the man who stole from a stall or a shop-window. He began to draw level, his eyes turning to keep her in view as she held up her skirts. Elaine tossed her fair hair and shouted angrily,

'Seen everything you want?'

The man strode ahead of her into the cobbled tunnel, then, as she entered, he turned to her and the light fell on his face. Elaine dropped her skirt and shrieked with a terror she had never known before. The man who stood before her was unmistakably Charley Wag.

The girl turned to run, but her limbs seemed deadened by shock. Then the Wag was upon her. He held her by the shoulders and shook her till her teeth rattled.

'Bitch!' he said savagely, striking her across the mouth. 'That for a cheating slut! That for a police-office whore! And that for good measure!'

Elaine staggered under the blows, falling in terror against the slime of the tunnel wall and slithering to a squat, gibbering with undiluted horror. It was Charley Wag in every detail, she knew that, risen from the grave to take his vengeance. He had drawn a cord from his pocket and was holding it taut between his two fists. In her paralysis of fear, the girl made no move to defend herself as the noose lay slack round her throat. She saw the Wag's features contort with rage, his hands seizing the cord. And then, as she fought for breath, there was a distant sound of footsteps. The air came freely and she was alone, vomiting with fright on the cobbles. One or two passers-by looked at her and saw a drunken slut, bedraggled and sick. Elaine stared wildly about, pulled herself together and then, still weeping with fright, began to run. She had no idea in which direction she was going. Her only desire was to run and run as far from Shoreditch, Charley Wag and London as her legs would carry her.

10

Marching side by side, their stout boots measuring the cobbled carriageway in equal strides, Verity and Samson entered the spacious piazza before London Bridge Station as the summer dusk began to gather. The first lights were showing in the bow-fronted little shops under the station colonnade and as the cabs waited outside, drivers nodding on their boxes, hats and whips askew, the warm tawny glow of the carriage-lamps glimmered like the riding-lights of distant ships.

'I got no business to be 'ere!' Samson grumbled. 'I got a pension to think of and a poor little wife to keep.'

'Last I 'eard,' said Verity with scepticism, 'all you got was Fat Maudie with a voice like Billingsgate.'

Samson shrugged.

'Common-law wife,' he said defensively, 'and she don't that often raise her voice.'

Verity beckoned a porter.

''ave the goodness to fetch two half-a-crown

Lewes-and-back, my man, and look sharp about it.'

Making a mental note of the man's number, he watched him scurry away.

'Body-snatching!' said Samson with a shudder.

Verity glanced about him, as though to ensure he was not overheard.

'Look, Mr Samson. When I was able to save you from a deal of unpleasantness over 'is 'ighness, you was quick enough to say 'ow you wished to return the favour. But the minute I took you up on it, there's a different song being sung.'

'Body-snatching!' said Samson again. 'You got any idea, 'ave you, the sentences they pass for it? Not including dismissal from the force and loss of pension!'

Verity paused, took the tickets from the porter, tipped the man a penny and led the way to the Brighton train.

'Mr Samson,' he said quietly but firmly, 'there ain't going to be any snatching done. I only want to see that all is as it should be, just as any constabulary officer might. There ain't no call for you to be in the tomb-house. Why, you might even stand at the wall and not set foot on Lord William's land. But I do need a pair of eyes watching for me while I work.'

'What I'll be,' said Samson glumly, 'is a necessary after the fact.'

Verity's plump jowls quivered and his moustache fluffed up a little under the impulse of windy chortling. He opened the door of a second-class carriage. As the two men sat down in the empty wooden interior he said,

'Mr Samson, there's accessories enough without you. I thought all about poor Lord Henry's scar jumping from leg to leg. Now, he never destroyed himself deliberate, though someone wanted me to think so.'

'Why should they do that?' asked Samson without much interest.

Verity chortled again.

'Why, Mr Samson! Fancy you 'aving to ask that! Ain't it plain? They wanted self-destruction talked of a-cos they knew poor sick Mr Richard was right. Lord Henry was

murdered. Mr Richard puts it down to his brother Lord
William, which is as may be. And then I'm took off the case,
the investigation is closed and I'm told to put it from me
mind. Well, now, Mr Samson!'

There was the ringing of a handbell on the platform, the
shriek of a whistle, snort of steam, and then with the sound
of fifty iron doors banging in quick succession, the little
steam-train jerked and jolted out of London Bridge.

'You wouldn't 'appen to know who murdered Lord 'enry
nor 'ow?' asked Samson sceptically.

Verity looked crestfallen.

'Not just this minute, Mr Samson. But once let me find
how and I'll soon tell you who.'

'Only,' said Samson, 'we know as every scrap of evidence is
on the other side.'

'I'll need a little time, Mr Samson.'

The train clattered through Croydon and the whistle of
the little engine shrieked again at the opening of the
Merstham tunnel. It was Samson who broke the silence.

'Course,' he said, 'a cove that couldn't have been
murdered, but has been murdered all the same, it ain't no
worse than a man what's dead and buried being so
inconsiderate as to get out and walk about the streets saying
how d'ye do to all his old friends.'

'Whatcher mean?' asked Verity, scowling.

'Charley Wag,' said Samson, 'what you coopered good
and proper, head split open, buried in Kensal Green. And
then presently, word goes round on the streets that there he
is saying hello to that little whore Elaine, feeling her in
Shoreditch and half strangling the life out of her.'

'Mr Samson!' said Verity, 'you never been took in by what
that little slut says? She'd sell her own mother, only her
mother's probably sold herself too often already!'

'She didn't act like she was lying,' said Samson
thoughtfully. 'Run screaming for her life and never sight nor
sound of her in London since.'

Verity thought about this.

'They couldn't a-buried the wrong one?'

'Not unless you killed the wrong one,' said Samson.

'Then your Miss Elaine is a lying little bitch,' said Verity with unaccustomed ferocity.

'Course,' said Samson again, 'today being your rest day, you wouldn't have heard the best bit what came into the division.'

'What's that?'

'Ziegler and Meiklejohn was questioning some of them prime little bunters up and down Haymarket. Charley Wag used to collect from a few of them personally. Took his money and had a serving of greens off them at the same time.'

'Huh!' said Verity disparagingly.

Samson smiled, as though the best were yet to come.

'Thing is,' he said, 'the morning after you done in Charley Wag, it seems his corpse left the Horseferry Road mortuary, and went the rounds of his girls collecting the money.'

'Gammon!' said Verity with spirit. 'Some bloody sharper that heard he was dead, got himself up like Charley and went for the dibs.'

'Verity, my old son,' said Samson softly, 'he was Charley all right. That doxy Adeline, with the docked tail of hair and the big bum, he had his greens off her in broad daylight. Cor, you no idea 'ow she took on this morning when Meiklejohn told her she'd been rogered by a corpse!'

'They must a-known Charley had snuffed it,' said Verity, still unconvinced.

'In a day or two they did,' said Samson, 'but not the very next morning. And that ain't all. One bunter who never heard the news for weeks had her pants took off by him a fortnight after he was put in Kensal Green. I do 'ope she was worth digging his way out for, Mr Verity. Oh-ho-ho-ho!'

Verity's small dark eyes glowered at him.

'Well,' said Samson triumphantly, 'whatcher going to do now, old friend?'

With all the dignity at his command, Verity pulled himself upright.

'What I'm going to do, Mr Samson, is think. If there was only a little more thinking done by constabulary officers such as yourself, the division wouldn't get into this sort of pretty pickle quite as often as it do.'

And, in frowning silence, Verity thought all the way from Redhill until the train drew, hissing and panting, into the station platform at Lewes.

After an hour and a half of walking through the warm, moonless night, Verity and Samson saw in the faint opalescent glimmer of starlight the low dry-stone wall surrounding the Jervis estate at Bole Warren.

'Now, Mr Samson,' said Verity kindly, 'o' course, you might wait here, by the wall, and never set foot on the Jervis lands. Only, standing out here in the open, you can't but cause suspicion, if seen. You'd best hop over the wall with me and stand in the dark among the trees.'

'And what of gins and traps and such?' asked Samson uneasily.

'Come, now, Mr Samson,' said Verity easily, 'them poaching traps is illegal, and you know Lord William as a gentleman that respects the law. In any case, we shall follow paths.'

He swung one fat trouser-leg over the wall and pulled himself across. They were clear of the main gates but the path which ran under the over-arching trees was close to the wall at this point. Verity led the way, still not daring to draw back the shutter on his dark-lantern. Samson walked, unhappily, a dozen paces behind.

'I was to be left on the public road,' he said reproachfully as the dark trees engulfed them.

Verity walked more slowly, peering ahead of him, searching to identify the darker silhouette of the mausoleum against the arch of starlit sky which indicated the end of the avenue of trees. Presently he saw it clearly enough, already closer than he had imagined.

'Now, Mr Samson,' he said gently, 'you might stay out here on the path. Only, as with the road, you'll be more easily seen here than if you was inside with me. And you no idea how much I should be obliged for your assistance.'

'What sort of assistance?' asked Samson suspiciously.

'Why,' said Verity innocently, 'only in moving doors what might otherwise be heavy and rusty in such a place as this is.'

He climbed over the links of the iron chain and walked slowly down the steps to the solid-looking door of the mausoleum itself. The dark bronze panels suggested strength and impregnability. But Verity knew that whatever the weight of the door, the lock on such a place as this would be a mere toy. It was made for a large and, no doubt, impressive key but those were always the first to fall victim to a cracksman of average ability. He probed the lock with a thin steel pick and felt the places where the tumblers moved. It was better than he thought, there was no need to shine the lamp upon the place yet. He was no cracksman but even so it was a child's game to him to open the lock on the heavy door. He stood up and pulled the double doors open towards him, motioning Samson inside. Then he closed the doors after them and, standing in total blackness, slid back the shutter of the dark lantern at last.

The mausoleum was the size of a small room, though the prevailing impression for Verity was of the sickly scent of rotting flowers. Funeral bouquets lay lank and dead, white petals long since turned to rust and the green stems to a dry brown. The dampness of the place gave an edge to the cold stillness which almost made him gasp. Already the walls which had been cleaned for Lord Henry's interment were fluffy and dusty, the spiders' webs hanging like tattered rags in the corners. The stone ledges on either side were capable of accommodating several generations of the Jervis family but there were only, as yet, two coffins in the entire mausoleum. They lay on opposite sides of the tomb-house at the lowest level. One of them, its wood darkened by damp and rot, its silver fittings misted over by neglect, was that of old Lord Samuel Jervis. On the other side, in light clean cedarwood and with silver which still shone like a new mirror, was the second casket whose polished plate bore the simple legend, 'Lord Henry Frederick Jervis, obit 4 May 1860'.

'Right, then,' whispered Samson, his voice trembling a little with the cold. 'You seen what you wanted to see, now let's get back to the road. It's all in order here.'

''ave the goodness to hole the lamp for me, Mr Samson,' said Verity firmly.

'Don't talk so loud,' said Samson, 'we might be heard outside.'

Verity chortled again.

'Why, Mr Samson! You don't do much thinking, do you? Suppose we was heard. Imagine what a voice from the tomb would do to Jem Rumer or his poachers, in the dead o' night. Why, they'd show such a clean pair o' heels that you'd never see 'em within a mile of the place again. Now, 'old that lamp steady, do, Mr Samson.'

Verity rubbed his hands together for warmth. He said more seriously,

'I 'ope the young gentleman could forgive what I gotta do. Where 'e is, I suppose he knows it's no disrespect but only to clear his honour and let proper justice be done him.'

He took his hat off, partly as a gesture of respect and partly to enable him to work more easily. The coffin had been fastened with large-headed and ornamental silver screws. Very imposing, thought Verity, and like most imposing things a good deal less efficient than they looked. The workmen of Pontifex and Jones of Finsbury, 'Undertakers to ladies and gentlemen of fashion', had taken such care with the silver, trying not to mark it, that the screws could almost be undone by hand. With the aid of an iron clasp which he had borrowed from Stringfellow, Verity did the job effortlessly.

'Lamp up a bit, Mr Samson, if you please,' he said softly to his companion, who was standing with head fastidiously turned in the other direction. The yellow glimmer of oil-light now fell squarely on the coffin top as Verity took it and slid it gently aside, propping it against the ledge. He shared little of Samson's horror of the dead. As a boy in Cornwall he and his father had paid their last respects to the bodies of miners crushed in the roof-falls and small tragedies of the tin-mines. In Her Majesty's Volunteer Rifle Brigade before Sebastopol, he had seen death in its most gruesome forms. What had to be done now was a necessary task, neither more nor less. A man must not shrink from that.

Despite the dampness of the place, the air of the coffin had been dry enough to preserve Lord Henry's body quite

well during the few weeks since burial. The odours of death
were strongly overlaid by spice and cedar, almost as if the
corpse were embalmed. Preserving the outer form of the
dead was a speciality of Pontifex and Jones. The mortal
remains of Lord Henry had been dressed in a black silken
suit, a single bandage about the head holding the mouth
closed. No rings remained on the folded hands, neither the
plain gold nor the bloodstone, but Verity knew they would
have been removed before burial. From the capacious
pocket of his ancient frock-coat he took a small razor and
made a careful slit in the burial suit, laying back a triangle
of cloth from the thigh.

'Have the goodness to keep that lamp up, Mr Samson,' he
said gently. Then he shook his head, as though it were too
much for him. 'Here's a rum go, all right,' he murmured to
himself.

Shrugging off a respectful immobility, he stepped aside to
avoid being in his own light and looked askance at the
right-hand side of the corpse, peering with a frown at the
head. The bandage customarily used to hold the jaw of the
dead man closed had been extended to cover the right ear
and the place immediately behind it, where the bullet had
entered. Verity eased the cotton forward and peered at the
wound with a grimace which conveyed sympathy rather
than distaste.

'Well I never!' he said presently. 'Then I wasn't hired for a
fool's errand after all!'

He had seen the wound before, on Dr Jamieson's
stereotype, and its contours were identical. But steel
engravings showed little more than contours and there was
something else which counted now.

'You seen all you need?' Samson asked nervously.

'What I seen, Mr Samson, some people is going to wish I
never had.'

He manoeuvred the lid of the coffin back into place and
tightened the silver screws.

'And what might you have seen exactly, Mr Verity?'
Samson judged it safe to turn and face his colleague once
more.

'What I seen, Mr Samson, is foul and beastly murder done, as sure as if I'd been standing with Jem Rumer and his crew the day poor Lord Henry fell. In fact, I seen it clearer, a-cos they was all took in by the plan of the devil that did it!'

'You never knew that just by looking at his poor head,' Samson said dubiously.

'You stick close to me, Mr Samson, and I'll show you what I know. For a start, whoever tried to put Lord Henry into them nasty photographic plates has given his game away. That forked mark on his leg – they knew of it but never saw it. In the pictures, the fork was high up, like a hay-fork. On his poor body it's much lower, more the shape of a "T" on its side. As for the rings, they might easy fake them.'

'If it was Lord William who faked it,' said Samson, 'he might have used the true ones.'

Verity nodded. The coffin-lid was fastened down and the two men were ready to leave the mausoleum. He took his cracksman's probe and slid the shutter across the little window of the dark-lantern. Then, in the pale starlight of the portico, he closed the doors of the grave and eased the tumblers into their locking position once more.

'Now,' he said, 'there's murder can be proved and must be investigated. As for Mr Inspector-bloody-Croaker, and telling me to forget all I ever heard at Portman Square, I'll stitch him into such corner that not all the seamstresses in Spitalfields shall pick him free!'

'Mr Verity,' said Samson softly, 'you ain't a-going to tell Mr Croaker what we've just done? We'd be put away for three or four years!'

'What we did,' said Verity sternly, 'was only to show me how murder was done. I can prove it was done without showing how. You ain't likely to be put away, Mr Samson.'

Verity strode resolutely towards the gamekeeper's lodge by the main gates. For all his protests over losing his place through poachers, it hardly seemed that Jem Rumer spent much of the night patrolling his territory. The lodge was locked and curtained, with every sign of the occupant being snugly in bed.

Verity walked slowly round its side and then returned.

'Back door, Mr Samson, 'ave the goodness to see the back door ain't used.'

Samson disappeared on this errand, his spirits rising now that the macabre business of grave-opening had given way to recognizable routines of police search and seizure. Verity approached the front door of the little lodge, raised its small brass knocker and thundered on the resonant panelling.

'Jem Rumer! Open this door in the name of the law! There's officers all round the house! We mean you no harm, but you shall open in the name of 'er Majesty!'

There was a pause, almost as though Rumer might after all be stalking his prey far across the dripping woodland of the Jervis estate. Then a candle wick glimmered at a crack in the curtains and there were movements within. A pair of bolts slid back and the door opened a fraction on its stout chain. Verity's lantern showed the emaciated features of Rumer, absurdly highlighted, under a white night-cap.

'It's me, Jem Rumer, Sergeant Verity, Scotland Yard division. We don't mean you harm but there's questions must be asked, and asked now.'

'You'm come at a funny time,' said Rumer nervously, taking care not to open the door further.

'Funny or not,' said Verity, 'we're here and must be admitted.'

Rumer rubbed his bristly chin.

'It ain't exactly convenient.'

'Don't you "convenient" me, Jem Rumer, or there's six constables here that'll have your door open on the hinge side.'

'Light at the back!' shouted Samson belatedly.

The sound of a second voice convinced Rumer. He pushed the door to, rattled the chain clear and then opened the door wide. Verity entered the warm hall with its lingering smell of dogs and cooked game. Followed presently by Samson, he made his way into the little parlour. Rumer sat on a chair in nightshirt and cap.

'It ain't exactly convenient,' he said with a twist of the mouth.

'No,' said Verity, 'and I daresay what happened to poor Lord Henry wasn't exactly convenient to him neither.'

Rumer wagged a finger.

'I told you, Mr Verity. These ain't Mr Richard's lands, and what happens here is none of his affair.'

'Mr Rumer, I ain't here for Mr Richard. I'm here for Scotland Yard and I'm inquiring into the murder of Lord Henry Jervis. The man that did it shall have a noose about his throat as sure as I say it. Witnesses that tells the truth has nothing to fear. Them that don't is liable as accessories to murder and, in course, must swing alongside the party that did it.'

Rumer swallowed. Just then there was a disturbance. A small closet door opened and a girl appeared. She was a blonde of sixteen or seventeen, her long hair worn loose. The blouse she wore left her sturdy young figure naked from the waist down. She took one look at the two sergeants and ran precipitately towards Rumer's bedroom. Samson followed hastily.

'Well!' said Verity. 'Well, Jem Rumer! And what's Lord William to say to a keeper that gives a poacher a night's hunting on the understanding that the poacher's daughter keeps his bed warm? I am right, ain't I, Jem? That is the way the bill do add up?'

'You leave my Jan Parry out of this,' said Rumer hastily. 'You ain't no cause to make trouble. Ask what you want to know.'

'Just this,' said Verity gently. 'Might there be any sand about here?'

'Sand?' said Rumer. 'Sand! You come waking me at three o'clock, taking me from my bitch, just to ask if there's any sand in these parts?'

'Yes,' said Verity simply. 'Any sand on the estate or anything like it?'

Rumer thought. In the interval, Verity heard Samson's voice from the bedroom.

'Oh no, miss you leave them off. You won't be needing

them while I'm in here. I ain't having such a pretty pigeon escape!'

'There's sand in a pile behind the stables,' said Rumer, 'where they do mix the cement for repairing some of the walls. Do 'ee mean that?'

Verity sighed with satisfaction.

'I fancy, Mr Rumer, I do fancy that's the very thing I mean.'

In the bedroom, there was a creaking of springs under sudden weight, a resonant smack and then the murmur of voices alternating with giggling.

'I 'ave been given to understand,' said Verity confidentially, 'that the fatal gun was kept in Lord Henry's private room here, never unlocked during his lordship's absence?'

Rumer nodded.

'And even during his lordship's residence,' said Verity with the hope still in his voice, 'the room was never unlocked and unattended long enough for the gun to have been took away and tampered with.'

'It was all gone through by the constabulary weeks ago,' said Rumer. 'Not a chance the rifle could a-bin took from the room, and the man as wanted to tamper with it in there would hardly have had five minutes. And he'd have to be a gunsmith. And there was no sign it had ever been tampered with. What you got on that gun is precisely nothing, Mr Verity.'

Samson's voice came from the bedroom.

'You ain't never in town, I suppose, Miss Jan? You no idea how much gold a girl with legs like yours might make in a penny gaff. Why, I happen to know a cove as runs the swellest of the lot!'

'Mr Samson!' called Verity, 'smartly, if you please!'

Samson emerged slowly from the room with only a single, reluctant backward glance. Verity motioned him outside, giving Rumer time to put on a coat. Then the three men set off to the place where the sand was kept. It was to one side of the main part of the house, which they reached just as the first light appeared in the sky to the east of them.

'Now,' said Verity, 'might there be a sieve hereabouts, Mr Rumer?'

Rumer shuffled off, entered a wooden lean-to by the stables and returned with a sieve and a trowel in it. Verity squatted, humming a nondescript little tune, and scooped the first trowel of sand into the sieve. The sand-heap was three feet high and a couple of feet long. He sieved with great care pausing only once to speak to Rumer.

'Mr Rumer, if I was a gaming-man, which I ain't and never would be, I'd wager you a sovereign that one of them rooms there is where Lord Henry had his apartment.'

'End of the first floor there,' said Rumer, not seeing the usefulness of such discussions.

Verity nodded, shifted his position slightly and continued his task. Presently he paused, listened, felt and handed something to Samson.

''ave the goodness, Mr Samson, to wrap that in your kingsman.'

Then he resumed his sifting, pausing occasionally to ease his cramped legs and knees. The sun had flushed the sky with pale summer gold, its warmth even detectable in the piles of sand, when he stood up and handed two more small objects to Samson. He gave the sieve and the trowel to Rumer.

'We ain't got cause to bother you further, Mr Rumer. I expect you'll be ready to get back to your bed. O' course, I'd appreciate your not mentioning last night's events to a soul, and, in return, I should prevail upon myself not to acquaint Lord William with 'ow his lordship's gamekeeper guards the estate of a night.'

'Can't answer for '*er*, however,' said Rumer hopefully, remembering the two sovereigns of Verity's previous visit.

'Then you must, Mr Rumer,' said Verity firmly, 'and if you can't leave a little sense in her head, then you must leave a little leather on your Jan's backside. One way or another, she ain't to talk.'

An hour later, as they entered Lewes among the market-carts and farm-wagons, Samson said,

'They could be from any gun, them three bullets what you found in the sand.'

'So they could,' said Verity, 'only they ain't. Them three

173

and at least one more was fired from Lord Henry's window into the sand. A man could hardly miss with a rifle at that range, and I don't doubt it was done when there was one of them firework evenings or whatever they have after summer hunting parties, so no one heard anything rum.'

'What for?'

'You look at them bullets, Mr Samson. They got the marks of the rifle on them but otherwise they're hardly more spoilt than before they went into Lord Henry's gun. It's the sand. It gives 'em a nice soft landing. Anyone who knows about guns knows that's the way bullets is fired for examination. That's why I asked Jem Rumer where there might be sand. Now, Lord Henry's murderer couldn't a-had it more convenient than just outside the window. Why, he never even needed to take the gun from the room, but just slipped in there while it was unlocked and empty for five minutes.'

Samson walked in silence for a minute. Then he said reproachfully,

'You never needed to bring me 'ere and make me a body-snatcher just to find that. And it don't get you far. A man can play with a flashy gun when no one's looking and still not be a murderer. Course 'e'd fire it into sand! He'd hardly shoot the 'orses or the groom, would 'e?'

Verity sighed with great tolerance, but kept silence until they were safely out of earshot of the other passengers and seated in a second-class compartment of the early train for London Bridge.

'I gotta tell you, Mr Samson,' he said generously, 'that I had to see the body first. When I saw that picture of the wound at Dr Jamieson's there was no sign of the little dark ring that sometimes goes round the wound.'

'Smokeless powder,' said Samson.

'No, Mr Samson, it ain't nothing to do with powder. It's the force of the bullet that bruises the poor skin round the 'ole it makes. The Rhoosians taught us that at Inkerman. All my poor friends who was killed there, them as was shot real close, showed this black bruise, thin as a wedding ring, round the wound. We saw it when we came to fetch in their poor bodies and I do remember the regimental surgeon saying how it happened. A man as ain't got that bruise has been shot from five or ten yards off. Now, Lord Henry's body on the picture didn't show it. But I had to see with my own eyes to be sure. There ain't a bit of that bruising, and it don't wash off like powder. Accidental or deliberate, he was never shot from his own rifle, unless he had arms that could reach out twenty feet!'

'Cor!' said Samson slowly, regarding Verity with awe.

The pink smugness of Verity's face deepened a shade. He said,

'And then, o' course, I saw it. If you pack the wadding right, you can fire a rifle bullet from a shot-gun. Only you never would waste rifle bullets that way unless you had some special reason. Now, a rifle bullet that was just fired like that could never have come from Lord Henry's rifle a-cos it wouldn't have the marks on it. But a bullet fired into sand, to get the marks of the rifle, but undamaged otherwise, might be fired from a shot-gun and look as if it was fired from Lord Henry's own gun. There'd perhaps be another scratch or two, which we'd have put down to it hitting bone, but there'd be no getting away from the marks of his own rifle barrel on it. Clever, wasn't it?'

'Then 'ow the 'ell,' asked Samson, 'did they hear Lord Henry's rifle go off when the real shot was fired somewhere else?'

'For all we know it may have gone off when he fell,' said Verity, 'but it didn't matter. There was four and a half feet of solid stone wall throwing the other crack back the way it came. Even if his own rifle never went off as he fell dead, they actually heard the sound of the gun that killed him thrown back from the wall he stood on. Though there was so many guns going off that morning, that I doubt if they noticed very much.'

'Course,' said Samson, 'you don't actually know yet that these bullets in the sand were shot from his gun.'

'No,' said Verity, 'but you wait till Mr Somerville sees 'em. All in all, Mr Samson, I'm ready to tell Mr Croaker that Lord Henry was murdered. Only thing is, I got no idea who done it.'

11

There was an unaccustomed stillness in Inspector Croaker's room, the calm broken only by the busy wings of a large fly, beating against a glass pane and striving for the open sky above the Thames at Westminster. Croaker put the tips of his fingers together, as he sat at his desk, and appeared to be framing a judgment in his mind. Lord William Jervis sat at his ease in a dun-leather chair by the empty grate, his youthful and black-whiskered face presented in disdainful profile to the other occupants of the room, as though the proceedings were no concern of his. Paraded at attention, though without an escort on this occasion, Verity waited before Croaker's desk. Presently, Croaker spoke, as though courteously airing a proposition in a philosophic argument.

'Sergeant Verity, you were under no misapprehension that your hire by Mr Richard Jervis was ended?'

'No, sir.'

'Yet you went, with Sergeant Albert Samson, to Lord Jervis' estate at Bole Warren. You entered those lands and broke in upon the gamekeeper, Rumer, in the middle of the night?'

'Trespass!' said Lord William, turning, half-profile, with an impatient twist of his mouth.

'With respect, sir, it ain't trespass for me nor any man to visit Mr Rumer. And now I know there were murder done, as Mr Richard swore, I must talk a little more with Mr Richard. You saying I'm not to see 'im again can't alter that, sir. With respect, sir.'

In his self-assurance, Verity settled his head a little lower and a flushed bulge of superfluous flesh began to form round the rim of his stiff collar.

'Murder!' said Croaker in exasperation, bringing his fist down on the desk. 'Lord Henry's body was medically examined by Dr Jamieson and the evidence was heard by a coroner's jury, who brought in a verdict of accidental death. What murder?'

''ave the honour to ask, sir, if Dr Jamieson might ever have been a military man.'

Lord William supplied the answer.

'No Why?'

'Just it, sir,' said Verity firmly. ''im being a gentleman that practised among the better classes in Burlington Street, he probably never saw a man that was shot to death. If he'd been a month in the Rifle Brigade, he'd a-told how far a man was shot from, what with, and who by. And he'd a-learnt all that without the expense of going to a medical school, sir.'

Momentarily, Croaker seemed prepared to indulge Verity with the aim of bringing him down in a harder fall later on.

'So you set yourself up as a pathologist, do you, sergeant?'

'No, sir. But I got two eyes and I seen the picture took of Lord Henry's poor head. If he'd been shot from less than twenty feet, there'd a-bin a dark ring of bruising round the wound. And there ain't

'Photographs don't always show every detail, sergeant.'

'No, sir, but then there's the bullets in the sand, sir.'

Lord William swung round.

'You fool! There were a hundred times when Lord Henry might have fired his rifle into that sand, merely to test the action. Of course there were bullets from his rifle there!'

Verity stared impassively ahead of him.

'It ain't just that, sir. The last thing Mr Richard Jervis swore to me, sir, was that his brother, Lord Henry, was murdered, that he saw it done with his own eyes, and he named to me the party that he accused. With respect, sir. Now, sir. Mr Richard may be mistook. The camera may be mistook. The bullets may be in the sand by mistake. I can believe one mistake, even two. But when it gets to three sir, then I say there's evidence enough for me to be allowed to see Mr Richard again and ask him what he meant.'

'No!' Lord William's voice rang across the room, as it might have done across the quarter-deck, and he sprang to his feet. 'By God, you shall not!'

'Don't see why, sir. With respect, sir.'

'Damn your thick skull!' shouted Lord William. 'Have I not told you before? My poor brother is more hurt in his mind than ever he was in his body! Richard Jervis, sir, is insane. Even you must have seen how brooding and impulsive and ill-balanced his conduct was!'

'Yessir, but a man can be all those things and still not be lunatic.'

'Fiddle-faddle!' said Lord William. 'Richard Jervis has the rage of a madman against the world. He might kill me, I suppose, for putting Jack Ransome over him.'

'Over him, sir?'

'Ain't it plain?' said Lord William more softly. 'Jack Ransome is his keeper. The little money that goes from me to Richard Jervis goes through Jack Ransome. Captain Jack don't get trusted with much but he's a power of attorney to Richard Jervis till the crack of doom.'

'I was 'ired to humour Mr Richard?' asked Verity, his plump face creased with incredulity.

'Something of that,' said Lord William gruffly. 'By God, had I been at Portman Square and not with the fleet, it should have been stopped.' He returned to his chair and sat, tapping his boot irritably with his cane.

'I shall 'ave to see Mr Richard just the same, sir,' said Verity gently, 'and ask the poor gentleman to explain his words to me.'

'He's in a strait-waistcoat,' said Lord William gruffly, 'committed to an insane asylum by Dr Jamieson and another physician. My family has suffered quite enough for Richard Jervis. Let the matter end there.'

'Don't alter facts, sir. With respect, sir.'

'Facts?' said Croaker, his face going a deeper yellow as he swallowed. 'Do I understand, sergeant, that in the name of your so-called facts you propose to interrogate a patient in an asylum?'

'Very sorry I am it should be so, sir. But I gotta be sure there ain't anything to what he says. Poor Mr Richard may not be a well gentleman. But he's still got his eyes and he swore that with them he saw murder done. Now, sir, murder was done all right. I gotta know what he saw. His reason may be touched but his eyes is clear.'

'Sergeant Verity,' said Croaker in a dry matter-of-fact tone which he reserved for giving orders, 'you are forbidden from making or attempting to make any contact with Mr Richard Jervis. If I hear that you have so much as tried to find where he has been committed, your dismissal from this force will follow the next day. Do I make myself clear?'

'Yessir. One thing to say, sir.'

'Yes, sergeant?'

'I was 'oping, sir, that me seeing poor Mr Richard might save Lord William and the family a deal of unpleasantness. Course, I can be forbidden from seeing him. But I can't be forbid from doing a citizen's duty, which is to go to the Westminster coroner and tell him what I know. There'd have to be a new inquest with poor Lord Henry disinterred. And then, of course, the newspapers must be full of it, morning and evening. You no idea, sir, how they like exhumations, though I never saw why.'

'I formally forbid you to reveal any of this to the coroner or anyone else!' said Croaker, his voice shrill and his eyes gleaming. 'Your oath of loyalty forbids it!'

'Couldn't say, sir. 'owever, I ain't the only one. There's Mr Rumer and a few others that knows it all. They ain't sworn oaths and might just as soon go to the coroner. The truth's out, sir, and had best be told.'

'I always thought,' said Croaker softly, 'that you would prove a scoundrel in the end!'

'Damned blackguard!' Lord William rose with cane in hand.

'Get out!' shrieked Croaker hastily. 'Get out of my sight!'

'Yessir!' Verity stamped about and marched out with a rolling, policeman's gait, half expecting to feel Lord William's cane on his shoulders as he withdrew.

He waited for reprisals, but when the noon watch paraded there had still been no sign of any. Inspector Swift beckoned him at the end of the parade.

'Superintendent Gowry's office for you, my lad. At once and smartly!'

Superintendent Gowry's room was on a higher level than that of the inspectors of 'A' Division in Whitehall Place, far above the smells of horse-dung and soot which pervaded the lower floors of the house so pungently. Gowry himself was an ex-cavalry captain and so a cut above Croaker, the former artillery lieutenant, in his origins. He was aged and whitened beyond his years but his manner was milder than Croaker's and he bore no particular ill-will towards Verity. As the sergeant entered, he looked up, brushed his white moustaches and waved away Inspector Swift. Verity came to attention.

'Sergeant Verity,' said Gowry, studying a sheet of paper.

'Yessir!'

Gowry looked up.

'You have been recommended to me, sergeant, for a particularly delicate undertaking which will require tact and judgment. I hope I may trust you to uphold the reputation of the division?'

''ope so, sir, I'm sure.'

'Inspector Croaker, who is an example to us all in the matter of methodical detection, has unearthed certain details concerning the death of the late Lord Henry Jervis. Frankly, sergeant, they point to the possibility of foul play.'

'Well I never, sir!'

'Unfortunately,' Gowry resumed, 'there appears to be no material witness. One such witness to the deed would make the case conclusive.'

'Sometimes 'appens like that, sir.'

'Quite, sergeant. However, Mr Croaker has devised a scheme of great ingenuity.'

'Yessir?'

Gowry brushed his moustaches again and allowed himself a smile of boyish pleasure.

'Yes, sergeant. Mr Richard Jervis, now sadly at Friern House Sanatorium, is the one witness whom a murderer would not expect the police to interview. The poor gentleman may not be a competent witness in court but his eyes may confirm what Mr Croaker's other evidence suggests.'

'Indeed, sir,' said Verity impassively.

'Mr Croaker suggests that you be sent to interview Mr Richard Jervis, accompanied by Sergeant Samson and backed up by a warrant authorizing search of the premises at Friern House, in case you should be denied access to the gentleman. Your warrant will be signed by two justices and counter-signed by two commissioners in lunacy.'

Superintendent Gowry sat back with the smile of a man who has revealed his master-stroke.

'Yessir,' said Verity flatly.

Gowry shook his head.

'Ah, sergeant, there are too few officers who acquire the skill and energy of Mr Croaker, let them rise never so high in rank. Think yourself fortunate to serve directly under the command of such a man, sergeant, for no other form of instruction can equal it.'

'That's a fact, sir.'

'We can all learn so much, sergeant, from men of imagination.'

'Yessir. Even in me own way, sir, I'm learning from Mr Croaker all the time.'

Where the twopenny bus ended and the horses were taken from the shafts and watered at the trough, Verity and Samson began their walk. On the outskirts of the city, half-built streets of houses spread on either side across pleasant fields. Gas-lights had been placed at long intervals and the gravel of the unmade road crunched under the boots of the two sergeants as they started on the half-mile to the more spacious villas beyond Shepherds Bush, each set in its own grounds.

When they reached Friern House, the building was visible from the road, though it was well back from the handsome iron gates. In appearance, it was a large square mansion, built of red brick with stone facings and corners. A metal plate by the bell-pull was embossed with the letters 'Ring and enter'. Samson pulled the iron handle and pushed open the side gate intended for visitors on foot. As the two men walked up the driveway, Verity noticed that a porter in some kind of livery had appeared on the steps promptly as soon as the bell was rung. Scanning the façade of the house, he also saw that the row of garret windows had been almost entirely hidden behind a newly-erected stone balustrade.

'Funny,' said Samson, 'I'd a-thought they'd have more bars and things to stop the softies getting out and running wild all over the neighbourhood.'

Verity grunted and led the way up the steps.

'Sergeant Samson and Sergeant Verity to see Mr Richard Jervis,' he announced to the porter. 'We're expected.'

The wiry, grey-haired little man bowed them into a spacious hall, lined with antlers and polished armour, as though it had really been the suburban villa of a successful lawyer or bill-broker. They passed up the left-hand flight of the fine sweep of a double staircase, crossed a landing with folding doors at one end of it and entered a finely furnished drawing-room which was partially darkened by Venetian blinds. The porter turned to Verity.

'If you'll have the goodness to be seated, gentlemen, I'll see Sister Liddell acquainted with your being here.'

When they were alone together, Samson spoke again.

'Funny. I never thought the place 'd seem so empty and quiet. There ain't sight nor sound of a poor lunatic anywhere.'

Presently the drawing-room door opened and a heavily-built woman of thirty or so came in. She was dressed in grey with white cuffs and collar, adorned with an insignia designed to suggest a nursing order.

'You are friends of Mr Jervis, I understand?' she said at once.

'We're police officers, ma'am,' said Verity sternly, 'and we come 'ere to ask certain questions of Mr Richard Jervis, relating to the death of the late Lord Henry.'

'That will be quite impossible,' said the woman.

Verity drew a sheet of paper from his pocket.

''ave the goodness to summon the proprietor of this place,' he said firmly.

'The proprietor,' said Sister Liddell, 'does not live here. He owns several houses of this kind, miles apart. He cannot live at all of them and therefore chooses not to live at any.'

'Then I must see the doctor that has charge,' said Verity irritably.

'The doctor called this morning,' said Sister Liddell. 'He comes three times a week from Acton and will not be here again for two days.'

'Then who has charge?'

'The head keeper, Mr Repington. But he is away just at present and I must deputize for him.'

'Ah,' said Verity, 'then you must likewise conduct me to Mr Richard Jervis and see to it that my questions are put to him.'

The woman planted her feet slightly apart, almost as if to bar the way.

'Quite impossible.'

'Then I gotta order here, signed by two justices and commissioners in lunacy, what makes it possible.'

Sister Liddell shook her head.

'You may come with an order signed by the Lord Chancellor himself, and it shall do no good. Mr Jervis will never understand a word put to him, poor gentleman.'

Verity glowered at her.

'You see 'ere,' he said softly. 'I spoke with Mr Richard Jervis not a fortnight since. Sick he may 'ave been, but he was rational enough to understand question and answer. And if he ain't so now, then someone shall account for it!'

Sister Liddell shrugged and turned away. She walked towards a large wall-mirror at one side of the room and spread her hand against it. To Verity's surprise the mirror swung back, revealing itself as a glass-covered door which led to the 'secure rooms' of the private asylum. He and Samson followed her.

By contrast with the comfortably-furnished drawing-room, the long plain apartment behind the mirror was drab and cold, its walls unpapered and hung with cobwebs. Verity observed that the attendant had a slender silver chain about her neck, from which hung an ivory whistle.

'The patients are all sent here for their own good by those to whom they are dear,' she said, with an air of having recited the same apology many times before. 'They come not as prisoners but as invalids to be cured and restored to the society of their anxious and affectionate friends.'

Verity said nothing. Now that they had passed the sound-proof door, there was a general, though distant, hubbub of voices, talking, sighing, groaning, sharply interrupted by the occasional cries or shrill laughter of the speakers. Though the windows were partly bricked up, there was space enough for him to see that the rooms allotted to the inmates overlooked a cobbled inner courtyard, from which cries and the sound of a struggle reached him. A dirty and bedraggled girl of indeterminate age was running barefoot round the yard, dressed only in a cotton shift. Two men and several women in uniforms similar to Sister Liddell were moving to pen her into a corner. Suddenly the girl looked up and shrieked.

'All you sane men and women who are imprisoned here! Come, fight for your lives! Rescue! Rescue!'

Ignoring Sister Liddell, Verity watched the sequel as open windows round the yard filled with pale faces, some grinning, some distorted by excitement, others exulting in the challenge, and all convinced of their own sanity. The uproar of voices was beyond belief. But the girl had given her pursuers a final advantage by pausing. They seized and carried her, struggling convulsively, to a large tank of cold water, some ten feet square and set partly into the ground. Four of them held her over it, horizontally and face down, while the others stood positioned to ensure that each time she was lowered her head and body were forced under for the full period of the immersion. Verity watched in horror as the victim was pressed right under and held there while the seconds ticked away. There was no way in which he could reach the yard and no means of intervening. When she was raised, choking and howling for breath, the attendants waited for the first scream of protest as a sign of recovery and then forced her under the cold water again. The process was repeated five times before the girl, struggling weakly and with her wet shift clinging to her, was led away.

Sister Liddell met Verity's indignation in her most philosophic manner.

'That's what they call "tanking",' she remarked. 'There's not a mad-house in the country where they don't tank from time to time. It keeps the poor wretches washed clean and helps to shock them out of their silliness a bit. Quiet as lambs they are after that.'

'She could a-bin drowned!' said Verity furiously.

'Not her,' said the woman. 'The art of it is to stop short of drowning by a bit.'

She opened a door.

'This is the day-room for the first-class patients,' she said.

Verity knew that asylums divided their patients into classes, like railway travellers, and treated them accordingly. Yet he looked with dismay at the first-class inmates, their trousers and petticoats absurdly short, their woollen gloves worn in holes, collars fitted high enough to cut their ears, their coats too short in the waist and too long in the sleeves. These grotesque costumes made them look even madder than they were and he wondered cynically what had become of the more expensive and elegant clothes in which many of them must have arrived. Two keepers, one a short stout man with red whiskers, the other tall and grey-haired, strolled up and down the length of the day-room, keeping order. Many of the patients had had their heads shaved which made it impossible to tell the difference between the sex of some of them except by the clothes they wore. To one side of Verity, a young man with manacles on his wrists was sitting on a plain bench being fed gruel on a wooden spoon by a lunatic with the muscular frame of a bargee. From where it came, Verity could not see, but a twisted scrap of paper landed at his feet. Ignoring Sister Liddell's outstretched hand, he unravelled it and read, 'Drink nothing but water at dinner'.

Presently, the woman left Verity and Samson under the gaze of the two keepers and went, as she said, to see if Richard Jervis was awake. While they were standing there, the young man with manacles on his wrists rose and shuffled towards Verity. He stood before him and said in a calm, level voice,

'Sir, I implore your assistance. I am the victim of a

conspiracy. They pretend I am mad. They are keeping me by force in a mad-house, a living tomb.'

''e don't sound mad,' said Samson softly to Verity.

The red-whiskered keeper approached.

'Take no notice, gentlemen,' he said, 'there's orders of committal and medical certificates enough and to spare for every patient in this house.'

'Don't be deceived, sir,' said the young man to Verity, almost on the verge of tears. 'I am put here that my uncle and cousins may enjoy my inheritance. The papers were signed by men who were bribed to sign them. For God's sake, put me to the test. Test my memory, my judgment, by any question you choose.'

'There now,' said the keeper, 'poor young gentleman. Don't agitate yourself so. It's all for the best, all for your own good.' He looked at Verity and Samson, shook his head, and added, 'Very painful, very painful.'

The young man shuffled off, twisting his wrists in the manacles, seeming uncertain how to proceed. Before he could renew his appeal, the two sergeants were beckoned by Sister Liddell. As the young man saw them leave, he shouted after them with sudden urgency,

'Help! Murder! If you are Englishmen, if you are Christians, for God's sake help me!'

Verity turned to the woman.

'Who might that poor lunatic be, ma'am?'

'Wilson Rust,' she said. 'Mad as a March hare.'

They followed her to a row of small inner rooms, which reminded Verity of his visit to question Ned Roper in the refractory cells at Newgate. Each door at Friern House had a small grill, through which the room with its truckle-bed could be observed. However, the first room was unoccupied, its bed piled with chains, iron belts, wrist-locks, muffles and screw-locked hobbles.

'You don't need to notice such contrivances as them, gentlemen,' Sister Liddell whispered self-consciously. 'That's only what was left by the last proprietor. None of it used since. Why, I dare say it's all rusted now so that it couldn't be used anyway!'

Verity said nothing. It was the next cell which was prepared for their visit. The gas was lit, glaring on whitewashed brick. Two cockroaches had been prudently squashed by the keeper's boot, close by the bed where they had been exploring the warm, helpless body of the occupant.

'Now,' said Sister Liddell, 'you shan't touch nor distress him. But if you think Mr Richard Jervis might be got to answer, put what questions you like.'

She withdrew beyond the door and Verity peered at the figure on the bed. His legs were hobbled and strapped to the bed's foot. His hands were laced into a leather muffler across his chest. The fact that he wore no strait-waistcoat was not a tribute to the tenderness of Friern House but the consequence of several patients having strangled themselves with the device after their keepers had left them for the night. Verity looked at the face and head, shaved of beard and hair, which seemed featureless and nondescript.

'Here!' said Samson.

''ave the goodness to leave this to me, Mr Samson. Mr Richard Jervis! Mr Jervis, sir! Can you hear me? Can you understand me?'

There was a moment's silence. Then the figure on the bed emitted an infantile burble, followed by a toneless laugh. Verity took a step closer. There was a menacing but frustrated roar, followed by another deranged laugh as the sergeant hastily drew back.

'It ain't. . . .'

'Not a word, Mr Samson!'

Then Verity called Sister Liddell.

'I fear, ma'am, we must own you in the right. Poor Mr Richard is so far gone that he'll never understand what's said to 'im, let alone make an answer.'

'So long as it puts the matter to rest,' she said with a smile that was almost too prompt.

'Well, ma'am, it don't go so far as that. I got one more instruction, which is to speak with Mr Wilson Rust, a first-class patient.'

She looked surprised and displeased.

'Why?'

'A-cos ma'am, I got a signed warrant here that empowers me to examine what persons and papers I choose. A keeper that stands between me and Mr Rust now is going to have a sharp taste of them manacles and leg-irons what the last proprietor left.'

It was said in the tone of a jest, but Sister Liddell gathered her skirts about her and swept back to the day-room.

'Stand back the far end of the room,' said Verity to the keepers and the woman when Wilson Rust stood, shaven-headed, before the two sergeants. Then he turned to the young man. 'Very well, sir. You wanted questions to put you to the test and questions you shall have. Not a few days since, one Richard Jervis, a first-class prisoner, was brought here under the escort of Captain John Ransome. It's all entered in the papers and regular, so you needn't fear talking of it. Might you have seen them?'

'Sir, there was not a man in Friern House day-room who did not. They watch every new arrival as he crosses the yard.'

'And Captain Ransome was with him?'

'Yes. He was spoken to by the doctor here as "Ransome".'

'Mr Richard was under restraint?'

'His wrists locked, but not leg-irons.'

'He walked?'

'Limped,' said Rust thoughtfully.

'But he had no sticks? Wasn't held at all?'

'Guarded round about but not held. They wouldn't trust him with sticks. Quite a tall fellow with power in his arms.'

Verity breathed out hard and said,

''ow might Captain Ransome look?'

'A quiet young man. No taller than you. Hair the colour of straw.'

'Right,' said Verity, 'if you told the truth I'll return the favour by letting it be known outside where the world may 'ear it.'

'Wait!' said the young man, and Verity nerved himself against another pathetic plea. 'You must hurry. Richard Jervis is raving and can't speak for himself. The keepers swear he's to be made a Chancery lunatic.'

'What's that?' Samson interjected.

The young man smiled.

'When a family wants to rid itself of a man for ever, it has his lunacy declared by the Court of Chancery. A Chancery lunatic is never cured and never freed, the law does not allow it. His wealth is consumed by other men and even if they chose to free him, he could not be found.'

'Whatcher mean?'

'Why, sir, Chancery lunatics are a good spec to be let and sub-let. When a sane man is signed into an asylum, the vultures who mean to feed upon his estates will pay the keeper £200 a year to have him. But the keeper lets him out to another and pays £150 a year for his board, pocketing the £50 and doing nothing to earn it. The second keeper puts him elsewhere for £100 a year and so on, until he ends packed in a ward with a hundred others, crawling with lice and vermin, for £40 or £50 a year. When he dies his very name is unknown, and however sane he began he ends raving mad.'

Verity seemed sceptical but the young man looked calmly at him.

'If you think me soft in the brain, sir, only ask if it is not so. Ask them outside, in the hospitals and courts. A week from now Mr Jervis may be a Chancery lunatic. A week after that he will be gone, God knows where, and not you nor all your officers will ever find him.'

They took their leave of the young man. Verity approached Sister Liddell again.

'I must see the book,' he said firmly, 'where Mr Jervis was entered.'

She led them to a small room outside the apartments of the patients and produced it. There were Richard Jervis' details, and the signature of John Ransome, as his escort, and Sister Liddell, as the person receiving him.

'Ma'am,' said Verity, ''ow might Mr Jervis have come here?'

'How?' she said uncertainly. 'By cab to the very door.'

'And just Captain Ransome with him?'

'Yes,' she said, 'but he had a muffler on his wrists and you should have seen how easily he followed Captain Ransome in.'

'Followed?'

'Why, yes. Just a step or two away and with our eyes close on him.'

'Much obliged, ma'am,' said Verity. 'And this was Captain Ransome late 73rd Foot, was it?'

'He might be any regiment that I know of,' she said.

'Fair or dark?'

'Fair more than dark,' she said.

'*Much* obliged, ma'am,' said Verity, and led the way back to the wide hall with its antlers and armour. The porter stood on the steps watching them, until they were in the roadway, beyond the main gates.

''ere!' said Samson, 'Jack Ransome ain't got fair hair!'

'No,' said Verity, 'and it's a few years since Mr Richard could walk without help and without a pair of sticks. That poor lunatic that was tied to that bed ain't Mr Richard, and the cove that brought him here was never Jack Ransome. Dr Jamieson sees off poor Mr Richard under guard of Captain Jack from Portman Square. But another man arrives here with a poor lunatic that's so deranged he'd never be able to say he wasn't Mr Richard. After they shave a man's head and face like that, it ain't so easy to tell his appearance anyhow.'

'Don't see the use of it,' Samson said with some resentment.

'It's a prime dodge, Mr Samson. And if we hadn't come here for quite different purposes today, it'd have worked. Mr Richard and Captain Jack is on the loose without anyone knowing. P'raps one may have coopered the other. But is it Mr Richard or Jack Ransome that's the villain of it all? I don't see it, Mr Samson, but there's a caper here that needs to be stopped fast!'

'Stopped!' said Samson derisively. 'You don't even know which to look for!'

'Mr Samson! Richard Jervis ain't got legs of his own. He must have a man to lean on. There ain't no question about it. Find Captain Jack and we'll find Mr Richard.'

'The old three-thimbles-and-a-pea caper,' said Samson. 'He'll be working it round every fair in the kingdom. Try that.'

12

Verity and Samson entered Brighton for the races. It was close enough to London, closer still to Bole Warren. If Jack Ransome had gone back to the three-thimbles-and-a-pea dodge, it seemed to Verity just the place he might choose to drive his trade. Making for the race hill, they joined a stream of people in the warm July morning, some walking, others riding in the close-packed traffic of cabs, donkey-carts, gigs, 'sociables', and the occasional phaeton or pilentum with its dashing lines and sparkling green or yellow paint. The balconies of every public house were crowded with gaily-dressed men and women eating and drinking, broad red faces looking down upon the road from every window. Shouts and gusts of smoke were emitted at every tap-room door, outside which were the stalls fashioned from blankets and poles, where gilt gingerbread was sold.

The brightness of the sea seemed to dance and sparkle on the freshly-daubed buildings of the town itself, among the tumult and confusion. The church bells were pealing and flags streamed from every roof and window. Waiters hurried to and fro across the courtyards of hotels, hooves clattered on the cobbles and the carriage-steps came rattling down as another guest debouched at the York or the Albion. The heavy smells of mid-day dinner and the unmelodious competition of two Irish fiddlers in adjoining public bars characterized the time of day. Verity paused and brushed down his coat indignantly as a four-in-hand dashed teeteringly round the verge of the other traffic, eclipsing the scene in a gritty fog and leaving the stragglers stunned and blinded.

At the approaches to the course, the two sergeants watched carefully as they passed each cheapjack and trickster. There was 'Jack-in-the-Box, three shies the penny', and presently the first of those who invited his dupes to guess under which of three thimbles, on the upturned barrel before him, the pea was to be found. They had *seen* which one it went under but, as Verity might have told them, it was now safely embedded under the sharp's long yellow thumb-nail. The trickster continued his chant with doleful enthusiasm.

''ere's the sort of game to make you laugh seven years arter you're dead, and turn every 'air on your head grey with delight. Three little thimbles and one little pea – with a one, two, three, and a three, two, one. Catch him who can. Keep your eyes open, and never say die! Never mind the change and the expense. All fair and above board. Them as don't play can't win, and luck attends the real sportsman! Wager any sum from a half-crown to a sov that no gentleman names the thimble as covers the pea.'

The sharp's stooge in the crowd swore it had gone under the middle thimble and regretted that he had left his own purse at home. Hesitantly, one of the dupes placed his half-crown on the tub. Verity knew the outcome before he even heard the trickster's voice.

'All the fortune of war, sir! This time I win, next time you win. Never mind the loss of two bob and a bender! Now then, ladies and gentlemen, here's the sort of game to make you laugh seven years arter you're dead. . . .'

The rigmarole began again, as Verity spoke softly to Samson.

'It don't mean Captain Jack ain't here too, Mr Samson. There's a pitch big enough for both of 'em on such a course as this!'

As they moved closer, the sharp looked up. Without a word he scooped up the thimbles, thrust them in his pocket and began to stroll off, a figure of top-booted innocence who was a mere spectator at the day's sport. Samson caught him by the shoulder and shepherded him along as though they were old acquaintances. The corner of a wooden barn hid them from view while Verity, as a matter of instinct in Samson's presence, kept watch. He heard a deep groan, which seemed of sorrow rather than of pain. After a few moments longer, Samson reappeared alone. He shook his head.

'Captain Jack ain't working his pitch here. Not that this sportsman knows of.' Samson breathed affectionately on the knuckles of his right hand.

'You can't be sure,' said Verity, 'not the way you go about it.'

Samson grunted.

'Much you know about that, my son! Show 'im reason once, then ask the question. Say you don't believe him, and apply the second argument, no matter what his answer. Let him speak a second time, and still don't believe him. The third reason has to have a lot of force behind it but if you still hear the same song being sung you must act half-believing. Only, afore leaving him, you must promise that if he's sold you gammon, you'll come back and qualify him to run in the gelding stakes.'

'Mr Samson,' said Verity nervously, 'you had no right to give him a seeing-to without provocation!'

'I'm the one as knows when I'm provoked,' said Samson firmly, 'and you no idea 'ow that thimble dodge do rile me.'

As they walked on, Verity glanced back uneasily over his shoulder. He was relieved to see that the sharp was on his feet, moving away from the barn, though he paused to wipe his mouth on the back of his wrist and when he moved on it was in a hopping run with hands covering his groin in a parody of classical decorum.

When they reached the course, the racing seemed the least important of the afternoon's activities. The brightly streamered tents and booths faced the long line of carriages on the turf. Men in silken vests and plumed hats appeared as mountebanks or jugglers. Girls in showy gypsy handkerchiefs for their hoods solicited as fortune-tellers. There were dancing dogs and men on stilts, ventriloquists and conjurers attended by pale women who held the sixpences and counted them repeatedly. An organ grinder and a brass band on either side were interrupted by the trumpeter of the Punch and Judy show, the booth carried on the back of the proprietor. Far off, a bell rang to clear the course, which had been roped off from the rest of the summer fair. Beyond the fluttering streamers and the white

193

tops of the booths rose distant shouts, the patter of drums at the start, and then the faint thunder of hooves.

'There!' shouted Verity suddenly in Samson's ear, pointing at a roll of canvas printed with large black letters.

ROLEY'S TOURNAMENT
KNIGHTS IN MORTAL COMBAT!!!
THE GENUINE AND ONLY TOURNAMENT
IN THE WORLD! ! !

Now Exhibiting Within

ROLEY'S is the Delight
of the NOBILITY & GENTRY!

The ROYAL FAMILY are
the Patrons of ROLEY's! ! !

At the beginning of the races the canvas booths had assumed an air of inactivity. There was no sign of Roley or his actors at that moment, only groups of thin and ragged children who ran or crawled, according to age, among the grime and dust of the donkey-carts and wagons. Verity pushed aside the flap of the canvas booth and found that even the stool where the money-taker collected the sixpences was deserted. Beyond that was another opening which led into a roped-off 'gallery' from which the spectators watched the antics of the riders in front of them. The grass area enclosed as the tournament-ground was no more than thirty feet across and it occurred to Verity that Mr Roley must be possessed of some very lethargic ponies if their energies could be confined in so small a space.

To one side there was a wagon quite concealed by the surrounding canvas walls. Upon it were hung overalls in woollen mesh, designed to simulate chain-mail. Verity motioned Samson forward and then prepared to cut off the escape of any occupant of the wagon who might elude Samson's grasp. He watched his companion move silently forward on the soft turf, to the rear of the covered wagon, and then heard him clamber rapidly on to the tail of it. There was the sound of a scuffle, a noise of wrestling, the click of metal cuffs, and then Samson's laughter.

'Why, Miss Elaine! After all that running, you had no more sense than to come back to your old trade, where you'd be sure to be looked for first. I half think you must have had a yearning to be caught and took back for Mrs Rouncewell's attention!'

'You bastards!' she snarled, 'I done nothing wrong!'

'Depends, I s'pose, what you think is wrong,' said Samson, as though giving the matter academic consideration. 'Blackmail notes and extorting money from gentlemen in cabs by menaces ain't exactly what they gives prizes for in dame schools, 'owever.'

'Bring her out here, Mr Samson, if you please,' said Verity firmly.

As he had expected, she was dressed for her part as a page in the tournament, every item of the costume identical to that in the glass-plate photograph of her which he had found in Lord Henry's bureau. Tossing her pale gold hair into place on her shoulders, she regarded him with thin-lipped and snub-nosed defiance. He recognized from the plate the white blouse which she wore as doublet and the skin-tight, greyish-blue trousers drawn into a narrow waist by the tight belt, still giving her rather large haunches the appearance of an almost complete circle from the rear.

'Now, miss,' said Verity, 'I can play this game two ways, and you shall decide which. I ain't much interested in you, only what you know about others. Answer sensible and I'll speak for you, p'raps even let you go your own way with Mr Roley. But cross me, Miss Elaine, and I'll see you straight back to Mrs Rouncewell with my compliments. And I'll make sure as I stand here that when she's finished welcoming you, you won't be able to bear a breath on you for the next week. That's the size of it, miss.'

She pulled at her lip with her teeth and then asked sullenly,

'What's the questions about?'

'That's better!' said Verity in his most encouraging manner. 'First off, about Charley Wag.' He saw the flicker in her dark, narrow eyes. At fifteen years old she might seem hard as brass to threats and even beatings, but the fear of the Wag was going to live with her for many years yet.

'Now,' Verity resumed, 'you wrote that letter for Charley, to blackmail Lord Henry, some time before his lordship died. When might it have been?'

'Dunno, exactly. Back just before the summer begun.'

'And just why might he want *you* to write it?'

'A-cos of the ring he heard I'd got. Another girl told 'im.'

'What ring?'

As though she had abandoned her animosity against them, Elaine's belligerent manner softened and she slipped into a rambling narrative.

'I had it when I was younger. Mother was going fine with a soldier and we was to sail with him, hoping for India or 'Straliar in the end. I don't remember exactly what happened, only that the boat we was on was wrecked and I was carried and put in a little boat with a lot of others. It was dark and in the middle of the sea. And then there was a fight and one of them in the boat was put in the sea for being a man. Then I don't remember more 'n half of it. We was days and nights in the boat, and seemed to sleep longer and longer. And I'd wake a bit and see no one else stirring. It was mother give me the ring, last of all. She said it'd come from the finger of the man that was put in the water. She made me take it and said I was to see what I could make on it if ever I found a story that could be told against the wretch. Course, I never really saw him nor had any idea who he might be. And it could a-bin any ring. There was writing on the inside, but not such as I could read. Foreign. Then we slept and when I woke I was on another boat. They said mother and the rest was on different ships, only of course I knew later they was dead. They didn't tell me at first, for fear of making me lose heart to recover.'

'And Charley Wag?' asked Verity.

Elaine pulled a face.

'I never did use the ring. 'aving been stolen from a man while they killed him, it wasn't worth the candle to sell it and be took for helping the murder. And there was no way to tell who he might be, no way I could find, so I 'adn't even the means to tell the tale to his family and see what might be made by that either. Only I told another girl in the spring and showed her what was engraved on the inside, which she wrote down. A few weeks later, though I never saw Charley Wag before, he came and gave me money for the ring and made me write the note. Later I heard he been coopered by one of the jacks from "A" Division. But he never was! I seen 'im plain as I see you now, every hair of his head and every look of his eye the dead spit!'

'Phantasm of a disordered imagination,' said Samson knowledgeably, 'Charley been snug in Kensal Green the past month. Why, the turf they laid over 'im ain't even been disturbed.'

Elaine tossed her hair again and said with adolescent defiance,

'Bugger you and your phantoms! Didn't I feel his hands round my throat? And ain't I got the bruise of his thumb there still? Look!'

There was no mistaking the faded shadow of the injury on her white skin.

''ave the goodness to keep her 'ere a minute, Mr Samson,' said Verity. 'I shan't be gone long.' He trudged out of the booth and disappeared among the tents and flags.

'Biggish, darkish cove, Charley was,' said Samson conversationally.

The girl nodded.

'That's 'im.'

'Only thing is,' said Samson, 'it was Mr Verity as coopered 'im and me that felt his heart stopped and saw his head broke in. And saw him buried, what's more.'

He stooped a little and peered at the bruise on her throat again. One of his hands went round her shoulders and sampled the soft weight of Elaine's young breasts.

'Course,' he said, 'in the matter of being returned to Mrs Rouncewell, you could have it hard or easy. And Mrs Rouncewell takes notice of what I say in such matters.'

The hand dropped, full-length, and began to travel up the backs of the girl's tightly-clad and sturdy thighs. Simultaneously, he planted a resonant kiss on her lips.

'Ain't no reason a good-natured girl shouldn't find things go easy for her,' he said.

She tossed her hair back furiously.

'Bastard!'

Samson's hand reached the fattened cheeks of Elaine's bottom, stroking and patting.

'Quite a big girl already,' he said optimistically, the hand darting between her tightly closed legs. 'And you ain't averse to a touching there by the feel o' things! Now, you'll have all the way from 'ere to London Bridge in a closed carriage to show just 'ow grateful you can be to a friend that's. . . .'

'Mr Samson!' said Verity from the opening of the booth. 'If you please!'

Samson released the girl reluctantly with a final lingering pat and a sigh. Verity was standing at the canvas flap with a little man who was a total stranger to Samson.

'This,' said Verity with an air of proud ownership, 'is Mr Adam Jump, Lightning Sketch Artist and Silhouette-Maker to the Crowned Heads of Europe. He been good enough to leave his tent for a bit to help us in the investigation.'

'Why?' said Samson, irritated by the intrusion on his private negotiation with a fifteen-year-old mistress.

'A-cos,' said Verity, 'Mr Adam Jump has a speciality, which is likenesses of Dear Departed Ones.'

'You'd hardly credit,' said Jump with soft owlishness, 'how they sell. Ladies and gentlemen describe a dear one to me and I fashion the likeness to suit. Seeing it done brings back all manner of other details even while I'm working on the sketch. It's a shilling in pencil and twice that if shaded with coloured chalks.'

Verity addressed Elaine sternly.

'Now, miss. Let's 'ear you give Mr Jump a notion o' Charley Wag. And remember what's waiting for you at Mrs Rouncewell's if it ain't a ringer for him.'

Jump sat on the steps of the wagon with his board, paper and chalks. He drew shapes of faces until there was one which, the girl swore, was the contour of Charley Wag's.

'Dark 'air, sort o' tight curls,' she said. Verity and Samson nodded at one another in agreement.

'Like that?' asked Jump, showing her the board.

'Bit bald at the front, though,' she said, 'and sort of grey, like it was powdered just on top.'

Samson looked at Verity in bewilderment, but Verity was grinning like a schoolboy. He put his mouth close to Samson's ear.

'I thought I'd got it, Mr Samson! And I have too!'

They watched the artist at work, peering over his shoulder.

'I'll be damned!' said Samson, as the finishing touches were added to the sketch.

'Very probably, Mr Samson,' said Verity jovially, 'and you'll still feel comfortable compared to this young person if she's told us a pack of lies.'

'I swear it!' she howled. 'Ask the other girls that saw 'im!'

'Charley Wag!' said Verity, his shoulders jogging with mirth.

'Captain Jack Ransome!' Samson murmured dismally. 'But *how*?'

'Ain't difficult, Mr Samson. He may have been in league with Charley or he may not. If he was, then some girls that paid their dues to Charley never saw him but in the person of Ransome. Natural enough to think he was the Wag if he said so. Then, if the law was ever to move in, Jack Ransome goes down and Charley stays free. Even when Captain Jack got his hooks into the Jervis family, he may have worked the dodge with Charley. The faked pictures of Lord 'enry was done on Charley's premises.'

'Then what you heard the night Charley was killed was thieves falling out?' said Samson.

'I half thought so, Mr Samson. No wonder Honest Jack was so quick to destroy the evidence! It was more faked letters to squeeze Mr Richard and Lord William. It must a-bin! And it was all to do with Lord 'enry or someone being put in the sea from a little boat after a ship went down. And then Jack Ransome made his mistake. Seeing the Wag dead, he goes straight out next morning, round all the girls, and this time he keeps for himself every penny that he takes.'

'And now he might cooper Mr Richard Jervis, seeing as he's got him.'

Verity shook his head.

'Not 'im! Poor Mr Richard's too useful to him for that! Why, even when three medical men found him lunatic, Captain Jack wasn't going to part with him but got some poor delirious wretch and had him entered at Friern House in Mr Richard's name.'

'He's never holding him to ransom?'

Verity shook his head.

'No. And it ain't for Mr Richard's little allowance that passes through Captain Jack's hands. There ain't enough and I daresay it stops altogether if he's supposed to be in an asylum.'

Dismissing Adam Jump and taking Elaine with them, the two sergeants retraced their steps towards Trafalgar Street and the train for London Bridge. As Verity chose a carriage, Samson escorted the girl to the refreshment room. The pair reappeared just in time to catch the train but not in time to reach Verity's carriage. With a shrug of resignation he heard them in the next compartment to his own. He tried to concentrate his thoughts upon Richard Jervis and John Ransome, upon the seemingly pointless compromising of the dead Lord Henry, and the charge of murder made against Lord William. From the other side of the wooden partition he was aware of the descending slither of cotton against female flesh, soft patting noises and the murmur of voices rising occasionally to audibility.

'You got strong hips for a girl just starting off,' he heard Samson remark, 'but I'm partial, meself, to a girl what's big in the right places.'

It was Verity's second meeting with Dr Jamieson, whom he had not seen since his preliminary inquiries into Lord Henry's death. But the atmosphere in the room with its partners' desk, Orléans clock and nymphs, the fine cabinets and the fire burning in the grate, was entirely changed. Dr Jamieson's meagre jowls and watering eyes expressed an incalculable weariness and melancholy. He had even invited Verity to take a chair opposite to him.

'Sir,' said Verity gently, 'I must have the truth this time, all of it. There's a man's life in peril, the law's already been broke, and if you was to conceal matters now, you might soon be accessory to the most serious crime of all.'

Jamieson nodded, as though he understood all this, and Verity resumed.

'The picture Miss Elaine gave of the so-called person Aldino, or Charley Wag, was shown to other girls that had "seen" him after he was killed. It was Captain Ransome in every case. And it was 'im that got the blackmail letter written to Lord 'enry, though his lordship was already dead.'

Jamieson sighed.

'No, sergeant. The girl wrote the letter, as you describe it, to the man who lost that ring in the struggle when he was put into the sea. It was not Lord Henry's ring but Mr Richard's.'

'See, sir.'

'I very much doubt that you do. Mr Richard was a subaltern with his regiment in 1852, shipped on the *Birkenhead* for the Cape. The truth of what happened has long been known to his brothers and I, as their physician. We knew it from his ravings and his nightmares, waking and sleeping, in the months after he was found. He was picked up after he had been carried shoreward clinging to a timber for support. The hours of cold and the battering of the reef had done such damage to the nerves of his body that he was never to feel, let alone use, his legs again. He had been struck a fearful blow on his spine, perhaps as he was being put into the sea. If he was a coward, sergeant, he paid dear enough for it. Ransome put the letter in Lord Henry's bureau to stop your inquiry.'

'Very sorry I am to hear it, sir.'

'The injury to his mind was worse than the damage to his body. He was possessed by hatred of his would-be murderers. Lord Henry was a loving brother to him but Lord William never forgave the cowardice. For nearly two years, from 1853 until 1855, Mr Richard was confined in a private sanatorium. In 1855 he was judged recovered enough to return home and, in time, Captain Ransome was employed to care for him, a comrade from his old regiment. And still the secret was kept. But who knows what ravings Ransome may have heard and how long he may have searched for the girl who had the ring and could tell her tale! Lord William thought Ransome a bluff honest fellow but I never held him in much esteem. He fed Mr Richard's obsession, till that young man loved Lord Henry and hated Lord William as his deadliest enemy.'

'And he charges Lord William with Lord Henry's murder, sir,' said Verity solemnly.

Jamieson shook his head again.

'Impossible. I was with Lord William and Captain Loosemore for ten minutes before the fatal shot, and when it was fired, and while we ran together towards Lord Henry's body.'

'However, sir,' said Verity persistently, 'Mr Richard says he *saw* it with his own eyes.'

Jamieson sniffed sceptically.

'And he said more often still, sergeant, that Captain Ransome was his eyes, ears and legs. If Ransome told him that he had seen Lord William shoot Lord Henry, Richard Jervis would regard it as the evidence of his own eyes.'

The Orléans clock chimed in a tiny silvery sequence.

'Someone shot Lord Henry, however,' said Verity, hoping not to provoke Jamieson's professional hostility, 'with a rifle bullet wadded into a shotgun. It ain't no disrespect to you, sir, that you didn't see it first off. It was done with great cunning.'

'And who do you suppose did it?' asked Jamieson, unconvinced.

'Well, sir, you, Lord William and Mr Loosemore swear each other's innocence. The two clergymen likewise. Mr Rumer and the beaters was all in one place. That leaves Mr Richard and Captain Ransome. But Mr Richard ain't likely to shoot the brother he loved more than any other creature. So that leaves Captain Jack for number one, sir. Though I ain't clear why.'

Dr Jamieson said, as though it were the simplest thing in the world,

'Shoot Lord Henry and foster Mr Richard's hatred against Lord William. Come to me, as Ransome did, urging that Mr Richard be confined again. Send another wretch into confinement, make off with Mr Richard and use him to accomplish the destruction of Lord William for a murder he never committed. Mr Richard, though lunatic, is heir to the Jervis lands but with Jack Ransome holding his purse. Arrange the transfer of the supposed Richard Jervis from one asylum to another, as a Chancery lunatic. It is the unknown wretch who leaves the first place, but it is the real Richard Jervis who enters the second, certified as irremediably insane. He is lost to the world forever, leaving Honest Jack Ransome as controller of the Jervis estates.'

'Why!' said Verity. 'Why, sir! You might be commander of the whole detective police with such an eye for a dodge as that!'

Jamieson shrugged.

'An eye for the laws of lunacy, sergeant, their use and abuse. God knows I have seen enough of it in my time.'

'Only thing is, sir, the dodge won't work. So soon as ever Lord William was brought to trial for killing Lord Henry, your evidence of being with him would set him free.'

'A man may be destroyed without trial, sergeant. Richard Jervis employed you, under Captain Ransome's advice. But every item of evidence, as Ransome arranged it, confirmed either accident or even suicide as the cause of Lord Henry's death. Who is to say what means of despatch might be found for Lord William? Mr Richard would no doubt prefer to see him drowned than hanged.'

''ow's that, sir?'

'In his raving, Richard Jervis heard how Lord William sneered at him as a coward for concealing himself among the women in the boat and he swore that nothing would please him better than to see his brother suffer as he had done during his time in the water, and die as he had nearly done.'

'In which case, sir,' said Verity, getting to his feet, 'Lord William had best be told everything at once, for his own protection.'

Jamieson laughed.

'I hardly think you need concern yourself for his protection as yet. He is on board HMS *Hero* for the gunnery trials, off Plymouth. There are ninety-one guns, a full crew, and a detachment of Royal Marines with him. I cannot suppose that Richard Jervis and Captain Ransome will come close enough to harm him there!'

'No, sir. Just so, sir,' said Verity tactfully and prepared to take his leave. At the door he turned a last time to Jamieson. 'Sir, you having seen such abuses of the law over poor lunatics, if you was asked to examine a man locked away but what was in all probability sane . . . if you was asked, might you be prepared to do it, sir? I shouldn't forget the favour easy.'

'Call on me for the service at any time,' said Jamieson gruffly, and the interview ended.

Verity, stiff at attention, heard Inspector Croaker pacing the carpet somewhere behind him.

'Your instructions are plain enough, sergeant, aren't they?'

'Sir?'

'You will proceed to Plymouth by third-class rail. You will meet HMS *Hero* at the dockyard on her return from gunnery trials, and you will deliver to Captain Lord William Jervis a despatch from me in which I have minuted the details of the police investigation and the evidence which has been elicited by the officers under my command. When you have delivered it, you will return forthwith. Do you understand that?'

'Sir!'

'You will not indulge in any heroics or sorties of your own, exhibitions of the sort by which you made yourself and your colleagues ridiculous in India. You will carry out your orders to the letter and I have the word of the commissioner himself that should you deviate one inch from them, your dismissal will follow at once.'

'Sir!'

'Finally, sergeant, you are to be accompanied by your

colleague, Sergeant Samson. His business in Plymouth is nothing to do with you, and yours is nothing to do with him. You will neither seek nor divulge details in respect of your two assignments. Just see that Lord William is warned of his brother and Captain Ransome. And see to it that he receives the warning in the form of my despatch!'

'Sir!'

'And don't try boxing clever, damn you!'

'No, sir.'

13

'A constabulary officer ain't nothing,' said Samson gently, 'not but what he ain't got discretion.'

He had pronounced the same judgment, with slight variations, a score of times during the day and a night in the third-class compartment of the train which had brought Verity and himself from London to Plymouth. Every time that Verity shifted on the hard wooden seat and tried some new approach in his endeavour to find out why Samson had simultaneously been sent to Plymouth, Samson remained unmoved.

'When a man gets employed on a 'igher class of duties, Mr Verity, it's best they ain't talked of.'

The two sergeants had just crossed the Stonehouse Bridge, striding towards the dockyard wall. The scattered quadrangle of the Royal Naval Hospital lay on the bank of the Tamar behind them. On the glittering water of Plymouth Sound, twenty or thirty warships rode at anchor. Their hulls, with rows of square ports along either side for the guns, had altered little since the broad wooden battleships of Nelson's fleet. But between the masts, whose white canvas shrouds were tightly reefed in the anchorage, each vessel showed a squat black funnel amidships. Here and there, the relics of a previous age, a large-rigged sloop and an old bomb-ketch, lay rotting on the mud of the shallows. Across the cobbled street, several luggers, made fast to the piles of a jetty, served as bum-boats to the fleet.

Leaving Samson at the gate, Verity showed his warrant-card and was admitted to the dockyard as a visitor to the Master's office. Once beyond the dockyard wall, he entered a world of rowdy and varied activity. On the slipways beyond the harbour basin of Hamoaze, three battleships were in differing stages of construction, surrounded by bustling timber-wharves and the metallic din of smithies. As a precaution against fire, many of the buildings were of iron, so that the noise rang still more loudly from the rigging-houses, sail-lofts, hemp magazines and the spinning-house for ship's ropes.

At the Dockyard Master's office, Verity checked the progress of the *Hero*. The ship had been at sea for two days on her gunnery trials. The trials would be completed on the following day. The ship would enter the Sound somewhen after midnight, and would dock later that morning.

It seemed a matter of mere routine as Verity began to walk back to the gate. Then he paused. To one side of him, where there was an open space beside the quays, he heard the sharp words of parade-ground command and the piping of a Royal Marine band. 'Hearts of oak are our ships, jolly tars are our men. . . .' He walked more slowly. The tune ended. An officer's voice, hoarse with exertion, roared out, 'General salute! Pre-e-sent *arms*!' Slow and subdued at first, but rising midway to a blare of trumpets, came the notes of the Anthem.

No one was watching him. He turned back and strolled towards the jetties where several ships which had recently been dry-docked were now taking on stores. On the deck of a frigate he spotted the bosun supervising the caulking of the decks by an unfortunate rating. The bosun's hair was done in ringlets, his brilliant white shirt-collar so high that it almost touched his cheekbones, and his keen eyes followed every movement of the seaman's. In his hand he carried the traditional 'persuader', three rattan canes twisted into one. He was yapping at the sailor in a sharp monotonous voice.

'You are spilling tar upon the deck, sir! A deck, sir, I had the duty of seeing holy-stoned this morning! You have defiled Her Majesty's fo'csle, sir! If you neglect your duty, then by God I must remember mine! Take that! And that! Will you not hold that bucket steady, you yelping, half-starved abortion!' He paused, as though belatedly aware of an intruder, and turned with a look of ill-tempered apology to Verity. 'You must excuse me, sir. The service makes brutes of us all. In my responsible situation, I am too often obliged to sacrifice my gentility. Your servant, sir.'

He performed an awkward little bow.

'Might you,' said Verity nervously, 'might you, bosun, have an idea when the guard of honour is to parade for HMS *Hero*?'

'The day after tomorrow, sir,' said the bosun sharply. 'Every man must know that. A fine ship, sir. Sent to shoot between Scilly and the Lizard, previous to crossing to America. If you choose not to wait for her return, why, you may watch the guard and hear the band now, for they have been at practice since early morning.'

Verity thanked him and turned away, a gleam of triumph in his eyes. The bosun returned to the pig-tailed sailor, his voice rising to a scream that was almost feminine in its shrillness.

'Spill one more drop from that bucket, sir, and you shall make the acquaintance of my swiving deck with your swiving tongue! Every inch, damn you, sir!'

Settling his frock-coat more firmly on his shoulders and patting Inspector Croaker's despatch in its sealed envelope, Verity returned to find Samson reading a printed bill. It was a warning to literate seamen of the disagreeable contagious diseases in store for the careless philanderer.

'All right?' said Samson innocently. 'Told yer all about when Lord William and the *Hero* docks, did they?'

Verity stared at him, and Samson laughed.

'Ain't hard to work it out, my son. You been sent here to tell Lord William that he's in peril of his life from Mr Richard and Captain Jack. You ain't quite got the art of concealing confidences. Takes a bit of learning.'

Verity beckoned his companion to the open gate.

'Mr Samson, 'ave the goodness to listen.'

As they stood there, the hoarse command echoed across the parade-ground again.

'Royal salute! Present. . . .'

'Mr Samson,' he said kindly, 'it ain't your fault you couldn't keep the secret. When there's royal salutes being practised by a guard of men that's to meet the *Hero*, a man don't have to be a detective officer to add it all up. Especially when the world knows that the young Prince is to

211

be sent to America in a few weeks more and that the *Hero* is the ship to take him. Only natural he should want to visit her first. When she docks the day after tomorrow, you'll just be escort to Windsor or St James', I daresay.'

'You had no business to meddle!' Samson's face flushed with indignation.

'That ain't meddling, Mr Samson. You may have cause to thank me yet. Two heads is generally better than one in this sort of caper.'

The two sergeants had been lodged in the Plymouth section-house during their three days' visit. To Verity it seemed like being back in the barracks of the Volunteer Rifle Brigade once more. He and Samson shared a room which was intended for four constables, the bunks being in two pairs, one above the other. There was pressed beef, bread and ale for supper, which was finished by seven o'clock. As they sat at the scrubbed deal tables and ate, Verity seemed deep in thought. Afterwards he spoke almost apologetically to his companion.

'I hope you ain't no objection, Mr Samson, but I got a feeling for going on the spree tonight. They leave the door open for the night watch, so it's no hardship to get back.'

Samson looked at him with suspicion.

'You? On the spree? You never been on the spree in your life, my son. You wouldn't know how!'

'I was hoping, Mr Samson, I was rather hoping that you might have the goodness to show me.'

Samson guffawed, shook his head, and then allowed himself to be persuaded. Arms swinging, they marched off to the centre of the town where the grog-shops blazed and reverberated with shouts and brawling which made them seem familiar as Wapping or the Ratcliffe Highway.

'Fetch a mop and a bucket of dirty water!' shrieked a woman from the grog-shop. 'I'll soon have the blade out of his fist!'

A crash and a shout of pain was engulfed in further

uproar. In the tawny oil-light, a hag with white-powdered face and dyed hair accosted them with the familiar greeting of dockyard towns.

'Come now, my fine reefers,' she said, wheedling them, 'how're you off for a bit of nice soap?'

'The minute that arm goes through mine,' said Verity conversationally, 'the darbies is going on your wrists so fast, you'll be down the cells before you hear 'em click.'

She drew back from him, the lines of her hag-face etched deeper with rage.

'Fucking jack!'

'Here,' said Samson reproachfully, 'we was supposed to be on the spree.'

'Something more flashy, if you please, Mr Samson. Where might it be that the high-class doxies do go?'

'Funny,' said Samson, 'one of the Plymouth officers was telling me about that this evening.'

He led the way to what seemed like a spacious public house which advertised cigars, billiards, pyramid and pool, in white appliqué lettering on the windows. Inside there was a well-furnished vestibule, its walls lined with looking-glass, two chandeliers hanging at either end and gas-brackets sprouting from pilasters between the mirrors. Marble-topped tables with wrought-iron bases were ranged along the walls, each table equipped with carafe and glass, cigar-cutter, bowl and toothpicks. A circular desk, with the sporting papers of the day spread upon it, stood at one end of the room.

Samson looked about him and then led the way through a pair of doors into a more dimly-lit room which was both dining-room and auditorium, tables set out in its centre and velvet divans, conveniently concealed by potted foliage, in the recesses of the walls. With tankards set before them on the little table, the two sergeants watched the amateur performers who stepped up, one by one, on to the platform at one end. An elderly man with a bluish nose and his face tied up to relieve the toothache provided such piano accompaniment as he could improvise. Verity seemed too distracted by the figures in the gloom to pay attention to the acts.

'I don't call this much of a spree,' Samson said aggressively.

'There's sprees and sprees, Mr Samson.'

'We ain't so much as spoke to a doxy!'

'Just let me find one that takes my fancy, Mr Samson.'

The evening passed until at length a thin girl, her pale red hair cut short as a boy's, her white skin and slant green eyes a perfect match for it, stepped forward on the platform. She was swathed in a narrow black dress, revealing her slim hips and thighs in a manner appropriate to her real profession. Yet she sang with a voice of limpid innocence.

> *There once was a merchant in London did dwell,*
> *Who had but one daughter, a most beautiful young gel.*
> *Her name was Miss Dinah, just sixteen years old,*
> *And she had a large fortune in silver and gold.*

Samson brought down his pot with a crash and joined the communal roaring of the refrain.

> *'Singing toora-li-toora-li-toora-li-ay!'*

Verity was not singing, but his face was illuminated by a smile of total satisfaction. Mademoiselle Claire, as she was introduced, trilled her way through the banal tragedy of 'Villikins and his Dinah' to the suicide of the lovers by poisoning, and the final moral.

> *Now all you young ladies, don't fall in love nor,*
> *Like wilful Miss Dinah, don't wax your guv'nor.*
> *And all you proud parents, when your daughters claps*
>   *eyes on*
> *Nice young men like Villikins, remember the p'isen!*

There was a professionalism about the act which set it apart from its predecessors. The red-haired girl left the platform to tempestuous applause. She sidled along the edge of the room, as though avoiding her male admirers and then paused. Verity reached forward and tugged his companion by the sleeve.

'Carefully does it, Mr Samson!'

Samson began to turn to where the thin girl with her cropped red hair was standing.

'Mr Samson! Have the goodness to keep your face hid in that pot o' beer!'

Verity himself had his face down, dark eyes watching furtively. As 'Mademoiselle Claire' passed one of the curtained recesses, the hangings were pushed aside and another figure, obscure in the shadowy oil-light, mbraced her.

'Now, Mr Samson!'

Samson hardly moved his head, but his eyes peered furtively upwards from the pewter pot. He squinted, blinked, and then looked again.

'Jolly!' he said, and looked once more.

'I was right, Mr Samson! Keep yer face in that pot! She knows the pair o' us once she sees us.'

The slim redhead with her slant green eyes was sitting tight against the other girl, her pale skin contrasting vividly with the gold tan of her partner. There were murmured exchanges between the two. Verity could just make out in the shadows the outline of the two girls. The darker, with her neat features and the almost Oriental elipse of her eyes, put her hand to Claire's pale, narrow face, and then kissed her, full and long, on the lips. The fair-skinned redhead got up, looked back once, and then strolled away.

'Mr Samson,' said Verity, his words rapid but distinct, 'I ain't got time to explain now. I thought I was on the right road, that they'd come here, if they was in Plymouth at all. And where Miss Simona and that are, Captain Jack must be. This is where the dodge is pulled, Mr Samson, and Captain Jack can't leave Charley Wag's two girls nor Miss Jolly behind once it's done. They know all about him and couldn't be left to tell the tale. If you want to see your precious Lord Renfrew safe again, you'd best do as I say.'

'What's this got to do with 'is 'ighness?'

'He happens to be in the line of fire, Mr Samson. And if you ain't a bit sharper than this, he's number one for being the bull's-eye. Listen! Behind that curtain, on that divan, is them three girls what was at the Temple of Beauty and

Ramiro's baths. Jolly I seen. Simona and Stefania is there, for a bet. When they leave here, you follow. Go where they go, but don't let 'em see you. I'll find you somehow. Now, I gotta go, Mr Samson.'

Verity slipped away from the table and followed where the thin pale redhead had gone. It was not hard to find her. She was not one of the street whores, like the painted and whitened hag who had accosted the two sergeants earlier on. Her haunt was the brightly-lit vestibule, where she posed and sauntered between her ingenuous solos on the platform of the inner room. Claire was still young, her light red hair cropped short in her nape to give her a look of boyish innocence, belied by her thin, knowing face and green eyes. Verity approached her.

'If you ain't otherwise engaged, miss, p'raps you'd care to spend a while with me.'

She looked at him cautiously. Her customers were generally men of commercial prosperity, young or old. It hardly seemed that Verity fitted their type. She studied him carefully, then swung about, as though inviting him to follow. He guessed that her room would be on the premises. She was no mere bunter who was obliged to find casual lodgings where she could. Claire led him through a door of the vestibule and up a spacious, carpeted staircase. At the top of this, she opened a nondescript door and went in.

Verity had seen the room a score of times before. The Coburg chairs, the Egyptian settee, plum-coloured velvet and gas-lamps in ornate brackets. Looking at her pale narrow face, he thought how set it seemed, as though she were capable of only one expression.

'Now, Miss Claire,' he said, ''ave the goodness to sit down and listen to me.'

'And who might you be?' Despite her soft, country voice, her words were as hard as her thin pale face.

'Me?' said Verity. 'I'm one as saw how fondly you kissed a certain other girl in the room below. And I'm one who knows how many crimes she's got to her name. Accessory to murder she's likely to be, which is a noose round her neck as sure as round the party that done it. And if you choose to obstruct my inquiries, then it's likely to be a noose round yours as well.'

Claire, who had begun to unbutton her dress as she sat on the settee, was now without motion or expression.

'Miss,' said Verity softly, 'I ain't concerned what you do with other girls. If you choose them for your lovers, that's your affair. But you stand in the line of accusation for murder.'

The slim red-haired girl lowered her head, as though she might be about to weep. But no tears came.

'Fool!' she said softly.

'Yes, miss?'

She shook her head without raising it.

'To please her,' she mumbled. 'To please her, I let her do what she would with me.'

Verity nodded wisely.

'Then she wasn't really a beau of yours, miss?'

'Promised me,' wailed the redhead. 'She promised I might be took to London and made a proper dancing-girl. But I must please her, in return. I'm not a girl's mistress, whatever you may think!'

Her face lifted towards him, and the green eyes seemed to darken with vindictiveness.

'I can believe that,' said Verity, 'a young person as comely as you.'

'She never did a murder.'

'She helped,' he said, 'and you best answer such questions as is put now. Where might she live, when she's in Plymouth?'

'She don't. Never was here more than a few days past, with them two flashy Italian girls. Hired the *Flora*.'

Verity stood up, crossed to the settee and sat down beside her.

'Now, Miss Claire, you just do them buttons up nice and tell me what the *Flora* might be.'

She turned to him, the doubt still in her narrow eyes and her teeth pulling at her lip.

'Pleasure steamer,' she said softly, 'the *Lady Flora* that Captain Joshua keeps at anchor off Great Western Dock.

They've got sweethearts on board, I daresay, but I never saw them ashore. Them three young ladies came on their own, for a bit of fun, and that dark one took some sort of a fancy to me, though I never gave her encouragement.'

'Captain Joshua,' said Verity, as though thinking deeply. 'Now what sort of a captain might he be?'

'Only the sort that hires himself and the boat to the quality. Fishing and that.'

'Might he fish so far out that he could bring his passengers alongside a French trawler? Just nod if you've heard that tale.'

She ducked her reddish hair quickly in acknowledgment. Verity sighed.

'Sort of captain that takes his folk anywhere, for hire, and then lies low in his bunk while they do what business they please? Snug in there with a bottle of rum?'

She nodded again.

'Or a high-class doxy?'

She bobbed her head.

'Why,' said Verity, 'why, Miss Claire, I half think you been paid once or twice, paid to keep him happy in his bunk, while the brandy and perfume and that was changing hands on deck! But you ain't to worry. Smuggling don't interest me, and you shan't be touched on that account. But if there's anything you've told me that ain't true, my young lady, you'd best beg pardon now. Otherwise, the most you can hope for is to be a transport in a prison settlement where the men put over you are cruel brutes and the women worse than the men. I ain't come to frighten you with what happens to you there, but you'll know the story of a young person with just such pretty hair as yours. The first week, their hands was never from her, and every strand on her head was shock-white at the end of it.'

She whimpered a little, in fright and misery.

'Now,' said Verity, 'it's me and me alone that can stand between you and such 'orrors, if I'm told the truth. Just where might this *Lady Flora* be?'

'Follow the path on Mill Bay,' she whispered, 'out towards Eastern King Point. Half-way between the dock and the point there's a broken jetty with an old landing. The gig comes ashore there and the *Lady Flora* lies off it. Captain Joshua has a mate that attends to the engines. There's stokers and other seamen that he picks up casual from time to time.'

Verity patted her hand.

'Why, miss, if you've been a truthful girl, I'll do more than stand between you and transportation. I'll see you rewarded from the police fund!'

She watched him, silent and suspicious, as he rose, opened the door, looked back at her and then slipped away.

The table where he had sat with Samson, and the alcove behind its velvet curtain, were deserted. Verity made his way quickly through the muddy, high-walled lanes which ran beside the wall of the Great Western Dock. The shoreline of Mill Bay was starlit and he could make out the path without much difficulty, the half-derelict jetty showing black against the opalescence of the rippling anchorage. Close to the spot, he paused and said softly,

'Mr Samson!'

There was a movement under the shadowy piles of the jetty, Verity preparing to ward off an attacker if necessary. But it was Samson's voice which answered him.

'Over here, Mr Verity! Them three doxies came down to the water, showed a lamp and was took out there in a little boat. Out where that steamer is.'

The outline of the *Lady Flora* was clear enough. The trim pleasure-craft seemed no more than a hundred tons, a tall buff funnel with black top rising amidships. The stern and the paddle boxes were gaily painted and embellished with gilt scrolling.

'Let's hear it then,' whispered Samson. 'Let's have the tale that's to be told.'

'Simple, Mr Samson. All the way from the London terminus, I been thinking more and more that if Captain Jack was to pull this caper, he must do it fast. Once Lord William and the *Hero* is docked, it may be too late. Ten to one, Lord William ain't going to America without stepping

round to Friern House and seeing his brother first. You or I
might have doubts as to Mr Richard's looks, but Honest Jack
Ransome can't take a chance that. Lord William wouldn't
know if it was his own brother or not. I been thinking all the
way from Paddington that he'd have to work the dodge now.
So he'd have to be in Plymouth, perhaps, but not let himself
be seen. Likewise, the girls in them blackmail pictures
couldn't be left to sing a song about it. When we was at the
railway station, I asked the railway constables if they'd seen
a sign of our friends. They hadn't noticed any such
passengers as Captain Jack or a poor cripple, who must have
come another way. But one of 'em saw a cab hired by two
girls that was Eye-talian and another what was a ringer for
Jolly.'

'You was quick, Mr Verity.'

'I was, Mr Samson. A-cos then I reckoned that Captain
Jack and Mr Richard would lie low. But them three bunters,
with a taste for a spree and an itch between their legs, they'd
never lie low for five minutes but must be out and about, by
fraud or force.'

'If you was to flash a lamp, Mr Verity, a boat would come
from that steamer. We might knock the man on the head
and get out there after 'em.'

'Not till I know who's there! Can you swim, Mr Samson?'

'No,' said Samson defensively, 'not actually *swim*.'

'Well I can. Sit 'ere in the shadow and look after these
things until I get back. Whatever you do, don't show a light.
If I ain't back in twenty minutes, or if you 'ear trouble, make
for the police office. Otherwise stay put. I shall need your
'elp.'

As he spoke, Verity discarded his frock-coat, shirt and
trousers. Either through modesty, or else as a protection
from the cold, he retained his long drawers. Where the piles
of the rotting jetty rose from the oily surface of the dark
water, the bottom sloped away gradually, deep in mud. He
waded through the clinging sludge until the black tide
lapped at the crease between his belly and his plump chest.
With a brief flurry of water, he kicked up his feet behind
him and paddled with his hands. After a while he regained

the art he had once known of keeping his hands and feet below water, where they moved almost as silently as fins. This, at least, was something which he could be sure those on the *Lady Flora* were not expecting.

Five minutes of cautious paddling brought him within ten yards of the dark shape of the *Lady Flora*'s hull. There were lights at some of the portholes, which ran in a single line round the ship, but the curtains were drawn at each. Two men, whose physique suggested brothel bullies rather than sailors, were in conversation on the deck. Parting the water as gently as he could, Verity came close to the stern, where the little gig was moored. In the slack tide, the *Lady Flora* turned forward and back in a slow semi-circle, whose centre was marked by the anchor-chain which ran down into the black dock-water at her bows.

He could hear the voices of the two men on deck, muted in a discussion of the female passengers.

'Three of 'em!' said the first man with soft incredulity. 'Cost you a duke's inheritance to hire three at once for the night! And that yokel-captain to have them all night and tomorrow! Just to look the other way when the dibs is paid out and the goods brought aboard!'

'What I saw,' said the second man, 'just before the door was closed, was them two Italian pieces. Naked as they were born, kneeling in front, fighting each other to get a kiss at the prize. Jolly, too. I seen that piece stooped naked, patting herself behind to get him to take her at a charge.'

There were muffled snorts of laughter.

'Bloody liar!'

Verity was holding fast to the wooden fender which ran back along the ship's side from the paddle-box, not twelve inches above the water. By shifting his grip he could pull himself along silently and also raise himself enough to bring his eyes level with the portholes. The after part of the ship seemed to be in darkness, until he came just to the rear of the paddle-box, where the lit circle of glass showed the little engine room with its single polished piston. A roughly-dressed man, no doubt Captain Joshua's mate, was attending to the piston-head with an oil-can. Verity slid back into the water and swam forward round the dark, dripping fins of the iron paddle, and he thought how neat the arrangement was. Apart from Captain Joshua and his mate, every man and woman in the caper was Jack Ransome's servant. And some means had been found of selling them the smuggling story so that they never questioned it.

Two forward portholes, belonging either to two adjoining cabins or else to one large saloon, showed light behind their curtains. He heard a man's voice, slower and gruffer than either Ransome or Richard Jervis. Muffled sounds of a girl were followed by the voice of a young woman, shrill with excitement.

'That way, signore! Now, like that! She like that a lot!'

And there was a chorus of feminine laughter.

Verity paddled round the bows of the *Lady Flora*, guessing what he would find on the other side. He had accounted for Captain Joshua, the mate, three girls and two bullies. There were probably two or three more bawdy-house toughs who had once worked for Charley Wag. But that was not enough. He swam soundlessly to the patch of shimmering light on the water where two other portholes shone red through their curtains. It was the stateroom opposite to that in which Captain Joshua was beginning to taste his reward.

Verity pulled himself up by the wooden fender and listened.

'It is justice, my lord,' said Ransome firmly. 'It is the justice you have long been owed.'

Verity frowned at the style of address. There was no room for a lord on the *Lady Flora* in his picture of events. But his brow relaxed as Richard Jervis answered, quickly and in great excitement.

'Call me your lord in jest, if you like. But tomorrow I shall be your lord in earnest!'

The voice and the personality were recognizably those which Verity had known. Yet now there was a shrill zest, as though Richard Jervis understood only what he said and was unable to comprehend much that was spoken by others.

'Punish the guilty and let the innocent go free,' he said mournfully.

Ransome's voice became humorously confidential, as though he might be speaking close to Jervis' ear.

'My lord, only the captain is required to go down with his ship. And so he must, unless you would have him commit you to the madhouse again.'

Something in this stirred Richard Jervis' humour. The laughter which followed was prolonged, as though with childish delight. Verity shivered and glanced towards the dark shore, where his colleague waited.

'Our own men will be secure,' said Ransome casually. 'Once the ports are closed over, no one shall see in or out. The hatches will be fastened. The worst tale they can tell is that they served us, hoping for a share of contraband, but found we were innocent yachtsmen. It convicts them, my lord, not us.'

Richard Jervis spluttered with laughter again.

'Brave Jack Ransome!' he said, as though even the admiration exhausted him. 'Oh, Jack, I am so tired! Oh, Honest Jack!'

Verity let go of the wooden fender, slid into the cold water of the anchorage and moved like a large pale fish in the murky tide. Ten minutes later, his teeth chattering with the chill of the air on his wet body, he stumbled ashore by the dilapidated jetty, where Samson waited. Samson had taken off his own coat and was holding it out.

'Wrap this round you, my son, and get dry on it!'

While Verity gratefully rubbed the worsted material against his back until the flesh glowed, Samson also produced a small flask. Verity took it without a word, tipped it back and emitted a choking gasp.

'Mr Samson,' he said breathlessly, 'it's the *Hero* they're after! There's Captain Jack and Mr Richard out there on that boat. They got them three young persons and a crew of Charley Wag's cut-throats, and Captain Joshua and his mate. Mr Richard still sounds half-asleep from laudanum or something. But I bloody heard Honest Jack promise to cooper Lord William by sending the *Hero* to the bottom.'

'Sounds to me like someone give you a dose of laudanum if you believe half of that,' said Samson, handing Verity his clothes. 'Sink a shipful of men in front of all them witnesses on the *Lady Flora*?'

Verity looked at him severely.

'They'll be battened under hatches, Mr Samson. But it wouldn't matter if they weren't. There's only two of 'em that's coming back from this little spree, and that's Captain Jack and Mr Richard. Can't yer see, Mr Samson? The *Hero* goes down with all hands, so no one thinks it's just Lord William that's aimed at. Captain Joshua sails away in the *Lady Flora* and never comes back. Mr Richard goes into Bedlam for good, leaving Honest Jack Ransome with the estates in his charge. And not a scrap of evidence closer than fifty fathom down. It puts 'is 'ighness fifty fathom down too, Mr Samson!'

Samson watched Verity dress. As though speaking to a slow-witted child, he said,

'If you think that even Honest Jack could sink the *Hero* with the *Lady Flora*, you ain't half got something to learn about boats, my son! A shell that wouldn't even dent a great ship like the *Hero* would blow a little pleasure-steamer to bits in firing it!'

Verity looked up.

'You never thought, Mr Samson, that whatever the device is might already be hid in some secret place on the *Hero* ready to blow her to smithereens?'

'No,' said Samson uncertainly.

'No,' said Verity. 'It ain't likely, of course, or they wouldn't need the *Lady Flora* now. Likewise, I suppose you never heard of a torpedo?'

'Torpedo?'

'I'm surprised a constabulary officer of your length of service ain't never took the trouble to familiarize himself with infernal machines. You don't have to fire a torpedo like a shell. You just tows it across the path of the target, so the bows of the other ship catches the trawl. It swings back smartly, banging the torpedo against the ship's side and up she goes. A pull on the tow might do it. Blows a hole as wide as a house. One of them great battleships like the *Hero*, she'd turn turtle with all hands in less than half a minute.'

'Dear God!' said Samson softly.

'Yes, Mr Samson.'

'Sooner we go for 'elp the better.'

'We *are* help, Mr Samson. We ain't paid to run for someone else. You walk out of here, and by the time we get back, that boat out there might have gone.'

'What then?'

'We'll just get aboard her and stay aboard.'

'I can't swim,' said Samson doggedly.

'Don't matter, Mr Samson. I'll just give 'em a flicker with the lamp and they'll come and row us across.'

'Course they won't. And if they did, they'd know us soon as look at us. Captain Jack, Mr Richard, them doxies. They all know us.'

Verity shivered audibly.

'Mr Samson, I had a good look at that boat, what was going on and what wasn't. They'll put to sea soon enough, but they ain't quite ready yet. I know a way to get on that steamer and stand face to face with Captain Jack Ransome, and him never say a word. Just get behind them bushes and keep yer head down.'

Ten minutes later, a blob of light swinging in the darkness showed the approach of two men from the direction of the lanes and taverns beyond the Great Western Dock. Their voices were loud and argumentative, and they stopped from time to time, as though to settle some matter in dispute. At the ruined jetty they turned the lantern seaward and flashed a signal. Bulky but silent, the shapes of Verity and Samson rose from the bushes, faces blackened as though for a night ambush. The two men on the bank knew nothing until they were seized, bent, and their wrists locked behind them. The breath was knocked from their bodies and by the time they recovered it, their mouths were securely stopped with wads of cloth. In little more than two minutes they were rolled behind the bushes, tightly trussed and naked, a worn but carefully darned frock-coat thrown over them as a gesture of decency.

Standing where their victims had been a moment before,

Samson and Verity adjusted their ragged garments and cheap caps.

'Back o' yer neck,' whispered Samson sharply. 'Rub some more of that black in! They'll spot it's too clean otherwise!'

The oarsman of the little gig glanced at them in the pale. starlight, two nondescript figures in their torn cotton breeches and jackets, faces blackened by the grime of the stoke-hold. The oars creaked and, without a word spoken, they clambered on to the stern of the *Lady Flora*. The after companionway was used by the crew, and Verity moved quickly towards it, as though from long familiarity. He kept in his mind the shape of the lower deck, its cabins and saloon for the passengers being well forward. The little engine-room was housed amidships, and just aft of it Verity saw the tiny door, plated with iron. The two men had to stoop a little to get through it and then saw by the light of their lantern the six steps down to the miniature stoke-hold. The area at the foot of the steps seemed hardly more spacious than the top of a dining-table. To either side of it, bunkers of coal, set back in two small recesses, sloped upwards to a small grimy porthole, tightly closed and level with the water-line. Facing them, at the foot of the steps, the dark cavernous mouth of the furnace awaited their attention.

'Mr Samson!' said Verity in a tone of reproach, 'you never mean those poor wretches live down 'ere?'

'Live down here?' said Samson thoughtfully. 'Yes, and die down here like as not. Pleasure-boats ain't quite the same thing when you're stood on deck as when you're here with nothing but the keel-plate between you and Davy Jones' locker. If this old wash-tub was to founder, you'd have as much chance of seeing daylight again as a coster donkey has of pulling the state coach.'

As he spoke, there was a reverberating clang of metal behind them and the sound of the stoke-hold being bolted on the outside.

'They never twigged us?' said Verity anxiously.

'No,' said Samson, inspecting the dead boiler-fire. 'Stokers is generally battened down for the duration of the voyage. Persons of quality don't like us dirty fellows coming up from hell's mouth and leaving chimney-black where it might touch the gentlemen's fine linen and the silk things of their ladies.'

'I 'ad no idea we was to be locked in, Mr Samson! You might have said a word! I never counted on this happening!'

'There's a lot a man don't count on, but what happens just the same,' Samson observed philosophically. 'Now, stop prosing and give me a hand with some fire. If we don't get that furnace going like two real stokers, you'll have more to worry over than that door being bolted!'

14

Long before the *Lady Flora* put to sea in the brightening dawn, Verity and Samson were stripped to the waist. On his chest and belly, Verity felt the scorching glow of the furnace, while his back was chilled by perspiration in a faint but persistent draught. Somewhere in the cramped stoke-hold there was an air-pipe, ventilating the space from above with an acrid smell of hot engine-oil and brass screws.

The flames of the furnace, roaring in the upward draught, provided almost the only illumination in the little hold. A wan daylight, filtering through the grime of the two bunker portholes, fell on the gleaming black bricks of coal and was extinguished. As the ropes were cast off, splashing into the oily water of the Great Western Dock, the thin iron plating of the keel shuddered so violently underfoot that Verity almost expected sea-water to spurt through the joints as they sprang open. With the crash of a mighty breaker, the finned paddle-wheels thrashed the sea, level with the men's shoulders, a few feet away on the far side of the fragile hull. The noise, added to the heat and grit of the hold, would have done credit to the casting-shop of a great foundry. Above the bunkers, green seas foamed and raced against the two small portholes as the paddles threw back their churning wake along the ship's flanks.

Verity shouted against the din.

'Mr Samson! I'll take one port, you the other! Have the goodness to see what you can make out as to which way we might be heading!'

Cutting his knees and shins on the sharp edges of the black slabs, he scrambled up the slithering mound of coal. It was something to find that the portholes, at this depth, could be opened. There was, of course, no question of risking this while the ship was moving and, in any case, they were far too small for Verity or Samson to squeeze through. The sea streamed constantly down the glass from the paddle-wake, but there were moments when the flow of water thinned sufficiently to show a blurred outline of waves and receding shore.

'Sun on this side,' gasped Samson, 'right in the face. Water on the porthole glass and not a sight of anything else.'

'Very good, Mr Samson. Being as there's land on my side, they're heading between west and south-west, which brings 'em somewhere off the coast of Cornwall, and a good way out.'

'Them two coves you heard on the deck was right, Mr Verity, and it was Mr Richard that got a load of old rope from Captain Jack. It's a smuggling spree, after all. You brought us on a fool's errand, old son.'

'They ain't the smuggling kind, Mr Samson. Honest Jack has murder to answer for. He's got too much at stake to waste his time with French perfume and kegs of brandy.'

'Much you know,' said Samson, unconvinced. 'Let 'im so much as wink at the *Hero* and see what happens. Them bullies of his, and them three little bitches, not to mention Captain Joshua and his mate, why they'll all sing Queen's evidence sweeter than a row of linnets.'

'Mr Samson,' said Verity with great patience, 'ain't you understood the tale yet? Lord William Jervis and several hundred brave men goes to their deaths. No one on this boat sees it or knows it except Captain Jack and Mr Richard. But Captain Jack don't take chances. Captain Joshua and his mate is coopered when the *Lady Flora* is a mile or two off Plymouth in the dark. The bullies that do it, say they're told to bring the bodies down here. No sooner are they down here than that door closes on 'em. P'raps the three doxies has their throats slit then, p'raps it's done before. There's a hundred ways it might happen. But the end of it is Captain Jack in the gig, rowing for the shore with Mr Richard, and the *Lady Flora*, with her sea-cocks open, lying so many fathom down that no one so much as looks for her.'

'He wouldn't find it that easy, Mr Verity.'

''ave some sense, Mr Samson! It's all too easy! Say there's four of them bullies. They'd do for the captain, his mate and the three doxies, and never ask why, if Honest Jack said the word! Him with his guns and the rest of it, he'd soon settle with four bullies, one by one.'

'All right,' said Samson grudgingly. 'What then?'

Verity was tearing at a strip of cloth, folding it into a pellet.

'They're going to open that door for me in a minute. Once I'm out, I'll have a look around and see how the land lies. There's a chance I might even pick up something to make it a fairer fight. When I come back, I shan't be watched too close. P'raps there won't even be someone there to lock the door right away. If I'm given a chance, these wads is going into the bolt holes, so when they do fasten the door, the bolts won't lodge too far in. A man that knows the art can always work a bolt if it ain't securely lodged.'

'How're you going to get out there?'

Verity walked carefully up the stoke-hold steps.

'You just watch, Mr Samson.'

He clenched his fist and beat on the iron door so that it echoed like a deep bell. After he had repeated the blows several times, the bolts rattled and the door opened.

'Gotta 'ave grease from the engine-room,' said Verity suddenly. 'Gotta fetch grease. Them portholes is leaking all over the coal again. Hour or two more and it'll be too wet to burn.'

One of the men who had opened the door stood back to allow him through. Verity ducked through the opening and straightened up, blinking in the stronger light. Even as he grew accustomed to it, he recognized the other man, who had been standing a couple of yards back from the door. The clothes were still a little shabby and crumpled, but the pouched red face with its greying black moustaches was alert and triumphant.

'Dammit,' said John Ransome with a snort of laughter, 'you do try a fellow, don't you?'

'Gotta 'ave grease,' said Verity, mumbling and keeping his head down. The heavy-looking gun in Ransome's hand he recognized as the new Colt revolver. One bullet each for four bullies and two over, without reloading.

Ransome laughed uproariously and spoke to the bully who had opened the door.

'But he does try, Scottie, don't he?'

'A jack 'as to try,' said the man sombrely, 'when he's caught interfering with honest sea-trade. He knows he can't go back alive, but it don't stop him trying.'

Ransome laughed again, as though it were a great joke.

'Sergeant Verity,' he said happily. 'Of course, it would be. Our little oarsman, Pineapple Jack, ain't as foolish as he looks. Why, we heard all about the two strange stokers who came aboard, but I never dared promise myself the pleasure of settling accounts with Sergeant Verity!'

'You're a bloody murderer Jack Ransome! You coopered Lord 'enry Jervis and the world knows it.'

Ransome sniggered and even the bully grinned at Verity's desperation.

'N' lis'n t'me, everyone that can hear! This ain't a smuggling spree! Captain Ransome means to sink HMS *Hero* with every soul on board, just to cooper Lord William Jervis! The Prince of Wales is on that ship! If he ain't stopped, Ransome will make you all the murderers of the Prince of Wales!'

Even as he shouted the words, Verity knew the futility of it. Two other bullies appeared from the companionway and watched him, grinning at the absurdity of his attempts to save himself. Jack Ransome turned to them, still smiling.

'Oh, he do try,' he said. 'Don't he?'

The first man, 'Scottie', had hold of Verity's arm.

'Right, you bloody peeler,' he said. 'Stokers you wanted to be, stokers you shall be. You may refuse and die now, the men here can do the job if they must.'

Verity braced his body against the stoke-hold entrance, struggling.

'We ain't the only ones that must die. N'lis'n. Never mind what the person Ransome told you. You try shooting a torpedo or shell from a hull like this, you'll sink yerselves. N'list'n t' me. . . .'

There was laughter all about him. One of the bullies approached and aimed a blow at his belly, driving him back into the dark stoke-hold, the wads of rag still clutched uselessly in his fists. He lost his footing and almost fell down the iron steps. Ransome, the Colt revolver in his hand, stood in the tiny opening, looking down at his two prisoners. He spoke softly, his words directed forward so that those outside would hardly catch a syllable of them.

'Dammit,' he said, 'if a fellow could win through by pluck without a brain in his head, I swear you'd do it. Now, be so good as to shovel away at that coal like a good chap. By and by you shall see them act a famous drama, "The Death of the Hero", outside your very porthole.'

'I'll see you in hell for this, Ransome!'

Ransome laughed.

'You may indeed, old fellow. But you shall reach that destination a deuced long time before me!'

He laughed again at his own wit. The two bullies, who had driven Verity back down the stoke-hold steps, slammed the iron door tight and closed the heavy bolts on the outside. There was a scraping of boots on the deck overhead, and then a long silence.

'You done it this time, my son,' said Samson, savouring a pet phrase.

'It ain't so bad as that, Mr Samson. I been worse off before. Why, me and Sergeant Martock was prisoners in a heathen fortress with guns pointing at us all round. I was even led out to death there, and still it was all right.'

The nuggets of coal rattled as Samson tossed them from his shovel into the glowing furnace. He grunted derisively.

'P'raps it was all right, there. But this time they ain't going to lead us anywhere. They won't even open that door again. Whatever happens, they got to get rid of us, and once the sea-cocks is open we're first to drown. This hold's the best iron cell a man could build. You can't bust out. Even supposing we could smash holes in them iron plates, we'd only let the sea in. As for that iron door and the bolts, your caper didn't half come a cropper.'

'I know *that*, Mr Samson. I know *all* that. I ain't *stoopid*.'

As he spoke, the engines of the *Lady Flora* seemed to race briefly, and then the churning paddles stopped, their wake hissing and bubbling into silence. The anchor splashed down into sunlit water.

'It's never fair,' said Samson, 'about pensions. If I'd married Church of England fashion, she'd have my pension. But common-law wives don't count. She ain't got a penny coming. It ain't fair!'

Verity tempered reproof with kindness.

'Mr Samson, it ain't the time to brood over Fat Maudie now. I daresay she's a good girl and true, but we gotta do something about all this!'

'All what?'

'Didn't you 'ear that person Ransome? The Death of the Hero, he said. He bloody admitted it to us! He's so keen to finish Lord William that he'll sink that ship with all hands. *All* hands, Mr Samson, in case you forgotten who else that includes!'

Now that the *Lady Flora* was at anchor, Samson was sitting on the heaped coal at the edge of the bunker. His elbows were on his knees and his chin in his hands.

'You don't 'alf lend your ear to some fucking rubbish,' he said moodily. 'There's ninety-one guns on that ship, any one of which could blow this hulk out of the water at a full mile range. There's hundreds of jolly jack-tars and two or three companies of Royal Marines armed to the teeth. Only thing is, p'raps your Captain Ransome had a man that he put on board her to set light to the powder magazine or something of the kind.'

Verity shook his head.

'It don't suit. Ransome's the only one who knows the whole score on this. In any case, if it was to be done on board, he'd never bring another boat out here like this. However, he did promise that we should see the whole thing from these little portholes, so he may as well be took at his word.'

Verity eased his way past Samson and clambered once again over the coal.

'Nothing this side,' he announced, 'just miles of empty sea and not a sight of land.'

He returned in a slithering avalanche of broken coal and began to climb up the bunker on the opposite side. For some moments he crouched at the top of the dark mound, peering through the grimy little circle of glass.

'Now that's rum,' he said softly.

'Is it?' said Samson, apparently still thinking of Fat Maudie.

'There ain't no land, but there's three things in the water. There's two quite close together, only a long way off, and then another much bigger, not half so far away.'

'What sort of things?' Samson got up and began to haul himself across the coal. Verity worked the porthole free and opened it for a clearer view. About two hundred yards from the *Lady Flora*, the first object was a metal, latticework tower, about twelve feet high, riding on a large buoy. It appeared to mark a wreck or an obstruction of some kind. Beyond it, at least half a mile off, floated the two much smaller buoys, each one the size of a man's torso but painted a distinct bright green and apparently bearing a lamp. Presently the two sergeants saw on their left, as though it had come round the stern of the *Lady Flora*, the white-painted gig, with one of Ransome's seamen rowing and another at the little tiller. A third figure sat in hat and cloak, his back to them, and Verity could not quite decide whether it was Ransome himself or not. Then he and Samson lay there, watching the progress of the little boat as the caps of the Channel waves chopped and smacked against its bows. Verity felt for his watch among the rags and checked the time. It had just gone two in the afternoon. He turned to Samson.

'If it was gone four when we left and almost gone two when we hove to, that's ten hours. She never did more than ten knots and probably not less than eight.'

'Somewhere about eighty miles south-west of Plymouth,' said Samson.

They watched the little gig rowing away from them and saw it pass the latticework tower of the largest and nearest buoy. Though the fires had been damped down in the stoke-hold, the perspiration was still heavy on Verity's round cheeks. He said,

'Supposing that HMS *Hero* was on this course for Plymouth Dock, and suppose she was expected there about three in the morning. Say she could make fifteen knots. That puts her here at about ten o'clock tonight, p'raps a bit after.'

'I could almost fancy it was smuggling after all,' said Samson. 'Them two green buoys further off, that's just the sort of caper. Fishing buoys that one party ties the cargo to, and then the other fetches it. Why there's even that iron tower there to show them the spot.'

'It ain't a proper tower, Mr Samson, it's floating. And the sea don't half splash about it, too, for such a calm day.'

The rowing boat had passed the latticework structure and was making for the two smaller green buoys. When it reached the first of them, the seamen pulled themselves alongside and began winding in a long chain attached to the buoy.

'Smuggling!' said Samson triumphantly. 'They're hauling up the kegs of brandy or that flash perfume, or whatever it is.'

'No they ain't, Mr Samson. They're taking that bladder in tow!'

Samson looked again. The little gig had made fast the nearer of the two buoys to her stern and was now heading towards the other. Despite the size of the green markers, they were no great weight and the men towed them easily. When both were secure, the rowing-boat began to pull slowly back towards the *Lady Flora*. But when it reached the tall latticework, which bowed and swayed as its own buoy rode the surge of the tide, the oarsman shipped his oars and the first green marker was unlashed. The iron chain with its cannon-ball weight splashed down, so that the conical buoy rocked and bobbed at its new anchorage. The gig skirted the latticework tower and left the second green buoy anchored on the other side. The three buoys now formed a line, about fifty feet long, with the tall latticework structure in the middle and the green markers equally distanced on either side of it.

As the gig began to pull away to the *Lady Flora*, Verity said softly,

'Mr Samson, might you be able to see what the writing is on them green things?'

Samson peered through the flurries of water which burst and dribbled on the glass of the porthole.

'It do go all round,' he said restlessly, 'you see a bit but not all. Board of something. Long word. Stop a bit. M . . . I . . . R . . . .'

'Admiralty,' said Verity abruptly, 'Board of Admiralty. Set out for the battleships to fire between. I seen it done once off Portsmouth when there was a naval review after the Rhoosian War. We of 'er Majesty's Volunteer Rifle Brigade was just landed and had permission to watch from the sea-wall. That's why Ransome come here. He knew the *Hero*'s markers would be set out and that she'd sail this way!'

'Not by dark she won't!'

'Mr Samson! 'ave the goodness to look at them green buoys! There's a light on each! Doncher see? It's for the night shooting! That's what's happening tonight! A display for 'is Highness on the last night out afore HMS *Hero* docks in Plymouth!'

'Night shooting?' said Samson doubtfully.

'Yes, Mr Samson. Like they did at Portsmouth that time. You have two marker buoys with their green lights. The battleship steams past, broadside on, and lets rip, so the water between the two buoys rises in a great spout where the shells land. Then she steams in a letter "S", curving back, passing between the buoys, steaming through her own spray, turning on the other side to bring her other line of guns to bear, and fires the second salvo. Speed, Mr Samson, accuracy, and a great ship turning on her heel like a dancing-girl. You no idea how our lads cheered 'em. A sight for 'is 'ighness, ain't it?'

'If the 'ero goes between them two buoys now,' said Samson, 'she'll 'it that floating tower!'

'She'll do more than that, Mr Samson. She'll take Lord William Jervis, and the Prince of Wales, and several hundred brave men, to the bottom of the sea in less time than it takes me to say it!'

'Never!' said Samson half-heartedly. 'That tower won't sink 'er!'

'Mr Samson, 'ave the goodness to look at the buoy under that iron tower and see what you can read.'

'I tried that,' said Samson, 'and all I can see looks like "Half" something or other.'

'Not to me it don't, Mr Samson. There's other words that ends in an "l" and an "f". We ain't just eighty miles from Plymouth, we're in a place what the villain Ransome has chosen very carefully indeed. Mr Samson, that tall thing out there is the warning buoy for the Wolf Rock!'

'Lord William ain't just going to run a bran-new warship on to a rock to please Ransome,' said Samson reasonably.

'So you been saying every minute for the last four hours, Mr Samson.'

Verity was alone at the porthole, watching intently. The long afternoon had passed and the sun was setting.

'All my childhood,' he remarked, 'all my childhood I 'eard men talk of the Wolf Rock, as though it was the devil himself. There ain't a more treacherous fang on any coast. When the tide's low, you see it just above water and the waves breaking on it, same as you did when you saw the foam about the buoy. But when the tide's high, it's just two feet under the water with long sharp ridges that might slice a ship in two. That's what they call the teeth of the Wolf. Any man that steams across it is going to find the bottom sheared off his hull easy as peeling the skin from an orange. It might be the flagship of the fleet, Mr Samson, but she wouldn't float twenty seconds hardly after that. It wouldn't matter whether or not she had lifeboats, a-cos there wouldn't be time even to order them lowered. Ransome ain't half got a mind for a caper like this! And, o' course, he must have been able to get every detail of the *Hero*'s rendezvous in his conversation with Lord William!'

'Lord William ain't going to prance about the Wolf Rock.'

'Not too close,' Verity agreed, 'but half or even quarter of a mile is deep water and safe enough. The target buoys is easier to find if he can track 'em down by the light of the Wolf Rock buoy.'

There was a ripple of oars and the little gig passed across their field of vision, heading for the three buoys several hundred yards from them. It seemed to Verity that the *Lady Flora* had been allowed to drift further off during the course of the afternoon, though he had not heard the anchor weighed. In the gathering twilight it was now possible to see the first glimmer on the water from the green lights on the target buoys. The three red lights in a vertical row on the latticework of the Wolf Rock buoy glowed in the semi-darkness. The gig was lost to sight in the gloom. Then, across the surging water came a sharp crack, followed by another. The highest of the three red stars was suddenly extinguished.

'Shooting 'em out!' said Verity for Samson's benefit. The report came again, and the lower of the other two red lights was gone. Two more shots and the third light died. Above the teeth of the Wolf there was nothing now but the green lights of the marker buoys, even the iron latticework of the floating tower having merged into the darkness. Almost at once, a red trace shimmered across the water, as three red lamps shone out from the foremast of the *Lady Flora* at an identical height to those which had just been extinguished on the Wolf Rock buoy.

Verity snorted with derision.

'Very clever! The *Hero* takes our mast-lights for the Wolf

Rock and the green lights as the place for Admiralty manoeuvres! They ain't to know, in the dark, that the whole set has been moved a few hundred yards to the left! She'll be doing full speed between them green markers, slice her clean as an apple! Honest Jack ain't missed a trick on this bloody caper!'

'There's always compasses,' said Samson hopefully. 'They'll check the course by 'em perhaps.'

'When they can see the lights, Mr Samson? A compass has to be set and it don't always stay true. After I heard of Mr Richard Jervis' adventure, I read the old report on the *Birkenhead*. It was compasses that did for her. Not being true, they drove her straight on to the reef. If her officers had used their eyes, they might all a-been safe. In a night like this, Mr Samson, a good sailor uses his eyes first and his compasses next.'

They lay on the coal, faces close to the porthole, watching the glimmer of red and green lights on the shifting waves.

'I keep thinking, Mr Samson. She'll be full ahead on both her engines. When they see that dark iron tower ahead of them, it'll be too late. And I keep thinking of the last minutes and the uproar, the brave men going down, sucked under by the ship sinking. And I keep thinking that one of them is otherwise to be King of England in his time.'

'Thinking might kill a cat, old son,' said Samson gloomily, 'but you ain't going to think your way out of here. They won't even open that door until it's all over and they come to blow us to Kingdom Come. You might let the boilers go out now, for all they care. When they've coopered us, their own men can stoke 'em up quick enough.'

Verity nodded, as though all this were entirely reasonable. He said,

'I ain't a man that enjoys thinking to no purpose, Mr Samson. P'raps I've thought my way out of here and p'raps I haven't. What I ain't going to do is sit here like the patience of Job and watch it all happen out there. There ain't nothing promised, but if you was to do as I say, we might have a fighting chance.'

'And what *do* you say?' Samson asked doubtfully.

Verity slithered down the heap of coal and picked himself up.

'They got coal enough to get 'em back to Plymouth, Mr Samson. So we may as well lend 'em a hand and start shovelling it in.'

'You ain't going to 'elp the bastards?'

'Do as I do, Mr Samson, and have the goodness not to argue.'

Verity paused a moment, shovel in hand. The two sergeants looked at one another. Across the surface of the darkened sea, as though from a great distance, came a strong insistent rhythm. Its dulled regularity sounded like the deep and powerful beat of a heart. They scrambled to the porthole once more and peered into the night. What they saw was so far away that it appeared to be almost beyond the first slight curvature of the horizon. But there was no mistaking the pattern of sound and the cluster of riding-lights as the great ship, with the Prince on board, churned towards them in her remote thunder of engines.

15

Without another word, Verity took his shovel, reversed his grip and forced open the porthole with a single blow of the handle. In the starless night, the dark water rippled and ran along the hull less than twelve inches below the little opening. To Samson's bewilderment, he loaded the shovel with as much coal as he could balance on it and shot the contents through the porthole. The black nuggets, varying in size from a clenched fist to a full brick, fell into the sea with a scattered and prolonged splash. Working with a sudden desperation, he loaded the shovel and repeated the procedure.

'Buckle to, Mr Samson! If we want to get out of 'ere, we must make 'em open that door and come down to settle with us! There ain't no surer way than by letting them see their precious coal going to the bottom! If they wait till the *'ero's* done for, there won't be a lump left! Fancy 'em stuck eighty miles out from Plymouth and being carried further and further to sea when the tide alters again!'

Samson said nothing, but the perfect simplicity of the idea was beyond question. Taking the second shovel, he opened the porthole of the other bunker and began shooting coal into the dark water in a long and vigorous slinging gesture.

'Kick up a row, Mr Samson! Let 'em see what we're doing.'

'Slap! Bang!' roared Samson. ''ere we are again! 'ere we are again! 'ere we are again! Slap! Bang! 'ere we are again! What jolly dogs are we!'

'That's it, Mr Samson! Let 'em think we're half seas over! It'll help to take 'em off guard!'

The coal was now falling into the sea with a rythmic splashing, first on one side and then the other. As he worked, the perspiration on his body icy cold in the night breeze from the open porthole, Verity heard the first sounds from the deck. There were voices in puzzled exchange, then a shout, and footsteps as someone strode towards the companionway.

''alf a minute more, Mr Samson! Keep shovelling while I get ready for 'em! When you hear the bolts go back, come and stand between me and them!'

Samson had hardly time to sling two more loads of coal into the sea before there were voices at the stoke-hold door and the tiny metallic scratching of the bolts being furtively eased back. Verity was in the act of driving his shovel into the glowing coals of the furnace when the iron door of the little hold was wrenched back. In the shadowy glare of the fire he half saw and half guessed the fate which Ransome had prepared for them.

'Bunker, Mr Samson!' he shouted, throwing himself to one side in the shelter of the little recess with its sloping mound of coal. There was no time to coordinate the movement, and as he sprawled on the slithering grit Samson's weight fell on him with an impact which knocked the breath from Verity's lungs. And in the same second there was an explosion which struck his ears with a ringing deafness in the confined and iron-walled space. But he knew his instinct was right, the air was filled with a bee-like singing as tiny lethal fragments of metal sprayed the area between the door and the furnace, even pitching and scattering on the lower slope of the bunkers themselves. It crossed Verity's mind that a man who was as expert as Ransome appeared to be in the matter of shot-guns would know that they were the unanswerable weapon against two men trapped in a small hold.

'Finish them now!'

It was Ransome's voice, the words precise and unperturbed. Verity guessed that the first discharge of shot had been fired by him but he must be accompanied by at least two of his seamen, each of whom was likely to be armed with a similar weapon. They would count on doing the job without even having to reload. He gripped Samson's shoulder, willing him to lie still, and felt rather than heard the throb of the engines which announced the approach of HMS *Hero*.

Two things alone were against Ransome and his bullies. The darkness, only half-lit by the fiery patterns of the furnace, made it difficult to judge a target, let alone aim at it. And even if Ransome knew where his two prisoners were lying, he could not be sure, after the first salvo, whether they were unscathed, wounded, or already dead. Moving his right arm gingerly, Verity chose the smallest attainable piece of coal. He lobbed it high, so that it moved in the darkness above the firelight, and heard it clatter in the opposite bunker. It would hardly deceive them into supposing that he and Samson were hiding there, but at least they would have to investigate. There were whispers beyond the door and Ransome said irritably,

'Go! They cannot hurt you now, and there is another gun here to cover your path!'

Unmistakably there were slow, awkward footsteps on the iron stairway from the furnace-hold door. The man would have a gun, of course, and there was another aimed from the door itself. But that, Verity judged, would be all. There could hardly have been time to snatch up, let alone prepare, more than three weapons. And if he could move quickly enough, the battle would be hand-to-hand before they might even reload the first. The footsteps were closer now, five seconds more and the man would reach the edge of the bunker and see his victims sprawled helplessly on the piled coal in front of him. Verity braced himself for what must come, his eyes on the furnace and his hand closing round the hard gritty contours of coal. In his mind, as though detached from all this, he was doing simple arithmetic. HMS *Hero* sighted at about eight miles distance, breasting the horizon. Steaming at, say, fifteen knots. Near enough thirty minutes away. Five minutes, at least, gone.

He pictured the man in the darkness, standing at the foot of the iron steps, far enough back to keep his gun free of any assault. Stalemate, it might be, but it was a stalemate which suited Ransome as the *Hero* thundered closer to disaster with every second that passed.

And then Verity moved with that speed which his weight and demeanour always made so improbable and which was only seen in moments of great peril. The second lump of coal rattled in the opposite bunker as he tossed it, accurately, through the darkness. It was a larger piece this time and it started a tiny avalanche, just as he had intended. Even now it would not deceive the hunter into thinking that his prey was hidden there, but he would not have been human if he could have suppressed the instinct to look in that direction as the mound of coal rattled and shifted in the darkness. The little avalanche trickled on for several seconds more, partially concealing the sound of Verity who flung himself from the opposite recess in a hefty spring. Samson watched him, dismayed to see that he made no attempt to reach the man with the gun but threw himself in the opposite direction, silhouetted immediately before the furnace door. In a continuous movement, Verity landed on his feet, seized the handle of the shovel where it projected from the bed of hot coal, and faced his adversary. Samson turned his head away slightly, knowing that Verity's bare chest and belly were about to be blasted to shreds of bloody flesh by the discharge of shot. There was no way that he could reach the bully with the gun before the trigger was pulled.

In the instant before the fusilade of metal fragments roared out from the muzzle, Verity stood four-square, as though about to put the weight at a village fair. In a massive arc, he swung the loaded shovel upward and forward, hurling a dozen white-hot fists of coal the length of the stoke-hold.

'Now, Mr Samson!' he shouted.

Samson took a standing jump into the arena of battle and saw the dark shape of the first man cowering backwards under the rain of burning coal. But, injured or not, he recovered his balance, levelled the gun and fired it as Verity's arm knocked the barrel upward. The hot blast of the explosion swept over Verity's head, a scalding pain from the metal barrel burnt his forearm like a brand, and it seemed that molten lead dripped on his bare shoulders as the shot was deflected harmlessly from the roof of the hold. But the gun was wrenched from the man's grip, Verity holding him and propelling him to the steps below the iron door. Ransome and another man were visible beyond the opening, and Verity could see Ransome taking something from his companion's hand.

'Mr Samson!' shouted Verity warningly.

The man he was holding saw it too, wrestling and twisting to free himself as he was forced backwards to the door. Ransome had raised the gun. The man Verity was holding screamed with terror. The long, metallic roar came again and the body in Verity's grip jerked convulsively, emitting breath in the long sigh of a punctured gourd. Something had hit and numbed Verity's left arm above the elbow but whether it was the shot he could not tell. The man in his arms became a dragging, downward weight. Several little pulses of warm liquid throbbed through Verity's fingers where they pressed on the man's back and then, presently, even that movement ceased.

It was not how he had planned things at all, and he saw that even before he could extricate himself from his gruesome embrace with a corpse, the stoke-hold door would be closed and bolted again. Once that happened, there would be no second chance for him, or Samson, or those on board the *Hero*. He could see that Ransome was drawing back from the opening, but then Verity was thrust aside by the weight of his colleague, Samson leaping the stairs in two great strides and hurling himself against the door as it began to close. His speed, added to his size, threw the door wide again for long enough to allow Verity to charge after him.

The foot of the rear companionway, just aft of the stoke-hold, was the scene of considerable confusion. There was no sign of Captain Joshua or his mate, but Ransome's men had come running from their posts at the sound of the shots. Four of them, with Ransome himself, now formed a semi-circle confronting the two sergeants. In the background were Simona and Stefania, grinning in anticipation at Verity and Samson and a darker figure in the shadows. Jolly, thought Verity, no doubt of that. Captain Joshua and his mate were either bound and gagged in their cabins or, perhaps, already dead. And then he noticed something else. Though the oil-lamps were lit below decks, every porthole had been tightly covered with coarse black cloth. The *Lady Flora* would have to be blacked out, apart from the Wolf Rock warning lights on her mast, if Ransome's plan were to succeed.

For what seemed a full minute, but must have been a few seconds, the sergeants and their antagonists stood motionless. It appeared to Verity quite absurd that Ransome's men made no attempt to come at them. But then he glanced quickly aside and saw Samson, levelling the shot-gun of the dead bully in the stoke-hold.

'Take it!' said Ransome with calm authority. 'It's not charged.'

'First one that makes a step this way is going to find out different!' Samson announced triumphantly.

Even Verity was deceived, though he knew it was impossible for Samson to have reloaded.

'Just aim at 'em, Mr Samson, while I have the coverings off them portholes.'

But even as he spoke, the men moved round and took up positions to deny him an approach to the tight black covers. The bluff of the unloaded gun would not last for much longer, certainly it would not survive an attempt to uncover all the *Lady Flora*'s ports. Even then, at a distance, she might be taken for a ship beyond the Wolf Rock, by the *Hero*'s look-out. Verity improvised a desperate plan.

'Mr Samson, shoot the person Ransome. Shoot low to avoid the head and chest, he may be needed for questioning.'

Samson concealed the bewilderment he must have felt.

'Right,' he said, levelling the gun.

There was no way in which Verity could convey his actual intentions to his colleague. Samson must gather them from what came next. The bullies watched motionless. They had been hired by Ransome, and they were prudently loyal to their paymaster, but not to the extent of taking the blast of a shot-gun on his behalf. Ransome, the four bullies and the three girls, stared at Sergeant Samson as though mesmerized. It was in this moment of uncertainty that Verity moved slowly round behind Samson and reached the companionway. Before any of the others could have followed him, he had set foot on the first step, climbed rapidly and gained the deck. From below him he heard the sudden movements and shouts of a struggle. The bluff of the unloaded shot-gun was over. But to have reached the deck evened the chances considerably. It was the one place where Ransome and his men dared not use a light, with the *Hero* no more than fifteen or twenty minutes away. A fight in the dark was infinitely to be preferred when it was one or two men against half a dozen.

In the few moments before his pursuers appeared through the entrance of the companionway, Verity busied himself with further improvisations. He mounted the port paddle-box and felt in the gloom for a smooth familiar cylinder. Carrying this to the stern, he set it down where he could find it again. The little gig, which had appeared from the stern when he and Samson had watched it altering the buoys, was still made fast there. It was equipped as the only life-boat of the *Lady Flora*, but it took two men to handle it properly, one at the oars and one at the tiller. However, he tied a line to the brass cylinder and lowered it carefully into the gig. Now he needed Samson.

There was a clatter of feet on the deck and Verity armed himself with the boat-hook which had been propped against the rail at the stern for use in the gig. The groan and struggle of two men wrestling together assured him that Samson was at least on the deck with him. Verity could make out a dim, ill-defined shape, which he knew must be the combatants, and then another man approached. Rising from the shadows, Verity drove the boat-hook hard into the face of the man as he ran forward, closing his mind to the appalling injury which the metal hook might inflict and thinking only of the *Hero* as she ploughed at full speed towards the teeth of the Wolf. The man screamed and fell back, hands to his eyes, as Verity swung round to see if there were any more of Ransome's men in the vicinity. He was about to go to Samson's aid when a figure, which must have moved with the stealth of a shadow, leapt at him from behind, clinging to his back like an incubus, sharp fingers scrabbling for his windpipe.

There was one way of dealing with such an attack, and he had known it since childhood. Making no attempt to resist, he threw himself further and violently forward, sending the attacker off his shoulders and over his head. But he need not have put such power into it, he decided, for his attacker was the lightest he had ever known. He was aware of a figure flying over him, somersaulting above the ornamental rail of the *Lady Flora* and hurtling towards the dark surface of the sea. In the instant before the falling body splashed into the waves, Verity stood motionless with a chill of astonishment as he heard his late antagonist emit a decidedly feminine scream. Her chance of success had been so remote that he could guess her identity and the sheer hatred which had prompted her to fly at him.

Knowing there would be little enough time when the moment came, he cast off the gig and let it drift slowly from the stern. At the very worst, it meant that Ransome and his bullies would now have no way of escaping from the ship if they attempted to sink it. He was satisfied to see that the tide carried it very slowly indeed.

The remainder of the deck seemed ominously silent. Then he heard Ransome's voice,

'Take him down and tie him fast.'

A body was pulled unceremoniously towards the companionway.

'Sergeant Verity! Come forward and give yourself up! Your friend will otherwise suffer greatly!'

Torn between loyalty to Samson and his wider duty, Verity looked about him. The lights of the *Hero* were clear now, the tall dark hull picked out by the row of lit portholes. Her engines beat strongly and the churning bow-wave as she cut the Channel tide was just visible in its white phosphorescence.

'Get clear, Verity! Get clear, for God's sake!'

Samson's words ended with the sound of a blow and a cry of pain. Verity could see that the others were coming towards him. They had searched the deck and they knew where he was. He backed against the rail, shivering in the tattered breeches which were all the clothes he wore apart from his boots. His plump flesh still shuddered with cold as he softly unlaced the boots and pulled them off.

'Take him!'

They must have seen his outline against the faint glow of the sea. Three of them came in a rush. But Verity was on the rail in an instant and, as their arms went for him, he jumped, feeling the rush of night air against his face, and then hit the water with a floundering splash.

He broke the surface, gasping. His first impression was that someone was, after all, trying to light a lamp on the deck of the *Lady Flora*. Then, as a single hail-stone seemed to plop into the water a few yards from him, he recognized the flash of Ransome's revolver. They were on the side of the deck hidden from the *Hero*, which explained the apparent rashness. He knew that the chance of hitting a man at such range was remote enough, even for a man of Captain Ransome's proficiency. And, of course, if they were going to fire at him, they could hardly risk sending one of the bullies in after him. Verity swam slowly, paddling like a dog, to the place where he last saw the gig as it drifted from the stern of the little paddle-steamer.

It was not until he could almost put his hand on the gunwhale that he thought of the girl. Her cry of terror, half choked by the water in her throat, would hardly have reached the steamer. He knew that if he swam to her and attempted to rescue her in the water, she would cling to him frantically, and he was not a good enough swimmer to keep them both afloat in that manner. With the puffing and shuddering of a willingly stranded whale, Verity pulled himself carefully into the little gig, near the stern. At all costs it must not be overset. Then he peered forward and saw the disturbance of water where the girl was struggling to keep her head free of the waves. She was no more than ten yards away. Taking the oars, he sculled forwards and drew as close as he dared, turning the boat so that its stern was nearest to her. She clutched wildly, her fingers slipping against the white-painted planks of the gig's clinker-built hull.

The gown she had been wearing, plum-coloured merino, was gone. Either she had struggled out of it in the water, or more likely its buttoning had been ripped away by the force with which Verity had thrown her over his head. She was wearing a pale blue bodice and knickers which he saw, as he hauled her in over the stern, were so wet that they revealed her body in as much detail as if she had been naked, even the coppery flesh-tones appearing through the clinging semi-transparency of wet silk. She writhed in the bottom of the gig, drawing breath in a muted howl, retching sea water, and then choking for air again. Verity seized her by a cold, slippery arm.

'Right, miss! You got one last chance to decide whose party you'm to belong to! There's been murder done on that ship, and there's worse still planned for the souls on that other boat that's bearing down this way! You and all Ransome's crew shall wear a rope collar and dance a polka in the air outside Newgate. . . .'

He saw the flash of the whites of her eyes as fear broke from her in a long wail.

'No-o-o!'

'Then you better join my crew sharply. Else it's over-the-water-to-Charley you dances, my girl. Eight o'clock sharp with the parson reading your burial service to you, and Jack Ketch pinching your bum most familiar as you goes through the trap.'

Her teeth were chattering, either from cold or fear, or both.

'I never knew they'd kill!' she shrieked. 'There was nothing said but brandy and perfume from France!'

'They'll hang you all the harder for lying,' said Verity, sitting on the little seat with his back to the bows and taking the two oars in his hands.

'I'll be the approver!' she cried. 'I'll give Queen's evidence, if I'm let! I'll say anything they want! Oh God, I will!'

'It'll go for nothing if I speak against you with the Crown lawyers,' said Verity gruffly. 'You'd best please me first, miss.'

Whimpering, she scrabbled at the waist of the clinging pants, about to wrench them down.

'No!' said Verity. 'Ain't you got a brain anywhere but between your legs? Hold that tiller and keep this boat straight till I tell you different!'

As he bent his back to the oars and pulled with all his strength, the gig drew slowly away from the lee of the *Lady Flora*. At this level, the prospect was less encouraging than it had seemed from the deck of the paddler. What had looked like a mere swell with occasional eddies of falling droplets was a different matter in the little gig, no more than eight feet long. On all sides they seemed menaced by steep seas, bitter wind, rain squalls and a surging tide. Verity knew that the lights of the *Hero* were at his back, the hammer-beat of her engines appallingly close. By his calculations she must be at least ten minutes from the Wolf Rock and the savage granite teeth now treacherously hidden beneath two feet of high water, yet the sound of her screws throbbing in the great ocean spaces seemed a good deal closer than that.

'Them green lights!' shouted Verity at the girl. 'Hold a course for them! Slap between, if you can!'

'Cold!' she howled. 'So cold!'

'If I have to stop,' Verity swore, 'you'll get such a hiding as 'll make sure you never feel the cold again! 'old that bloody tiller straight!'

A smother of rain, spray and seas came drenching over the bows of the gig and fell with the pain of hail on his bare back. The ache in his arms and shoulders flamed as though the muscles and ligaments were being systematically torn apart by the strain of rowing into the squall. But the *Lady Flora* was dropping away astern, nothing visible of her at a distance but the three red lights at the masthead, treacherously simulating the warning buoy. Quarter of a mile, Verity thought. How far had they gone, and how fast? If they could only move at a slow walking speed, it would be enough, but with every surge of the dark water he felt the effort of his rowing countered. The gig seemed to be stock-still in the middle of a great ocean with the dark, curling seas racing past.

Then, to his dismay, he saw the *Hero*, her outline clear against the faint luminosity of the sky. The frigate and the gig were now on parallel courses, which would bring them broadside-on to the two green marker-buoys, though on different sides. There was no mistaking one of the newest and fastest of England's warships. Behind the curling bow-wave, the dark stalwart sides of the great ship rose menacingly from the water, the square gun-ports open and lit, the guns themselves rolled forward and ready for action. There were two rows of gun-ports on either side and tiny circles of light under each, indicating the portholes of the lower deck. The lights on the deck showed the three tall masts and the short, squat funnel amidships. Verity guessed that Lord William Jervis and his visitor would view the gunnery practice from the quarter-deck, which was on the high poop at the stern. There were two or three life-boats hanging from davits by the poop, but there would be no time to lower them once the bottom of the ship had been torn away by the granite teeth and by the force of her own speed.

Both the warship and the gig were close to the green lights

of the marker-buoys, the *Hero* about to overhaul the rowing-boat. Verity shipped the oars and seized the smooth brass cylinder which he had purloined from the paddle-box of the *Lady Flora*. He slid back the shutter, praying that it was already lit and would not need a flame kindled. To his relief it was. The gig would hardly remain steady if he stood upright, but on his knees he held aloft the red glow of the port riding-light from the *Lady Flora*. Surely they would see. Surely someone would see. He waved the light to and fro as hard as his aching arms could manage. The *Hero* was no more than two hundred yards off, the great ship thundering past in the darkness. But every eye on the quarter-deck was on the firing range marked out by the two green lights. The gig rocked in the swell of her passing, and soon she appeared only as a squat stern and a flurry of broken water above her twin screws.

Verity put the lantern down.

'Gotta tie it to that iron tower above the Wolf Rock buoy,' he said furiously, as though it mattered to the girl as much as it did to him. Seizing the oars he began to row strongly across the remaining hundred yards or so of water which separated them from the first buoy. In a matter of seconds, he knew his error. From behind him there came a whisper, which grew louder than any stage-whisper he had ever known. The sea ahead of them erupted with a crash into a great water-spout, sending a wave so powerful that it almost stood the little gig on its stern. The girl screamed and fell, but her hold on the tiller saved her from being thrown into the sea. In her terror she was beyond all reason and all control, beating at Verity with her little fists, her dark eyes flashing with panic, shrieking at him to save her.

Flame lapped the ports of the *Hero* again. There was a whisper, a roaring, and then a new thunder of spray was thrown skywards, drenching the occupants of the gig and almost swamping the fragile craft. But away from the flame and the storm of water, Verity was engaged in simple arithmetic once more. Ninety-one guns, say forty-five a side. Two rows on each side, say twenty-two each. They'd never fire off more than a single row at once, then reload that while the other was being fired on a second manoeuvre. Twenty-two. He counted the fourth and fifth. And the water-spouts would move further and further on as the *Hero* passed the target area. Now! It must be now!

Seizing the oars again, he pulled strongly for the first of the green marker-buoys. It would help to have extinguished it, but there was no time and, in any case, they would assume it had been accidentally hit by the guns. He rowed on towards the darkened warning buoy above the Wolf Rock with its black swaying tower of iron latticework. Just able to make it out in the gloom, he brought the gig alongside. The *Hero* was turning in a foaming sweep of water to race back between the green markers, loop round and discharge her other guns from the opposite side.

Clumsily, for the numbness of his hands, Verity made the gig fast to the buoy, threaded the handle of the riding-light on his right arm and tried to grab the iron latticework of the swaying twelve-foot tower. He was aware of the girl shrieking in terror behind him, but the time had come to put such things from his mind. He tried the buoy itself, but the slippery surface rolled away from under the pressure of his foot. Then the surge of the tide dipped the latticework tower far enough towards the gig. Verity seized it, felt at once that it would bear his weight, and rode with it forwards and upwards.

He seemed suddenly high above the water, in a world where the cold was more bitter and the air was full of screaming, whether of the wind, or the girl's terror, or sea birds in the dark, he could not tell. His feet were as numb as his hands, but they were securely lodged in toe-holds on the iron framework. His left arm was threaded into the latticework to hold him to it. Gripping the handle of the red port-hand riding-light in his right fist, he held it outwards and upwards as far as he could.

The *Hero* had turned completely, her broad blunt bows head-on to the dark tower. The water rose in two cresting plumes on either side as the powerful ship gathered full speed from her massive engines and bore down on the black and treacherous rock. Almost sobbing from the ache and the chill, Verity waved his tiny lamp and prayed.

On the quarter-deck of the *Hero* the thunder of the ship's engines was discreetly muted. Lord William Jervis, in the splendour of cocked hat and gold braid, stood close to General Lord Bruce, surveying the froth which now marked the surges after the firing of the first salvo. Lord William spoke to the elderly General Bruce, who wore the plumed hat of a British staff officer, but the other officers on the quarter-deck had not the least doubt that his lordship's aim was to engage in conversation the young man who stood at the General's side. He was a dark-haired adolescent, rather too weighty, with a round face and a heavy mouth. The mouth gave him an appearance of perpetual sullenness, which was unfortunate since he had made every effort to be as agreeable in his behaviour as he might be, ever since boarding the *Hero* at Plymouth several days before.

As the green lights seemed to rush upon them, General Bruce inquired,

'You find markers of great use, my Lord William, on such occasions as this?'

'Use, sir?' said Lord William, smiling confidentially at the General's young companion, who seemed a little embarrassed by such public intimacy. 'Never try a ship without 'em! Why, sir, only think of the scandal when they steamed battleships over the measured mile at Maplin Sands. Damme, there were posts stuck in the sand for the ships to steam past, out to sea. By altering his angle, a commander could steam a measured mile that was a hundred and fifty yards short! And he might set a course for another ship that was a hundred and fifty yards long. Why, there were ships that did the same speed but one was noted as two knots faster than the other! Now, sir, when the course is from buoy to buoy. . . .'

'Red warning light dead ahead, sir! Range two hundred yards!'

Lord William clapped a spy-glass to his eye, dropped it on the deck, and turned to his subordinate, crouching as though he might actually spring at the man.

'Hard a-starboard!'

The urgent shout echoed across the quarter-deck. Lord

Bruce stood rigid and deathly pale, the young man beside him seemed tense but nonplussed by it all. The deck beneath their feet slewed and canted as the ship swung in a churning suction of water. The men on the quarter-deck braced their feet against the angle of the ship as she turned, and then there was a mighty thump which suggested the meeting of two blunt surfaces.

'What in God's name . . . ' said General Bruce, but Lord William ignored him.

'Stop engines!' he shouted down the voice-pipe. 'Go astern!'

A breathless lieutenant appeared from below.

'Struck an unknown obstruction in turning, sir. No major damage apparent. Passing blow, sir.'

Lord William Jervis shook his head, as though to clear it. He went to the rails of the quarter-deck as the *Hero*'s searchlight sprang across the water in a blinding shaft of magnesium brilliance. The beam probed the dark water.

'What the devil's that?' said Lord William suddenly.

'It's the Wolf Rock warning buoy, sir.'

'Dammit, can't I read for myself?' said his lordship ungratefully. 'But what's the bloody thing doing across the bows of *my* ship?'

Verity almost wept with relief as the great dark shape of the *Hero*, looming the height of a house over the warning buoy and its tower, turned in a surging thunder of foam, shearing away at the last moment from the savage sharpness of the long rock. But the relief was soon overwhelmed by other considerations as the wash from the mighty hull and the powerful screws struck the buoy with the force of a sea driven by a gale. The riding light was spun from his hand, hitting the water and sinking at once. He lost his footing, his right hand brushed uselessly against the cold wet metal and, as he fell, his weight tore his left arm from its grip on the iron struts. In the second between falling and hitting the water he thought, for the first time since leaving Plymouth, of Bella and Paddington Green.

Carried down into the trough of the waves and then up on the next crest, he had hardly the breath to cry for help. As the water bore him up, he saw the iron latticework now brilliantly lit, but there was no sign of the gig or the girl. He had not the strength left even to cry for rescue. The sea had taken him at last, an unresisting victim to be borne to his death wherever the tides drew him.

And then there was a terrible pain in his eyes as a white radiance seemed to hit him with the force of a blow. He longed only for the ease of darkness, and darkness came. It was followed abruptly by the same cruel brilliance, the sound of voices, and something falling. The voices were closer, the words quite clear.

'Back starboard! Down port! Give way together!'

For a long moment he was alone in the painful white light. Then a voice, almost at his shoulder, said,

'In bows!'

Though his body was numb, he could just feel the hands which took him under the arms and pulled with such strength that Verity's portly body seemed to flip effortlessly into chill air and then to fall on to the boards of the ship's cutter.

'Girl,' he said drowsily, 'Jolly, girl in the water.'

'Could have been swept anywhere by now,' said one of the men doubtfully, though not addressing Verity. Verity attempted to shake his head.

'Was in boat, tied to warning buoy.'

There was more shouting and the bright beam of light again. Someone said,

'Still in the boat? No. Capsized. Hanging fast to it! Dead ahead! Give way together!'

Verity opened his eyes. Someone was wrapping a blanket round him. Two other men were leaning over the side. They had seized Jolly by the back of her bodice and the seat of her pants and were hauling her in over the side. Despite her second immersion, her eyes now shone with dark suspicion of the boatload of men. Presently the cutter glided and bumped alongside the steps which had been let down the *Hero*'s side by davits and chain. Verity had to be helped up at first but, to his surprise, he found that when he reached the main deck, he could actually stand unaided. With the girl following, under heavy escort, he was led to the quarter-deck. The dark young man had gone below and the stage was held by Lord William Jervis, with General Lord Bruce standing back in the shadows.

'What's this?' asked Lord William, as though he might have been reprimanding a light-fingered butler.

'Sergeant Verity, sir. Metropolitan Police, "A" Division, Private-Clothes detail, sir. 'ave 'ad the honour o' making your acquaintance before.'

'You!' said Lord William indignantly. 'What the devil are you doing here? And by what right have you tampered with the Wolf Rock warning buoy?'

'Ain't, sir. Captain Ransome and his crew done that, and towed the green markers there to decoy your ship on to the rocks. It's you they want dead, sir, so's Ransome can get his hands on everything that would come to Mr Richard. Mr Croaker knows that Ransome murdered Lord Henry and he sent me to warn you as soon as the *Hero* docked. Only I'd a-bin too late to save you then, sir, you and your men, and 'o course 'is 'ighness.'

Lord William looked sharply round at General Bruce. The General nodded his elderly, distinguished head, as though the time for anger or irritation were long past. He came forward and laid a hand on Verity's shoulder.

'Well done,' he said. 'Well done, sergeant.'

And then General Bruce went below.

'Sir,' said Verity. 'Gotta say one thing more. What you think is the warning buoy, over there, is a pleasure steamer called the *Lady Flora*. It's got Ransome and several of his men and two of his girls on it. And it's got poor Mr Richard. No, sir, the poor creature as went to the mad 'ouse near Acton was never Mr Richard. Honest Jack Ransome saw to that. And, sir, there's two sailor-men on there, Captain Joshua and another, and there's Sergeant Albert Samson. Ransome may have cut all their throats by now, and if he hasn't already, then he soon will.'

Lord William nodded.

'You may be an unconscionably fine detective, Sergeant Verity, but give us credit for knowing our own business. The searchlight picked out that vessel as soon as we hove to. Quarter of an hour ago, a cutter with two dozen blue-jackets put off. She's to be boarded and taken into Plymouth. See for yourself.'

'Then they ain't even had time to get steam up!' said Verity thankfully.

He turned and peered through the darkness. Presently, the first lights sprang alive on the deck of the *Lady Flora*. There were sounds of distant commotion, but in regular succession, the little circles of light at the portholes appeared, as Lord William's boarding-party took the steamer and her occupants into their custody.

'I never thought they'd cooper me,' said Samson with great confidence. 'Not after you'd got clean away. You'd have had a tale to tell. They'd never risk it. They had me and Captain Joshua and his mate, and them two doxies, Simona and Stefania, all tied up in one cabin with a cove as threatened to slit our gizzards if we gave trouble. However, the moment the *'ero* went down, they was going to slit 'em anyway. They saw the *'ero* stop dead, and couldn't tell if she was on the rocks and sinking or not. Course, the searchlight flashed about, as it might if she was going down. And then, just as they decided she wasn't on the rocks, there's footsteps all over the deck. I swear I never even 'eard them blue-jackets come alongside, let alone climb on to the deck. Well, being as there was only Ransome and three of his coves, it was over in a minute. Soon as the coves saw the marines, why they couldn't a-bin more 'elpful. Bless you, they even wanted to change sides without being asked.'

'You 'ad quite a little adventure, Mr Samson,' said Verity, pulling at the rum which had been brought to the cabin on Lord William's orders. 'Cor, I 'ate this stuff! 'ow you can drink it for pleasure, I shall never know!'

'*I* had an adventure!' snorted Samson. 'What you had was twice that, and a doxy that's now got to be admitted Queen's evidence. Not the first time she's saved her lovely skin that way!'

'Don't seem right, after all she's done, Mr Samson. Why, she'll get clear away!'

'Not *clear* away,' said Samson with a thoughtful smile. 'She won't hang, she won't be transported to 'Straliar, nor anything like that. But while there's Mrs Rouncewell and the steam laundry, and while I'm in Mrs Rouncewell's good books, I think I can promise as Miss Jolly won't get *clear* away with what she done.'

16

The windows of the drab houses were aflame with the reflection of dawn, the trees in the squares bright and green against a sky of pale, brilliant blue, as Verity and Samson turned into Snow Hill. Even the smoke of Samson's penny cigar rose in a white unruffled plume in the stillness of the new day. The 'Magpie and Stump', which had blazed with light since the previous evening stood with doors open wide and tables strewn with a litter of ale-glasses and jugs, carcases of cold fowl and rabbit, remains of kidneys and lobster, and pickled onions in jars. A scattering of scraps and the butts of cheroots lay among the sand of the uncarpeted floor.

On the roofs of the houses, makeshift galleries had been formed overlooking the street, where men with matted hair and grimy hats cocked on one side, lolled and drank with laughing girls whose white scarves had been pulled down to reveal the pallor of bare shoulders. At the windows of the rooms below sat parties of young subalterns, among sleeping dandies and the brokers of the 'Swell Mob'.

As the two sergeants turned the corner there was the humming of thousands of voices, a packed and impenetrable crowd of men and women filling the length and width of Newgate Street and Snow Hill. Several uniformed constables at the rear of the crowd were enduring volleys of ribaldry from stunted and sallow youths of sixteen or seventeen, while the dandies at the upper windows stroked their moustaches, twirled their cigars and shouted their encouragement of this sport.

Well back from the rear of the crowd, family parties of respectable-looking tradesmen and their wives sipped tea as calmly as if they had been in their own parlour, never taking their eyes from the sight on which the gaze of the entire throng was soon directed.

High up in the blank grim wall of Newgate Gaol was a tiny door, never used except on a Monday morning, and only on such Monday mornings as this. A black-draped platform had been built out from it, carts with posts and planks still rattling up Snow Hill as late as four in the morning to conclude the work. The final clatter and hammering died away as the carpenters completed the erection of two black-painted posts on the platform with a stout cross-beam between them and a dark iron chain dangling from its centre. Long before the arrival of Samson and Verity, the coach carrying the sheriffs had made its way through the crowd and the doors of the great prison had closed behind it. Now the hands on St Sepulchre's clock stood at ten to eight. Verity shivered in the chill of the summer morning.

It seemed an age until the minute hand rose to a perfect vertical and the bell of the tower tolled out eight times. A silence fell upon the crowd.

'They'd have knocked the irons off his legs in the press-yard by now,' said Samson doubtfully. 'Surely he never been respited nor done away with himself in his cell?'

But the little door opened and a man's head appeared briefly and vanished. He reappeared, a single figure dressed all in black. A group of young men in the crowd set up a hissing, but it soon faded into silence. Four more men followed in a close group, the first on to the platform was black-suited but with his shirt open. His hands were strapped together in front of him and, as he stood there, he opened his palms once or twice in a helpless little gesture. The voice of the man behind him carried faintly across the multitude of onlookers.

'I am the resurrection and the life. . . .'

'Hurrah for Honest Jack Ransome!'

The voice of a gaudily-dressed young swell at one of the upper windows of the 'Magpie and Stump' echoed across the street, provoking a mutter among those below, which swiftly fell to silence again. The condemned man placed himself quietly beneath the beam. Then the other man, who had come alone on to the platform, pulled him round to face the crowd, took from his pocket a white night-cap and drew it down firmly to cover the victim's head. There was not a sound from the crowd as the hangman stepped back and gave a signal to his assistant below the platform. The bolts of the trap were drawn away and the hooded figure seemed to stumble, rather than fall, into the dark well which opened under him. As he dropped to waist-level in the opening, the rope which connected the noose and the black chain shuddered taut. It seemed that the pinioned body twitched but those watching from the upper windows and balconies were able to see the last refinement of humane execution, the hands of Jack Ketch's apprentice reaching upwards to pull with vigorous jerks on the legs of the hanged man until the choking and the twitching ceased.

Samson let out the breath which he had been holding in the tension of the moment. He turned to his companion.

'Yer eyes is closed!' he said incredulously.

Verity nodded.

'Never thought I'd feel for Jack Ransome,' he said throatily. 'He never did much actual harm to me, though. Funny enough, he once spoke up for me, to Mr Richard, and I could a-thanked him.'

'The villain would have coopered us both, if he'd had his way!'

Verity nodded again. There was a resurgence of noise and movement in the crowd. Captain Jack's body was required by law to hang for a full hour. But the excitement and the spectacle which had drawn men and women in their thousands was now over.

Samson nudged Verity, as though to cheer him up.

'Breakfast! I know where there's hot breakfast kept for us!'

He led the way to Ludgate and London Bridge, Verity walking in silence beside him. Samson said conversationally,

'Your Mr Richard was lucky, though. If he hadn't been mad as a hatter, he'd a-swung with Honest Jack. Now he'll end his days in Broadmoor Asylum. A cove told me that it's all new built, a real palace. It's on a hill, so you look clean over the walls and see the countryside around you, just as you might be at home on your own estate.'

'What good's it to a man, if it ain't his own estate?' asked Verity with uncharacteristic bitterness. 'Poor young Mr Richard might a-bin better off going down with the *Lady Flora* or keeping Jack Ransome company on that trap just now. No, Mr Samson, I only got one thing to shout about, and that's what I got Dr Jamieson to do for that mistreated young fellow Wilson Rust, who swore to us he was sane in the asylum near Acton. There's a man that was wrongly held prisoner and is set free at last. And there ain't another thing I should wish to remember from this whole sorry business.'

'You'll come round, however. See if you don't!'

And Samson was right, at least to the extent that the gloom of witnessing the execution seemed to be passing from Verity's mind by the time they marched through the gates of Mrs Rouncewell's converted workhouse. The ruddy-faced and muscular proprietress greeted them with enthusiasm.

'There's breakfast awaiting for two brave officers!' she said jubilantly. 'Sich devilled kidneys as you never dreamed of.'

'Much obliged, Mrs Rouncewell,' said Verity softly, 'and I ain't particular about much breakfast just now.'

'Gammon!' said Mrs Rouncewell sharply, and she sat the two sergeants at the parlour table with her. 'Take a mug o' porter with it. That's all you need.'

Samson ate with gusto, and Verity took a mouthful or two in order to oblige the former police-matron who had been of assistance to him several times in the past.

Samson munched at a kidney impaled on a fork. He said,

'Pity about that Miss Elaine of yours. It didn't quite suit Mr Croaker and the Division to have her brought back here, else you might have apprenticed her hot and strong.'

'Apprentices!' Mrs Rouncewell's solid bosom heaved with mirth. 'I ain't complaining of apprentices, not after what some of the officers in the Division done for me!'

She stood up, pulled back the curtain on the glass door of the little parlour, and beckoned Verity with an impatient wave of her arm.

Beyond the glass was an open lobby, which broadened into the steamy vista of the washing room. Two scrubbed wooden benches with a dozen tubs let into each ran the length of the room. A score of women, their ages between fourteen and forty, stooped in varying states of undress over the tubs. Simona and Stefania, blouses discarded and smocks peeled down to hang loose from their waists, pummelled and snatched in frantic rivalry at the contents of the same steaming tub. Not a yard away, one of Mrs Rouncewell's brawny lieutenants watched them in stern disapproval. And then Verity saw the other girl. She was working at a tub on the second bench, her dark hair pushed up in a tall coiffure, the pale gold of her bare back and shoulders glistening with the heat of the room. Once she paused, straightening up, her sharp features turning and her almond eyes flashing a look of spite and loathing over her shoulders, just as Verity had seen when the sailors hauled her into the *Hero*'s cutter. As on that occasion, she was naked but for bodice and pants. Now she stood furtively, wiping her hands against herself, hands whose caresses, Verity knew, had given infinite pleasure to a great number of men, and even a few chosen girls. There was a sudden shout from the powerfully-built woman who watched over the scene from a desk on a horseshoe dais. Spite and loathing vanished from the girl's face, her lip quivered and she plunged her hands back again into the frothing water.

Mrs Rouncewell let the curtain fall and drew back into the parlour.

'Apprenticed to righteousness,' she said piously. 'That's how I see them frail fallen creatures when they're in my 'ouse. The wholesome gospel of honest work is what they're sent to learn. And you can rest easy, Mr Verity, that when I'm finished with 'em, they can recite it backwards in their sleep! Six months more and them three little sluts might be fit for class-leaders at Paddington Chapel. More a work of mercy than anything else, that's what I'm doing here.'

And Mrs Rouncewell opened her cavernous mouth, leering in appreciation of her own wit.

As he marched smartly across the room to Superintendent Gowry's desk, and came to attention before it, Verity was disconcerted to see Inspector Croaker standing at ease on one side. Now that the affair of Captain Ransome and the Jervis family was over, he had no idea what his fate might be. Clearly, he had been summoned before Superintendent Gowry in order that he should find out, but the sight of Croaker standing there did nothing to reassure him.

Gowry looked up from his chair at Verity, the bleak eyes and the careful set of his moustache betraying nothing of his intention.

'Before I say anything by way of comment on the events in which the men of the Private-Clothes detail have involved themselves,' he said smoothly, 'I am instructed to read the following passage from a letter received this morning by the Commissioner of Police for the Metropolis. The letter is signed by the Honourable Sir Charles Phipps, Secretary to His Royal Highness Prince Albert.'

At the mention of the Prince Consort's name, Inspector Croaker, who was still standing at ease, sprang quiveringly to attention. Gowry unfolded a sheet of stiff blue notepaper, heavily embossed, and read the passage in question.

His Royal Highness is obliged to the Commissioner for his long letter in which certain matters relating to the recent visit of the Prince of Wales to HMS Hero are set forth. His Highness has heard some account of these from the Prince himself, but is indebted to the Commissioner for other details, including the part played in guarding the Prince of Wales by officers of the Private-Clothes detail, Metropolitan Police.

It would not be appropriate for His Royal Highness to comment on events which have been made the subject of criminal proceedings. None the less, he is instructed by the Queen to convey the deep appreciation felt by Her Majesty and His Royal Highness himself to those officers whose personal courage and resource contributed so greatly to the safety of the Prince of Wales. It is the wish of Her Majesty that these sentiments should be made known to the individuals concerned.

Verity stood breathless at attention, flushed with pride, his eyes bulging and gleaming with the exhilaration of the moment. He wondered why Samson, too, had not been informed of the royal 'sentiments' at the same time, but he was almost overwhelmed with emotion and quite unable to consider such things systematically. Superintendent Gowry cleared his throat and read on.

> As the Commissioner will be aware, the Prince of Wales is shortly to embark on HMS Hero to undertake a tour of Canada and the United States of America as Her Majesty's personal representative. His Highness will be accompanied by the members of his household and, on this occasion, by a group of officers responsible for the safety of His Highness. It is the wish of Her Majesty and of His Royal Highness Prince Albert that the officer responsible for defeating the late attempt on the life of the Prince of Wales should be attached to the royal bodyguard for the forthcoming tour.

With that, Superintendent Gowry laid the sheet of paper down and Verity, his eyes furtively downcast, made out the signature of Sir Charles Phipps and, to one side, the single and magisterial word of endorsement: 'Albert'.

Inspector Croaker slackened his stance in order to snap to attention again, his voice cracking out across the room as though on the square at Woolwich.

'Sir! As officer commanding the Private-Clothes detail and, therefore, responsible for ordering the warning to HMS Hero, I should deem it the greatest privilege to serve His Royal Highness in any capacity that might be chosen for me, sir!'

The breath went from Verity's body, as though he had been struck by a mighty fist. Superintendent Gowry shuffled his hands together awkwardly.

'Mr Croaker, I understand — the Commissioner understands — that the duties anticipated for an additional officer of the Prince's bodyguard would hardly be of a dignity to match such a rank as your own. . . .'

'Sir!' said Croaker, swallowing greedily, 'there is no duty I would consider beneath me in the service of Her Majesty and His Highness!'

He looked, as Verity later remarked to Samson, as though he might be about to fetch up his dinner all over the Superintendent's carpet. Gowry shook his head.

'Commendable though your sense of duty is, Mr Croaker,

I fear the private instructions from the Prince Consort are very plain. It is the officer who reached the Wolf Rock buoy and shone the red light there who is wanted as part of the bodyguard. He will, of course, be subordinate to the other officers and will mess with the royal servants. But it is Sergeant Verity who has been asked for.'

Croaker's porcine little eyes went very round and bright, as though expressing unfathomable agony.

'Sir!' he said, exhaling the word protractedly and investing it with all the submission and hate, obedience to duty and loathing of the fat complacent sergeant, which surged and mingled in his tormented mind.

'Why?' asked Bella, with a scepticism which almost bordered on resentment, 'I don't see why it should be a reward to take you from home and a wife that loves you, and send you off to foreign parts again. You only just got back from Portman Square and Plymouth, and all that!'

The moonlight streamed through the thin curtains of the open window, while scents of the summer street, distantly obnoxious, lingered in the warm air. In the cradle at Bella's side, the infant Verity snuffled, woke and began to shift about protestingly at the sound of voices.

'A man gotta take such duty as its own reward,' said Verity firmly.

'Eye-wash!' she said, determinedly turning her back.

'No it ain't, Mrs Verity. It's the truth, and you know it is! Your father brought you up to know that all right.'

Her voice was half muffled by the pillow when she replied.

'Pa says there's some duties ain't as bad as you make out. He says. . . .'

'Yes, Mrs Verity?'

''e says,' she blurted, 'when you was hauling that unfortunate young person about in that rowing-boat . . . 'e says he bets you gave her a good touch-up in the right places!'

Appalled at such a repetition from Bella, it took him a moment to regain his composure.

'Yes,' he said at length. 'Well, I got a great respect for your old father as, in course, I'm obliged to have. But there ain't no question that Mr Stringfellow's mind stands in need of a bit of refinement.'

They lay apart, in careful isolation from one another, for several minutes. Then Verity turned caressingly towards her.

'After all,' he said softly, 'it ain't for long, Bella. Only a month or so. Nothing like going off to 'indoostan that time!'

'But why've you got to be a bodyguard, Mr Verity?'

'Well,' said Verity, as though no less puzzled than his wife, 'there's Canadians that don't like belonging to us, a-cos of being Frenchies. And there's Yankees wot don't much like us neither. Some do, some don't. But it's a secret that he's going to such places as New York. He's going under an alias, and you ain't to say a word about it, not even to Mr Stringfellow. You wouldn't want 'is 'ighness foully murdered, would you?'

'No,' she said meekly.

Verity's hand patted Bella's plump little thigh consolingly.

'Well, then,' he said. 'It'll be all right, you see if it ain't. And I'll be back in no time at all. And we gotta behave a bit more special now, being members of the royal 'ousehold, in a manner of speaking.'

Bella gasped.

'Are we? Members of 'is 'ighness' household?'

'In a manner o' speaking,' said Verity hastily. 'But it means behaving very proper and setting an example round here.'

'You and me and Mr Stringfellow?' she whispered wonderingly.

'Well,' said Verity doubtfully, 'Mr Stringfellow might have to be a bit more genteel first.'

Bella began to giggle. Verity held out at first, and then emitted a snorting guffaw. The bed shook violently under their mirth and there was an angry wail from the cradle. Bella ignored it as they wrestled softly together.

'I 'ope,' she gasped presently, 'I 'ope that when the poor young Prince comes back safe . . . I 'ope, Mr Verity, that you're sent to live home for always and always!'